FANGS FOR THE MEMORIES

The sea serpent reappeared, nose to nose with the prow of the ship. Twin fangs gleamed like ivory in that pink, gaping maw. There was a groan and wrenching deep in the ship. The sound of splintering wood, breaking bolts, and snapping joists rose above the terrified cries of men. With an effortless contraction the sea serpent ripped the carved prow away, taking the foredeck and part of the hull with it.

Without any warning, Caspar found himself spinning head-over-heels through the air. He hit the sea on his back with jarring force. Water filled his nose and mouth. He gave a kick and struggled toward air, but the weight of the chains on his arms—and the strong tow of the sinking ship—worked against him.

He opened his mouth to scream, and a rush of bubbles rose before his face like startled fleeing birds.

Other Avon Books in the
INFOCOM™ Series

ENCHANTER® *by Robin W. Bailey*
PLANETFALL® *by Arthur Byron Cover*
WISHBRINGER® *by Craig Shaw Gardner*
STATIONFALL™ *by Arthur Byron Cover*
THE ZORK® CHRONICLES *by George Alec Effinger*

ROBIN W. BAILEY

THE LOST CITY OF
ZORK ®

A Byron Preiss Book

AN INFOCOM™ BOOK

AVON BOOKS ◆ NEW YORK

THE LOST CITY OF ZORK is an original publication of Avon Books. This work has never before appeared in book form. This work is a novel. Any similarity to actual persons or events is purely coincidental.

Special thanks to Marc Blank, Dave Lebling, Richard Curtis, Rob Sears, John Douglas, David Keller, and John Betancourt.

AVON BOOKS
A division of
The Hearst Corporation
105 Madison Avenue
New York, New York 10016

Cover and book design by Alex Jay/Studio J.
Cover painting by Walter Velez
Edited by David M. Harris

CHAPTER ONE
THE ROAD TO BORPHEE

CASPAR WHISTLED A sweet melody as he strolled down the tiny, dusty road that would eventually take him to the great port city of Borphee. The sound floated over the broad, grassy plain, announcing his coming to the butterflies and bumblebees that flitted among the fiery blossoms of wild dragondil flowers and the more delicate white blooms called gryphon's breath.

Everywhere he looked, the world was full of beauty. He drew a deep breath and grinned happily. The air was rich with the blossoms' perfume. Adjusting the small pack that contained his few belongings, he bent and plucked a dragondil, inhaled its fragrance, and stuck it behind his ear without ever missing a note of his song.

Overhead, billowy clouds drifted languidly through a blue sky while the sun gently warmed the land. A pair of firebirds circled playfully, their plumage shimmering red and yellow, as they rode the air currents in their graceful mating flight. Caspar watched as they gyred lower and lower, wingtips almost touching. Then, brushing the top of the high grass, the birds climbed again and flew eastward.

Borphee lay to the east, too, and Caspar took it as a favorable sign that such beautiful birds were going his way. He knew in his heart he'd made the right decision to leave his small village in the Peltoid Valley and strike out to seek his fortune. Not that he'd had any choice. A pang of regret still filled him when he remembered the angry and accusing faces of former friends and family as he walked away, and he still felt the sting of his uncle's whip on his shoulders.

But never mind that, he thought to himself, pushing those unpleasant memories aside as he finished his tune. He'd never really been cut out to be a farmer anyway. And it was too fine a day to dwell on regrets. He paused long enough to open his pack and extract a small canteen of water, from which he drank sparingly. Lifting his head, he gave an experimental blow, liking the quality of the whistle. His daddy had taught him that good music was a source of joy, and Caspar knew it was true. He put the canteen away, adjusted his pack on his shoulder again and hurried on at a jaunty pace.

In the far distance, the tops of Borphee's highest towers rose into the summer sky. The fleecy clouds seemed to hang upon those slender spires like speared sky-fish. Caspar paused again and stopped his whistle as his jaw gaped. Slowly, a big grin spread over his face and a thrill shivered through him. All his life he'd heard stories of Borphee. At last, he was going to see the city for himself.

It was all he could do to keep from running, but he knew the city was still farther than it appeared. He could not see the high wall that he knew surrounded the city, for instance. Nor could he yet smell the tang of the salty sea when the wind blew. Not that he actually knew what the sea would smell like. He'd never been out of the Peltoid Valley. But he'd heard stories, and he'd dreamed dreams. More than anything, he wanted to see the Great Ocean. That was why, from among all the cities of Quendor, he'd chosen to begin his life anew in Borphee.

The road led up a low rise. As Caspar reached the summit, he spied another traveler coming up the hill toward him. It was an old man, to judge by the way the figure leaned on his thick staff. It was hard to be sure, though, for despite the summer heat, the traveler was almost totally concealed in a dusty brown cloak and hood.

Caspar stopped his whistling and waited for the old man to join him at the top.

"No, no! Don't stop!" the old man called as he trudged the last few steps to the summit. His voice was firm and throaty, though it betrayed a certain weariness that put Caspar at his ease.

"That was a chanty, wasn't it?" the old man continued as he stopped before Caspar and leaned heavily on his staff. "I used to love chanties. Knew 'em all by heart, I did."

The man looked up and brushed the hood back from his head. His blue eyes sparkled like sapphires, and a thick iron-gray mane flowed down over his neck, past his collar and into the cloak. There was a jovial kindness in his face, and he had the features of a man who laughed a lot.

"Not a chanty, but a work song," Caspar answered. "The folks in my village sing it all the time when they're planting their crops."

The old man shrugged as he reached under his cloak and unslung a leather bottle, which he unstoppered. "Well, I don't know what words your farmers sing, but in these parts that tune you're whistlin' is a sea chanty. I know that tune down to the note." He tossed back his head and gulped a mouthful from the bottle and swallowed noisily. A thin trickle of red liquid purled down his chin. "Ah!" he sighed. Then he closed his eyes and shook himself, grinning with smug satisfaction, before he wiped the trickle away with the back of his left hand. "Good wine is a source of joy!" he uttered, leering at Caspar.

Caspar started at the slightly altered version of his own favorite proverb. "I suppose your daddy taught you that?" he said.

The old traveler gave an indignant snort as he folded his legs under himself and sat down in the dust by the side of the road. He set his morgia wood staff aside and wrapped his cloak about himself as if he were cold, though that was impossible on such a hot day. "I taught it to daddy," he answered with a curt nod and a wink. He cupped a hand to his mouth, and in a conspiratorial whisper, he continued. "It was momma who taught it to me. She could drink any three men under the table, and frequently did. Stout old sow, she was, may she rest in peace." He took another quick nip from the bottle and hammered the stopper back in place with a thump of his fist.

"Now where was I?" he went on. A twinkle ignited in his blue eyes, and he began to sing.

> *"Dance me laddies to the riggin's hum*
> *When the moonlight's ridin' high,*
> *And the wind is wild, and the sails are full,*
> *And the waves are sweepin' by.*
>
> *Dance me laddies to the canvas crack,*
> *and the creak and groan of timbers.*
> *'Round and 'round—we're goin' down,*
> *This ship and all its members!"*

The song ended, and the old man gave a sad, thoughtful look before he threw back his head and laughed heartily. There was a strained, bitter tone in his laughter, and Caspar began to wonder who this strange old man was.

"It's the same tune," Caspar conceded when the old man grew quiet again and looked at him. "But I know it this way." He sang the song the way he knew it.

> *"The maids are in the corn, boys,*
> *Shucking off their dresses,*
> *And the wind is making free, boys,*
> *In their long, silky tresses.*
>
> *So off to the corn we go, boys,*
> *And don't forget your hoe.*
> *We've lots of hard men's work to do,*
> *And lots of seed to sow."*

Caspar finished with a quick shuffle, a little sidestep, a flourish of his hand, and a bow. "That's how *we* sing it," he said with an exaggerated air of superiority.

The old man regarded him from under raised eyebrows. "Well, that's how it is with folk music, I guess," he responded at last. "One man's chanty is another man's smut." He jerked a thumb over his shoulder toward the distant spires of Borphee and changed the subject. "You headin' into the city?"

Caspar nodded enthusiastically.

The old man peered at him queerly, then one corner of his mouth turned upward in a crooked grin. "First time, too, isn't it. Fresh from the hayfields, I'll bet. What's your name anyway, boy?"

Caspar frowned at the "boy" business. In fact, he didn't know his exact birthdate, but he was certainly of an age to be out on his own. On the other hand, he reasoned, calming himself as he regarded the face before him with its deep wrinkles, this old man probably called everybody "boy." It was one of the few privileges of age.

He made another small bow as he introduced himself. "Caspar Wartsworth," he answered.

The old man chuckled. "Wartsworth? How'd you get a name like that?"

Caspar frowned again in irritation. He didn't much like being mocked, especially by a stranger. Age as an excuse for rude behavior went only so far. He wasn't very happy with his last name, either, but it was the name his village had given him. He still remembered clearly that first humiliating day when the townspeople deemed him old enough to be sent to the fields with the rest of the village boys and he'd gotten lost among the stalks of corn, which were taller than he was. They'd had to come find him, and someone remarked later that he'd never be worth much as a farmer, and someone else added, "Maybe what a wart's worth." And the name promptly stuck.

Well, now that he'd left his village and was out in the world he'd earn a new name soon enough. He just shrugged in answer to the old man's query.

"Never mind," the old man replied, apparently realizing he'd touched a sore spot. "Didn't mean to seem so nosy. I got a name that's causing me some problems right now, myself." He held out a gnarly hand to shake. "Won't tell it all to you, but you can call me Zil."

Caspar hesitated, then shook hands.

"You be careful if you're going into the city. There's trouble brewing. That's all I'm goin' to say." Zil looked back over his shoulder toward Borphee, and a soft mist stole over his eyes.

"What kind of trouble?" Caspar prodded, suddenly concerned. He, too, turned to stare toward the city.

"There's chaos in the streets," Zil answered. "Chaos, I tell you. There's soldiers everywhere, an' people disappearing, an' new laws against everything but pickin' your nose, an' that'll be illegal tomorrow. But that's all I'm goin' to say. You take it as a warning."

"But I've got to go to Borphee!" Caspar insisted as he knelt down in the roadside dust beside Zil. "I've got to find a job. I want to be a sailor!"

Zil turned to look at him with something like a concerned sneer. "Nice green farmboy like you? They'll eat you up down there. Lot of trouble right now, an' unrest. Soldiers in the streets, I tell you. All the gates guarded. House-to-house searches. Lot's of folks have just vanished without spit nor warning." He pointed a shaky finger and wagged it under Caspar's nose. "Borphee's become a dangerous place to be this past month. You go down there, you better be careful. That's all I'm goin' to say."

Caspar stood up, rubbing his chin worriedly, looking from the old man to the city spires, from the spires to the old man. How much should he believe Zil, he wondered? What if he really was walking into some kind of trouble? Borphee had been at the center of his heart's dream for most of his life. He *had* to go on, no matter what.

The old man must have noted his determination. "You'll be sorry," Zil said as he stiffly rose and brushed the dust from his cloak and garments.

"Is that all you're going to say?" Caspar asked wryly, reaching out a hand to steady the old man as Zil bent down to retrieve his walking staff.

The old man winked at him as he straightened and leaned on the staff. "I earned that, didn't I? Well, you're young, and full of the eagerness of your years, so I don't blame you for not heeding an old fart like me." He grew serious again. "But Borphee is not going to be the party place of Quendor that you've heard about in the past. It's got a new host on the throne now, and he's strip-searchin' everybody at the door. You be careful, and that's all I'm goin' to say."

Caspar started at the bit of news concealed in all that. "What do you mean Borphee's got a new host?"

Zil backed a step, holding both hands up and shaking his head. "That's *really* all I'm goin' to say about it. Having outstayed my welcome, I'm off to find a new life." He reached into an inner pocket of his cloak and brought out a deck of painted playing cards all bound together with a silk ribbon. He riffled them with a flourish. "I've invented a card game, you see. *Double Fanucci*, I call it. Thousands of rich bored old people in retirement homes across the country are going to love it. And I'll make a quiet, personal fortune publishing the rule books and strategies and variations on the strategies, not to mention playing fees I'll collect from workshops and demonstration games." He waved a hand disdainfully at Borphee's spires. "It'll certainly beat my old job."

"And what was that?" Caspar asked, still hoping to extract more information from the old man.

Zil put his cards away and smiled secretively. He arched his eyebrows twice sharply with a "heh-heh" kind of expression as he pulled his hood back up over his head. "A small government position. Nothing worth mentioning," he said. Almost under his breath he added, "any longer."

Zil started to turn away, then once more he glanced back at Caspar. "Speaking of things not worth mentioning," he said from under the concealment of his voluminous hood. "There's no real need to tell anyone you saw me out here on the road, either. We just had a pleasant little conversation. Let it go at that, all right." His eyes, or what Caspar could see of them under the heavy drape of material, narrowed darkly. "It could be the worse for you if you do otherwise."

Caspar stared in hurt confusion. Then he bristled. "'Is that some kind of threat?"

Zil was already down the road. He didn't stop, but he waved with his staff as he called back. "For your good, as well as mine," he shouted, "that's all I'm goin' to say."

Caspar watched from the top of the hill until the old man was out of sight. With a sigh, he turned and prepared to resume his journey for Borphee. But instead, he spied the old man's small leather wine bottle lying in the dust where he'd been sitting. The strap was worn and had broken. The old man probably didn't even know it was missing. The bottle itself, though, was in fine shape and still half full. He examined it, admiring its craftsmanship and the elaborate initial "Z" carved into the front of the bottle. Caspar wasn't much of a wine drinker, but he figured at the very least he could sell such an exquisite object to some dealer. After all, he was down to his last zorkmid coin, and he knew he'd need money in the big city. So he tied the two frayed ends of the broken strap together, slung it over his shoulder and started off again.

CHAPTER TWO
THE BIG CITY

THE DUSTY ROAD WIDened as it descended out of the hills and stretched across the broad Plain of Borphee toward the city gates. From the south a pair of vegetable carts laden with cabbages and turnips trundled down another road until they joined the main one and caught up with Caspar. From the north came a huge wagon pulled by four horses and loaded with freshly cut lumber from the great forests. Caspar hailed each of the drivers with hearty greetings.

"No riders!" shouted the driver of the first vegetable cart as he passed by.

"But I wasn't asking for a ride!" Caspar called uselessly at the departing man's back. He braced his hands on his hips and stared in surprise and annoyance at such rudeness. After a moment, though, he merely shrugged it off. The man had probably come a long way on that uncomfortable buckboard.

"No freeloaders!" scowled the second driver in answer to Caspar's friendly wave. He cracked his lash over the back of the cart pony, leaving a slack-jawed Caspar in a cloud of soft dust.

"No hitchers!" cried the bearded driver of the lumber wagon before Caspar could bid him more than a pleasant good day. "No bums!" added his partner, sitting beside the driver. The man pointed at the small blue bundle of belongings tied to the stick on Caspar's shoulder.

"Now wait just a minute!" Caspar shouted resentfully at the two men. He increased his stride and managed to keep pace with the heavy lumber wagon as it creaked and groaned and rattled its way down the road toward Borphee's great, high wall. "I didn't ask anybody for a ride, and I certainly didn't ask for all this abuse!" The driver and his partner squirmed uncomfortably on their rough seats and refused to look at him. Caspar raised his voice insistently. "What's wrong with trying to be friendly on a nice day? I'm a stranger in these parts!"

"No strangers!" snapped the partner, who kept his eyes straight ahead toward the city.

"No strangers!" the driver agreed with a dark glower. He set the heel of his boot firmly against Caspar's shoulder and propelled him into the ditch. Caspar gave a yelp as he tumbled into a prickly patch of weeds. The driver snapped his reins and kept on going without so much as a backward glance.

Muttering, Caspar picked himself up and tried to brush the dirt and dust and leaves and bits of grass from his clothes. The strap of his canteen and the worn strap of old Zil's leather bottle had wrapped themselves about his neck, and he nearly strangled himself trying to untangle them. That done, he retrieved his blue bag of belongings from the bush where it had landed.

Still muttering, he stepped back onto the road and found a half-wilted dragondil blossom lying at his feet. With a sigh, he bent and picked it up. Some of its perfume yet lingered. He drew a deep breath, tickling his nose with the flower's limp, but still velvety, petals, and his anger abated somewhat. In the distance, the lumber wagon disappeared inside Borphee's gates. Caspar stuck the dragondil behind his ear again where he'd worn it most of the day, and tried to push the whole incident out of his mind. After all, he told himself with an inward frown, he *was* a stranger here. Maybe he'd inadvertently done something to offend them.

The sun was high in the sky by the time he approached the gates. The towering wall that surrounded Borphee stretched as far as he could see in either direction, and he was close enough now that he could no longer see the buildings and spires that lay secure behind it. His breath caught in his throat. He'd heard that Borphee was big, but he hadn't dreamed! This was magnificent!

A pair of large guards stood watch on either side of the gate, their red and gold uniforms and their polished helmets dazzling in the sunlight. A smaller, officious-looking little man in a long red robe stood with them, the sun gleaming on his polished bald head. The guards eyed Caspar suspiciously as he came nearer, but the little man put on a thin smile and patted a huge red book, which he kept under his arm.

"Ah, a traveler!" the little man said with a nod toward Caspar's bundle. "Will you step over here, please?" He bent slightly at the waist, barely a bow, and made a sweeping gesture with his hand. He passed the red book to one of the guards. Caspar spied a small table in the shadow of the wall where another large black book, writing materials and ink wells were spread. The little man sat down in the only chair, and Caspar blinked sharply as the sun reflected off the fellow's bare scalp.

"That's quite a twitch you've got there," the little man said, regarding Caspar as he reached for a pen and opened the black book. A long list of names were written in a spidery hand with scribbled notes of information under each one. This little man was a Gatekeeper, then, one of the king's officers, whose job it was to monitor traffic through the city's several gates.

The Gatekeeper stabbed his pen down into the nearest ink well and shook the nib. But there was no excess to shake off. The ink well was dry. He gave a low snarl and stared at the small blackened jar. He picked it up. Then he stared down into it, lifting it up to his eye. With another snarl, he flung it sideways, and it shattered against the massive stones of the city wall.

Stunned, Caspar's gaze followed the bottle's short flight and its destruction, and he noted also a number of old black stains on the wall and the accumulated shards of other glass bottles and ink wells sparkling on the ground.

The Gatekeeper smiled again nervously as he glanced

up at Caspar and reached for another open jar of ink. A bead of sweat trickled down his bald scalp, headed for the little man's right eye, but the Gatekeeper flicked it away with insect quickness. "It's the damned heat!" he muttered apologetically as he dipped the pen. "The ink evaporates faster than I can use it."

Again, the nib came up dry. The little man's face screwed up as if he had been personally and direly insulted. He swept up the bottle and dashed it against the wall, and for good measure, he seized up two more unopened bottles and sent them after the first. Rich, black ink splattered over the stones and ran downward in glistening streams.

The Gatekeeper fell back in his chair breathing heavily, his eyes unfocused, a bland expression on his slack face. Then, gradually the thin smile returned and he looked up at Caspar. "Now then," he said in pleasant exasperation, "what did you say your name was?"

Caspar told him, and added helpfully, "Might I suggest, sir, the sun wouldn't dry your ink if you stoppered the bottle after you finish."

The little man looked at Caspar. The thin smile faded. The pen slammed down on the table so hard that several ink bottles fell over and a sheaf of white papers slithered into the dust. The Gatekeeper rose out of his chair and leaned over the table until his nose was almost against Caspar's.

"Well, Mister Expert-On-Everything Caspar Wartsworth!" He snapped his fingers under Caspar's chin and two guards quickly snatched Caspar's bundle away and grabbed him by his arms. Their grips were like steel. Caspar glanced hastily from side to side, not liking the twisted smiles on their faces. "We'll just have to find us some ink that won't dry up in the sun, won't we!" There was a crazy, strained note in the little man's voice, and Caspar began to tremble inside as he stared into those narrow little eyes. "Then, we can get you all signed in nice and proper," the Gatekeeper continued as he sat back down again. "Can't have you running around our city without signing in, you know!"

The guard on Caspar's right side began to force his hand closer to the table. The Gatekeeper bent and picked up one of the white pieces of paper that had fallen to the ground. He laid it out neatly, the smile returning to his face as the muscular guard forced Caspar's hand down upon it.

Caspar trembled for real now, but the guards held him firmly. The Gatekeeper opened a small drawer and extracted a long dagger with a gleaming point. His thin smile broadened as he looked at Caspar again and closed the drawer.

Caspar tried uselessly to pull his hand away. "Uh, I think there's still ink in that one!" he said, nodding toward the several remaining bottles.

The little man leaned forward thoughtfully, examining Caspar's outspread fingers on the white paper, tapping them each with the flat of the dagger as he pursed his lips and rubbed his chin. "I think there's ink in this one!" he answered gleefully. He made a short stab with the dagger's point. Caspar gave a yelp of pain and blood began to ooze from the tip of his first finger. "Yes, I thought so!" the Gatekeeper cried as the guards chuckled. He gripped Caspar's wounded digit between his thumb and forefinger and squeezed so that the blood flowed faster. A red pool quickly formed on the white paper.

"Now then, I think we're ready!" The Gatekeeper sat back again, picked up his pen and dipped the nib into the smear of blood. He made a couple of red scratches on the white paper, smiled and rewet the nib as he drew the book with the list of names toward him again. "Now, Caspar Wartsworth, where are you from?"

The guards let him go. Someone handed his bundle back to him. Caspar barely noticed as he thrust his bleeding finger into his mouth. "Djabuti Padjama," he said around the finger.

The Gatekeeper's eyebrows went up in surprise that turned quickly to suspicion. "What's that?" he said.

"Your dirty pajamas," one of the guards supplied. "I think it's some kind of insult!"

The Gatekeeper reached for the dagger again.

"No!" Caspar cried, taking his finger out of his mouth and curling his hands into tight fists. "Djabuti Padjama! It's a tiny village far east of here. That's where I'm from!"

The Gatekeeper scowled doubtfully, but another guard saved Caspar. "I know it," the guard offered, but the sneer in his voice was unmistakable. "Passed through there, once. It's over in the Peltoid Valley, several days away. Bunch of backward farmers live there, and none of 'em pleasant. I say stab him again."

"Wait!" Caspar shouted, pointing to the pool of blood on the paper. "There's still plenty of ink!" Then, realizing how close his pointing finger was to the dagger, he snatched it away again and clutched his hands to his chest. "It hasn't dried yet," he added sheepishly.

The Gatekeeper's mouth twisted up one side of his face as he studied Caspar, but at last he dipped the nib in the blood and scrawled the information into the book of names. Caspar bent forward just enough to notice his wasn't the only name in red ink. He swallowed hard. Some of the names had a lot of information written with them.

The Gatekeeper finished writing, closed the black book, and set the pen aside. "Well, Caspar Wartsworth from Djabuti Padjama in the far east." He leaned back, rocking his chair on its two back legs as he folded his hands over his stomach and sternly regarded Caspar. "There've been a lot of changes around here. A lot of new laws."

One of the guards brushed aside the paper with Caspar's blood smear and set down the thick red book, which the Gatekeeper had originally carried under his arm. The guard opened it to the first page and turned it so that Caspar could read.

"These are the new city ordinances," the Gatekeeper continued as the smile came slowly back to his face. "I helped write them myself, actually. I've got a novel at home I'm working on, too, but it's hard, holding down a job and all." He waved a hand before his face. "But never mind that. You'd do well to take a moment to acquaint yourself with our laws and regulations before you actually enter the city. Once you step across that threshold you're subject to every one of them."

"The least infraction of which will result in dire consequences," volunteered the guard who had set down the book. He leered at Caspar, and Caspar felt suddenly like a piece of steak.

"What kind of dire consequences?" he swallowed hard and dared to ask.

The smile on the Gatekeeper's face flickered and faded, and his whole expression took on a new menace. "We make it up as we go along."

Caspar swallowed again. "That's comforting," he answered weakly as he glanced down at the page. It was covered with line after line of teeny tiny handwriting. Caspar had to squint and put his nose almost to the page to read the wispy script.

HONOR THY FATHER AND THY MOTHER, THAT THEY MAY REMEMBER YOU IN THEIR WILLS, read the first rule.

Caspar scratched his chin and glanced at the Gatekeeper. "That's a good one," he mumbled. And easy to keep too, since he didn't have a father and mother anymore, and they'd already willed what little they'd had, including their son, to a nasty old uncle.

THOU SHALT NOT COMMIT ADULTERY WITH UGLY WOMEN, NOR WITH UGLY MEN, NOR WITH UGLY COMBINATIONS THEREOF. NEITHER SHALT THOU FORNICATE WITH FARM ANIMALS, NOR WITH FUNDAMENTALIST RELIGIOUS PRACTITIONERS LEST THEY MULTIPLY BEYOND THEIR NUMBERS.

"That pretty much covers it," Caspar commented, rubbing his eyes before he went on to the next rule.

THOU SHALT NOT STEAL UNLESS THY INCOME BE ALREADY IN THE UPPER TENTH PERCENTILE.

Caspar pursed his lips and glanced sheepishly from the page. Fortunately, the Gatekeeper had not asked him why he'd left Djabuti Padjama. Well, sometimes it was better to just keep your mouth shut, and now was one of those times, he reasoned. The past was behind him, and so was that pathetic little village.

He continued to scan down the page. There were all kinds of *Thou shalt nots* and *Honor* this and *Honor* that.

"What about *Thou shalt not kill?*" Caspar said thoughtfully as he thumbed the pages. "Seems to me that would have been a good one."

The guard near Caspar's right side snorted derisively, and the Gatekeeper's jaw fell slack. "You must be living in some kind of fantasy, boy," he said, openly sneering. "This is the real world we're dealing with."

Caspar closed the book slowly and pushed it back. There were simply too many rules for him to remember, and the strain on his eyes from reading the fine text was too great. He'd just have to be careful as he moved about Borphee. "May I go through the gate now?" he asked, trying his best to sound humble.

"After you pay the tax," the Gatekeeper said. He leaned forward in his chair and thrust his hand across the table, palm up. The smile returned to his face once more.

"What tax?" Caspar yelped. "How much is it?"

"A one-time gate fee," the Gatekeeper explained patiently. His open hand hovered expectantly in the air, while he pointed with his other hand to the black Book of Names. "See, I'll put a check mark by your name when you've paid so you won't be charged again."

"That's a relief," Caspar said worriedly. "But I've only got one zorkmid to my name."

The Gatekeeper smiled again. "What a coincidence!" he said, raising his outstretched hand until it was just under Caspar's nose. He didn't need to say more, so Caspar dug out his last coin and regretfully placed it into the open palm. The hand closed like a hungry clam around fresh prey. An instant later the coin disappeared down the front of the little man's tunic.

Caspar gave a sigh and remembered the leather wine bottle he'd picked up on the road. He gave it a pat and felt the half-full contents slosh around inside. "I'll have to find a buyer for this pretty quickly now," he said to himself.

The Gatekeeper eyed the bottle from behind the table

until Caspar noticed his interest. He covered it with one hand, afraid the little man would suddenly remember another tax he'd forgotten to levy and demand the bottle as his price.

"That's a nice little piece of workmanship," the Gatekeeper commented, his attention still on the bottle.

"I'll be going now," Caspar said, quietly backing away from the table. "Nice meeting all of you."

The Gatekeeper and the guards watched him as he backed a few more steps. Finally, he turned around and headed for the gate. The massive stones arched above his head as he crossed the threshold and entered Borphee. Almost instantly, he forgot the unpleasant experience with the Gatekeeper and let the magnificence of the city sweep him up.

On either side of the wide street buildings soared into the air. The sandy-colored stone structures shimmered in the sunlight, and real glass gleamed in all the windows. Tall towers loomed against the heavens, and slender spires pierced the clouds. Banners and pennants of many colors fluttered from poles and parapets; some were draped across the street itself from one building to another.

A rickety old cart piled high with hay trundled by, and Caspar jumped out of its way. The street was filled with merchants hawking goods from apron pockets or baskets tied to their hips. Caspar stared with wide eyes as these sellers pushed shells under his nose, or wooden spoons, or copper nails, or bone needles, or beads. And then he was past this throng. Suddenly booths and small tents lined the street. Here, the goods were larger. Ripe fruits and vegetables waited in large barrels and flat baskets to be examined by shoppers. Bolts of cloth lay sprawled carelessly for anyone to handle. Brooms and rakes and hoes stood in stacks.

The smell of food nearly overwhelmed him. Up ahead, some merchant had set up a grill. Slender, finger-sized strips of beef and pork sizzled on skewers over the open heat. Caspar watched, his mouth watering, as a busy shopper passed over a coin and walked off munching the tasty snack. On the other side of the street, another merchant sold loaves of bread and fat rolls. In the booth beside him was a cheesemaker. Across from that was a fishmonger.

Overcome with sudden hunger, Caspar clutched the leather bottle. He hadn't eaten anything but a few berries and a biscuit from his bundle since morning when he woke by the roadside after walking for three days. Now it seemed like nothing at all. He had to find a buyer for his fine bottle before he starved.

He spun about seeking the three familiar balls of a pawn broker. It was then he spied the two guards he'd encountered at the gate and two others. The Gatekeeper was right behind them, his red robes hiked up above his ankles as he hurried along. His little face screwed up as he saw Caspar. He pointed an accusing finger and screeched something that Caspar couldn't make out over the street noise.

Nevertheless, he didn't much like the sound of it. He thrust his wounded finger unconsciously into his mouth and sucked it, wondering what to do. *In the face of adversity*, he decided swiftly, *Thou shalt run like hell*.

He spun about again, but too late. Four guards hit him all at once, and he found himself crushed on the ground under their combined weight. He cried out desperately, but another four also piled on, and the Gatekeeper danced around the mound of bodies, waving his arms and shrieking hysterically.

All Caspar could hear was the roaring of his own blood as it pounded in his ears. A red haze filled his vision. He couldn't draw a breath. More and more guards appeared from somewhere and threw themselves atop the growing heap. He was almost grateful for the onrushing darkness as the world rapidly slipped away.

CHAPTER THREE

ROYAL HOSPITALITY

CASPAR AWOKE ON A bed of wet, foul-smelling straw. A dim light shone through the bars of his cell door, barely enough to let him see the far side of his small confinement. He ached from head to toe. The smallest movement caused him pain. Slowly, he pushed himself into a sitting position and rubbed his temples. His head throbbed. For a moment the room spun crazily, and he thought he would throw up. Fortunately, he'd had nothing to eat.

Someone had taken his clothes. He found himself naked in the near darkness and hugged himself for warmth as he looked around. There was nothing else in the cell, not so much as a stool or a slop jar. Abruptly, he realized why the straw smelled so bad. With a groan of disgust, he got to his feet and brushed himself off.

He didn't know exactly how long he leaned against the wall, or when exactly he made his way to the cell door. He grasped the bars and peered out. Not far away, a smoky torch burned in a sconce on the wall. Near it, he spied a peg where hung a ring full of keys.

"Help," he called out weakly, sure that no one could have heard him. His knees buckled. Only by grasping the bars did he manage to stay on his feet. He pulled himself upright again. "Help!" he cried with greater volume, his face pressed to the bars.

A roach crawled across the back of his hand. With a violent start, he shook it off. The creature landed on his leg, however. Frantically, he snatched at it and caught it in a tight grip. In almost the same motion he flung it against the far wall. A satisfying pop marked the roach's demise.

"Hey, bucko! What'cher doin' to me pets in there?"

Caspar turned toward the door. A face was pressed up against the bars from the outside. A very ugly face. Half the teeth were missing, the nose had been broken at least twice, and a large earring dangled from a distended left lobe. A key grated in the iron lock. An instant later, the door swung outward.

"Howdja like me ta splatter yer guts all over the wall like that, ya little creep?"

Caspar's eyes widened in fear as the jailer squeezed through the doorway and entered the cell. The fellow was at least a half-blooded giant! The dim torchlight gleamed on biceps as thick as Caspar's waist, on fists large and powerful enough to twist his head off like it was a cork in a beer bottle.

He retreated immediately to the far side of the cell. "Uh, sorry?" he said hopefully.

The giant leered. "Maybe I oughta jus' bang yer head on the floor a couple o' times ta give ya the flavor of it," he growled as he advanced toward Caspar. "Them little bugs don' hurt nobody. They's my friends down here. The only friends Olio's got."

Caspar felt the cold stone wall against his spine. "Olio?" he said, putting on his biggest smile. "Is that your name?" He held out his hand, hoping the giant would take it as a chummy gesture. "Well, Olio, I'll be your friend. How about that? We can talk if you want. Trade life stories. Won't that be nice?"

Olio came closer, his eyebrows knitting together, a snarl on his lips. One hand reached out for Caspar.

"We could hang out together!" Caspar suggested anxiously. He shot a glance toward the corridor. There was no chance at all he could get around the giant and bolt for the door. The aches in his body told him he'd never make it. "Wanna check out some babes?" he said. "We could double date!"

Olio hesitated and appeared to think it over. The giant rubbed his chin, then tugged at the thin queue of braided hair that sprouted from the right side of his scalp and hung down his shoulder. Finally he reached out for Caspar's hand. For a brief moment Caspar smiled as he felt Olio's hand close warmly around his own. But before he could so much as let go a sigh of relief the giant jerked him forward, spun him about, and twisted his arm high up between his shoulder blades. Caspar let go a surprised cry of pain and found himself bent forward and dragged toward the door.

"Ya already got a date, bucko," Olio told him with a sneer. "An' I thank me lucky stars I ain't involved in it wit' ya."

"Wait!" Caspar pleaded as Olio steered him into the corridor. Just beyond the torch was a small table. Spread upon it were his clothes and the contents of his blue bundle. "At least let me get dressed!"

Olio twisted his arm higher still, and Caspar let go a sharp groan. "Now me little roach friend didn't get a chance ta dress 'fore ya splashed his innards on the wall, did he?" The giant let go a mean, throaty chuckle. "What makes ya think ya deserve better?"

"It was only a bug!" Caspar cried in pained exasperation.

The giant clucked his tongue chidingly. "That's real egocentric o' ya," he answered smugly, employing the largest word in his vocabulary. "I suppose yer one o' them kind what sees a bug an' ya just got ta swat it." Without warning, Olio delivered a stinging slap to the back of Caspar's head. The sharp smack echoed loudly in the narrow corridor, as did the shriek it elicited from its recipient.

Olio leaned forward and put his mouth close to Caspar's ear. His breath reeked of onions and turnips, but Caspar barely noticed. "Ya better realize real quick, bucko. Yer jus' another bug around here. Jus' another roach. An' with Duncanthrax, you'll be real lucky if ya get off wit' the same fate as me little squished pal back there."

"Dun—Duncanthrax?" Caspar stuttered fearfully. "Who's he?"

Olio pushed him roughly forward, using the twisted arm to guide and hurry him along. "'Ya'll find out right soon enough." He gave Caspar another slap and chortled. "Boy like you," he laughed, "you'll look jus' fine all splattered an' stuck on a wall. Now march!"

They moved through a maze of dank corridors. The stone floor was moist and cold against Caspar's bare feet, but he didn't think much about it. Everytime he slowed or hesitated, the giant dealt him a painful smack. Nor could he do anything to relieve the pressure on his arm. Up a spiraling flight of steps they went. Once, they passed a crenelation, which gave Caspar a brief glimpse of the outside world. The sky was an iodine blaze as the sun sank behind the spires and towers of Borphee.

Olio steered him through a wooden doorway and down another corridor. A bevy of scantily clad women, all draped in strategically placed silks and satins, came from the opposite direction. A long, delicate chain of gold joined them all by their wrists. Despite his uncomfortable situation, Caspar was struck by their beauty. Each lady was perfect of form and face, elegantly coiffed and jeweled with smears of rouge in the cleavages between their plump breasts. A cloud of perfume filled the air.

Concubines, Caspar realized.

The women began to giggle and stare as soon as they saw him. Immediately his cheeks began to burn. In fact, all of him began to turn red with embarrassment. He was still naked! He did his best to cover himself with his one free hand, and Olio thoughtfully helped by twisting his arm even harder, forcing him to bend almost double.

"Oooh, he's a cute one!" cooed one of the women in a low husky voice. Despite his predicament, Caspar noticed the slender gold key she wore on a silk cord about her neck. She had a look of authority about her, and he decided she must be in charge of the others. She noticed him noticing, and gave him a wink as she pulled a strand of jet black hair over one eye, pushed out her lips, and struck a suggestive pose. "You send him to me,

Olio. When Duncanthrax is through tenderizing him I'll really cook his meat."

The giant jailer's scowl only evoked more laughter from the ladies.

"And you can come, too, Olio!" suggested another of the concubines, a flirty little girl with blond curls that spilled down the small of her back. She batted her lashes playfully at the jailer.

But the girl next to her nudged her sharply in the ribs. "Olio can't come!" that one scolded the blond girl. "He's got nothing under his apron. His dangle-bobs are hanging on a nail in Duncanthrax's trophy case!"

The ladies laughed uproariously, threw more taunts, and made rude gestures at both Caspar and Olio as they passed on down the corridor and vanished through a large doorway. Olio growled deep in his throat and took his anger out on Caspar's twisted arm. Caspar gave a shriek as he found himself lifted onto the tips of his toes.

"Give me a break!" Caspar screamed.

"I just might, bucko!" the giant answered brutally, but he eased the pressure ever so slightly as he glanced back at the door the women had gone through. "I hope they suffocate on all that cheap cologne."

At the end of the corridor was a large pair of ornately carved doors. Olio rapped twice and pushed them open. With a shove he propelled Caspar into the center of the room. Caspar stumbled and fell on the plush carpeting. Near tears, he rubbed the elbow he had landed on, but at least his poor arm was finally free.

He glanced around quickly, taking in his surroundings. The room was large, the walls hung with richly embroidered tapestries, the floor piled with thick, woven rugs. An elaborate candlelabrum hung suspended on a fat chain from the ceiling. A score of candles burned there, filling the room with a warm light. Besides a few plush chairs and some small tables there was no furniture. There was, however, another room just beyond.

"Is that him?" said a harsh voice from the other room.

Caspar twisted around just in time to see a short,

plump little man, not much more than four feet tall, all dressed in a heavy red velvet robe, fancifully embroidered, with yellow felt slippers come from the side chamber into the main room. The man's hair was flaming red, as were his bushy eyebrows, which nearly met in the center of his forehead above a bulbous nose. His cheeks and lips were cherry red. But for the cold gleam in his dark eyes, it was the face of a cherub. An unpleasant cherub.

Olio made a curt bow and said loudly, "Soon as he woke up, I brung him, Majesty."

Caspar's eyebrows arched sharply. *Majesty*? Could this little man really be Zilbo the Third, King of Quendor and last ruler in a dynasty dating back more than six centuries to Quendor's founding father, the Great and All-powerful Entharion the Wise? He frowned again, but this time in disappointment. Despite the obvious costliness of his garish garments this guy hardly looked like Caspar's idea of a monarch.

A hand slapped him roughly in the back of the head. "Lower yer eyes, ya damn dog, when King Duncanthrax looks at ya!"

Caspar had had about enough of being smacked around by the jailer. His eyes flared angrily. He barely managed to bite back a sharp insult. Instead, he looked at this Duncanthrax character and said with far greater calm than he felt, "You should teach your eunuch better grammar, sir." He looked over his shoulder at the red-faced Olio. "It's *you* damned dog. Try to say it without sounding like you've got your finger down your throat."

Olio barked a short curse and rained a storm of blows around Caspar's head and shoulders. Caspar, for his part, could do nothing but curl up in a ball to protect himself. At last, he cried out, not from any real pain, though there was plenty of that, but because he figured the jailer would not stop until he gave him that satisfaction.

"You're such a brute, Olio," Duncanthrax said with an exaggerated sigh as he went to a decorative table on the far side of the room. Caspar uncurled cautiously and peeked out under one arm to watch. Duncanthrax picked up an item that Caspar recognized immediately. It was the leather bottle.

"Now, young man," said Duncanthrax. There was a hint of impatient boredom in his voice that made him sound all the more dangerous as he held the bottle up. "Perhaps you'll tell me where you got this? Speak up. Or shall I have Olio give you another massage?"

Caspar swallowed as he stared at the bottle with the letter "Z" carved so delicately upon it. He pursed his lips as he began to realize just how much trouble he was in. Olio had called this Duncanthrax *majesty*. Except Zilbo was supposed to be the king of Quendor. As Caspar hesitated, the gleam in Duncanthrax's eyes sharpened, and Caspar didn't much like that gleam.

"Now wait a minute," he said to Duncanthrax as he slowly rose to his knees, but no farther. He clutched his hands in his lap in an effort to conceal his nakedness. He felt exposed enough as it was. "I suppose you're looking for a little old guy." Duncanthrax nodded, listening with an intent expression, and Caspar continued. "Blue eyes. White hair down to here, right? A staff made of morgia wood?"

Both Duncanthrax and Olio nodded enthusiastically. Caspar felt the first beads of sweat pop out of his brow. "And I suppose you're going to tell me that old guy was King Zilbo the Third, right?"

Duncanthrax laid a finger to the tip of his nose and nodded. Olio frowned, however. "Don't much like the way he says *King* Zilbo," the giant commented. "Sounds like a loyalist."

Caspar studied the leather bottle in Duncanthrax's hand, thinking fast. There had been a change of power, that much was certainly clear. He'd met Zilbo on the road. The old man was leaving town, perhaps on the sly, considering his lowly appearance and lack of entourage. It seemed equally clear that Duncanthrax had taken the old man's place. It also seemed clear from his tone of voice and his interest in the bottle that Duncanthrax wanted Zilbo found.

It would be better for you if you didn't tell anyone we met, Caspar heard the old man who had called himself Zil saying as they parted on the hilltop.

On the other hand, Duncanthrax didn't look in a very good mood, and Olio was almost twice Caspar's size. Caspar looked from one man to the other, feeling like a mouse with a cat on his left and a trap on his right. He examined his options. He could do the noble thing and keep his mouth shut. Or he could do the smart thing.

He settled on the smart thing. "I'm not a loyalist," he answered quickly. "I'm a *Casparist*. If you want Zilbo, he's on the east road beyond the hills. I talked to him a few moments, but he called himself Zil. He left the wine bottle behind, and I picked it up. I figured I could sell it for a few zorkmids." He made a deep bow, touching his forehead to the floor before he looked up again. "That's all I can tell you, Majesty." *Might as well get used to the sound of that*, he decided practically. *King Duncanthrax*. It had a ring.

"What a wimp," Olio commented disgustedly to his king. "Didn't even get ta use the rack. An' all those hot coals wasted. What am I supposed ta do with the rest o' the evenin', now?"

"I have a suggestion about that," Caspar muttered. He swiftly cringed as Olio raised a fist over his head.

"Stop!" Duncanthrax commanded. He put the toe of his felt slipper softly under Caspar's chin, forcing him to raise his head ever so slightly until their eyes met. "You seem to have a ready grasp of the situation you find yourself in," Duncanthrax said. "Where are you from? Answer me, and don't mutter."

"Djabuti Padjama," Caspar answered quietly.

A flicker of a smile danced across Duncanthrax's face. "Yes, I am cute in pajamas," he said with a wink. "But you can't buy your way into my heart that easily."

"He's a little deaf," Olio whispered, nudging Caspar with a toe as he rolled his eyes ceilingward.

"No, your Majesty!" Caspar enunciated more clearly.

"Djabuti Padjamas! It's a small village in the Peltoid Valley in the eastern part of the kingdom."

Duncanthrax waved a hand in annoyance. "Yes, yes!" he said. "And the keeper at the east gate tells me your name is Caspar Wartsworth?"

It was Caspar's turn to nod.

"Well, you've done me a great service, Caspar Wartsworth." Duncanthrax swirled his red robe about himself and walked a few paces away before he turned back. "Zilbo was no longer fit to rule Quendor," he continued in a harsher voice. "He preferred to spend his days playing card games, instead of managing the bureaucracy and looking after the business of the kingdom. Ambassadors and dignitaries were left waiting while he dealt hands with gossipy little blue-haired old ladies." Duncanthrax paused and looked thoughtful. "Not that I have anything against gossip, mind you. It's just that it was never *interesting gossip!*"

"So you kicked him out," Caspar said sympathetically. He'd personally sat around with far too many farmers not to know first hand the mind-numbing effects of dull gossip.

Duncanthrax smiled and looked at Olio. "He is quick, isn't he?" he said. "He's quick." He looked down at Caspar on the floor and came closer. "I like that. You're quick."

Then, Duncanthrax bent down, grabbed a handful of Caspar's hair and jerked his head back sharply. "The word is *deposed*, you little backwoods sheep chip! I *deposed* Zilbo. For the good of Quendor, you understand?"

Caspar did his best to nod. "Yes, sir!" he shouted.

Duncanthrax clucked his tongue and wagged a finger under Caspar's nose. "Your Majesty," he said quietly, but firmly.

"Yes, your Majesty!" Caspar answered, acknowledging the correction.

Duncanthrax sighed and let him go, then stepped back a few paces and brushed his hands. A few strands of Caspar's hair floated to the carpet. Eyes smarting, Caspar reached back and patted the crown of his head, expecting to find a bald spot the size of his hometown.

Duncanthrax folded his arms across his chest, yawned, then stretched. "Because you're quick," he said looking at Caspar with an almost paternal expression, "and because I like you, and because you've done me such a service by telling me which way that old fool Zilbo headed, I've made a decision in your favor."

Duncanthrax pushed his hands into the voluminous, embroidered sleeves of his red velvet robe and did his best to look regal, though at just over four feet Caspar thought he only looked like a plump dwarf with a bad fashion sense.

"I'm going to let you continue to serve me," Quendor's new king went on. He turned his back, then, and strutted toward the side chamber from where he had originally appeared. But he waved a hand casually at Olio as he departed and said, "Take him to the galleys."

CHAPTER FOUR

ANTHARIA ON FIFTY LASHES A DAY

CASPAR HAD COME TO Borphee to be a sailor, but this wasn't quite what he had in mind. The heavy shackles had been on his wrists for less than an hour and already they chafed. He gazed upward at the star-speckled heavens and rattled his chains in frustration.

His bench-mate, a grizzled but tough old man with scraggly hair and beard woke up and gave him an elbow in the ribs. "Quiet, damn ye!" he growled, eyes burning in the dim moonlight. "Wake me again an' I'll twist your fool head off! Get some sleep while ye can! We sail for Antharia at first light!" The old man curled forward over the massive oar and cradled his head on folded arms. He appeared to fall asleep at once.

Caspar groaned inwardly, filled with despair. The gentle rocking of the great battle bireme did nothing to lull him. He stared toward the dark outline of the city. He had barely seen anything of it. On the other side of the ship stretched the vast black expanse of the sea. The rolling waves gleamed, kissed by the moon. It was beautiful, but horrifying and unknown.

A cool wind blew in from the sea, chilling him. The guards had given him no more than a loincloth to cover himself before they'd chained him to his bench. Most of the other oarsmen had already been asleep. A few looked up from their uncomfortable slumber as the pins were hammered through his shackles and the chain locked in place. They eyed him dully, then went back to their dreams. He gazed sadly at them now. Poor men, old men, weary men. Where had they come from?

A word popped unexpectedly into his head. *Loyalists*. That was the word Olio had used. These were the men still loyal to Zilbo. Duncanthrax had found a convenient way to dispose of them. Let them be as loyal as they wanted. They would still serve the New Order.

Caspar gritted his teeth as despair slowly became a smouldering rage. He strained at his chains again, though quietly, testing their strength. He couldn't break them. Yet, he swore, they would not hold him long. Somehow, he would find a way. He would be free.

He leaned forward on his oar and rested his head. Sleep wouldn't come, he knew. Yet he forced himself to rest and be calm. His time would come. He closed his eyes and listened to the creak of the wharves, the groan of the bireme's timbers, the quiet, endless lapping of the water.

Just before sunrise someone placed lighted torches in the fore and aft parts of the ship. A slender young man emerged from a rearward cabin and moved down the central deck passing out crude wooden bowls and slapping the heads of those who still slept. Some of the slaves growled curses at him and gave him sullen looks, but he paid no attention. His gaze was almost blank, his features utterly passive.

He hesitated only a moment at Caspar's bench. "You're new," he grunted, soft-voiced. Then he shoved a bowl into Caspar's hands and moved on.

It was the first thing anyone had said to Caspar since he came to the ship in the night that wasn't a threat or an order. He watched the dark-haired youth as he worked his way up the deck. He moved with a lithe, lean-muscled economy of motion on the gently rocking deck, yet he had a beaten, abused look.

"Who is he?" Caspar whispered to his bench-mate.

"Sunrise," the old man answered gruffly, glaring at the youth's back.

Caspar frowned. "That's a strange name."

"Not his name," the old man answered. He looked away and spat over the side of the ship. Then he turned back. "Jus' what we call 'im. Nobody gets a name here. He's the one what wakes us up, always jus' before sunrise. So that's what we call 'im. You'll learn to hate 'im soon enough, like the rest of us."

"What do you mean, nobody gets a name?" Caspar asked, leaning closer to his bench-mate, the better to whisper and still make himself heard. He realized he hadn't yet learned this old man's name. "You've got a name, haven't you?"

An ugly leer turned the corners of the old man's mouth upward, showing two missing teeth on the left side of his mouth. "I'm Number Twenty-three," his benchmate growled. He drummed the tip of his left index finger down on the bench between them, showing Caspar a numeral mark burned into the wood there. "An' yer Number Twenty-two." He leaned just far enough across Caspar to point out another numeral near the place where the bench joined the central deck. "Now we're introduced proper."

Twenty-three turned away again and looked out over the harbor. Caspar gazed that way, also. It was still dark. Dawn was only just beginning to color the sky. Yet, he could see the spots of firelight out upon the water. Torches, he realized. When he stared hard he could just make out the black outlines of prows and masts and oars. There were other ships out there. Lots of them.

He leaned close to Twenty-three again. "What are we doing here?" he whispered. "What's going on?"

Twenty-three made a disgusted face and looked at Caspar as if he was the stupidest dog in the kennel and maybe should just be tied in a bag and dropped in the river. "You some kind o' fool, boy? That's a navy out there, an' we're part o' it. Ol' Duncanthrax, curse his eyes, has taken it in his to try an' invade Antharia. We git to go 'long for the ride."

"But nobody's ever invaded that island!" Caspar

hissed. Even a poor dumb inland farmer knew that. Antharia was the strongest sea-power on Zork. Others had tried to invade it before, but its cliff-lined coasts and heavily fortified harbors made it a tough clam to crack.

"Where's that damn food!" Twenty-three growled, leaning forward on his oar, clutching his bowl. "It's puke, but ye better eat it. It's all we git."

A few moments later, Sunrise strode back down the deck and disappeared through an aft door. Shortly, he reappeared, lugging a heavy black kettle from which he ladled a sticky, bland-looking mass into each man's bowl. The youth looked Caspar directly in the eyes again, seeming to study him, as he filled Caspar's bowl, but he passed on without a word.

Caspar stuck two fingers into his bowl and lifted a portion of the thick, grainy cereal. He wrinkled his nose. It had a foul, pungent odor. He stuck his tongue out and touched it to the mixture. It was all he could do to keep from spitting. Still, he hadn't eaten for a full day. He ate little by little, forcing himself to swallow each bite. He tried his best to ignore the taste by observing the vessel on which he found himself.

He had never seen a sailing ship before, let alone one of Quendor's mighty battle biremes. The prow swept upward gracefully. The shipbuilder had fashioned it in the likeness of one of the fearsome sea serpents that haunted the Great Ocean, even painting large, white eyes that from a distance no doubt appeared real. There were cabins both fore and aft, but their doors were kept shut, and Caspar couldn't guess what lay within, except that food came from the rearward. On the roof of the forward cabin stood a massive drum. Caspar didn't need to be told what it was for.

He took another mouthful of cereal and continued his study in the dawn's growing light. A tall single mast rose from the center of the deck. The furled sail was tightly wrapped and bound around the boom. They would not be using that until they were out of the harbor. There were piles of supplies scattered about the deck, but most were covered with heavy cloth to protect them from wind and water. Stacks of weapons, though, he recognized. Bundles of arrows, racks of spears and javelins, pitch-balls to be ignited and catapulted at other ships.

It was true, then. They were bound for war with Antharia. He quickly counted rowers. Thirty men. But a bireme had two rows of oars. There would be another thirty, then, on a lower deck. Come time for combat, the sail would be stowed away. They would be the power that drove the ship to battle.

As he finished his meager breakfast, Quendoran soldiers, each bearing weapons and a rolled pack, began to come on board. Over a gang-walk from the edge of the wharf they filed, stepping onto the roof of the rear cabin, climbing a short ladder to the deck. Some disappeared through an aft hatch into the bowels of the vessel. Others moved to various stations on the upper deck. Some vanished inside the cabins. Shortly after them came the officers, three men, resplendent in gold battle armor, red uniforms and black cloaks upon which were embroidered the great eagle emblem of the Quendor nation.

"That's Cap'n Chulig," Twenty-three whispered, nudging Caspar in the ribs and nodding toward the largest of the three officers. Chulig was not only tall, but grossly fat, with heavy jowls and several chins. His cloak and armor and crested helm only made him seem heavier still.

"I thought I felt the ship list a bit when he stepped on board," Caspar whispered with a barely hidden grin.

Twenty-three was not amused. "He's mean. Ye best watch 'im," he cautioned.

The officers disappeared inside the forward cabin. While the other soldiers and sailors made their preparations Sunrise collected the breakfast bowls from the rowers. Through the timbers under his feet, Caspar could feel activity in the deeper bowels of the vessel.

The deep blue of morning peeled back the last edges of night. Out in the harbor, the first of twenty ships dipped its oars in practiced unison, turned, and moved out toward the open sea. The sun sparkled on the water that rilled from the oars as they rose and fell. The ship's prow cut through the sea, leaving behind a white, foaming wake.

Despite his predicament, Caspar felt his heart sing! During all those nights when the cloying smells of stables and barnyards and dusty silos had filled his nose he had dreamed of the sea. How many times had he held a rake or a hoe in his hands and pretended it was an oar or the tiller of some great ship? How many times had he stared at a pond or a lake and tried to imagine high tides and distant shores?

He lifted his head, felt the wind on his face, and smelled the smells of the sea. Without thinking, he shifted on his bench, the better to see that first great vessel pass between the horns of the harbor, but the heavy clinking of the shackles on his wrists reminded him that this was not the dream he had dreamed.

The door to the forward cabin opened and Chulig stepped on deck again. He wore a scowl on his ugly face and ground his right fist into the palm of his left hand. He stared toward the wharfside of the ship, and his scowl deepened.

"Get aloft!" Chulig ordered one of his sailors. A soldier in full armor scrambled hand over hand up a rope, one of many attached to the single mast, until he reached the boom. He grabbed hold and pulled himself up until he straddled it. "Any sign?" Chulig called.

The man shouted enthusiastically. "He's coming!"

Chulig smashed his hands together angrily. "I'll have his ears and the nails off his big toes!" the captain growled. "He was supposed to be on board already!"

The soldier slithered back down the rope and landed on the deck as Chulig continued to pace and scowl. An air of expectation hung over the ship. The soldiers glanced nervously at one another, eager to be under way. Even the slaves at the oars mumbled among themselves.

Suddenly, all conversation ceased. The abrupt hush was almost chilling in its effect. Caspar saw the others around him turn and stare toward the rear of the ship, and he turned, too.

A willowy stick of a man stood upon the roof of the aft cabin, his hands folded inside voluminous sleeves, his blue robe and cloak fluttering about him. It was difficult to see a face under his hood. The man stood there, completely still, calm and commanding as he surveyed the vessel and its crew. Only when he was apparently satisfied did he mount the ladder and climb down to the deck. With a slow, measured stride he moved toward Chulig.

"Well, you took your damn fine time getting here!" the captain raged, shaking a fist in the air. "The other ships are already heading out, and we're still tied up at the frogging wharf!"

The blue-robed figure made a gesture of indifference as he moved sublimely past Chulig. "Then I suggest you cut the ties and cast off," he said with more than a hint of sarcasm as he opened the forward cabin's door and went inside.

Chulig turned red-faced and started after him, but with the very first step he tripped, cried out awkwardly and fell on his face. A great roar of laughter went up from sailors and slaves alike, but almost at once they realized it was the captain they were laughing at. A tense embarrassed silence settled as Chulig sat up and glared around. One of his soldiers went to his aid, but Chulig cuffed the man away and leaned forward to untie his bootlaces, which had mysteriously tied themselves together. With as much dignity as he could muster, he rose, adjusted his cloak, tunic, and breastplate, set his helmet aright on his head, and strode toward the forward cabin. The slamming of the door as he went inside jolted the entire crew.

One of the junior officers emerged on deck a moment later. "Take her out!" he called at the top of his lungs. The order echoed back toward the rear of the ship, passing among at least ten men, which Caspar estimated was eight more than was necessary.

On the starboard side, a pair of axes cut quickly through the ropes that held the ship to the wharf. The oarsmen on that side then used their oars to push away while the tillerman at the rear did his part.

"Granted there's been a long tradition of military waste," Caspar whispered to his bench-mate, "but why don't they just untie the ropes, or lift the loops off the bollards?"

Number Twenty-three gave him a sidewise glance and raised an eyebrow. "Hey," he muttered. "These are *real* men." He leaned on his oar and gave a weary sneer. "Besides, the welfare of our country *depends* on military waste and overspending. Without it, thousands of bureaucrats and politicians, not to mention half the admirals and generals, would be out of the kind of work that keeps their conniving minds occupied, and otherwise turned loose on a hapless and unwary public."

The vessel's prow swung away and pointed toward the sea. Caspar and his bench-mate leaned on their oar, holding it high out of the water, as did the others on their side of the ship, until the turn was completed.

A loud *thump* sounded from the roof-deck of the forward cabin, and Caspar looked up to see an iron-thewed figure there behind the huge drum with a mighty gavel in each fist. He slammed one of the gavels down, and another *thump* shivered across the ship. At a barked command from the junior officer all rowers dipped their oars and the ship shot forward.

Caspar felt the muscles in his back pop as he strained at his oar. He turned his gaze toward the great drum, anticipating the fall of each gavel stroke. The city of Borphee disappeared from his field of vision. He had seen nothing of it, anyway.

They were coming up on another ship, one of those waiting to leave the harbor. He watched it growing larger on his right. Too fast, he realized with a clenching moment of terror. Too fast and much too close. Twenty-three gave a fearful cry and jerked hard on the oar. The long shaft went shooting across the deckway, and the dripping blade slammed hard up against the oar hole. The other leeward rowers did the same, all screaming and cursing.

A terrible splintering and shattering filled the air as they crashed through the oars of the other bireme and rushed on by. Caspar had a fleeting glimpse of the stricken faces on the other ship and of a captain standing in stunned disbelief as his vessel was crippled and left behind.

Chulig rushed out on deck and stared over the rail. There was a sheepish look on his fat face, and he chewed one nail. Then he forced a smile and waved to the captain of the disabled ship. "Tough luck, there!" he called. "Better luck next time!"

Then, Chulig turned to his junior officer and crooked a finger. Like a frightened puppy, the officer slunk to his captain's side, clutching his hands in front of him and staring at the toes of his boots. "Sorry, sir!" he muttered, shamefaced.

"Assume the position!" Chulig barked.

A look of fear crossed the young officer's features, but obediently he climbed up on the rail and balanced there, his toes at the edge, his arms extended like a diver preparing to leap. "Whenever you're ready, sir!" he called timorously down to his captain. He bit his lip, waiting.

"I'm sorry it's come to this," Chulig said. "You'd have made a good captain someday."

The young officer struggled to keep his balance as the ship rolled under him. "Thank you, sir," he answered. "I don't suppose there's any chance of forgiveness?"

"None," Chulig answered.

The officer nodded. "I understand, sir. Standards to maintain, and all that."

Chulig planted his hand on his officer's rump and gave a little nudge. The officer grabbed his nose with both hands as he tumbled over the side. The sun flashed briefly on his armor, and his cloak fluttered around him like the broken wings of a bird.

"There's a good man," Chulig declared over the sound of the splash. He turned around and pointed at one of the regular soldiers, who instantly turned pale.

"You're first mate now," Chulig announced, and the soldier swallowed. "Don't disappoint me."

"Hope he can swim," Twenty-three whispered to Caspar. "Chulig goes through mates like a fish through water."

"No faith in monogamy?" Caspar suggested.

Chulig left the deck again, leaving the new first mate to tremble at his good fortune. Finally, he turned and shouted to the rowers. "Get those oars back in the water! What do you think this is, a pleasure cruise?"

"Great," muttered the slave directly behind Caspar. "This one's got a sense of humor."

The drum cadence began again.

CHAPTER FIVE

THE SCREAMING QUEEN
GOES DOWN

ONCE THE VESSEL achieved open sea, the rowers shipped their oars. A brisk wind blew, and the sail was swiftly hoisted. The canvas snapped and cracked, and the rigging hummed as the white sheet was drawn upward. A huge Quendoran eagle, emblazoned on the sail in red and gold, shone brilliantly in the morning sunlight.

All the ships in Quendor's navy flew the same eagle, and Caspar had to admit it was quite a stirring sight as he glanced to either side. Nearly thirty ships, minus the disabled one left behind in the harbor, rode the waves close by. They hugged the coastline, sailing a southward course, spreading out upon the sea as they went.

"Does this ship have a name?" Caspar whispered to his bench-mate as another vessel approached on the leeward side, overtook and passed them by.

"The *Screamin' Queen*," Twenty-three answered. He leaned down, put his mouth close to his oar hole, and drew a deep breath. He let it go and drew another.

"Why are you doing that?" Caspar asked, intrigued.

"Fresh air," Twenty-three answered without looking up. He continued to fill his lungs, inhaling and exhaling noisily and with great show.

Caspar frowned. "That might make sense down below," he admitted. "But this is the top deck. There's plenty of fresh air." He drew a deep breath himself, and exhaled it.

Twenty-three sat up and gave him a stern look of disapproval. "Ye've absolutely no sense o' drama, boy," he declared as he brushed back the locks of gray hair that blew across his face.

"But he does have nice shoulder blades," commented Number Twenty-four, the slave on the bench behind Caspar.

Caspar twisted around, raising an eyebrow. The man winked at Caspar and put on a smile.

Twenty-three ignored the interruption. He tried again to brush back an unruly lock of iron-gray hair that snapped at his nose like a small whip as the wind blew. He fixed Caspar with a hard gaze. "As a galley slave, it's your lot to suffer. Your liberty has been taken from you. Even your name. You're Twenty-two." He rattled his chains and gave the oar a shake as he warmed to his speech. "Your freedom has been raped. You've been forced into a dehumanizing situation without recourse or appeal to justice."

Twenty-three jabbed Caspar's arm with a steely finger to drive home his point. "Even when you're not suffering . . ."

"Don't worry," came a whisper behind Caspar. Twenty-four leaned as close as his shackles allowed him. "You'll suffer. How you'll suffer! And me, I'll just sit here alone, and you'll never turn to me for help."

". . . you have to pretend like you are!" Twenty-three continued earnestly over the comments of Twenty-four. "You have to look the part. Look as miserable as possible. Look awful! Act abused!" He leaned forward on the oar shaft and glared at the back of the nearest soldier. "Never forget, it's a slave's duty to make his masters feel as guilty as possible."

"What happened to your accent?" Caspar asked quietly, scratching his chin as he regarded his bench-mate with sudden puzzlement. "All that gruff sailor talk?"

Behind Caspar, Twenty-four gave a low chuckle. "That's part of his act, too, dearie!"

"Shut yer froggin' mouth, maggot!" Twenty-three

snapped, falling into character as he whirled around to face his fellow slave.

But before Twenty-three could do or say more a shadow fell across them all. Caspar turned slowly and stared up at the huge figure of Captain Chulig. The brightness of the sun behind his head caused Caspar to squint and shield his eyes. Chulig's features were black with anger.

A chilling silence fell over the ship. Chulig hooked his thumbs in his belt as he glared at Twenty-three. "You know my rules about talking, Twenty-three!" he roared.

The old man glared back defiantly. "Damn yer rules, an' damn yer eyes!" he hissed. "I am not a number. I am a free man!"

Chulig gave a low, unpleasant chuckle as his first mate and several other officers gathered around. "You're a prisoner," Chulig answered coldly, "of Quendor, and a slave aboard my ship. But you obviously need to be reminded of that." He snapped his fingers and called out. "Sunrise!"

The youth walked nervously down the deck in answer to Chulig's summons. In his right hand he clutched a coiled whip, and his gaze darted from side to side as the other galley slaves glared sullenly at him. He said nothing, but his eyes fell on Caspar as he stopped at the captain's side, and Caspar saw to his surprise that the boy trembled. "Yes, sir?" he said apprehensively.

A thin smile flickered over Chulig's face. "Twenty-three has been insubordinate," he said firmly. "Teach the dog the error of his ways. Ten lashes."

Behind Caspar, Number Twenty-four clucked his tongue. "Oh no, Captain," he said grandiosely. "Spare him, please. I started the conversation, so whip me, instead. I've been bad. I deserve it."

"No," said another slave from the other side of the deck. "Whip me!"

The first mate stepped forward and made a curt bow. There was a strange gleam in his eyes. "Actually, Captain, it's all my fault. I should have been keeping a closer eye on them. If anyone should be whipped, I guess it's me."

Several of the sailors abandoned their tasks and rushed forward, raising their hands. "No, me!" cried one. "No, me," shouted another. "Gimme a taste o' that lash, mates!"

Caspar stared in confusion at all the eager faces and all the hands volunteering for punishment. At first, he'd thought the slaves were merely trying to divert the captain's attention away from a fellow slave, a very courageous and selfless thing for them to try. But with the sailors and soldiers, even the officers all stepping forward, he hardly knew what to think!

Sunshine licked his lips, hesitating, awaiting an order from his captain. When none came the coils of the whip slipped from his fingers and uncurled on the deck. The youth glanced at Caspar again, and his trembling increased as he drew back with his arm and prepared to strike.

Twenty-three gave up all pretense of defiance. He screamed suddenly and covered his head with both arms as he cowered down over the oar. Caspar saw the stripes of previous whippings on his exposed back.

"Wait," Chulig ordered before Sunshine could deliver the first lash. The captain braced his hands on both his hips and put on a pouty expression as he leaned forward. His shadow fell directly on Caspar. "Well?" he said impatiently.

Caspar realized Chulig was addressing him. "Well, what?" he answered lamely.

Chulig's face turned almost as red as his hair. His eyes burned like coals as he bent down over Caspar. "Don't you want to volunteer too? Don't you fancy a bit of the long Betsy, here?" He caught a piece of the whip's length in his hands and slid the braided leather over one palm.

The question stunned Caspar. Without thinking he looked up from the whip and met Chulig's gaze. "One of us is having a severe personality lapse," he suggested with quiet gravity.

The captain's face went from red to purple. "Sunrise!'' he shouted angrily. ''Twenty-two has decided to stand punishment for his bench-mate. He'll take the ten and five more.''

''Oh please!'' shrieked the slave behind Caspar. ''Don't mark those beautiful shoulders! Well, not too much, anyway!''

Twenty-three gave his chains a vicious shake. ''Leave 'im alone, ye mongrel seadog!'' he hissed, rising from his bench. The shackles on his arms, however, allowed him no more than a pathetic crouch. ''He's new here, an' don't yet know what a nasty pig's arse ye are!''

Captain Chulig's face contorted with rage, but he mastered his temper and allowed a tight little smile. ''Compliments won't make me change my mind, Twenty-three. However, since you ask for them so eloquently, you may have your own fifteen.'' He snapped his fingers. ''Sunrise!''

The boy raised the whip, but his eyes met Caspar's, and he bit his lip. He hesitated, trembling, torn between his captain's order and something else. Yet his fear of Chulig finally won out. The whip slashed downward. Biting fire shot across Caspar's shoulders. He gasped and jerked his head away to protect his face.

The lashes came in rapid succession. Caspar howled and did his best to cringe away, but his chains held him to the bench. The stinging pain filled his mind, and the cry that issued from his lips sounded far away. He sagged across his oar and prayed for it to end.

The crack of the whip was unrelenting. It took a few moments, though, for him to realize the screams he was hearing were no longer his own, that it was no longer his bare back that suffered the lash's bite. He turned his head aside and through a red haze saw his bench-mate. Twenty-three snarled curses between each blow and screamed his lungs out each time the leather ripped his flesh.

Then, for a blessed instant there was no sound at all.

Captain Chulig pushed Sunrise away and bent down. He wore a big grin as he said close to Caspar's ear, ''There now, you kind of like the long Betsy, don't you?''

He patted Caspar's head and rumpled his hair. "I could tell you were the type. That wasn't so bad at all."

Caspar pushed himself up and tried to focus on the captain's face, but the effort nearly made him sick. His head swam, and he felt nauseated. "No, no sir," he managed weakly. "But you'll have a devil's own time sanding my nail marks out of this oar." He slumped forward again as Chulig's laughter roared in his ears.

"By all the seas, Twenty-two, you've got spirit!" Chulig roared mirthfully. He gave Caspar an appreciative slap on the back, eliciting a sharp cry of pain and surprise from Caspar. Chulig laughed again and marched across the deck toward the forward cabin.

Caspar lifted his head and watched him go through tear-blinded eyes, swearing to somehow get his revenge.

"Let it go, lad," Twenty-three muttered. His breathing was labored, his words a harsh rasp. "There's a time fer anger, an' a time to lick yer wounds. Be thankful there's wind in the sail an' we don't have to row."

But Caspar wasn't thankful at all. "What happened to all that philosophical bluster about slaves and masters?" he said bitterly.

"Right now, it's bleedin' out me back," Twenty-three sighed as he put his head down on the oar.

Caspar stared past his bench-mate at the distant coastline, avoiding the pity-filled eyes of the other galley slaves and the mocking glances of the sailors and soldiers. Every wind that blew across his back fanned the fire in his flesh and the hatred in his heart. Slumped over his oar, he felt the weight of the shackles on his arms and fought to hold back tears. How long, he wondered, before his anger turned to despair? How many lashings did it take to beat the fight out of a man?

He flinched suddenly as someone touched his back, but the sensation was cool and soothing. "I'm sorry," someone whispered in his ear.

Caspar twisted around enough to see Sunrise behind him. The boy held a jar of grease in one hand. With his other hand he applied the black, viscous substance to Caspar's wounds. From the smell and the look, it was the same grease used around the oar holes to keep the oar shafts from wearing against the wood. His back felt better instantly. Caspar, though, turned away.

"Chulig makes me do it," Sunrise explained regretfully as he smeared the thick balm. "If I refuse I get the lashes and worse. All the slaves hate me because he makes me give the punishments. But I'm just trying to survive, too." Finishing with Caspar, he began applying the grease to the back of Number Twenty-three, who scowled and muttered a curse, but nevertheless accepted the youth's ministrations.

"Why do you keep looking at me the way you do?" Caspar didn't turn to face Sunrise. It was hard to sympathize with the one who had dealt him so much pain, no matter what the boy's circumstances. The fact that now he sounded apologetic and played the role of healer did little to mollify Caspar.

"You're going to get me off this crazy ship," Sunrise answered without hesitation. He came back to Caspar and smeared more of the grease upon the lash marks. His touch was feathery soft, strangely tender as he worked. "You're not like the rest of these tired old men," he said. "You're younger and stronger, and you're angry. I can see it in your eyes. You're going to find a way out of this, and when you do you're taking me with you."

"You're crazy," Caspar said, falling back over his oar. The beating had left him drained, and he felt a blackness creeping up over his senses. "I can't even save myself."

"You'll see," Sunrise told him in a terse whisper as he took the pot of oil and prepared to leave. "You'll see. And you'll have your revenge on Chulig, too."

For most of the morning the wind filled the sail and carried the *Screaming Queen* down the coast. Caspar could make out enough of the shoreline to guess how far they'd come.

A light mist wafted over a dark forest that lined the shore, and tendrils of fog drifted among the old trunks like wayward ghosts. Mauldwood it was called, this great, dense woodland that grew along the border between the provinces of Gurth and Frobozz. By legend it was a haunted place, full of grues and nabizes and hellhounds and other terrible beasts. Caspar had never been there, but he'd heard stories. There were only a few old roads through Mauldwood, and fewer still were the men who dared to travel them.

They were not yet past the southern edge of Mauldwood when the wind died suddenly. The first mate barked a command. Grimfaced, the barechested cadence master took up a position behind the great drum at the ship's fore as the galley slaves bent to their oars. The cadence master set the rhythm, slamming the gavels forcefully, his huge forearms bulging as sweat broke out upon his body. The ship itself throbbed to the mighty drum's pulse.

Caspar almost welcomed the mindlessness of his labor. For a while he lost himself in the back-breaking work. With the oar in his hands there was no need to think or worry. He merged into the stout shaft of wood, matching his efforts with his bench-mate's. The beat of the drum became his heartbeat, and for a time nothing mattered but the smooth flight of the ship upon the water.

Then, as a stinging drop of sweat fell into his eyes and he flung his head back to shake away the pain, something off to starboard caught his attention. A school of dolphins raced playfully alongside the vessel, the sun flashing on their sleek, silvery forms. But beyond them something else, some shadow, glided just under the water's surface. Caspar continued to labor at his oar, and when he looked up again the shadow had vanished. Only the dolphins remained, and in the distance, the other ships of the Quendoran navy.

"Did you see that?" Caspar asked his bench-mate. But Twenty-three was oblivious to everything but the oar and the rhythm of the great drum.

A moment later, the underwater shadow returned. It glided smoothly through the water. A long, thin ribbon of darkness beneath the rippling surface, it kept effortless pace with the ship, seeming to draw ever closer while the dolphins moved farther and farther away.

"I have a bad feeling about this," Caspar muttered to himself.

"About what?" Twenty-three grunted as he strained at the oar. He gave Caspar a queer, accusing look. "Do yer part, boy. I can't handle this thing by myself."

"Didn't you see it?" Caspar exclaimed in a tense whisper as he put his back into the rowing, trying to take more upon himself to ease the effort on his bench-mate.

"See what?" Twenty-three snapped irritably. "Can't see nothin' for the sweat in my eyes!"

Caspar threw a disbelieving glance over his shoulders. He couldn't have been the only one to see the shadow! Yet, the other slaves worked at the oars, groaning and gasping with each muscle-wrenching stroke, oblivious to all else. The soldiers and sailors on deck also seemed unaware of the underwater shadow.

He twisted around to peer past his bench-mate over the side again. The dark, smoothly swimming shape was gone.

The frayed end of a rope lashed down suddenly and stung Caspar's back. The pain seared through his already wounded flesh as if he'd been touched by the smoking end of a white-hot poker, and he cried out.

"Row, you damned pup!" The first mate stood above him, his face a twisted mask of nervous worry as he coiled the short rope in his hand and shook it at Caspar. "You make me look bad before the captain, and I swear you'll go headfirst over the rail before me!"

Caspar redoubled his efforts, trying once again to lose himself in the mesmerizing throb of the cadence drum. His tender hands were blistering around the rough wooden oar, but he gritted his teeth and tried to compensate by adjusting his grip, pushing with his palms, pulling with his fingers, yet that was futile. Silently cursing, he gripped the oar with his whole hand, pulled with his entire strength and tried to ignore the agony.

Suddenly, the door to the forward compartment

slammed open. Sunrise came flying out and crashed head-over-heels to the deck. Chulig stormed out after him. The front of the captain's trousers were soaking wet, as if he'd not made it quickly enough to his chamber pot. Several of the sailors noticed it right away. Those who were not standing too close pointed and snickered.

Chulig was too angry with Sunrise, though, to notice. He dealt the boy several kicks. Sunrise tried uselessly to scramble away. There was no place for him to go in the crush of men and supplies that crammed every spare corner of deck space. At last he simply curled up in a ball.

"You'll be more careful how you pour the wine next time, you useless little boot licker!" Chulig kicked him again. Then, seizing the short piece of rope that still dangled from his first mate's hand, he lashed Sunrise with it. The boy gave a loud whimper, but made no other sound as he huddled defenselessly at the captain's feet.

Chulig continued to beat him without mercy. "You're the worst cabin boy . . ." He drew back to strike with the rope again, but as he did he chanced to look up. His arm froze in midair, and his curse went unfinished. A shadow fell across him.

The monstrous head of a sea serpent appeared over the prow directly in the path of the ship. The sunlight gleamed brilliantly on its wet emerald scales and on the pair of dorsal crests. It twitched its whiskers once, and its great wide eyes, so white and round, blinked at its own likeness carved and painted on the *Screaming Queen*'s prow. Then it slid back beneath the waves.

A hundred cries of terror went up from slaves and sailors and soldiers. The cadence master forgot his drumming and dropped his gavels as he jumped down from his exposed position atop the forward cabin. Half the men who were not in chains ran to the rear of the ship, thinking to seek safety there. The other half surged to the rails to keep a watchful eye out for the monster's return.

"I told you I saw something!" Caspar shouted over the panic to his bench-mate.

Twenty-three wasn't listening. Like the rest of the slaves, he abandoned his oar. He pulled and tugged desperately at the chain that held him to the bench, fighting uselessly to pull it loose, to get free.

"It'll sink the ship!" someone cried in Caspar's ear. He turned and stared into the face of Sunrise. The boy bled from the corner of his mouth, and one eye looked dark and puffy, but he scrambled on his hands and knees to find the lock to Caspar's chain. A ring of keys jingled in his hand, and he quickly inserted a key when he found the lock. "I stole it from Chulig," he hurriedly explained. "I poured the wine on him to distract him, and I plucked the ring from his belt. He hasn't noticed yet!" He twisted the key. Nothing happened. He withdrew it, and inserted another.

A chorus of screams went up from the forward rails. With a collective gasp the soldiers fell away. The sea serpent thrust up from the waves, directly in the ship's path. Higher and higher it stretched its immense form until it loomed above even the tip of the single mast. Carried by its own momentum, the *Screaming Queen* plunged ahead, destined to smash against the beast. Only moments before impact, though, the serpent slipped back beneath the sea.

There was not even time for a relieved sigh. The beast rose again just off the leeward side of the prow. Instead of slipping back under the waves, this time it lunged forward, striking the water forcefully with its diving length. The wave rocked the ship as if it were a toy.

"Why are you doing this?" Caspar cried to Sunrise. While the boy struggled with the keys and the lock, Caspar began to tug on his chain as the same panic that infected the others began to claim him.

"I told you!" Sunrise answered with a grim calm as he tried yet another key in the salt-rusted lock. "You're going to get me off this ship!"

One of the soldiers suddenly took notice of what Sunrise was trying to do. Even as the sea serpent raised its head another time before the prow, the soldier swal-

lowed his fear and grabbed Sunrise by the shoulders.
"Here now!" he shouted. "What do ye think yer . . . !"

Sunrise twisted with surprising speed and pushed the
unwary soldier. At the same time, the sea serpent smote
the water again, sending a great wave that bounced the
ship up and down. The soldier lost his footing and fell
into the laps of the galley slaves behind Caspar.

A shriek went up from Twenty-four. In an instant
the slave had his chain around the soldier's throat.
"Loves it, I does!" he screamed hysterically. "My precious!" The soldier's gurgling and the snap of his neck
was audible over the general tumult.

At almost the same instant, the key clicked in
Caspar's lock, and it sprang open. The chain that held
him to his bench slithered to the deck between his feet.
His hands, however, were still shackled. Not locks, but
bolt pins closed the manacles about his wrists. There was
nothing Sunrise could do about those. At least, if the
ship went down, Caspar wouldn't be dragged with it.

"Over the side!" Sunrise shouted as he dropped the
keys in the lap of Twenty-four. The slave gave another
cry as he pushed the dead soldier's body aside. He and
his bench-mate immediately began to fight over the keys.

Sunrise stepped up onto Caspar's bench and prepared to jump overboard, but Caspar caught his arm and
stopped him. It was a long swim to shore, and there was
still the sea serpent to think about. He had no desire to
be eaten by that monster!

In the fore of the ship, a group of archers and spearmen waited for the monster's inevitable return. Heart
hammering, Caspar waited, too. When the creature
thrust suddenly up out of the water the breath caught
in Caspar's throat. Involuntarily, he jumped backward,
stumbling over his own bench. Instantly, hands were on
him, but whether they tried to right him or hold him
down he couldn't tell. He lashed out with fists and feet,
fighting off any who tried to touch him.

At the forward rail, the archers and spearmen fell
back in terror. A flurry of tiny shafts poked harmlessly
from the sea serpent's body. The serpent seemed not

even to notice. A few of the bravest archers set arrows to their strings and prepared to fire again.

But suddenly, the odd blue-robed figure who had been the last to board before the ship left port, ran out of the forward cabin. "Stop!" he shouted, high-voiced, as he waved his arms in the air to draw everyone's attention. "Weapons can't hurt it!"

Chulig scurried to the man's side at once. "What can you do, then?" he demanded frantically, trying to sound like a captain though panic was on his face as plainly as anyone's.

"What can I do?" the figure shouted indignantly, sweeping back his hood to reveal a shining bald head and old, darkly glittering eyes above a fishhook nose. "What can I do?" His voice took on a shriller, sarcastic tone. "I am Satchmoz the Incomparable!"

"Well, do something incomparable!" the first mate shrieked as he tore out a handful of his own hair and stared toward the serpent-shaped prow. "I knew that thing would bring us nothing but bad luck! Whoever saw a prow like that? Curse the architect, and curse Duncanthrax!" He whirled on Chulig and spat on his captain's boots. "And curse you, too, Captain Piss-pants! I'll throw myself overboard!" With that, the first mate sprang up onto the rail and launched himself outward in a graceful dive.

"We should do the same!" Sunrise shouted desperately in Caspar's ear.

Yet Caspar watched as the blue-robed old man strode to the fore of the ship, climbed the small ladder to the roof of the forward cabin and positioned himself beside the mammoth cadence drum. As the sea serpent rose yet again from the waves, the old man pushed out his arms. His sleeves snapped back up to his elbows, and a white energy crackled from his fingertips to tickle the monster's nose.

The sea serpent looked stunned for an instant. It stared down at the ship, and its great eyes blinked. A moment later, it slipped back under the sea.

"You did it!" Chulig cried, and a cheer went up from

the soldiers and sailors. The captain went to the foot of
the ladder and seized a rung, preparing to climb. "What
did you do?"

"A vaxum spell!" the old man shouted proudly in
answer. "I prepared it down in the cabin. A potent little
sucker that makes even the nastiest beastie friendly."

Caspar wondered, however. The serpent had slipped
underwater before only to surface again. Still, he eyed
the blue-robed figure hopefully. The man was a wizard!
Maybe one of the powerful Circle of Enchanters that
Caspar had heard about. He knew that many of the finest
universities in Quendor taught the fine arts of wizardry.
But stuck way out on a farm in a small town in the
Peltoid Valley, he'd never actually seen magic done!

There was little time to marvel, though. The sea serpent reappeared, nose to nose with the serpent-shaped
prow of the ship. It blinked and opened its mouth. Twin
fangs gleamed like ivory in that pink, gaping maw. The
mouth closed, and the creature planted its thin, translu-
cent lips right up against the prow's carved serpent head.

The ship jolted at the impact. Men went sprawling
all along the deck. The wizard, in the act of pulling some
kind of scroll from an inner pocket of his robe, tumbled
backward and pitched off the cabin roof with an awkward yelp. The next instant, the monster coiled a loop
of its sensuous form around the serpent-shaped prow.

There was a groan and wrenching deep in the ship.
The sound of splintering wood, breaking bolts, and snapping joists rose above the terrified cries of men. With an
effortless contraction the sea serpent ripped the carved
prow away, taking the foredeck and part of the hull with
it. The monster turned away then and swam dreamily
off, embracing its prize.

The *Screaming Queen* lifted its stern high in the air as
water rushed in the gaping forward rent. The rattle of
chains and the dismayed shrieks of the galley slaves filled
the air. Angry and vengeful, they grabbed at the nearest
soldiers and sailors and clung with all their might, determined to drag their captors down, too. Some soldiers

flung themselves over the rail, heedless of the armor that would only drag them down into the sea's depths.

Without any warning, Caspar found himself spinning head-over-heels through the air. He hit the sea on his back with jarring force. Water filled his nose and mouth. He stared upward, salt water stinging his eyes, toward light and toward the surface. He gave a kick and struggled toward air, but the weight of the chains on his arms, and the strong tow of the sinking ship worked against him. He opened his mouth to scream, and a rush of bubbles rose before his face like startled fleeing birds.

CHAPTER SIX

A DAY AT THE BEACH

SOMETHING ROCKETED UP out of the murky depths below Caspar. Instinctively, he shot out a hand and felt his fingers close around a piece of rope. His weight barely slowed its rise, and it dragged him toward the light. An instant later, his head broke the surface. Gasping, coughing, he sucked in precious air.

It was the great drum that had saved his life. Somehow, it had torn loose from the ship's deck, and he found himself clinging to one of the ropes that bound its massive hides in place. Hollow and air-tight, it bobbed on the water, sometimes threatening to roll over on him. He quickly learned, though, that by kicking with his legs, he could generate enough force to keep his head above water and prevent the drum from pushing him under.

Little by little, other debris began to bob to the surface. Broken crates and splintered planks, a piece of sheeting that might have been part of the sail. Here and there, a body floated into view.

Then, he heard another desperate cough and a choked gasping, the first indication so far that he wasn't the only survivor. The sounds, however, came from the other side of the galley drum. Maintaining his hold on the rope, he worked his way around, letting go long enough to swim around the gavel-scarred hide. Now he could see the shore in the distance. There was a lot of debris between him and it.

Someone hailed him, and a thin hand waved weakly in the air from behind a crate. He had to squint against the sun's glare on the water before he spied Sunrise. He waved back as best he could with shackled hands, and the youth swam over and took hold of the drum.

"My benefactor!" Sunrise managed, smiling weakly.

"My ass!" Caspar answered. "You're the one who saved my life. I'd be fish-food if it wasn't for you."

"No," Sunrise protested, facing Caspar as he clung with one hand to the drum and treaded water with the other. "I had a feeling about you from the first!"

Caspar gave a kick to keep the massive drum from rolling on them. Nevertheless, a wave dashed him unexpectedly in the face, and he swallowed a mouthful of seawater. "Forget it, kid!" he sputtered, wiping at his eyes. "No one can see the future. This is a rational world!"

"That's not actually true, young man."

Both Caspar and Sunrise started at the sound of another voice. A moment later, the bald-headed wizard, Satchmoz, his blue robes floating about him like the open petals of a flower, drifted into view. He clung to a broken beam that might have been part of the *Screaming Queen's* hull.

"There's a certain spell called *vezza*," he continued in his best professorial voice, "developed by the wizards of the northern city of Thriff, which does give limited power to foresee events. But it's very esoteric, and quite difficult to master."

Caspar stared cautiously at the wizard. He was one of Chulig's men, after all, and by extension, loyal to Duncanthrax. But the old man appeared to offer no threat.

Suddenly, though, he thought about his bench-mate, Twenty-three, and all the other slaves chained to their benches at the bottom of the sea. "What did you do to that monster?" Caspar demanded.

The wizard looked askance and rolled his eyes in some embarrassment. "Yes, that was a mistake, wasn't it?" he said apologetically, and he clucked his tongue. "You see, the *vaxum* spell is designed to make a hostile creature friendly. But if the creature is already friendly, it can make it positively, well, affectionate."

"You mean, it fell in love with the prow?" Caspar exclaimed, recalling how the ship's prow was fashioned.

The wizard rolled his eyes again and shrugged. "It's just a guess," he answered defensively. "It might have attacked the ship anyway."

"No!" Caspar snapped. "I remember now. It kept rising up in front of the prow, like it was playing with it!"

"Or flirting with it!" Sunrise shouted. "I saw it wink!"

The wizard put up a hand. "All right, all right!" he said disgustedly. "Make me feel bad! Can't anyone make a mistake anymore?"

Caspar was about to hurl an answer when he felt a nibble on his back. "Ouch!" he muttered in surprise. Forgetting momentarily about his shackles, he tried to slap one hand over his shoulder. The chain snapped taut, flicking salt water into his eyes again. Another sharp nibble pricked his shoulder. With a yelp, he inadvertently let go of the rope to wipe his eyes and slipped underwater with his mouth open.

Sunrise thrust out a hand and caught him by the hair. Caspar struggled to grab the rope again. "Damn!" he cried. "Something's eating me!"

"Who knows what evil lurks in the briny deep," Sunrise commented with a smirk.

But Caspar wasn't listening. Dozens of finny mouths took nips at his shoulders, at his back, at his sides. He did his best to fight them off with his elbows as he twitched and splashed and kicked his feet. But nothing frightened the mouths away, and his eyes grew wide with panic.

Sunrise pushed himself under the water and surfaced a moment later. "Fish!" he cried, grinning. "Tiny fish! They must be attracted to the grease I smeared on your back." He covered his face with one hand to hide his laughter.

Caspar yelped again. He had to admit, though, the bites didn't really *hurt*. They just—ouch!—well, frightened him. Sunrise laughed out loud. Even Satchmoz wore a sheepish grin. Caspar felt the heat of his own embarrassed blush.

"We'd better head for shore," he suggested angrily. "One of the other ships will come to investigate as soon as it's plain the sea serpent has left the area." He twitched violently again, somehow trying to rid himself of the tiny, busy mouths. "I have no desire to be picked up and chained to a bench again."

"So you're drumming yourselves out of the service," Satchmoz said as he gave a kick and pushed against the great floating drum.

"Let's just swim for it," Sunrise suggested, letting go of the rope and treading water. "It's not that far."

Caspar gave another sharp twitch. "Pardon me," he muttered through clenched teeth. He lifted one arm to show off his shackles. "I'd just as soon hang on to the drum, if you don't mind. We can push it to shore."

"I'm not such a great swimmer, either," Satchmoz admitted.

Sunrise nodded and grabbed hold of the rope again. The three of them began kicking, propelling the drum ahead of them as they worked their way toward the distant coastline. Caspar kept one eye over his shoulder, watching for any approaching ship. The few vessels he could see, though, all kept their distance. There was nothing to be done for Chulig's ship, and no one apparently wanted to risk a similar fate.

"Why don't you get rid of those heavy robes?" Sunrise, on Caspar's left side, suggested to Satchmoz. The wizard, on Caspar's right, only shook his head. Though he was old, he did his part without complaint.

You live to serve this ship, Caspar thought as he watched the wizard and recalled the faces of the many galley slaves who now lay dead on the sea bottom. *Row well, and live.* Then, a particularly sharp and well-placed nibble brought him back to reality. *Damn fish!* he cursed as he gave a twitch.

The drum scraped to an unexpected stop against the sandy bottom, and the three survivors piled into it. Nevertheless, they were grateful to have made it ashore.

Caspar let go of his rope, splashed wildly through the surf and fell to his knees on the sand.

"Free at last!" he cried joyfully. "Free at last!" He looked over at Sunrise as the youth fell down beside him. For the first time he noticed how bone-thin and undernourished the boy appeared, and he wondered how long he'd had to survive on no more than bad mush. He didn't ask, though. Instead, he turned on his side and rubbed as best he could with shackled hands at his back. "I was beginning to feel like live bait," he confessed.

"You tell it right, and it'll make a good story," Sunrise told him, grinning, as he rolled over, sand-covered, and brushed a lock of wet, darkly blond hair from his eyes. He lay on his back and opened his arms to the warm sun. "You'll never have that many mouths on you at one time again."

Caspar gave a chuckle even as he raised an eyebrow. "For one so young, you have a nasty little mind," he said with barely concealed appreciation.

Sunrise raised up on one elbow and made a face at a seagull that flew overhead. "You spend a month on a slave ship as a captain's cabin boy," he muttered in a low tone that was only half amusement. For a long moment, he let the comment hang. Finally, he picked up a handful of sand and hurled it lazily toward the surf as he muttered, "Well, you either learn to move very fast, or develop an appreciation for Quendoran seamen!" He gave Caspar a wink. "I am extremely fast."

Caspar let that go and glanced around for Satchmoz. The wizard was a little farther up the beach. He had his blue cloak spread upon the sand. To Caspar's surprise, the inner lining seemed mostly to consist of pockets. As he watched, Satchmoz removed scrolls and vials and all manner of strange things. The scrolls, he immediately began to spread upon the ground, making little mounds of sand to hold the corners down so they would dry in the sun.

Caspar got up to have a closer look. "What's all this?" he asked.

Satchmoz glanced up at him as he opened a vial, sniffed it, and stoppered it once more. "Tools of the trade, my boy," he answered. "None of it ruined, either, bless my luck! No sea water got into my potions, but the scrolls will have to dry."

"What about your clothes?" Caspar suggested wryly.

"Good idea!" Satchmoz agreed. Quickly, he stood up, pulled his long blue garment over his head, gave it a twist and a wring, and tossed it up on the sand without so much as a second thought. Then, wearing only a small blue loincloth, he bent his spindly legs, and returned to the inspection of his cloak's many pockets.

Caspar stood by as the wizard unrolled another wet scroll. The ink upon it appeared to have run slightly, yet the spidery handwriting was still legible.

"What was a wizard doing on Chulig's ship?" Caspar asked abruptly as Satchmoz carefully spread the scroll out to dry.

Satchmoz gave him a sharp look. "What was I doing?" he gasped indignantly. "What was I doing? My boy, I am Satchmoz the Incomparable!"

Casper blinked. "Pleased to meet you," he said drily. "But what were you doing?"

Satchmoz snorted. "Where've you been all your life?" he asked rudely. "On a farm? I suppose you think Duncanthrax just planned to sail over to Antharia, shoot a few arrows in the air, and declare the birth of the Quendoran Empire?" He snorted again as he reached into another pocket and pulled out something that looked like a child's multi-colored windmill. Indeed, when he held it up by the narrow stick, a small puff of wind caught the blades and set them spinning.

"Of course not!" Satchmoz snapped as he set the toy aside. "We wizards were his weapons. One of us on every ship. Every member of the Borphee guild. Against our magic, Antharia's navy wouldn't have been worth *that*." He gave a snap of his fingers.

"Worth *that*?" Caspar said, snapping his fingers, too.

"Not worth *that*," Satchmoz emphasized proudly.

Caspar folded his arms across his chest, and the

chains of his shackles gave a clank. "Well, your magic sure turned the trick with that sea serpent," he said with a bit of a sneer.

Satchmoz sat back on his heels, sighing, and his old face crinkled up in a frown until he resembled a dried prune. "How long are you going to hold that against me?"

Caspar sucked on his lower lip. "I haven't made up my mind," he answered, turning away. He walked back to join Sunrise. The youth lay stretched on his back, his eyes closed, basking in the sun. The smile on his face was unmistakable.

"Don't sit in my sun," he chided as Caspar plopped down beside him, his shadow falling across the younger boy's face. Caspar muttered an apology and moved. "There were times," Sunrise continued without looking at Caspar, "when I thought I'd never enjoy anything again. Now, I could lie here all day."

"How long were you Chulig's prisoner?" Caspar asked as he stared out over the sea. There was no sign of any ship on the horizon. Duncanthrax's navy had left them behind and sailed on to their war against Antharia.

"A little more than a month," Sunrise answered. "Since the first day Duncanthrax claimed the throne after Zilbo walked out. His soldiers rounded up all the waifs and orphans, all the homeless people who lived on the streets, all the vagrants with no employment, and he put them on the ships, whether they wanted to go or not."

"A month?" Caspar exclaimed. "But I met Zilbo on the road outside Borphee just the other day."

Sunrise gave a shrug. "Then he finally managed to sneak out of the city," he said disinterestedly. "Rumor had it he was hiding somewhere waiting for a chance to make his break."

Caspar scooped the sand between his legs into a mound and idly sifted it with his fingers. "I must say, I'm surprised by all this," he said quietly. "Back in Djabuti Padjama, we heard nothing about Zilbo's overthrow."

Sunrise turned over and leaned on one elbow. "Overthrow?" he said sharply. "Who said anything about an overthrow? Zilbo just decided to walk away from his throne one day." He rolled his eyes and made a wild gesture. "Left things in a fine mess, too, when he did. Didn't say a word to anyone. Just left a note. *I resign*, it said. Duncanthrax—he was General Duncanthrax then—had to step in to prevent total chaos!"

Caspar smashed his fist down against his pile of sand, sending a shower of particles flying. "You talk as if you blame Zilbo!"

Sunrise sat up defensively. "Well, who else should I blame?" he shouted back. He drew his feet in close and crossed them at the ankles as he leaned forward. "He was the king! His family had ruled Quendor for six hundred years, all the way back to the great Entharion himself. It was Zilbo's job to be king!" Sunrise's face wrinkled up with sarcastic anger as he rocked back and forth with his hands on his knees. "But no! He has a bad day, or he feels a little bored with his work, or maybe it's a midlife crisis. So he just quits! And where does that leave us, his subjects?" He didn't wait for an answer. "On a galley ship bound for Antharia, that's where." He settled back smugly, and some of the red color drained from his cheeks.

"All right, all right," Caspar said in a calming voice. "Maybe Duncanthrax didn't bounce Zilbo out on his ear. He's still a crazy tyrant."

Sunrise shrugged again and stared up at a flock of seagulls that flew by. "Maybe the power went to his head," he muttered. Finally, he looked back to Caspar. "So where do we go from here? Home?"

Caspar looked away quickly. "I can't go home," he said.

Sunrise didn't miss much. He uncrossed his legs and bent forward. "Some trouble?" he asked quietly.

Caspar stood up suddenly. "Nothing I want to talk about," he answered. His shackles clinked as he extended a hand to help Sunrise up. "Come on, let's join our incomparable wizard. Maybe he has some idea."

Sunrise let himself be helped up. "Yeah," he said doubtfully. "Maybe he can tickle another sea serpent."

Caspar grinned and nudged his young friend in the ribs. "How long you going to hold that against him?"

Sunrise set his mouth in a firm line as they moved up the beach. "I haven't made up my mind," came the straight-faced answer.

Satchmoz was bent over one of his scrolls, his mouth close to the old paper. The afternoon sun glinted on his bald head, and his pale skin showed evidence of burning without the protection of his robes. He seemed oblivious, though. His cheeks puffed and puffed as he blew a stream of air onto one particular scroll. He looked up, red-faced, as they approached.

"It's almost ready," he said excitedly to Caspar. He picked up the scroll and waved it in the air. "I've got a little surprise for you, boy."

Caspar faked a quiver, caught Sunrise by the shoulders and put the boy between him and the wizard. Sunrise quickly ducked and pulled free, though, and stepped well away. "Go ahead," he called to Satchmoz. "Surprise him. It should be safe. I don't see any sea serpents."

Satchmoz frowned and gave the youth a sharp look. "Everybody's a wiseguy!" he complained under his breath as he spread the scroll on the sand again and bent over it. He appeared to study the writing for a moment, his lips moving as he read. Then, he closed his eyes, folded his hands, huddled down into a little ball, and grew very still.

Caspar looked at Sunrise. Sunrise looked at Caspar. Finally, Caspar leaned forward and tapped the wizard on the shoulder. "Are you all right?" he asked.

Satchmoz gave a wispy little sigh and sat slowly back on his heels. He didn't answer. Instead, he reached out and touched the tip of his right index finger to the chain that dangled between Caspar's wrists. A spark of blue fire shot out from the old man's finger. Tiny lightning bolts crackled over the links, twining round and round as they raced in both directions toward the heavy metal cuffs.

Caspar gave a fearful cry. "What have you done!" he screamed, jumping away from the wizard. He held his arms rigidly straight out from the rest of his body as he stared, wide-eyed, at crackling chain.

The blue lightnings reached the cuffs and scurried over and around them like frantic glowing serpents until they found the bolt pins that fastened them tight. Caspar gave another scream. Magical energy sizzled, and a bright azure flash surrounded both his wrists.

When the flash faded the shackles fell off and clattered to the sand at Caspar's feet.

"I did it!" Satchmoz cried gleefully. Then, he clapped a hand over his mouth and swallowed hard as he recomposed himself. "There now," he started again as he folded his arms smugly over the sparse, wiry gray hair on his narrow chest. "That wasn't so bad, was it?"

Caspar didn't answer right away. He felt both his wrists. Then he counted his fingers. When he found nothing broken and nothing missing, he allowed a faint smile. "No, not so bad," he mumbled sheepishly, still unable to believe he wasn't at least burned.

Sunrise ran forward. "That was great!" he exclaimed. But he pointed to a pile of gray ashes on the sand between the old man's knees. "What happened to the scroll?"

Satchmoz rocked himself ever so slightly as he basked in Sunrise's admiration. "I'm afraid the scroll crumbles away once the spell written on it has been cast," he answered.

"You mean, you can only do that once?" Caspar asked, trying not to sound too hopeful. Actually, he had to admit, a spell that could open any locked object was a handy thing to have. He could see all kinds of possible uses.

Satchmoz looked like an old cat that had just eaten a fat meal—ready to curl in a window, lick his paws, and let the world go by uncaring. "That was my only *rezrov* spell," he answered, nodding.

"All of these," Caspar pressed, waving a hand toward all the other scrolls drying on the beach. "You can only use them once?"

Satchmoz nodded again. "Of course!" he answered,

falling into his professorial voice once more. "That's the nature of magic. No wizard can memorize more than two or three spells. They just won't stay in the human head. So you have to write them down, and not on just anything, either. It takes a special, magically embued paper. Unfortunately, once the spell is cast, the scroll dissolves. Some wizards over at Galepath University are experimenting with reusable scrolls—eventually, they even hope for some kind of spell book—but that technology is years in the future."

Abruptly, the old wizard stood up, reached down his loincloth, and gave himself a scratch. "Now, if you'll excuse me," he said with great dignity, "I'm going to wash off. Some sand seems to have gotten in here."

He walked down the beach and strode into the waves. When the water was above his waist, he unwound his blue cloth and gave it a brisk rinsing, all the while humming loudly to himself.

"I'm just curious," Sunrise said, folding one arm across his chest and stroking his chin as he leaned closer to Caspar. Together, they watched the old man from the shore. "Did he seem just a little bit surprised by his success when the shackles fell off?"

Adopting his young friend's attitude, Caspar folded one arm across his chest and stroked his chin. He leaned toward Sunrise until their shoulders touched. "Would you say he was as surprised as I was?" he asked quietly. "Or would you say he was more surprised?"

CHAPTER SEVEN

SATCHMOZ THE INCOMPARABLE EXPLAINS IT ALL FOR YOU

INCE IT WAS LATE IN THE
afternoon, not long before dusk, they decided to spend
the night on the beach. The flames of sunset licked across
the western sky while purple clouds crept out of the
east. The tide moved in, and the white-capped surf rolled
higher and higher on the sand.

Caspar sat hugging his knees to his chest. He stared
toward the water, watching a trio of gulls beat their
wings uselessly against a potent gust of wind. For
minutes they simply hung in the air above the waves,
making no progress at all, until the stiff breeze weak-
ened, and they raced away.

A low rustle rose over the sound of the surf. Caspar
turned and glanced over his shoulder toward Mauldwood. The leaves of the trees shivered and the branches
scraped on one another. For an instant the whole wood
seemed alive with motion. Then the wind died again,
and Mauldwood became ominously still.

Caspar peered at the dark places between the great
old trunks, hoping the things that stirred there in the
shadows were no more than shrubs and bushes. Uneasily, he turned his back to the forest and tried to forget
all the tales he'd heard, but as twilight deepened, the
growing chorus of insect noises only increased the atmo-
sphere of strangeness.

A splash and a laugh from down the beach caused

Caspar to look around. Sunrise stood waist deep in the water and teased the trio of gulls, which had returned, by launching barrages of water at them as they skimmed the waves. The birds seemed as enthusiastically playful as the youth as they circled around him, coming back again and again to dare his assaults. Sunrise had spent most of the afternoon swimming and sunning himself, enjoying his new freedom.

"I see you found enough wood," said Satchmoz, coming to Caspar's side. He still wore his blue loincloth, but his cloak had sufficiently dried, and he wore that now around his shoulders. His scrolls, too, had dried, and when he moved, Caspar could see the tops of them poking out of the many pockets in the cloak's lining.

"Fortunately, I didn't have to go very far," Caspar confessed. "There was plenty of stuff lying around at the edge."

"Then you know the stories, too?" Satchmoz said, glancing toward the woods.

Caspar nodded.

Satchmoz changed the subject. "Here, I made these for you and the boy. They're pretty crude, but it'll get cooler as the night comes on." He held out a pair of makeshift blue sleeveless tunics, which he'd fashioned from his one long garment. They were little more than wide strips torn from the original with holes ripped in the center to fit over the head and thinner strips to tie around the waist. Nevertheless, Caspar rose and put his on over his loincloth, and thanked the wizard as he tied the belt.

Satchmoz set Sunrise's tunic aside and pulled out a scroll. "If we're going to have a fire, I'd better get busy while there's still light to read."

Caspar quickly grabbed up a few pieces of the driftwood and dead branches he'd gathered and arranged them at a point halfway between the woods and the water's edge. Satchmoz, studying his scroll in the fading twilight, knelt down beside the small pile, his mouth in a thin tight line. A moment later, the wizard closed his eyes. Soundlessly, he mouthed words.

The letters written on the parchment in Satchmoz's hands began to shine. A tiny flame sprang up and raced over the page, following the line of script. Satchmoz's pale face and hands reflected the ruddy glow of the fire, yet he held on, unburned as the scroll was consumed and the ashes fell onto the sand between his knees.

Satchmoz opened his eyes. "Now comes the impressive part," he stated. His whole face screwed up with concentration as he stretched out his left hand toward the small pile of wood. For a moment it seemed that nothing happened. Then, a great rushing fountain of fire shot out from the old man's fingertips. Caspar felt the heat of it on his skin and threw up an arm to protect his eyes. The air crackled and took on a terrible stench, which the wind quickly carried away.

"A bit overdone, I'd say," Caspar commented when the gush of flame faded and it was safe to approach the smoking pile of ash that was all that remained of the wood.

Sunrise came running up. "Don't let him cook the steaks," he said to Caspar as a grin spread over his face.

"What steaks?" Caspar answered wistfully. His stomach grumbled at the thought of food. The only thing he'd had to eat all day was the bowl of bad porridge.

"A little too much *presence*," the wizard commented as he leaned over the results of his handiwork and stirred the ashes with a finger. "I'll have to correct that next time." He jerked his hand back suddenly. "But look, there are still some hot spots and coals. Bring some more wood. We'll have a campfire yet."

Sunrise danced up the beach and grabbed a few of the smaller bits of bark and dead branches from the supply Caspar had scavenged. "What did you mean, too much *presence?*" Caspar asked as they all gathered around the ashes. Sunrise bent down to blow on the coals as Caspar broke a piece of bark into small fragments and fed them into the heat.

"The Three Principles of Thaumaturgy," Satchmoz recited formally, and he drew his cloak about his narrow shoulders as if it were his dignity. His face took on the appropriate solemnity of a lecturer. "Presence, Incantation, Unusual Effect," he continued as his younger companions worked. "The most important of these is, of course, presence, which is the will and the determination of the enchanter or wizard to make the incantation work. Some instructors would substitute *personality* for the word, *determination.* Others, *desire.*" Satchmoz allowed a small grin as a genuine flame began to grow among the pieces of bark. "In any case, it's that inward part of the wizard, himself, that actually powers a spell."

Sunrise looked up, red-faced from blowing on the coals, and said somewhat dubiously, "You're telling me you reduced this pile of wood to cinders because you have too much *personality?*"

Caspar gave the youth a shove that sent him tumbling sideways. "I think the word, *desire* is better applied here," he told Sunrise. "Satchmoz *desired* this campfire so that all sorts of wild animals with big teeth don't come crawling out of the woods tonight and eat you up."

Sunrise rolled lithely to his feet, turned toward Satchmoz, and made a sweeping bow. "No offense intended, O Mighty Enchanter," he said grandly.

Satchmoz chewed one corner of his lip, aware that he was being teased. "I'm just inexperienced with the *radnog* spell," he said pensively. "It's not in my normal repertoire."

Caspar sat back as the flame began to flicker and burn and spread among the pile of bark he had created. He added several twigs and a small piece of driftwood. "Just what is in your usual repertoire?" he asked.

Satchmoz shrugged and glanced aside uncertainly. "Well, I'm awfully good at tying people's shoelaces together," he answered. "I don't even need a scroll for that one. I've got it memorized."

Caspar recalled how Captain Chulig had tripped on his bootlaces shortly after delivering an insult to the late-arriving Satchmoz. "I thought you said spells couldn't be memorized?" he replied. "You said they wouldn't stick in the human head."

"No," Satchmoz answered. "I said most spells

wouldn't. But an enchanter can sometimes memorize one or two of the simpler spells. A really talented wizard might memorize three. But never more."

"Which is it, in your case?" Sunrise said, kneeling down by the fire once more. "One or two?"

As a reward for his clever insolence, Caspar gave the youth another shove, again toppling him. Sunrise giggled as he fell over.

Satchmoz looked at them both for a long, silent moment, and an odd sadness—was it disappointment?—filled his old eyes. Sheepishly, he gazed down at the sand and held up one finger. Then, he curled his hands into fists and put them in his lap. A small sigh escaped his lips.

Caspar gave a sigh, too. How had he come to this, he wondered, stranded in nowhere-land with a strange kid and a one-trick wizard? Was what he'd done back in Djabuti Padjama bad enough to warrant this? He sat back in the sand, unfolding his legs, which had begun to tingle and ache.

Sunrise came and sat quietly beside him. The boy seemed to have run out of things to say. On the other side of the campfire, Satchmoz kept his silence also. He hadn't looked up since his confession. The firelight reflected on his face, casting shadows around his eyes and in the hollows of his cheeks. The only sounds were the crackling of burning wood, the soft susurrus of the surf, and the wind in the leaves of Mauldwood.

Caspar regarded both his comrades and gave another sigh. He wasn't really being fair. Without Sunrise, he'd be fish food on the sea bottom. And whatever his short-comings, Satchmoz, too, had managed to survive the sinking of the ship. They had survived. Whether through skill or luck, it didn't matter. They had survived.

"So what if you've only memorized one spell," Caspar said, breaking the silence. "You've still got your scrolls."

Sunrise spoke, too. "You're like an archer," he added, sliding a few more branches into the campfire. "Only better. All the arrows in your quiver are magic."

Caspar looked at Sunrise and nodded. "That's right,"

he agreed. "Only right now I wish we had a real bow and some arrows so we could hunt up some food." He rubbed a hand briskly over his stomach as he rose to his feet. "I'm starving."

Sunrise stood up and glanced uneasily toward the shadows of Mauldwood. "I suppose I should have looked for some berries or something, instead of lying in the sun all day," he said without much enthusiasm.

Satchmoz made a little sound to clear his throat. He pursed his lips tightly together and reached one hand into a pocket of his cloak. Then he frowned and reached into another pocket. The frown only deepened, and he tried yet another. "Frog it!" he muttered under his breath. "I know it's here someplace!" He tried two more pockets before the frown turned into a smile. "Ahem!" he repeated as he drew out a small vial of green liquid. The bottle was as long as his index finger, and securely stoppered.

"Figuratively speaking," he said as he used his nails to pry loose the cork, "I have a few tricks up my sleeve that don't require scrolls." He lifted the open vial to his lips and took the tiniest sip. Immediately, his eyes lit up and his smile broadened. He gave a sigh of satisfaction as he wiped the back of his free hand over his mouth. "Try it," he said, passing the bottle up to Caspar.

Caspar bent down again and held the vial toward the firelight. "What is it?" he asked dubiously as he raised it to his mouth. He poured a thin trickle onto his tongue without waiting for Satchmoz to answer. "Fudge!" he cried in surprised delight a moment later.

Sunrise snatched the vial. He gave it a sniff, then ran his tongue around the rim. His brow crinkled in an expression of thoughtfulness, and he smacked his lips. Then, he gave a joyful shout. "Spenseweed milkshake!" He threw back his head and raised the vial again.

Satchmoz leaned across the fire, nearly burning himself as he grabbed the bottle from the boy. "*Berzio*," he said, naming the potion as he hammered the stopper back into the bottle with his fist. He dropped it into a cloak pocket. "It always tastes like your favorite food. That's the magic of it."

"And it fills you up!" Caspar observed in amazement. He stared downward toward his navel. "I feel like I've eaten a whole meal!" He grinned at Satchmoz. "Well, a whole pan of fudge!"

"Milkshakes!" Sunrise insisted, folding his arms across his stomach. "Three of 'em, at least! Thick ones with real whipped cream on top, I swear!"

"Just remember," Satchmoz warned, "it's not very nourishing, and we'll have to find real food sooner or later. This can keep us going a few days, though, if we use it sparingly."

Caspar walked the few steps up the beach to the pile of wood he had gathered during the day. Picking up several large pieces, he placed them on the fire and sat down again. Sunrise got up and brought back an armload, which he deposited on the sand within easy reach. The firelight danced in his dark eyes as he stretched out on his side and supported his head with one hand.

The stars burned like perfect jewels in the black sky. The *Jester*, a particularly bright constellation, shone directly overhead, and next to it, the huge and misty cluster known as *Entharion's Hair*, which according to legend is where all the ancient king's hair truly went when he lost it in his thirties. Thereafter, Entharion the Wise became Entharion the Bald. In the north the *Great Wheel*, with the hub-star *Bobol* gleaming at its center, slowly turned the heavens.

In all the world of Zork, Caspar doubted there was a more beautiful sky than the one above his head just then. Back on the farm in Djabuti Padjama he had loved the night, and he had learned all the constellations by name and all the farmers' various stories about them. Learning was not something his uncle encouraged, though, and he had beaten Caspar several times for it and called him a "fool dreamer!"

"I suppose we should discuss what we're going to do in the morning," Caspar said abruptly. There was no point in thinking about Djabuti Padjama anymore. He couldn't go back there. All its residents had made it clear they didn't want him.

Sunrise pushed himself up onto one elbow. "If I strip some bark from a morgia tree tomorrow," he said without looking toward Mauldwood, "I can roll the fibers into twine. It'd need an afternoon to dry in the sun, but then we could fish for our dinners. While I'm doing that, you two could rig some kind of shelter."

Caspar raised an eyebrow. "You talk like you want to stay here?"

Sunrise shrugged self-consciously. "Why not?' he insisted. "It beats the back alleys of Borphee where I grew up, and if we went back there, Duncanthrax would just toss us on another galley ship."

Caspar scratched his chin. He knew they were somewhere near the border between the provinces of Frobozz and Gurth. If they went south they should eventually come to Gurth City. It wasn't much of a town, though, he'd heard. Mostly an industrial center for the Big Three farm wagon manufacturers—Board, General Toters, and Priceler. Caspar had left Djabuti Padjama to seek his fortune. Assembly lines, rude bosses, and six-month layoffs didn't fit into his plan.

Farther south, though, was the province of Mithicus, said by some to be the birthplace of Quendoran civilization. It was renowned for its artisans, and its cities were said to gleam with fantastic and beautiful structures. The greatest works of art and music all came from Mithicus.

Caspar loved music. Perhaps in Mithicus he could seek his fortune.

"I'm going south," he told his friends. He glanced at Sunrise. "There are far better beaches in Mithicus, and all the back alleys are well lit."

Satchmoz drew his cloak about his shoulders as he stared into the fire. "I'm afraid I must go back to Borphee," he announced. "I have no choice."

"Why?" Sunrise snapped, uncurling with a feline grace and quickness. "Because you're loyal to that short little sheeplover, Duncanthrax?" He glared at the wizard and looked as if he might leap across the campfire and go for his throat.

"Sheeplover?" Satchmoz gave a snort of amusement. "I have it on good authority he's allergic to natural fibers."

"Worse and worse!" Sunrise shouted disgustedly.

Caspar tried to restore calm. "Why do you have to go back?" he asked.

The wizard bit his lip and looked askance. "For the sake of Quendor," he answered nervously, "and perhaps the world."

Sunrise puffed himself up and made a sarcastic face. "Oh well, in that case . . . !"

"You don't understand, you little snot!" Satchmoz snapped uncharacteristically. His eyes narrowed with genuine anger and he pointed a long, crooked finger at the boy. "Now sit and shut up, or I'll turn you into a pile of ripe guano!"

Sunrise's eyes widened with surprise. Then, obediently, he folded his legs under himself and sat down on the sand, his hands clutched in his lap. He glanced at Caspar from the corners of his eyes, but he said nothing more.

"That's better," Satchmoz said. He paused for a moment as if to collect his thoughts. "I'm not saying you have to come with me," he told them. "Go south, north, east, or west, wherever you will. That's up to you. But there's something I've got to do. Something I suddenly and unexpectedly find myself in a position to do, because with the sinking of the *Screaming Queen* everybody in Borphee must think I'm dead, and that gives me an advantage that just might offset my natural bumbling."

Caspar shook his head and started to speak, but the wizard waved him off. "Oh, I know I'm something of a bumbler, and a coward, too. Believe me. I've known it for a long time." He hesitated again and swallowed before continuing. "Before I rushed up on deck to try to tackle that sea serpent I made damn sure to cast a water-repelling *louganis* spell on myself. I couldn't have drowned if I'd wanted to. Couldn't even sink. When the ship went down I bobbed to the surface like a cork. That's what kind of a coward I am. I thought of myself first."

Caspar chewed a corner of his cheek. So that was how the old man had managed to survive when all the others had gone down. Still, it didn't really strike him as a cowardly act. Just a smart one. Satchmoz sounded like a man trying to prove something to himself.

"Are you going back because you're afraid of Duncanthrax?" Sunrise asked quietly and politely.

Satchmoz frowned. "I'm afraid of him," he answered, meeting the younger boy's gaze across the campfire. "There's more to that little man than meets the eye. But I have a greater fear of something else."

Caspar gave a twitch. At mention of the word *fear* he glanced over his shoulder at Mauldwood and adjusted his position so he could keep one eye on its closest shadows. He put another branch on the fire.

The frown on Satchmoz's face deepened. The fire cast shadows that gave him an eerie expression. "Many hundreds of years ago," he started as he drew his cloak about his shoulders, "in what has come to be known as *The Empirical Age*, all knowledge and lore of magic mysteriously disappeared. For generations, the schools and universities of Zork studied only the so-called natural sciences."

"What's this got to do with Borphee?" Caspar asked impatiently. "Or with you, for that matter?"

Satchmoz, however, would not be rushed. "You must realize," he went on, "that it was only a little more than a hundred and fifty years ago that the great scholar, Bizboz, a fellow at Galepath University, wrote his seminal work, *On the Presence of Incredibly Weird Stuff Going On*, which in time gave rise once more to the study of the *unnatural sciences* of magic and thaumaturgy." Satchmoz gave a shrug and pushed his right index finger into his right nostril. "Unfortunately," he added, "Bizboz committed suicide only two years later."

"And that's what we'd be committing if we went back to Borphee," Sunrise commented.

"I said I'm not asking you to go," Satchmoz

reminded him. "But I must. You see, Bizboz was a great mind, and his death was an incalculable loss. These days, there are many students of magic, but like myself, most are bumblers. We're all stumbling around trying to recreate the magical wheel. But most of our wheels are squares."

"Or hexagons," Caspar suggested with a raised eyebrow.

Satchmoz looked at him queerly, then allowed a tiny grin. "Or hexagons, as you say. But there's one mind as great as Bizboz's. Perhaps greater. He has already given the world five new spells. Most wizards only dream of finding one."

"So who is this incredibly wonderful person?" Sunrise asked as he stretched out again on his side in the sand.

"His name is Berknip," Satchmoz answered, "He's the heart and soul of our guild, and he's Duncanthrax's prisoner."

Sunrise made a face and tossed a handful of sand into the air. The soft breeze caught the particles, which showered down on everyone. "Well, then, how great a wizard can this Berknip be?"

"Potentially," Satchmoz answered in an offended tone, "he could give magic back to the world. I don't mean mere tricks, like tying shoelaces, or even starting a fire. But truly great magic."

Caspar leaned closer until the heat of the campfire threatened to scorch him. But Satchmoz and his talk of magic had captured his interest now. "Yet from what you've told us," he said, "the wizards of Borphee are cooperating with Duncanthrax. Why did he imprison this Berknip?"

Satchmoz got suddenly to his feet and began to pace before the fire. "It's precisely because he's imprisoned that the other wizards are cooperating." He ground his right fist against his left palm as he spoke. "Borphee is the only place where a group of wizards and enchanters have dared to come together to share study and do research. It's the only guild of its kind anywhere. For the most part, that's because wizards are notoriously unco-operative, stingy and private characters. Most of us would rather give our mothers the flu than give away the secrets of a spell." He stopped his pacing. The fire cast an orange glow on his rail-thin body as his cloak gaped open. "It's Berknip that's pulled us together. We'd do anything for him, and anything to protect him. We don't like Duncanthrax any more than you. But while he holds Berknip, Duncanthrax knows he can command our loyalty."

"So you're going to crawl back like a bad puppy and lick your master's feet," Sunrise muttered. He threw another handful of sand into the air, but this time at least the wind carried it away.

Satchmoz didn't respond immediately. He folded one arm across his chest and brought the fingers of his other hand up to his lips. He chewed thoughtfully on a nail and turned to stare out toward the sea. "I'm going to try to free Berknip," he said at last. "The sinking of the ship gives me a chance. If everybody thinks I'm drowned, nobody will be watching for me."

Caspar regarded the old man with a new respect. He rose and went to stand beside Satchmoz. On the far horizon, a fiery red full moon began to climb over the rim of the ocean. It cast a trail of light upon the rippling waves that led straight to the place where they stood. "You say this Berknip is an important person?" he whispered.

"Five spells," Satchmoz said as if that was answer enough. "Bizboz himself only gave us five."

Caspar folded one arm across his chest and lifted the fingers of his other hand to his lips. He began to chew one nail. He thought, and slowly he nodded his head. He had left his home to seek his fortune. Adventure, though, was an acceptable substitute. What, besides a bunch of effete, bent-nosed artists could he really expect to find in Mithicus anyway?

"I think I'll come with you," he said softly. "I didn't get to see much of Borphee the last time I was there."

"Maybe you should think about what happened the

last time you were there!'' Sunrise shouted angrily. Caspar had been unaware that the youth had come up behind him. He turned to find Sunrise trembling, his fists clenched at his sides. ''We can't go back! It's too dangerous!''

''He's probably right,'' Satchmoz agreed.

Caspar gazed from Satchmoz to Sunrise. He could feel the boy's fury like blows on his chest. He reached out a hand to reassure Sunrise, but it was batted away. Sunrise whirled and ran down to the water's edge. He stood there a moment before splashing head-first into the next cresting wave. He surfaced a moment later and simply stood, hugging himself and shivering as the ocean surged around him, staring at the red moon.

Caspar sat down by the fire again and watched Satchmoz's back and, farther out, Sunrise's still, wet form. Troubled, he hugged his knees to his chest and gently rocked himself as he wondered what to do. Though he didn't quite understand it, Satchmoz's quest offered him a purpose, a strangely appealing direction that his heart told him was right. On the other hand, Sunrise had saved his life, and he couldn't just abandon the boy.

It didn't take him long to make his decision. In the morning he and Sunrise would head south for Mithicus. It was not what he wanted, but perhaps it was for the best. He gave a sigh and leaned his head down on the tops of his knees and closed his eyes. It was nice to have a peaceful moment alone by the fire.

It was then he felt the delicate jab of a spear-point at his back, and a small, high voice said from behind him, ''Hello, sailor! New in port?''

CHAPTER EIGHT
THE FUR STARTS TO FLY

CASPAR RAISED BOTH his hands in the air and slowly twisted around. It wasn't a spear that jabbed at his back, but a tiny trident. The hand that held it was attached to a sticklike arm that sprouted from a fat black furball perhaps three feet high and just as thick. A pair of gleaming red eyes blinked at him from that mass of fur. Its wide mouth parted and flashed a white, toothy smile.

"You're a Kobold?" Caspar said with careful awe. He'd heard stories about such creatures, but Kobolds dwelled in deep caverns and dark forests, never in such plain, dull places as the Peltoid Valley.

"Tha's a fac', Jack!" the creature answered. It blinked again, and its grin widened to almost half the width of its body. "An' youse the tastiest lookin' little morsel I's seed today!"

Caspar lowered his hands and glowered as he turned around, the better to face the creature. Sitting on the sand as he was, he looked it directly in the eyes. "Who's calling who little?" he said with amusement.

The Kobold rested the middle point of its trident on the tip of Caspar's nose. Its red eyes narrowed as it wagged a finger. "Don't git smart-moufed, youse!" it threatened. "Youse hurt my feelin's, an I'll jus' give youse a little prick wit dis sticker an' let some o' that hot air out like youse was a cheap balloon. Now, jus' call yo' tall, skinny friend back here nice an' quiet-like."

Caspar moved his hand upward very slowly and pushed the trident slightly to the side so that it no longer rested on his nose. The Kobold was actually kind of cute in an ugly sort of way. He hoped he didn't have to hurt it. "Do you think you can capture all three of us by yourself?" he asked, trying to hide his grin.

The Kobold brought two twiglike fingers to its lips and gave a soft whistle. Nine sets of bright red eyes suddenly snapped open at the forest's edge. An instant later, nine tumbling furballs came rolling over the sand. They stopped a few feet behind the first Kobold and sprouted arms and legs. All of them carried tridents, and they all grinned broadly as they rolled to their feet.

"Hi, guy!" said one.

"Um, tenderloin," said another, smacking its lips.

By this time, the commotion had attracted the attention of Satchmoz. The wizard came hurrying up the beach as fast as his old legs would carry him, his fists clenched at his sides as he ran. He stopped next to Caspar and stared at the strange assembly.

"Icky-do!" shrieked one of the Kobolds in disgust. It gestured at the top of Satchmoz's head. "No hair! Man, where's your modesty?"

"Old meat," said another. It wrinkled up its face as it studied Satchmoz. "It'll be tough."

"Good jerky," suggested yet another.

The Kobolds began to close in, forming a circle around Caspar and Satchmoz. Caspar bent down swiftly and lifted a brand from the campfire. Crouched down, he waved it at the nearest foe. "How about a little fire, furball?"

The Kobold made a loud hack and spat such an incredible wad that Caspar's small torch was immediately extinguished. The creature's saliva splashed up on Caspar's hand. He dropped the useless brand reflexively and wiped his hand over his blue tunic. "Oh, yuck!" he moaned. He'd never felt anything so slimy in his life.

"Chow time!" Satchmoz shouted suddenly. "Come and get it, boys!" The wizard opened his fists and tossed a pair of vials into the air. With surprising agility the unsuspecting Kobolds all sprang up, two higher than the rest. One caught the first bottle and swallowed it with a gulp. The second creature snapped his jaws down loudly, crunching glass and cork in midair, smacking its lips before it ever touched the ground again.

A queer look came into the eyes of the first Kobold. It dropped its trident and struck a dramatic pose, clapping one gnarly, three-fingered hand over its hairy breast, folding the other arm behind itself. Coyly, it turned to the side and regarded its fellows over a shyly raised shoulder. "My soul is rumbling," it stated in a low, theatrical voice. "My spirit hungers. Flowers on the breakfast table. A bowl of waxed fruit nourishes nothing." It turned a narrow-eyed, seductive look over its comrades, then made a curt bow.

The Kobold who had won the second vial licked a fragment of glass from its lips and burped. An instant later, its eyes snapped wide open. It gave a small moan, then a loud moan. It clutched its chest with both hands as its breathing began to shorten. Clutching itself, it sank back on the sand. "Ooooh!" it sighed. "Aaahhh! Oh, my!" Abruptly, its furry face screwed up in a most obscene expression. Oh yes!" it cried. "Yes! Yes!"

Some of the Kobolds bent over it in bewilderment. The first one began to compose another poem. Striking a new pose, it glanced down at its tiny feet. "A lusty young Kobold named Larry," he said, "liked gals who were shaggy and hairy."

"I think we should make a retreat," Satchmoz whispered in Caspar's ear.

"Wait," Caspar replied shrugging free of the old wizard's grip on his arm. "I want to hear this. I love these things!"

"With a lamb or a ewe," the Kobold continued, "the fur really flew, but a ram, best of all, proved extraordinary."

Satchmoz grabbed Caspar's arm again and compelled him backward in tiny surreptitious steps toward the surf. Five of the Kobolds were clustered worriedly around the one who lay writhing and sighing on the sand. Two more were busy applauding and encouraging the poet.

"Youse!" shouted the one who had first come up

behind Caspar, whirling as he saw the humans trying to sneak off. He lifted his trident and prepared to throw it at Satchmoz. Satchmoz and Caspar froze in their tracks. "What'd youse do ta dem? Tell me, or I'll skewer ya like raw kabobs!"

But before the little Kobold could carry out his threat, a rather large conch shell came flying through the night and conked him squarely on the forehead. The little creature's eyes rolled up, and he plopped over without another sound.

"This way!" Sunrise shouted, his silhouette barely visible in the moonlight as he waved to them from up the beach. "Run!"

The other Kobolds took note of their fleeing captives and started to give chase. Satchmoz and Caspar ran as fast as they could toward Sunrise, who waited impatiently at the edge of the forest. A pair of tridents hissed by Caspar's head as he crashed into thick foliage. The savage yells and trillings of the angry Kobolds rang in his ears.

Branches and limbs scraped his arms. Bushes clawed his bare shins. Roots tripped him. Each time, Caspar scrambled up. All around him the Kobolds plunged through the woods. Surely, he thought, there were more than ten! In panic, he ran, dimly realizing Satchmoz was no longer with him. Nor was there any sign of Sunrise.

A large tree loomed up unexpectedly in his path. Unable to stop in time, he slammed into it. The darkness swirled about him for a moment, and dim colored stars filled his vision. He teetered and reached out to the tree for support.

The Kobolds sounded closer than ever. A desperate idea occurred to him. Glancing upward, he spied a stout branch. Could the little cannibals climb? he wondered. If they could, then he was chopped liver, and spleen and kidneys, too. He decided to risk it, though. He couldn't continue to run through the dark woods. His bare feet were already cut and bleeding. He leaped and caught the branch. Without looking down again, he clambered into the highest limbs and prayed the thick leaves would hide him.

Trembling and cramped, he waited, not daring to move. A pair of Kobolds rushed by on the ground below, and he held his breath. Soon, though, the night was quiet again. He climbed halfway down and settled himself on a thick branch. Without making a sound he loosened his belt and retied it around both the branch and himself. There was no point in descending to look for his friends. He couldn't call out to them. The Kobolds might still be too close. And he'd never find them by blundering around in the dark. No, the best thing to do was to make himself as comfortable as possible in the tree and wait for morning.

He didn't sleep, though. Didn't even nod. Soon, the insects and night creatures, their songs disturbed and silenced by the Kobold attack, began to sing again. As Caspar listened, every note took on an ominous quality. A cricket's rasp made him jump. A low growl caused him to shiver. His eyes darted this way and that into the shadows that stirred around him. The wind rattled the leaves.

The music of Mauldwood. If he hadn't heard stories about this forest he might have found it beautiful. Instead, it sounded menacing. He rubbed at the goose-flesh on his arms. For the first time since leaving home he thought about the soft hay that made his bed in his uncle's barn loft. Those first few days had been fun, rather idyllic as he whistled his way down the road from Djabuti Padjama to Borphee. The last few had been anything but. He wondered if this was how his life was going to be from now on.

That was too depressing a thought.

A lusty young Kobold named Larry, he said to himself, making an effort to dispel his fears, *was tricked by a wizard contrary*. He tried several more lines, seeking a good finish that would lift his spirits. At last, though, he gave it up and nestled down as comfortably as he could on his branch.

The Kobolds had been kind of cute. Too bad they

had proven so unfriendly. He knew so little about them. So little about the world.

But, he thought grimly, *I'm learning fast.*

Dawn, filtering down through the leaves, cast a disturbing beauty over Mauldwood. Sunbeams shattered into dazzling bursts of light on droplets of emerald dew. The faintest wisps of fog lent a surreal haziness to the morning shadows. In many nearby trees tiny white parasitic flowers sprouted surprisingly from the dark damp bark, their petals open wide to catch the new light. A rich earthy smell permeated the air, and an absolute hush hung over the forest.

Caspar let out a slow breath and bestirred himself from his rough nest. His tunic was dew-damp, his skin cool and sticky with moisture. With stiff fingers he untied the strip of cloth that secured him to his treelimb perch and retied it around his waist. Slowly, he climbed down.

The earth felt spongy under his bare feet, and the odor of chlorophyll wafted up from the crushed moss as he took his first hesitant steps away from the tree where he'd spent the night. He thought of calling out to his companions, yet he feared alerting the Kobolds. They might still be near, or perhaps their camp or village, wherever Kobolds lived, was close by.

He scanned the trees around him, hoping that Sunrise or Satchmoz might also have sought refuge in the high branches. That was an idle hope, however. He had no idea how far they might have run into the woods, or even if they had escaped their strange attackers. At last, unable to formulate a better plan, guided by the slight tang of salt that rode the breeze, he traced his way back to the shore of the Great Sea.

A flock of seabirds, startled by his sudden appearance, scattered into the air as he emerged from the woods. A few circled overhead, scolding him, as he walked down to the edge of the surf and stared both ways. There was no sign of his friends, nor any sign of their camp. No doubt he was somewhere above it or below it. But which?

He turned to his left and walked up the beach. The sun, beating on his face and bare arms, promised a hot day, and he thanked his luck when he came upon a small stream that trickled out of the woods and into the ocean. It had a salty taste as it caught the ocean's backwash, but following it back among the trees for a short distance he found it sweet enough to drink. Refreshed, he returned to the beach and resumed his search.

A little further on he found an old trunk, some broken boards and a length of rope rigging. Certainly, he told himself, it was debris from the *Screaming Queen*. He took time to pick over the wreckage. The rope might come in handy, he thought, so he freed as much of it as he could and coiled it over his shoulder.

Then he turned to the trunk. It was still securely locked. Too large and heavy to carry, he looked around for anything that might help him break the mechanism. Attached to a piece of broken planking he found some kind of metal joint. At least, he assumed it was a joint. What did he know about shipbuilding? Carefully, he dragged the plank toward the trunk. It was too long and unwieldy for him to use as a tool, nor could he free the joint from the plank itself. Instead, he rested one end on the trunk and found a second, far heavier piece of planking. Lugging it into position, he dropped it sharply on the angled plank, snapping it.

The joint was still bolted to a section nearly as long as his forearm. He looked it over and nodded with satisfaction. It would give him added leverage as he slipped the flat edge of the joint behind the lock. He planted both his feet against the trunk, grasped his tool in both hands, and pulled with all his might. The lock popped open with ease.

Caspar gave a triumphant yelp and sprang to his feet. Hinges groaned as he threw back the trunk lid. Inside he found a number of uniforms, some military cloaks, and extra clothing of a more civilian nature. There were also a few pieces of light armor, a short-bladed sword, and a pair of plain daggers.

Grinning at his find, Caspar ripped away the crude

blue tunic Satchmoz had made for him and cast the scraps on the beach. All of the trousers he found in the trunk were too long for him, so he chose a sturdy pair and used the sword's keen edge to cut away the legs. Next he drew out a short-sleeved white linen tunic and pulled that over his head. Finally, he found a light quilted jerkin. Drawing it on over the tunic, he fastened it around his waist with a thin leather belt.

Everything was wet, but it would dry soon enough in the sun. In fact, the jerkin might prove too warm. He would wait and see, though, before he discarded it. He rummaged through the trunk's contents again, deciding what else he would take. The sword and daggers, of course. He wouldn't be caught helpless by a bunch of furballs again. He fastened the sword's belt around his waist, then added the sheathed daggers, which hung on separate belts. He knew nothing at all about armor, and the only piece he took was a small gold arm guard, which caught his fancy. He strapped it around his left wrist and looked at it admiringly.

Unfortunately, there was nothing for his feet. Nevertheless, he was in better condition than before, and he almost felt like whistling as he started off up the beach again. He had clothes, he had rope, and he had weapons. Things were looking up again.

He had begun to wonder if he had chosen the wrong direction, that perhaps he should have gone *down* the beach, when he heard the sound of tears. He stopped and listened closely. Male tears, he realized. The rarest kind.

"Sunrise?" he called tentatively.

The crying stopped instantly. A moment later, the bushes rustled a few paces ahead, and a bleary-eyed Sunrise walked out of the woods and stared at him. Instantly the boy wiped his eyes and grinned. "You got away," he said with quiet restraint. "I thought I was the only one."

Caspar grinned too as he walked toward the boy. "That was a nice shot with the conch shell last night. Great aim. Not only did I get away," he said. "I brought you back a present as a reward." He unfastened one of the daggers and tossed it to Sunrise. "And if you're interested, I found a cache of clothes back down the shore away."

Sunrise held out his hands and put on a mock-pout. "There something wrong with the way I look?" he asked in a hurt voice.

Caspar folded his arms across his chest as he shook his head. "You're very becoming in rags," he answered, "especially filthy ones covered with mud that you've slept in all night."

"Who slept?" Sunrise answered with a roll of his eyes. "I was too afraid of falling out of the tree."

Caspar laughed out loud, then related his own similar experience. Together, they headed back to the wreckage. It was harder to find anything in the trunk to fit Sunrise, but soon they settled on a light blue linen tunic. Belted around his waist, it fell almost to his knees, and the long sleeves offered his arms some protection.

"How old are you anyway?" Caspar asked Sunrise.

"Fourteen, I think."

"You think?"

Sunrise only nodded as he strapped on his dagger, and Caspar remembered the boy had lived most of his life in the back alleys of Borphee. It was quite possible Sunrise didn't know his age or birthday, and such a thought saddened Caspar. After all, he didn't really know his own birthday, either.

"What's your real name?" he asked suddenly. "I mean, the name you had before they sent you to the galley?"

"Something stupid," the boy answered as he began to throw everything out of the trunk.

Caspar raised an eyebrow as he watched Sunrise. "Something stupid?" he repeated sarcastically. "That was your name?"

Sunrise looked up from his examination of the trunk's interior long enough to stick out his tongue. "I've decided I like Sunrise better than my old name, despite how I came by it." He bent back inside the trunk. A moment later he rapped his knuckle on the left inside panel. "Bingo," he said, raising up again and gesturing for Caspar to look.

A small drawer had popped open at the bottom of the trunk's rear corner. Ten gold *zorkmids* and another ten silver *zorkles* lay within, glittering in the sunlight.

Caspar regarded Sunrise with a look of dubious surprise. "How'd you know those were there?"

Sunrise gave him a wink and reached within to scoop up the coins. "I wasn't always a cabin boy," he said, jingling his newfound wealth between his cupped palms.

Caspar grabbed a discarded tunic, ripped out one sleeve and quickly fashioned a rough purse for Sunrise to put his coins in. "Oh?" he said, "and just what were you?"

Sunrise flashed him an easy smile. "Maybe I'll tell you someday," he answered. "But a trunk like this?" He put on a proudful sneer. "There had to be a hidden compartment. I'm surprised you overlooked it."

Caspar smiled inwardly. How tough and competent the boy acted now. And his speech was always so flippant. Yet, only a little while before he'd been crying in the bushes, thinking himself stranded alone. Actually though, it was easy to reconcile the two images. Sunrise had all the fear and bravado of a growing youth.

"I want to go back to our campsite," he said as they started up the beach again. "Maybe Satchmoz is there waiting. It would be the logical place to regroup."

"If he got away," Sunrise said doubtfully. "He's an old man, remember? Those Kobolds were fast little suckers."

"He's not just an old man," Caspar answered. "He's Satchmoz the Incomparable. I'll bet you he's there, impatient because we haven't shown up."

It was a bet he would have lost, had Sunrise accepted it. They found the blackened smouldering remains of their campfire, but there was no sign of the wizard. Caspar picked up the conch shell with which

Sunrise had bashed one of the Kobolds, and looked toward the edge of Mauldwood.

"You'd better hang onto this," he said quietly, unable to hide his disappointment. He handed the shell to Sunrise. "You might need it again."

Sunrise took the shell. His gaze, too, roamed the border of the woods, and a frown creased his mouth. He tossed the conch aside. "What now?" he asked, kicking sand.

"We wait," Caspar answered firmly. "He'll come. I'm sure of it." Without another word, he began to unfasten all his belts, let his weapons slide to the sand, and pull off his clothes.

Sunrise made a wry face. "Is there anything about you I should know?" he asked with a mischievous lilt.

"Yeah," Caspar answered, taking a swing at the boy's backside with his foot. "You need a bath worse than I do." He turned and strolled toward the surf. "Last one in is a Kobold furball."

Sunrise scrambled out of his new garments, but Caspar was treading water before the boy ever hit the waves. Sunrise swam out to join him. "Do you really think he'll come?" he asked intently as he stretched out and floated on his back.

Before Caspar could answer the air exploded with a loud *bamf* and a horrid stench of brimstone. For an instant, Satchmoz was right there beside them. Then, the wizard gave a startled cry and sank beneath the surface.

Caspar caught Satchmoz's floundering hand and pulled him up again. The wizard coughed and gasped and spit out water as Sunrise caught his other arm and helped him until he could stay afloat on his own.

"Damn, damn, damn!" Satchmoz cursed as he tread water. "I finally get that stupid *aimfiz* spell to work! Ten tries it took, and I couldn't even start until it got light enough to read it." He rocked his head back and forth and wrinkled up his nose so that his voice took on a nasal whine. "Then, all I had to do was think of you, and it would bring me straight to you. And where do I find you?" He slapped his hand on the water's surface, splashing them all. "In the middle of the damned ocean! Now, I'll have to dry all my scrolls again!"

Caspar looked at Sunrise and winked. "Told you he'd come," he said.

Sunrise made a clucking sound. "And he didn't even have to click his heels three times. What a world."

The three of them swam to shore. Sunrise chuckled while Satchmoz fumed and muttered under his breath. At least it was still early morning, Caspar thought as he began to dress. They could dry the wizard's scrolls and still get well away from this spot with plenty of daylight left.

CHAPTER NINE

MAULDWOOD

HAT WAS IN THOSE bottles, anyway?" Caspar asked Satchmoz as they strolled up the beach. The sun sat just over the tops of the trees on their left. The blue water to their right sparkled. A ribbon of golden sand stretched before and behind.

Satchmoz grinned to himself and scratched his armpit. "I couldn't think of anything else," he chuckled. "When I saw the Kobolds had you surrounded I just reached into a couple of pockets. It was too dark to read a scroll, so I grabbed a couple of potions at random. But I knew Kobolds. They tend to use those big mouths like they use their hands—for biting, grabbing, holding. I was pretty sure they'd catch the potions that way and swallow them."

"Pretty smart," Sunrise acknowledged. "But what was in 'em?"

The wizard shrugged. "Judging from the effects," he answered, "one contained *sirano*. It's a potion that makes the drinker recite bad poetry for hours on end. The other, I'm sure, was *flaxo*, which can only be described as exquisite torture in distilled, liquid form."

"Ah," said Caspar, nodding. "I wondered. I was almost embarrassed watching its effect."

"Some of the other Kobolds were pretty intrigued, too," Sunrise recalled.

Satchmoz rubbed at a speck of sand that had gotten into the corner of his eye. "Well, you know Kobolds," he said distractedly. "Before they turned fierce their idea of a good time used to be to roll up to a farm house late at night pretending they were tumbleweeds and peek through the farmer's keyhole."

Sunrise gave a lopsided grin and arched one eyebrow, a trick he was picking up from Caspar. "I used to do that," he admitted with a tilt of his head. "Only we had to make do with apartments and boarding houses."

Caspar gave him a disapproving look, but he said, "I'll bet you took notes, too."

"Nope," Sunrise confessed. "Can't write a word, myself." Then, he tapped his temple and winked. "Got a good memory, though."

Satchmoz gave the boy a dubious look, then glanced at Caspar. "Duncanthrax didn't toss him on a galley as punishment," he said. "I think he was put there for safe-keeping."

A little farther up the beach they found another stream and followed it back into the woods far enough to refresh themselves. They didn't rest, though, until they returned to the shore. Caspar hated Mauldwood. Something about its gloomy recesses and strange stillnesses made his skin crawl. It was beautiful, sometimes, in its lushness. Yet he sensed nothing but danger.

On the beach again the sun shone brightly, and the sky was clear as sapphire. The breezes blew clean and sweet, and the smell of the sea spray was like perfume. Though it was hot and sweat ran off him like rain, he stayed in the sun and avoided the shadows of the trees.

Clumps of grass and weeds began to pop up through the sand as they continued northward. The strip of beach grew narrower. They came upon another stream, and not much farther, still another. The water ran crisp and cool, and they took time to sit and soak their feet.

Little by little, the ground began to change. Soon there was more grass than sand. The edge of the forest receded on their left, though the tall morgia trees still loomed against the sky. They pushed their way through a patch of reeds as the earth turned spongy under their steps. For the first time, insects became an annoyance.

"If Quendor has a national slop jar," Sunrise said

with some exasperation as they stopped by yet another stream, "this place must be it." He scratched at a couple of midge bites and made a face. "Where are we?"

"Some kind of delta," Caspar suggested, his expression growing more troubled. He glanced to the left. It seemed the woods were closing in again. For the umpteenth time, he readjusted his sword. Wearing a weapon wasn't half as much fun as he'd always imagined it. The damn thing had slapped him in the thigh until he was bruised. So he'd slung it by its belt over his shoulder. Now the strap was rubbing him raw, and his spine was taking the bruising. "I'm beginning to wish Satchmoz had saved his teleportation spell," he grumbled.

"If I'd saved it," the wizard reminded him gently, "I might still be running around in the woods, and you might still be sitting on the beach by a cold campfire."

"Naw, we'd have abandoned you by now," Sunrise reassured the old man.

They pushed on, trying to stay close to the sea, but the terrain kept forcing them inland. It was no longer sand beneath their feet, but moss and mud. Water began to squish up from the earth around their steps. Little streams and branchlets flowed like some kind of crazy, wet lacework. Cattails and saw grass sprang up to impede their progress.

Sunrise gave a startled yelp and jumped against Caspar. Off to the right, a snake as long as the youth was tall slithered into a clump of reeds.

"I want to go home," Sunrise muttered nervously. "I'll even think about going back to Chulig."

Caspar hugged the boy around the shoulders and stared at the last place he'd seen the snake. "Chulig is on the bottom of the sea," he reminded.

Sunrise bit his lip and looked thoughtful. "Well, never mind then," he said without much conviction.

Caspar frowned and looked back the way they had come. For some time he had been watching for a place to camp for the evening, but no good spot had presented itself. On his left, Mauldwood seemed closer than ever. He could smell the ocean, but he could no longer see it.

He waved a hand in front of his nose to drive away a fly the size of his thumb. "I don't suppose you have a scroll or anything that might get us out of this?" he said to Satchmoz.

The wizard shook his head. "I've got a spell to make liquids turn dry," he reported, "but not *this* much liquid." He lifted up one muck-covered foot and made a face. His felt slippers were ruined. With a low moan of disgust, he cast both slippers away. "Someone up in Thriff has been working on a flying spell," he continued, "but nothing's come of it, yet."

Caspar cursed. "If I didn't know better," he muttered, "I'd say the land itself is conspiring to force us into the woods. But that would be nonsense." He clutched his fists tightly at his sides and gritted his teeth. "This is a rational world!" he added as if to reassure himself.

They pressed ahead, fighting bugs and saw grass, ever alert for snakes. The water rose over the tops of their toes, then over the tops of their feet. Caspar could no longer smell the ocean. The air was full of the wet stench of decay.

Abruptly, they halted. Before them stood a copse of tall cattails and slender morgia saplings. Draped among the reeds and branches were hundreds of incredibly elaborate, not to mention large, webs whose silken strands glittered in the late sun. Among those silver threads hung scores of the fattest, ugliest spiders Caspar had ever seen. He knew it was his imagination, but in his mind he thought he could feel their eyes upon him, feel them smile as the silly humans stood and gawked.

"I am not having a good time," Sunrise said emphatically, clutching the hilt of his dagger.

Caspar glanced left. Mauldwood had grown closer than ever. The advancing edge of its shadow was almost upon them. "Let's go that way," Caspar suggested, gesturing to the right, a way that led around the spiders. "Maybe we can find the shore again."

"I don't think so," Satchmoz murmured worriedly. "I've seen this kind of country before, farther up north."

They moved away from Mauldwood and away from the laughing spiders. Caspar began to grow truly afraid, and he knew that Sunrise shared his fear. The old wizard said nothing, but his bald head turned right and left, and his eyes searched in all directions. At the slightest sound they all jumped.

The shrill, characteristic calls of a flock of firebirds sounded in the remote distance. Caspar spied them as they appeared in the northwest, a dark cloud at first. As they drew nearer, though, their bright plummage caught the sun's rays and filled the sky briefly with fluttering reds and oranges and golds. Gradually, the flock wheeled southward and disappeared. Their calls could still be heard after they were gone. Then that too faded.

A smile lingered on Caspar's face as he remembered the pair of firebirds he had spied on the way to Borphee. "Firebirds are good luck," he told his friends.

Sunrise gave him a smug look. "Luck? This is a rational world, remember? You said so."

Something splashed in the water off to their right, and they caught a fleeting glimpse of something big swimming off into the reeds. It was quiet for a moment, then suddenly the water behind those reeds began to churn with a frenzy, and the reeds shivered and cracked. Then, it grew quiet again, except for the sound of something feeding.

Caspar looked down as the ripples broke against his ankles. He swallowed and looked at his comrades. A feeling of guilt began to gnaw at him. At first, he'd mistaken it for hunger. But there was no denying it now. He'd chosen the direction. He'd gotten them lost in this damned swamp. And he was likely to get them all eaten.

Satchmoz licked his lips, then rubbed a hand over his stubbled chin. With a glance toward the setting sun, he started off in the direction they had been going, hopefully toward the sea. He hadn't gone but three steps when he cried out with a despairing *awp*, threw out his hands in a vain attempt to stop himself, and plunged over his head into some unseen drop-off. Both Caspar and Sunrise rushed to his aid. Caspar, too, fell in.

The wizard surfaced sputtering, slapping the water angrily, and cursing in languages neither Caspar nor Sunrise knew. "Not again, damn it!" he shouted in dismay. "Not my scrolls!"

Caspar clambered out onto safe elevation again, and helped Sunrise extract the wizard from his predicament. "This might be the ocean," he told them. "It gets deep very quick."

"You're telling me?" the wizard shrieked. "I found it out first." He grabbed the hem of his cloak and gave it a wring.

"Nothing but reeds and clumps of reeds!" Sunrise complained. "And in the reeds snakes and spiders and things with big teeth!"

Caspar felt the weight of his friends' anger, though he knew it wasn't directed at him. His chest felt tight, and his breathing came in shallow gasps. Nevertheless, he turned and stared toward Mauldwood. No matter how far they traveled eastward, the shadow of the woods, and the woods itself seemed to pursue them.

He bit his lip and swallowed hard as a breeze blew over the land. The tallest morgias swayed gently, beckoning them. "I don't think we've got any choice," he said at last. "If we can make it into the forest by dark, we might at least find solid land to sleep on."

"I'll settle for another night in the branches," Sunrise said, "as long as I can be dry."

"As long as *you* can be dry, boy?" Satchmoz snapped as he started off toward Mauldwood without them. "What about my scrolls?"

Sunrise scowled as he watched the wizard's back. "I'm going to tell him what to do with his scrolls," he muttered to Caspar before they both started after Satchmoz. "They don't roll 'em in those tight little cylinders for nothing."

Caspar didn't say anything. It worried him how quickly they seemed to be progressing toward the wood. It should have been farther away. Already its shadow chilled him and shut out the sun, and still the wind blew, almost like a whisper, and the trees beckoned.

"I feel like I'm surrendering to it," Caspar whispered as they climbed toward dry land. His gaze roamed through the tree tops, through the gloom-filled spaces between the dark old trunks. They were well into the forest before the swamp finally gave way. Twilight was upon them, and they had still found no place to make camp.

There was no path. They wandered among the old trunks, picking their way as they went, sometimes pushing through underbrush that scratched and tore at their clothing. Poor Sunrise's unprotected legs took the worst of it. Caspar had his trousers, and Satchmoz kept his cloak hugged close about himself.

"If we're going to keep going," the wizard said when they stopped for another rest, "I have a spell that can create a usable light." He glanced up toward the sky, what little of it could be seen through the leaves. "It's getting pretty dark, though. If I don't use it now it'll soon be too dark to read the scroll."

"Light?" Sunrise said. "What about a campfire?"

Satchmoz shook his head. "I only have one copy of most of my spells. I used the *radnog* last night."

"Great," Sunrise scowled. He gazed slowly around into the forest depths and hugged himself, though it was not yet even cool.

"Never mind," Caspar told the youth. "We'll make a fire the old fashioned way. But I'd like to go on until we find another stream and water to drink. It shouldn't be too far; we've found plenty of streams."

"Then we'd better move on," Satchmoz suggested. "When night falls in these woods it's going to fall like a fist."

Caspar led the way, using his sword to hack through some of the denser undergrowth. He felt better with the weapon in his hand, anyway. Well, not better, but more secure. Well, not secure, but ready. Well, not really ready, either. He chewed his lip. Damn, if Satchmoz just hadn't used that blasted *fist* metaphor!

Just as they had the night before, the crickets and tree frogs began their evening paean. Caspar was unused to woods. The Peltoid Valley was mostly fields and meadows. It unnerved him to hear so much sound and yet see nothing of the sound*makers*. He kept looking up into the trees, and consequently tripping over sticks and roots in his path.

"I've been meaning to ask," Caspar said to Satchmoz just to divert himself. "That teleportation spell . . ."

"*Aimfiz,*" Satchmoz supplied.

"Right," Caspar replied absently. "You said all you had to do was think of Sunrise and me, and it brought you right to us. Why can't your guild find this Berknip character the same way? How could Duncanthrax possibly hide him from you?"

The wizard rubbed a hand distractedly over his chin. "A good question," he answered. "We tried *aimfiz* . . ."

"Let me guess," Sunrise interrupted. "It *aimfizzled.*"

Satchmoz frowned. "The brat does have a way of putting things in colorful terms," he said to Caspar.

"Brat!" Sunrise protested.

"Keep your voice down!" Caspar scolded. "We don't want every living thing in the woods to know we're here!" Though, somehow Caspar felt they already did. In fact, he felt sure he was being watched. He glanced up into the trees again and promptly jambed his toe on a moss-covered rock. "Damn!" he shouted. In a rage, he picked up the stone, flung it as hard and as far as he could, and listened to it crash as it landed in thick foliage.

"Good shot," Sunrise smirked. "You killed a bush."

Caspar's eyes narrowed as he regarded Sunrise, but he held his tongue and resumed the lead again. It had been a tough day, and their tempers were growing short. They'd walked a long distance without anything to eat. Only brief sips of the *berzio* potion kept their bellies from complaining.

It was with great relief, then, that they came upon a small clearing on the bank of a shallow stream. Sunrise collapsed at once on the soft grass, uttering no more than a sigh as he closed his eyes. Satchmoz went immediately to the bank, sat down, and put his feet in the cool water. "Ahhh," he said, rolling his eyes upward.

Caspar longed to fall to the grass, too. His arms and legs felt like weights. Yet, he could not shake the oppressive mood of the forest. He began at once to gather handfuls of dry grass and small sticks, which he placed in a pile near the stream bank. There was almost no light at all left in the sky, and he worked quickly.

Satchmoz understood Caspar's purpose, and looked a little embarrassed that he had not thought to help. He drew one foot out of its soothing bath as he turned and started to rummage in his cloak pockets. "Wait," he said, "I may still be able to read the *frotz* spell."

"No!" Caspar said sharply as he deposited another pile of sticks on the bank. "It's foolish to waste a spell that we might have greater need for later. You know how to make a fire?"

The wizard pushed out his lip a bit and shrugged. "I told you, I'm out of *radnog* spells."

"I mean naturally," Caspar said with some exasperation as he wiped a trickle of sweat from his brow. "We can do some things for ourselves, can't we? Magic doesn't make the world go around."

"Wanna bet?" Satchmoz muttered under his breath. He picked up a pair of dry sticks and began to rub them together as Caspar resumed his task. In no time he was huffing and puffing and getting nowhere.

Caspar came back to his side again, not with more kindling, but with a long stripped sapling which he had cut with his sword. Quickly, he showed the wizard how to make a bed of dry leaves and grass and how to rub the sticks properly to produce the necessary friction. Satchmoz did his best while Caspar, using one of the daggers he had taken from the trunk, went about carving a sharp point on the end of his sapling. In the end, of course, he wound up setting his would-be spear aside and building the fire himself.

"That's wonderful!" Satchmoz exclaimed as Caspar blew on the first tiny spark. It flared like a precious jewel in the utter darkness that now surrounded them. A wisp of smoke curled up from the leaves, stinging his eyes. Then a small flame flared with a sputter. The wizard wasted no time feeding new bits of grass and leaves into the fire, as Caspar had instructed him.

"Your *radnog* is quicker," Caspar admitted as he sat back to catch his breath.

Satchmoz smiled as he continued to nurse the fire. "Yes, but I can tell by the look on your face that you have a real sense of accomplishment."

"I'd rather have a good linament," Caspar answered wearily as he massaged his palms and fingers. They were still tender from his time at the oar. He thanked his luck that farmwork had toughened his hands and they hadn't blistered. His legs ached from the long walk. And his shoulder, where the sword strap had chafed him. In fact, he hurt all over. He sagged back on the grass and threw his arms over his head.

The flickering campfire made strange shadows in the leaves above his head. Everytime a breeze blew the shadows twitched. Tired as he was, Caspar watched them uneasily. That shadow looked like a cat, he thought, giving a little start. Then it disappeared. That one looked like a face, eyes and everything. The wind blew, shaking the leaves, and it vanished.

Caspar gave up. He drew his dagger again and reached for his half-finished spear. The point was not yet sharp enough, and he began to whittle with a vengeance, and shavings flew in all directions.

"Sword, dagger, lance," Satchmoz said as he put his feet back in the water again. "Maybe you can start a fort next."

Caspar glanced across the stream into the darkest part of the woods. "I might," he answered curtly.

The two of them fell silent again. The sounds of the crickets and frogs swelled louder than ever as the night deepened. The only other sounds were those made by the steady strokes of Caspar's knife and Sunrise's snoring.

When Caspar was satisfied with his work, he sheathed the dagger, squatted closer to the fire, and held the newly carved point of his spear in the flame. The fire would harden it, he knew, and make it more reliable. He watched carefully, roasting the point slowly. It would defeat his purpose to let it char and burn, for that would only weaken it.

At last, it was done. He held the point close to his eyes, feeling its warmth on his face, and examined it. Rising to his feet, he hefted it in one hand and tested its balance. As a throwing weapon, he decided, it stank. But in a close fight with an animal or an enemy he could use it to jab and thrust. Finally, he sat down again and put the spear aside.

Satchmoz passed him the unstoppered vial of *berzio*. Caspar thanked him with a wordless nod and took a sip. The taste of fudge exploded in his mouth. What would happen, he wondered, frowning as he passed the bottle back, when after a few more drinks of Satchmoz's elixir he could no longer stand fudge? He felt full—the potion's magic was still as effective as ever—but he was beginning to long for the taste of a steak.

On the bank, Satchmoz drew one foot out of the stream, crossed it over his knee and began to massage it. He let out little sighs as his gnarly fingers worked, and his face took on a sublime look. If the stories about Mauldwood bothered the old wizard, he didn't show it. He might have been on a fishing trip with good friends for all the concern he displayed.

If he breaks out in a camp song, Caspar thought unkindly as he hugged his knees to his chest and rocked back and forth, *I'll roast his toes and see if they taste like fudge*. He grimaced, admitting the meanness of that, irritated with himself.

It was safe to relax a bit, he told himself. He had figured out all the possible directions something could come at them, all the routes danger could take. Still, he watched the shadows and measured the dark places. He listened to the sounds of the woods, alert for any warning snap or rustle. But loudest of all in his ears was the sound of his own pulse.

All the while, he kept one envious eye on the wizard's back. Satchmoz sat contentedly, almost enjoying the night, soaking and paddling his feet in the water as if he didn't have a worry in the world. Finally, Caspar could stand no more. His tension would strangle him if he didn't do something to ease it. He rose and undressed and waded out into the stream. Satchmoz might find a footbath soothing, but Caspar needed a real bath. The water was quite cool, yet he felt better instantly.

"It's amazing how quickly he fell asleep," Caspar said to Satchmoz as he nodded toward Sunrise's still form. "You'd think he was on a family picnic, or a hunting excursion."

"Speaking of hunting," Satchmoz said, "I wonder if he's ever heard of snipes?"

Caspar caught the odd, sneering note in the old man's voice, and paused in the act of washing himself. Why would Satchmoz think of that old prankster's game now? No one in his right mind would send a boy alone into this woods in the dark.

Slowly, Satchmoz turned his head and looked at Caspar from under a pinched and shadowed brow. The firelight touched the corner of the old man's eye and filled it with a subtle gleam, and his lips turned upward, not in a smile, but in something more feral. The wizard gave a low chuckle, then looked down again and resumed his foot massage.

The wind blew, chilling Caspar, and the water suddenly seemed cold as ice.

CHAPTER TEN

"YOU MEAN, WHISTLE A HAPPY TUNE?"

CASPAR AWOKE WITH A start, aware that something was moving around the camp. Surreptitiously, he groped for the spear by his thigh, curled his fingers around it, then sat bolt upright, ready to fight.

Sunrise stuck out his tongue as he bent down by the ashes, all that remained of their campfire. He dropped a small armload of strange-looking plants on the ground and brushed dirt from his forearms. "Spenseweed roots," he said. "I didn't think I could take any more of the old man's potion."

"You said you liked spenseweed milkshakes," Caspar reminded him as he put down the spear and stretched. He'd fallen asleep leaning against a tree. He felt stiff all the way down his spine, and his neck had a kink in it.

"Not three times a day," Sunrise grumbled.

Caspar stood up. Every joint in his body made an audible pop or crack. "So you brought back spenseweed roots?"

"Complain, complain!" Sunrise snapped. "They're all I could find. The stuff grows like crazy around here. And at least you can *chew* these." He threw one to Caspar with a little more force than was necessary. "Here, give your jaws something to do besides flap."

Caspar made a face. The root was still covered with dirt. He didn't say anything about it, though, just carried it to the stream and gave it a quick rinse. Cautiously, he took a bite of the hard root. Its full flavor burst in his mouth as he chewed and crunched noisily. With his back to Sunrise, he put on a wicked grin. For him, it was a welcome relief from fudge.

"You might at least say thanks," Sunrise muttered as he brought over two handfuls of the roots, knelt down, and began to cleanse them.

"For what?" Caspar answered sharply. "It's about time you pulled your weight. Satchmoz has helped with his magic. And I've done everything else—got us clothes, hacked our way through the swamp, obtained weapons. I even made the fire last night. The least you can do is find breakfast without grumbling about it."

Even as he said it, Caspar didn't quite believe the words coming out of his mouth. He knew his criticism was unfair. He owed his life to Sunrise. But the damned kid was getting on his nerves. From the look on the youth's face, Caspar might as well have hit him. He couldn't bring himself to apologize, though, so he turned away and nibbled self-consciously on his root.

"Choke on it, then!" Sunrise hissed. He got up, carrying his roots back to the ashes of the campfire, where he laid them down again on some broad morgia leaves he had placed there. Angrily, he rolled several of the roots in the leaves and placed them in the heart of the ashes, which were still warm. In no time, the smell of warm, moist spenseweed wafted through the camp.

Irritated both with himself and Sunrise, Caspar tried not to watch the boy. The delicious smell, however, soon made his mouth water. He munched a few more half-hearted bites, and let the rest of his raw meal fall into the stream while he told himself he wasn't hungry anyway.

The rich odor did what all their talking had failed to do. It woke Satchmoz. The wizard crawled out from under his cloak and rubbed his eyes with his fists, looking ever so much like a bald-headed, hawk-beaked, bleary-eyed child. "Food?" he said hopefully.

"You wash first!" Sunrise ordered, pointing to the stream with one hand as he kept a careful eye on the leaf-wrapped roots. "You stink like a back-alley corpse!"

"Why not?" Caspar said with a sneer. "He's been dead to the world for hours."

Satchmoz looked from one to the other, and his sleepy face recomposed itself into a harder mask as he stood over Sunrise and the smoldering ashes. "That's hard cheese in a glass rathole, coming from you, little boy," the wizard said flatly to Sunrise. "You have a certain pungent fragrance, yourself."

Sunrise glared up at him over one shoulder. "I bathed this morning before either of you stirred!"

Satchmoz turned up his nose as he put his cloak carefully aside. "And quite obviously you went digging in the woods *afterward*. You're covered with dirt and mud."

Sullenly, Sunrise picked up a stick and jabbed it into the ashes. With a few quick flips of his wrist he turned the roots over. A thin smoke and a puff of ash swirled up into his eyes.

Caspar had been just about to add another jibe of his own when the boy flung a hand up to his eyes and sat back on his haunches. It was only the smoke, Caspar told himself, his sense of guilt deepening for no good reason. Yet it looked almost as if Sunrise was about to cry.

Caspar frowned again. He watched Satchmoz strip off his sweaty loincloth and squat down in the stream to wash. Sunrise recovered and went back to his cooking and his sulking. When the roots were done, he carried one in his bare fingers to Caspar and placed another on the bank close to the wizard. He dug his own out of the ashes, then, and took it to the far side of camp where he could eat alone.

Caspar unrolled the leaves slowly, and steam rose up around his hands. The root was buttery soft now. He stared at it, lying on its green bed on his palm, and inhaled its sweetness. He raised it to his lips and started to take a bite. Then, he hesitated. "Thanks," he called to Sunrise. But even that small word had a grudging tone.

After that, all three ate in silence. When they were

full, Sunrise rinsed off the remaining roots and dropped them down the front of his tunic to eat later. Meanwhile, Caspar bent over the stream and washed his face and hair. Satchmoz, using a stick, scattered the ashes of the campfire so they would not continue to smolder.

When at last they were ready to leave, they headed, not into the woods, but up the course of the stream. It was easier than pushing through the tangled undergrowth, and they would have water to drink for as long as the stream bed took them generally the way they wanted to go.

The morning sun shone down through the leaves, casting spears of light all through the forest. Birds darted among the trees and squirrels scampered from limb to limb, chattering at the humans that passed by. Mauldwood shimmered with shades of green. It seemed in so many ways a paradise.

Yet Caspar felt uneasy. Neither Sunrise nor Satchmoz had spoken since breakfast. Sunrise waded along, wearing his sullenness like protective armor, barely glancing up at all as he put one foot in front of the other. The wizard, on the other hand, seemed even more agitated than Caspar. He stopped frequently and peered from side to side, up into the trees or back the way they had come. He carried the hem of his cloak draped over one arm to keep it and his precious scrolls out of the water. A permanent frown had carved itself on his face. He wrung his hands or clenched them into fists. His eyes never fixed on anything for too long, but shifted suspiciously toward the slightest movement of leaf or branch.

"What's wrong with you!" Caspar snapped when he could take the wizard's queer behavior no more. He shook the tip of his lance at the old man. "If there's something out there, say so!"

"Can't you hear it?" Satchmoz shouted back, his face purpling with rage. "It's like . . ." he hesitated, searching for the word. ". . . breathing!"

"That's preposterous!" Caspar responded, his gaze sweeping all around, nevertheless. "I don't hear anything! Now stop slowing us down, and let's just move!"

He led the way upstream again, gritting his teeth so hard his jaw began to ache. Without quite knowing why, he found his right hand constantly straying toward the hilt of the sword he wore on his back. Each time he stopped himself before actually grasping it. After a while, without really thinking about it, he began to curl his fingers around the hilt of the dagger at his belt.

What's wrong with me? he wondered to himself as he searched the trees ahead for any sign of danger. He let go of the dagger and forced his jaw to relax. He rolled his head a bit, trying to loosen the knots of tension in his neck and shoulders. *Why are we all shouting?*

From the bank close to Caspar's left came a sudden ominous rattle. "Snake!" Caspar cried in alarm. He leaped aside, forgetting he stood in calf-deep water. With a second, awkward yelp, he fell, drenching himself and splashing Sunrise.

"You rot-brain!" the boy shrieked, wiping his face and eyes. "It's just a coin bush!" He pointed toward a peculiar plant, perhaps as tall as a man's waist, that grew by the side of the stream. Its dark red leaves, almost black, hung stiff and thin and round as coins from its branches. An easy breeze blew, and the coins shivered with a rasping rattle.

"Well, at least it wasn't me who fell this time," Satchmoz smirked.

Soaking wet, red-faced with embarrassment and anger, Caspar got to his feet. Sunrise, though, wasn't quite finished. He snatched up the crude spear, which Caspar had dropped and which now floated on the water between them.

"I thought you were my friend!" he screamed at Caspar. "But you're not! You're not! I trusted you!" Without warning, he swung the spear at Caspar, catching him a glancing blow on the side of the head. Again he raised the weapon, wielding it like a quarterstaff. Caspar took the blow on his arm as he sagged under its impact.

A third time, the boy prepared to strike. Desperately, Caspar flung himself at Sunrise, and they both fell backward. In a red haze, Caspar struggled with the youth, tearing the spear from his hands and flinging it aside, locking his fingers around the boy's throat, pushing his head under water as he straddled his small chest.

Sunrise scratched and clawed uselessly at Caspar's wrists. Through the crystal clear water, Caspar saw fear widen the boy's eyes. A rush of bubbles shot upward from Sunrise's mouth. Satchmoz, standing to one side, threw back his head and laughed.

It was the laughter that somehow snapped Caspar out of it. He froze for a confused instant. Then, he cried out with a terrible dismay and dragged Sunrise to the surface. He threw his arms around the boy, hugging him tight. Sunrise coughed and sputtered against his shoulder, while at the same time struggling weakly to free himself from Caspar's grip. Nevertheless, Caspar refused to let go.

"Forgive me!" he begged, half-sobbing. "Forgive me!" He glanced over the boy's shoulder at the wizard. Satchmoz was no longer laughing. He stood dumbly, rubbing his head, obviously sharing the confusion. "What are we doing?" Caspar screamed. "What's happening to us?"

As if a deep fatigue had come over him, the old man waded to the shore and sat down on the grassy bank. He unlaced his cloak from around his throat and set it aside. His head sank into his hands, and he rubbed his temples.

"It's Mauldwood," Satchmoz said at last. "I told you I heard breathing before. I'm a wizard, and wizards—any magic users—are sensitive to even the most subliminal enchantment." He looked up and swallowed hard before continuing. "My skin has been crawling. Now I know why." He made a broad sweeping gesture. "It's this place. It's alive! More than just plants and animals. The woods, itself, is alive and evil. And it's affecting us!"

"I wanted to kill you," Sunrise's voice was a timid whisper. He rubbed his throat with one hand as he clung to Caspar. "I tried to reach my dagger," he went on, giving a small cough, "but you were sitting on it, holding me down!"

Caspar squeezed the boy again, pressing his face down into the hollow of Sunrise's neck in shame. "We've got to get out of here!" he said.

"How?" the wizard shouted, his voice taking on a sharp edge again. "We're lost!"

"Then we've got to hang on!" Caspar shouted back. Then he forced himself to be calm. His breathing came in rapid, shallow gasps, and he felt the knife edge of panic against his heart. He fought it back and rose to his feet, keeping Sunrise's hand tightly locked in his. "It's the woods," he reminded Satchmoz. "It's making us afraid, and it's making us fight with each other. We've got to resist it!"

The wizard bit his lip, trembling visibly. "Yes, you're right," he said.

"Remember, it's the woods," Sunrise said hoarsely. "I don't really hate either of you." He glanced up at Caspar and forced a weak smile. "Though right now I feel like I do."

"Just hang on," the wizard repeated to himself as he folded his cloak into a clumsy bundle and clutched it to his chest. He rose and waded into the stream again, his old body seeming paler than ever. "Just hang on."

They started upstream at an urgent pace. Pretty soon, though, Sunrise tugged his hand free from Caspar's grip and reached down the front of his tunic. His mouth was curled up at one corner and he made an unpleasant sound.

"What's wrong?" Caspar asked worriedly, still full of guilt for nearly drowning the boy.

Sunrise grimaced. "You squashed the spenseweed," he answered, drawing up one of the crushed roots from the neck of his tunic. It fell into the stream with a plop. "Things are getting kind of sticky down there."

"Don't throw them away, you stupid boy!" Satchmoz scolded as he snatched the discarded root from the water. He caught himself almost instantly. "Nice little boy," he corrected in a calmer tone. He forced a smile, though it was an obvious strain. "Better to lunch on these now, no matter what their condition, than to just throw them away. Right?"

Caspar made a curt bow and a flourish. "Can Satchmoz the Incomparable ever be wrong?" he asked grandiosely. "Let's have lunch. Let's have a song, too. Let's have a good time!"

"Let's do something to attract the Kobolds," Sunrise added with a sarcastic lilt as he fished out another spenseweed root.

"It's worth the risk," Caspar insisted quietly. "Maybe if we try to have some fun, it'll work against the magic of Mauldwood."

Sunrise made a face. "You mean, whistle a happy tune?"

Caspar shrugged as he took the root from Sunrise and bit off a mouthful. "Why not?" he said, munching.

"I've heard it said," Satchmoz joined in, "that when you walk through a storm you should hold your head up high . . ."

"Yeah," Sunrise interrupted, but he was grinning despite his caustic tone. "It makes a better target for the lightning."

Satchmoz stuck out his tongue at the boy. "How can you be so cynical at your age?" he asked as he raised to his lips the root he had rescued from the water and prepared to bite.

Sunrise shrugged as he recovered two more roots from inside his tunic. "It's in my blood."

Caspar raised an eyebrow and swallowed a mouthful. "The cynicisms of the father?" he suggested.

The mood turned jovial, and no one mentioned that the humor had a strained quality. Satchmoz still watched the trees, and Caspar still felt uneasy and vaguely frightened. He kept his fears to himself, though, and took extra care not to let it show.

Sunrise seemed to have the greatest, genuine fun. He fished all the spenseweed roots out of his tunic one at a time, but before he gave them to his friends to eat he used his thumb nail to carve some shockingly naughty word into the pulp. "Here, this is what you're eating," he'd say, passing the root over. But even his humor had its subtle edge. "And remember," he'd add, "you are what you eat."

Shortly after that they found true cause for rejoicing as the stream cut suddenly and unexpectedly across an old road. Caspar gave a whoop as he ran splashing ahead of the others and stepped onto the hard-packed earth.

Sunrise rushed up behind him. "We're not lost anymore!" he cried excitedly. "A road has to go *somewhere*, doesn't it?"

Satchmoz nearly dropped his cloak as he climbed out of the stream. Fortunately, he caught it before it got wet. "Hmmm," he said quietly as he bent and peered at the road. "Nobody's been this way in a long time," he announced. "Look, the old ruts where wagons used to cross the stream and roll up onto the bank again are nearly worn away." He pointed also to thick clumps of grass that grew in the middle of the road. "Must have been a lot of traffic through here once to pack the earth so hard," he added, "but not in recent years."

Caspar gazed up and down the old road. It was really no more than a well-beaten path just wide enough for a farm wagon. His immediate joy slowly ebbed, and he sensed his apprehensions closing in again. Just a way ahead, the road appeared to curve in the proper northward direction. It might follow a course parallel to the stream. It made sense to take it. Yet, standing in the center of the wide path, he suddenly felt awfully exposed and vulnerable. The trees loomed on either side like gnarly black hands waiting to grab him, and the laughing shadows that swallowed the road murmured taunts he couldn't quite hear.

It's just the woods, he reminded himself, mastering his fear. Even so, he wished he'd taken time to recover the spear he'd lost in his mindless struggle with Sunrise. Unconsciously, he rubbed at the bruise on his right arm where the boy had landed a blow.

Sunrise noticed. "Some walking sticks might be useful," he suggested, raising an eyebrow exactly as he had seen Caspar do. There was no doubt from his tone, either, that he was really thinking of a weapon.

"I'll cut one for each of us," Caspar agreed, drawing his sword. He stepped to the side of the road, found a reasonably straight sapling about Sunrise's height, and chopped it close to the ground. "Use your dagger to strip the smaller branches," he directed the youth as he selected another for Satchmoz, and yet another for himself.

In no time, they each had staves to help them along the road. The going was far easier, allowing a brisk pace. It didn't take long, though, before Satchmoz, far older than the others, showed signs of tiring and began to lag behind. Caspar listened to the old man's labored breathing and forced himself to slow down.

"We're running," he admitted with sudden understanding. "Letting the woods and our fear propel us. Stay calm, and keep a steady pace." He touched Satchmoz's arm, offering support. "Do you need to rest?" he asked.

Satchmoz shook his head. "I haven't yet seen the day I can't keep up with a pair of boys," he huffed.

Caspar leaned closer to the old man's ear. "You know, I wish you'd drop this *boy* business. I'm nearly nineteen summers old."

Satchmoz rubbed his chin, and his eyes narrowed a bit. "Ah, let's see now," he said, loud enough for the squirrels and birds to hear. "Yes, nineteen. I remember. Just old enough to feel like a man, and young enough to need reminding that you're not really."

Insulted, Caspar stepped back. "What do you mean by that?" he demanded angrily. Then, he gave a sigh and forced himself to relax. "Sorry," he offered, massaging one temple. "Just the meanness of the woods."

"It wasn't the woods," Satchmoz told him as he leaned on his staff and started down the road again. Caspar walked on his left, Sunrise on his right. "It was the truth. Eighteen, nineteen, twenty . . ." He waved a hand and made a face. ". . . fifty or a hundred. Years don't make a man. That recipe takes time and experience and some accumulated learning." He put on a big smile then, dropping his serious tone as he clapped both his comrades around the shoulders. "You're not men yet," he said winking. "But don't worry. By the time we get through this and rescue Berknip you will be."

"You're sure about that?" Caspar replied with sarcastic good nature.

The old man nodded. "Trust me," he answered. "It's a kind of magic."

CHAPTER ELEVEN

THE CASTLE AND THE SMART-MOUTHED STATUE

IT WAS NEARING SUNSET again when they discovered the castle. They saw it first through a gap in the trees. Further down the old road a narrow, seldom-used footpath branched off through the underbrush and led up to it. The sun lent a fiery orange gleam to the highest parapets of the castle's four great towers, though the stones of its walls were black with age. Its gate, a massive structure of wood and rusted iron, was shut and locked with a massive mechanism. There was no kind of knocker, nor any guards on the ramparts to call out to.

"Well, what now?" Caspar said when they had shouted themselves hoarse trying to attract someone's attention. He stared in frustration at the lock. It would soon be dark. He had entertained thoughts of finding some hospitality here, a host who would, perhaps, be kind enough to offer them decent food, and something resembling his memory of a bed for the night. He didn't really relish the idea of sleeping in the open woods again.

Satchmoz shrugged. "There doesn't seem to be anyone home. Unfortunately, I used my only *rezrov* spell on your shackles. Otherwise, I could hex the lock open."

Caspar gazed around again. The high defensive walls were indeed old. Ivy vines grew over part of it with roots that were deeply anchored in the ancient mortar. The vines were delicate and not strong enough to climb. He'd already tried twice and wound up with nothing for his trouble but a bruised backside.

"You don't by any chance have a magic pole-vaulting spell in one of those pockets?" he asked with a weary smirk, pointing to the wizard's blue cloak.

"I've got a potion to cure impotency," Satchmoz replied, "but I don't think that's what you had in mind."

Sunrise hadn't said anything for several moments. He stood studying the lock and rubbing his chin. Then quietly he drew his dagger and inserted the sharp tip into the keyhole.

"What are you doing?" Caspar asked. "You'll snap that blade if you're not careful!"

Sunrise didn't look around. He wiggled the dagger's point in the keyhole with an experimental twist of his wrist. "There are a few things about my past you don't know," the youth said. He gave the dagger another twist, and let out a sigh of satisfaction. Leaning his shoulder to the gate, he strained. The hinges creaked, but the gate swung inward an inch or so. It was enough for Sunrise. He turned back to his comrades and made a deep bow. "I used to make my living this way," he announced proudly.

Satchmoz raised a hand to his lips thoughtfully. "You were a locksmith?" he said.

Sunrise stuck out his tongue.

"A doorman?" Caspar tried.

Sunrise made a rude gesture. "A thief!" the boy shouted, stamping his foot. "One of the best in East Borphee! Why, I could pick a lock faster and more subtly than you can pick your nose in heavy traffic!" He waved a hand toward the partially opened gate. "This was nothing," he boasted. "Silly people think the bigger a lock, the stronger it is. Actually, the bigger the lock, the bigger the keyhole usually is, and the easier to spring."

"And that's the kind of talent that earned you a ticket on Chulig's Luxury Cruise Lines," Caspar quipped. *"See Antharia on fifty lashes a day."*

Satchmoz moved between them and put his weight against the heavy gate. "Since it is open," he muttered as he strained to push it wider, "I suggest we go inside and politely introduce ourselves. It's starting to get dark."

Caspar and Sunrise agreed. The gate eased open under their combined strength, and they stepped inside a high-walled courtyard which was overgrown with weeds and grass and small saplings that had poked up through cracks and breaks in the once polished and beautiful granite paving stones. Just a few yards inside the gate stood a tall slender statue, carved from a deep, rose-colored marble and set upon a pedestal. It was a figure of a young man. Its arms were folded across its wide chest, and it seemed to be tapping one foot impatiently.

Intrigued, Caspar took a step closer.

"Now you've done it," the statue said.

Caspar jumped back, nearly falling over Sunrise, who had come up behind him.

"Now I've done what?" Sunrise protested, thinking it was Caspar who had spoken.

"It wasn't me, kid," Caspar said in a hushed tone. He pointed, hiding the finger of his left hand behind his right palm and nodding his head in the direction of the sculpture. "He said it."

"Like, gate-crashers," the statue said distastefully. There was the barest semblance of life in its stone face. Perhaps the eyes looked down at them. Its lips and mouth were the only parts that moved for certain. "I mean, can you believe it? Mondo boorish!"

Satchmoz crept forward to the foot of the statue and stared upward in amazement. "It's some kind of sentinel," he declared, "and wonderfully clever!"

"Well, like, you needn't speak as if I'm not standing right here in front of you!" the statue answered in a voice that was pure sneer. "That's just so uncool. Were you raised in a barn, or what?"

"I was," Caspar confessed.

The sculpture seemed to gain life as it spoke. Its eyes rolled down to focus on Caspar. Its massive stone chest began to rise and fall as it drew breath. Its nostrils flared ever so slightly. "Then you've, like, been there and know first-hand," the statue went on, "what I mean when I tell you that you've really stepped in it this time, man."

Caspar thought he heard just a little bit of a threat in the statue's tone. "But we come in peace," he assured the strange creature. "We mean no harm. We've gotten lost in the woods, and need directions, that's all." That *was* all, too. He'd eat spenseweed roots or drink *berzio* potion and sleep under a tree again before he'd spend the night in a place that kept a talking statue for a watchdog.

"So, you, like, picked the lock and just walked in uninvited, like you were some big celebrity or something," the statue responded indignantly. "How stoned do you think I am? I mean, what kind of a pebble-head do you take me for?"

"Marble, that's obvious," Satchmoz answered. "Rose marble. From the southern valley area of Mithicus, I'd say."

The statue's voice brightened a little. "You, like, know Mithicus, man? The Big M?"

Satchmoz shrugged. "I've vacationed there a time or two."

The statue let out a sigh, and its shoulders sagged a bit. "Oh, wow," it said. "I was like born there—sculpted, anyway—in this bitchin' little shop on Blasterberry Street in Mithicus City by this really torched-out old geezer with two gold front teeth and wispy gray hair fine and shiny as a spider's web in sunlight." The statue sighed again, then sniffed and whispered something that sounded suspiciously like, *daddy*. "Like, he was really into a far space of his own, but that was cool, and I was, like, real mellowed out standing in the sun in a corner of his shop until he sold me. Let me tell you, it's been a bummer since then." Once more, it sighed and sniffed. "But that's, like, neither here nor there, man. You broke in, and now I've got to sound the alarm."

"Wait!" Caspar cried.

"Oh, come on, dudes!" the statue interrupted in a sudden whine. "Like, don't bring me down! Like, it's my job, you know?"

"And we wouldn't want to get you fired," Caspar interrupted, thinking fast. "But would you mind telling us just who you're alerting?"

The statue gave him a sharp look and tried to shake its head. "Oh, you don't want to know *that*." A shudder actually ran through its stone form! "If I were you, I'd, like, use those blades you're carrying. Do yourselves now, man. Right here. Make it quick. No barfy muss, no fuss."

Sunrise stepped forward. "Don't threaten us, you hunk of rock."

The statue looked down its nose at the youth. "Please," it replied haughtily. "Hunk of rock? What a dweeb. I am a work of art."

"I'll say," Satchmoz sneered.

"Suppose," Caspar pressed, attempting to avoid any unpleasantness, "we just turn around and walk out of here?"

The statue put on a pained expression. "I wish you'd understand, man!" it complained. "Like, it's my job."

A loud *thump* made them turn around. The gate had shut by itself. Sunrise ran to it and cursed. There was no lock or keyhole on this side, nor even a handle or iron ring to pull it open. The boy slammed one fist against it. Then he kicked it.

"Gotcha!" the statue said with a little laugh.

"Open it up!" Caspar demanded, his heart hammering. "Open it, or so help me . . . !"

"What, dude?" the statue interrupted with a superior air. "I'm a sculpture, for Zork's sake. What can you, like, do to me?"

"You're a rock with an ego problem!" Caspar shouted angrily, "and I'll show you what I can do!"

With that, he lunged at the statue, planting both hands squarely against its heavy base. Straining, he managed to tip it ever so slightly before his strength gave out, and it settled back into place again.

"Nyah, nyah!" the statue said rudely.

Madder than he ever thought he could be, Caspar hit the base again, putting his shoulder to it. It tipped, but not far enough, he knew. With a loud groan he pushed with all his might until he felt his joints and muscles pop, and a red haze filled his vision. He squeezed his eyes shut and gave a cry. Suddenly, with an ease that surprised him and almost caused him to fall, the statue teetered backward. He opened his eyes again, and found both Sunrise and Satchmoz straining with him.

"Oh, come on, guys!" the statue said, trying to sound reasonable. "I mean, like, three against one! That's not even cool! Hey, guys? Ohhhh!"

The statue crashed backward. Caspar, Sunrise, and Satchmoz stood huffing and puffing. On the ground, the statue rolled its eyes. Then, a smile creased its lips.

"Oh wow!" it exclaimed. "Oh wow! Thank you! My feet were killing me! I mean, do you have any idea how long I've been standing on my feet? What a relief! Oh wow!"

Caspar ignored the statue and glanced up at the castle. It was dark as far as he could tell. No light of any kind burned in any of its windows or crenelations. Nor did he hear any sound or see anything move. It was almost night. The first stars were already winking on.

He turned to his friends. "We can't get out," he said grimly. "I think we'd better go knock on the door."

"After what that thing said?" Sunrise protested. "I'd rather sit out here by the gate!"

"And do what?" Caspar snapped. "Starve? The walls are too high to scale, and we can't open the gate. The only way out," he continued, pointing to the castle, "is in."

"I'm afraid he's right, boy," Satchmoz said quietly, obviously not relishing the prospect anymore than Sunrise. "Let's just hope we can charm our host enough to let us go."

"You charm him," Sunrise grumbled, drawing his short-bladed dagger. "That's more your line. Me, I'm gonna give someone a double-edged enema at the first sign of trouble."

Caspar touched Sunrise's arm and motioned for him to sheathe the blade. "First we try the charm," he said, "then the enema." Side by side, they started off across the courtyard toward the castle's massive front doors.

"Thanks dudes!" the statue called after them. "But like, before I forget, there's something I should add."

Caspar frowned, but he stopped and looked back. "What's that?"

The statue began to rock violently from side to side. "Warning! Warning!" it shouted at the top of its voice. "Danger! Alien life-forms approaching! Danger! Warning!"

"You refugee from a gravel quarry!" Sunrise screamed.

Caspar caught the boy's shoulder and turned him around before he could finish his curse. The three of them strode the rest of the way across the courtyard, up a wide flight of stone steps and stopped before a pair of doors each twice as tall as any normal man. A great iron knocker hung on each door. Caspar reached out and touched the cold metal. He hesitated, regarding his friends and licking his lips. Then, he raised the ring and slammed it down once.

The sound vibrated through the great door and rang across the courtyard. When it faded a vast silence took its place. Caspar turned and glanced toward the gate. The toppled statue was merely a statue again.

The left door creaked open just wide enough for them to enter. From inside came the amber gleam of torchlight. A slight musty smell wafted out. They stood there, waiting, peering around the door's edge into the gloom for someone to appear, something else to happen.

"I guess that's all the invitation we're going to get," Satchmoz whispered at last over his comrades' shoulders.

"I've got a very bad feeling about this," Sunrise muttered. His dagger was half out of its sheath.

"That's my line," Caspar said quietly as he stepped across the threshold.

"You stole it," Sunrise charged. He hesitated, unwilling to follow until Satchmoz gave him a little push.

"Hey, you're the thief," Caspar reminded the boy good-naturedly.

When they were all inside, the door closed again. It didn't surprise any of them, yet they each gave a little jump, and Sunrise's dagger came the rest of the way out of its sheath.

They found themselves in a large hall. A pair of torches, mounted in sconces, glimmered on each wall, revealing a curving staircase of polished morgia wood that rose directly before them. Its topmost steps disappeared into darkness. There was not a piece of furniture in the hall, not even a chair or a coat rack. To the left and right, corridors led to other parts of the castle. On either side of the staircase, too, were gloomy corridors. Four ways out of the hall. Five, if they took the stairs.

"Why aren't I having a good time?" Sunrise complained in a bare whisper, his eyes searching the shadows in rapid, darting little glances.

"Beats me," Caspar answered, moving into the center of the hall and turning slowly around and around. Overhead, hung an old chandelier. He could barely make out the pale stubs of candles and the drippings of tallow wax. "The place is a regular carnival," he added.

"A carnival, right," Sunrise replied nervously. "And we came straight to the crazy house."

Caspar glanced over his shoulder and forced a grin. "Hey, we hit a few thrill rides along the way, don't you think?"

Sunrise stared at him in disbelief. But then he, too, forced a small grin as he put his dagger back in its sheath. "You can be so irritatingly calm sometimes," the boy said, coming to his side.

Caspar gave an airy wave of his hand and answered in a lilting imitation of Satchmoz's voice. "Why do you think they call me Incomparable?" Inside though, he thought, *Thank Zork the kid's easy to fool.*

Abruptly the weak light shifted and flickered. Alarmed, Caspar and Sunrise whirled. It was only their wizard comrade carrying a trio of torches he had taken from their sconces. He passed them around until they each had one.

"Perhaps we should split up and each take a corridor . . ." Satchmoz started to suggest.

"Not in this life," Caspar quickly answered. "We stay

together until we know who owns this place. Somebody let us in, and that somebody obviously wants to play games or they'd have come to greet us. The question is, which way do we go?''

Satchmoz pursed his lips thoughtfully. "Well, that depends on which you consider more pressing, food or sleep. If you can stand the *berzio* potion again, the stairs probably lead up to bedrooms. If, on the other hand, you want to take a shot at finding real food, then it's one of the corridors. Nobody in their right mind puts a kitchen upstairs.''

"Think about where you are before you say things like that," Sunrise warned.

"I don't think I'm going to get much sleep," Caspar said. "Let's try a corridor. How about that one?" He pointed to the left.

No one voiced an objection, so they started across the hall, their bare feet slapping softly on the cool stone tiles. Caspar led the way with Sunrise at his side and Satchmoz following right behind. Their torches provided plenty of light, though there was little to see. The featureless walls were of pale, milky stone, devoid of tapestries or paintings or any decoration.

Thirty steps along, it took a sudden bend to the right. The air grew cooler, the musty smell stronger than ever. A drafty little breeze rattled down the passage. Straight ahead was a door. Caspar reached out and turned the iron knob. It vanished in his hand, taking the door with it. He stared in fear and wonderment before summoning his courage and stepping across the threshold.

"I don't believe it," he said in a muted whisper. He turned to his friends and beckoned them to come on.

They were back in the main hall. There was the great morgia wood staircase, and there were the doors to the outside. Caspar moved to the center and counted the corridors. Four, as he knew there would be. Overhead, hung the old chandelier.

"We only made one turn," Sunrise stammered. "We can't be where we started.''

"There's no door on this side, either," Caspar pointed out. "Only on the other side."

"This way," Satchmoz said. He led them to the right, almost running across the hall. Obviously, he didn't share Caspar's and Sunrise's fear. The wizard had found a puzzle. His curiosity was piqued, and his excitement easy to see. Before he entered the new corridor he lifted his torch high and examined the entrance from top to bottom. "Nothing," he said with a disgusted frown.

They started down the new corridor, and soon passed a door. Satchmoz grabbed the knob and jerked it open. To everyone's relief, the door didn't disappear. Inside, they found a room with a spindle propped up in one corner and a pile of raw wool beside it ready to be made into yarn. In another corner of the room stood a loom with a half-finished tapestry. From the accumulated dust, however, it seemed doubtful anyone had worked here for a long time.

"You seem almost disappointed," Caspar whispered to Satchmoz as he wandered about the room. He ran his hand along a fireplace mantel and made a face at the dust that clung to his fingers. "Did you think we would end up back in the main hall?"

"I don't know," Satchmoz answered glumly. "But it was magic that took us back there a moment ago, not a feat of architecture."

Sunrise gave the spinning wheel a spin. With a noisy clickety-clack the axle grated within its hubs. The wooden spokes blurred as they whirled around and around until the wheel gradually slowed and stopped.

They turned to leave the room and stopped. Cautiously, they approached the doorway and stared across the threshold. It was not the corridor on the other side, but the main hall again.

With a growl of frustration Caspar stepped through the door. He looked down at his own footprints in the thick pounce on the floor. "We take the staircase this time," he said, leading the way.

They climbed the winding stairs, holding their torches high, and found themselves on a balcony overlooking the main hall. There was also a door, however. They eased it open and started down yet another passageway. Several more doors waited close at hand. Caspar pushed them open, finding bedrooms and sitting rooms. After each examination they stepped back into an unchanged corridor.

Until the fourth room, anyway. It was just another bedroom with a large canopy bed with blue satin drapes and comforter. A draft blew in through the cracked shutters that covered the two windows, and dust motes swam in the air. There was a dressing table with a hand mirror and an elaborate hairbrush shaped like a flamingo, several pins beside a vase of dead, brittle flowers, and a scarf so old it disintegrated at Sunrise's touch.

"Leave that," Caspar ordered when he saw Sunrise fondling the hairbrush.

Sunrise pouted. "Surely you don't believe somebody still lives here," he said. "This stuff hasn't been touched in ages."

"Leave it," Caspar repeated. "It's just a trinket. And if we meet the owner of this place I don't want to be accused of theft." He watched and waited until the boy finally put the hairbrush down. "Don't touch anything," he stressed, "unless it's food. And then we'll leave a coin to pay for what we take."

Caspar beckoned for them to move on, and found himself back in the main hall. "What the flamin' Zork?" he shouted. On his right were the great doors to the outside. On his left the staircase. He'd emerged from the first corridor they'd explored! He whirled quickly in time to see Sunrise step across the threshold. Satchmoz joined them a moment later.

"What is this?" Caspar demanded irritably.

"Fantastic, that's what it is!" the wizard answered, wide-eyed. "It's a magical maze! You can't find your way out because every twist and turn leads you right back to the beginning!"

"Are you telling us there is no way out?" Caspar said, feeling the fear and desperation rising again.

Satchmoz frowned and waved a hand, dismissing

him. "Oh, shut up, boy!" he snapped. "I have to study this. This is great and true magic!" With that, he handed his torch to Sunrise, wrapped himself in his cloak, folded his legs under himself and sat down on the hallway floor. His eyes rolled up inside his skull until only the whites could be seen. Then his eyelids fluttered like nervous birds and shut entirely.

"Great!" Caspar fumed. "We're in the deep doojahs, and he takes a sudden vacation to never-never land!"

Sunrise caught Caspar's hand. "Hey, it's all right," the boy said with unexpected gentleness. "Let's keep searching. At least we can't get lost if we always end up where we started."

Caspar had to admit there was a certain logic to that. "All right," he agreed, drawing a deep breath and calming himself while Sunrise returned Satchmoz's torch to an empty sconce. "Which way this time?"

"Let's try the staircase again," Sunrise suggested, leading him by the hand. We made pretty good progress up there, and there were still more rooms we didn't get to explore."

They took the steps quietly, their bare feet making almost no sound on the polished morgia wood. Up and up they went, carrying their torches like umbrellas against the darkness. Then, Sunrise's grip tightened on Caspar's hand, and they stopped. A pair of large green eyes glared down at them from the highest stair.

Mowrrrr?

The eyes blinked, then blinked again. A moment later the largest, ugliest, most mange-ridden black housecat either of them had ever seen padded silently down the steps.

CHAPTER TWELVE

CASPAR FINDS A SLEEPING BEAUTY, AND THINGS TURN NASTY

THE CAT RUBBED UP against Caspar's leg, then Sunrise's as they stood unmoving on the stair. Its fur felt like the bristles of an old, stiff brush. It let go a long, rumbling purr and rubbed Caspar again. Then with a languid grace it sprang up two stairs, turned and stared at them with liquid glowing eyes.

Sunrise let go a sudden sharp sneeze.

"I think it wants us to follow it," Caspar said, raising his torch a bit higher so its light reached to the top of the staircase. He bent down and gave the cat a quick scratch between its ears. "Is that what you want, kitty?"

The animal whirled and bounded up two more stairs and waited for them. Sunrise and Caspar exchanged glances, then shrugged and started upward. At the top, the cat ran onto the balcony that overlooked the main hall. It poked its head between the railings of the bannister and stared downward at Satchmoz. It let go a demanding *meow*, a sound that knifed through the silence of the castle and echoed in all its corridors.

Seated on the floor below, the old wizard didn't stir.

The cat called once more, louder, more insistent. Then it waited. When Satchmoz didn't react, the beast drew back. The hair rose straight up on its high-arched back. Its ears flattened. Fangs glittering in the torchlight, it gave a hiss that curdled the blood in Caspar's heart.

"My sentiments exactly," Sunrise muttered as he gazed over the bannister at Satchmoz. Abruptly, he gave another sneeze.

The cat turned and quick-padded down the long corridor at the top of the stairs. Caspar and Sunrise hurried after it, passing the rooms they had already explored, then rooms they had not. The cat ran just at the forward edge of the torchlight, taking them to a bend in the passageway and leading them into a part of the castle they had not seen yet.

The cat turned a sharp corner and vanished from sight. Then, as if realizing it had left them behind, it reappeared again, sat down and waited for them to catch up. It licked one paw with a pale pink tongue and rubbed at its whiskers as it turned those big eyes up at them. Then it sprang up again and ran down the next corridor, turned a corner and vanished. Again, it reappeared and waited.

"Cat and mouse," Sunrise muttered as they caught up with the cat and it took off again.

"Usually, it's the mouse that gets chased," Caspar reminded his friend. His voice took on a graver tone. "It's leading us farther and farther away from Satchmoz. I don't like being separated this way."

"It was the wizard's choice," Sunrise answered with a shrug. "What were we supposed to do, just stand around while he counted the lint balls in his navel?"

The cat reappeared again and sat down. Its tail swished back and forth, stirring the pounce on the floor. "Meow?" it called invitingly as it lifted one paw and rubbed at a gray bald spot just above its left eye.

"Besides," Sunrise said, moving toward the cat. "How can you not trust a face like that?"

Before Caspar could answer they were giving chase again. The cat ran ahead of them, its tail held straight up. Abruptly, the corridor ended. A new flight of stairs rose before them. Apparently, Caspar guessed, they had come to one of the four towers they had seen from the outside.

Cautiously, they began to ascend. The dust on the steps was thick enough to make them slippery, and Caspar leaned one hand on the wall for support. Up and up the stairs wound. They came to a landing and a closed door, but the cat passed it by. So, then, did they. Higher still they went. The amber torchlight gave the dust an almost glittery quality. A wind swept through a broken shutter on one of the crenelations. The torches fluttered, and for an instant the steps shimmered with a surreal beauty.

Caspar paused by the broken shutter and drew a deep breath of good fresh air. Sunrise, a few steps higher, stopped and waited for him.

"Meow?" called the cat impatiently. The sound echoed down the stairs, amplified to an unnatural degree by the narrowness of the space in which they found themselves.

"Meow!" Caspar answered back in a mocking imitation of the cat's voice. The beast looked down at him from above and raised one doubtful eyebrow. Then it twitched its whiskers and bounded upward, two steps at a time. Caspar drew one final breath of clean air and motioned for Sunrise to follow their guide.

Two more narrow landings and two more doors. They didn't stop. The cat called to them each time to make sure they didn't. At last, the steps went no higher. There was one final door, and nowhere else to go. The cat sat down and let go a sharp, mournful wail. It turned and stared at Caspar and Sunrise, its tail swishing.

"I think it wants us to go inside," Sunrise commented, bending down to pat the cat's head. It leaned into him, accepting the stroke. Then it walked in a tight circle around his legs, rubbed his shins and went back to the door. Sunrise's eyes widened, he looked around wildly, then covered his nose and sneezed. "Yuck," he said disgustedly, wiping his hand on his tunic.

Caspar made a face and examined the door. There was no handle or ring to pull it open. There was, however, a little space between the edge of the door and the jamb. If it was not locked he might be able to pry it open with his sword. He handed his torch to Sunrise and drew the blade from its sheath on his back. The metal gleamed in the flickering light.

"You look so heroic when you do that," Sunrise said with sarcastic good humor.

"Image is everything," Caspar replied as he inserted the sword's point into the space.

Sunrise nodded agreement and pursed his lips studiously. "Your biceps are good," he noted. "We'll have to build your lats, though. Still, you may have a career."

"Professional hero," Caspar grinned as he leaned cautiously on the blade, being careful not to snap it. "What's it pay?"

Before Sunrise could answer the door slipped open. Caspar gave a sigh and examined his sword. The blade was only bent a little bit up near the hilt. He made an effort to straighten it as the cat dashed over his feet through the gap and into the room beyond.

Sunrise pulled the door the rest of the way open and let the torchlight shine within. He caught his breath. "Oh wondrous oyster that hides so great a pearl!" he exclaimed.

"Oh pul-lease!" Caspar retorted, grabbing his torch back from the boy. Then, he gave a gasp of surprise as he saw what Sunrise had seen. Slowly, he crept forward.

In the center of the room lay a crystal coffin, and within, a young girl. Her head was cradled on a pillow of pale blue satin, and her hair, black as night, billowed around her face. Her cheeks still held a hint of roses, and her lips were red as blood. Her gown of creamy silk, all embroidered with white and red flowers, was draped gracefully about her still form, and her slippers were of black velvet.

The cat leaped up on the coffin and gave a loud, despairing meow.

"She's beautiful!" Caspar whispered.

Sunrise shrugged. "She's dead. Don't go necrophiliac on me."

"That's absurd!" Caspar answered, repulsed. Still, he bent over the glass coffin and stared at the girl. There was a kind of beatific light that seemed to emanate from her. The cat paced back and forth on the lid. It rubbed against Caspar's cheek, brushed its tail under his nose, and gave another loud meow.

Sunrise picked the cat up and scratched its ears. "Poor kitty," he murmured, nuzzling his face against the top of its head. Abruptly, his eyes pinched shut and he gave a sneeze. The cat sprang out of his arms to the floor, gave him an insulted glare, and leaped back atop the coffin.

"I think you're allergic to him," Caspar commented, still staring at the girl in the coffin. He leaned one elbow on the glass lid and gave a sigh.

Sunrise sneezed again and rubbed his nose. "Go on, kiss her," he said in a taunting voice.

Caspar frowned without looking up. "Don't be silly," he said quietly. Her lips were so red, though. He wondered how they must have tasted when she was alive.

Sunrise grinned and folded his arms across his chest. "I dare you," he said.

Caspar didn't answer. He reached out and idly stroked the cat as it paced back and forth.

Sunrise tapped his foot. "Chicken," he said sharply.

"I am not!" Caspar answered, finally glancing up.

"Are too!"

"Am not!" Caspar grasped the side of the lid and lifted it. The cat gave an awkward squawk. Its claws scratched on the glass as it slid off. In midair it twisted desperately and landed on both feet. There was nothing complimentary in the meow it gave out, but it leaped back inside the coffin and curled up at its mistress's feet. The sound of its purr filled the room.

"Kiss her!" Sunrise urged, bending closer. "Or you're chicken!"

Caspar glared at the boy, heat rising in his cheeks. He leaned over the girl, trembling. He swallowed. Closer he bent until his lips were almost on hers. The smell of silk and satin crept up his nose. Pale blue veins made a fine tracery in the milky translucence of her eyelids. Yes, she was beautiful. She was also *dead!*

He straightened suddenly, grimacing. "You kiss her!" he shouted at Sunrise. "Go on, unless *you're* chicken!"

Sunrise looked as if he'd been betrayed. Then his expression hardened, and he stepped up to the coffin and lifted his torch higher. He had to raise onto tiptoe to bend over the side, but he brought his face close to the girl's. He hesitated a moment, licked his lips, then planted a quick kiss on her lips.

The girl's eyes flew open and she stared in horror at Sunrise. "Rape!" she screamed. Sunrise gave a loud grunt as a surprisingly fast uppercut caught him under the jaw and sent him reeling backward. His torch went skittering and sputtering across the dusty floor.

"You're alive!" Caspar exclaimed.

The girl grasped the sides of the coffin and sat up. "That's more than I can say for your friend when I get out of this thing!" she snapped as she put a hand on Caspar's chest and pushed him away. "Of all the nerve! I'll twist his scrawny little head off!"

"But he thought you were dead!" Caspar explained.

She shot him a look and froze in the act of swinging one leg over the coffin's side. "That's disgusting!"

Caspar tilted his head and gave an embarrassed nod. "That's my boy," he answered sheepishly.

The cat bounded into her lap before she could get her other leg over the coffin's side. She wrapped her arms around it and hugged it close. "Poor Meezel! You've grown so old!" She looked around suddenly, noting her surroundings. The anger left her face, replaced by a look of doubt and confusion. "How long have I been asleep?" she wondered aloud as she stroked Meezel's fur.

"Asleep?" Caspar said, sharing her confusion. "Who are you?"

Sunrise groaned as he pulled himself up from the floor and massaged his jaw. He looked at Caspar, his eyes still unfocused, and groped for his torch. Groggily, he rose to his feet. He kept a respectful distance, however, when he saw the girl glance his way and clench her fist.

"My name is Esmerelda," she said, turning back to Caspar. "This was my father's castle until he died." Her eyes snapped wide suddenly. She dumped Meezel to the floor and sprang up into Caspar's arms. "Oh dear! My step-mother!" she cried in alarm.

"Step-mother?" Caspar replied, trying to calm her obvious fright. "There's nobody else here but us. Well, except Satchmoz downstairs."

Esmerelda pushed herself free from Caspar's consoling embrace. "Then she's out," she answered whirling desperately toward the door. "But she'll be back. Nasty's not one to leave her home for long."

"Nasty?" Sunrise said, heading toward the door himself.

"Nasturtium," Esmerelda answered. "A real witch if ever there was one!"

Sunrise kicked the door back. The cat Meezel ran over his feet and down the stairs ahead of them. In no time the little beast was beyond the range of the torch's light. "You said there were no such things as witches!" he shouted at Caspar.

"There isn't!" he shouted back as Esmerelda flew down the steps after her pet. "This is a rational world!"

"Tell it to Nasty!" Esmerelda called back breathlessly. "She's the one who put me to sleep and shut me in that stupid casket!"

Caspar hurried to keep up, nearly slipping once on the dusty steps. "She probably did it with a perfectly scientific spell," he insisted. "There're just no such things as witches."

They rushed toward the darkness at the bottom of the stairs. Esmerelda stopped suddenly, causing Caspar to collide with her. Sunrise slammed into him, and they all went tumbling.

Caspar realized at once they were not in the corridor where they should have been. For one thing, there was a windy, swirling draft. For another, Sunrise's and Esmerelda's voices echoed too much for a corridor's confines.

"Were your mother and father by any chance brother and sister?" Esmerelda shouted at the boy.

"You're the one who stopped without any warning!" he screamed back. "Besides," he added, pointing at Caspar, "he ran into you first!"

Esmerelda lifted her nose haughtily. "Well," she answered, hesitating, "he's cuter."

Sunrise smirked. "Chulig didn't think so."

"Never mind!" Caspar interrupted, getting to his feet and offering his hands to pull them both up. "We're in trouble again. Where are we?"

"I don't know," Esmerelda said, her voice growing soft and little-girlish as she looked around. "It looks like father's library. But where are all the books?"

"Forget the books!" Caspar whispered tensely. He didn't believe in witches at all. But Esmerelda was certainly afraid of her stepmother, and the statue at the front gate had warned them about somebody. Every bone in his body suddenly cried that it was time to opt for the better part of valor. He caught Esmerelda by the arm. "Where's the way out!"

"I don't understand," Sunrise grumbled. "Every time things shifted around before we wound up back in the main hall!"

"That was downstairs," Caspar reminded the youth. "Maybe this is where all the upstairs rooms lead."

"I don't understand any of this!" Esmerelda wailed. "What's happened to Father's castle?"

Meezel appeared at her feet, gave a loud meow and leaped into Esmerelda's arms. The cat's presence, at least, seemed to calm her. She hugged the cat until his luminous green eyes bugged out, but Meezel only purred.

"There should be a door," Esmerelda said quietly, "in the west wall, I think."

Caspar hadn't the vaguest idea which way was west, but he turned in a circle with his torch held high until he spied the twin morgia wood panels that formed the library doors. "Let's go," he urged.

They rushed through the door only to find themselves back in the library. "This is crazy!" Caspar exclaimed, pounding his forehead. "Back that way!" He waved them through the door again. This time they emerged into the corridor. "How did you ever get around this place?" he said as they ran.

"This is new to me!" Esmerelda answered breathlessly. "One of Nasty's tricks."

They made it to the balcony overlooking the main hall. Satchmoz sat on the floor, his legs still crossed. Some strange whirling light hovered in the air before him though, throwing off streamers of color that reflected on the walls and floor around him. He talked to it, and it answered back!

"I'm beginning to think the *Screaming Queen* was an oasis of tranquility," Sunrise said to Caspar.

Meezel bounded down the stairs, and Esmerelda gathered her skirts and chased after him. Sunrise glanced at Caspar and rolled his eyes. He didn't bother with the steps. He hopped up on the staircase railing, gave himself a slight push and slid to the bottom, leaping clear at the last instant and landing lithely on his feet.

"Never can resist that," he said with a grin as Caspar hurried down behind him.

Esmerelda and Meezel ran to the door. Caspar and Sunrise rushed to Satchmoz's side. The whirling light cast strange, multi-hued shadows on the old man's face. At first, he didn't seem to notice them. He spoke quickly into the glow, using the Old Quendoran tongue: In a low, throbbing voice the light answered him.

Caspar shook the wizard's shoulder. "I think it's time to leave," he said with barely controlled urgency.

"Not yet!" Satchmoz answered. "I've almost got it! It's fantastic!"

Esmerelda gave a small scream. "The door won't open!" she called. "I can't budge it!" Sunrise was at her side in an instant, and the two of them pulled with all their might on the great iron rings. Between them, Meezel went to work with his claws on the expensive wood.

Caspar stared at the whirling light, but he felt little sense of wonderment. Esmerelda's urgency had infected him. After all, she lived here. She knew the dangers better than he did. He shook the wizard's shoulder again. "Satchmoz, let's go!"

Satchmoz frowned as he reached out and thrust his hand into the light. Immediately the glow died, and Caspar blinked. The wizard held nothing but a child's pinwheel! He remembered now seeing it among the things the wizard kept in his cloak pockets. An infotater, Satchmoz had called it.

"I've got it!" the wizard cried excitedly. "A wonderful new spell! I'll be the envy of the Borphee guild! Of wizards and enchanters everywhere!" He got to his feet and thrust the pinwheel into a pocket. "Did you find food?" he asked, his tone changing.

Caspar jerked his thumb toward Esmerelda. The girl was still banging and pulling and kicking at the door with Sunrise and Meezel aiding her. "Does she look like a tuna sandwich to you?" Caspar said sarcastically.

Satchmoz rubbed his stomach with one hand and appeared to think about it.

"Never mind!" Caspar said, yanking the wizard's arm. "She says it's best not to be here when her stepmother returns."

"Ah!" Satchmoz answered hurrying toward the door. "The old *wicked stepmother* story!"

Before they could reach their friends the door began to shimmer with a weird blue radiance. The hair on Meezel's back stood straight up, and the cat gave a shriek. Sunrise and Esmerelda both screamed as the energy knocked them on their backsides. Caspar grabbed the girl as the old wizard bent over the boy. Meezel ran under the hem of Satchmoz's cloak and hid.

The blue radiance faded away, taking the door with it. It was as if there had never been a door, only the solid wall.

"I'm baaaack!" a high-pitched voice called from the top of the staircase. A long cackle followed that announcement.

"You can't imagine how thrilled we are," Caspar muttered as he turned around.

Nasturtium—it could only have been her—stood at

the top of the staircase, a particularly nasty smile upon her fat-jowled face. Her gray hair swept upward and moved with every slight motion she made, as if it were bleached seaweed growing underwater. Her back was half bent, and warts grew upon her needlelike nose. She was swathed all in black—dress, cloak, even a pointed hat.

"Madam," Satchmoz called to her indignantly, "must you actualize every bad stereotype of your profession?"

Esmerelda interrupted him. Despite the terror she had evidenced earlier, there was something of a smirk on her face. "Why, mommy, dear!" she said with wicked delight. "You've grown old! Quite ugly, too!" She gave a low chuckle.

The witch gave a look of surprise. "You!" she shouted, pointing a long thin finger. "And your little cat, too, I see!" She crept halfway down the stairs and leaned on the railing. Then she glared hatefully at Caspar and Sunrise. "Which one of you little brats woke her up? You'll pay for this!"

Sunrise pointed at Caspar. Caspar pointed at Sunrise.

The witch turned her fury on Esmerelda. "I could have kept you young and beautiful forever!" she ranted. "But here you are, running off with the first little masher that sticks his nose in your casket. You little tramp!"

Esmerelda drew herself up. "Oh, stick it, mummy!" she cried, her fear giving way to indignation. "That spinning wheel business was a dirty trick, and you know it. That needle hurt! There's still a red mark on my finger! I'll probably have a scar!" She turned up her nose, put one hand on her hip and patted her hair. "You just wanted to get me out of the way because you were jealous of my beauty!"

"Dirty trick or not!" the witch shrieked, "you fell for it. You little bimbo! You never did have the brains of a tree stump!"

"Ladies," Satchmoz interrupted, stepping forward, "if I might interject a calming word . . ."

"Shut up!" both women shouted at the same time. The wizard paled and stepped back.

Caspar looked at Sunrise. Sunrise shook his head. "What a world!" the boy muttered, half to himself.

"Look at you!" the witch screamed, "running off with the first boy that comes along! If your poor dead father knew he'd rise up from his grave and snatch you bald-headed!"

Esmerelda tut-tutted. "Daddy was such a fuddy-duddy!" she answered. "But he never tried to lock me away in a casket!"

The witch's face purpled until it resembled a wrinkled prune. "I spent a lot of money on that casket!" she said defensively. "It was the finest in Quendor! You always had the best of everything!"

Esmerelda stamped her foot. "It was a mean thing to do!"

"How else was I to stop you from throwing yourself at everything in pants?" Nasturtium demanded. "A mother has a responsibility!"

"Oh, yak, yak, yak!" Esmerelda said cleverly, tossing her head from side to side. "I don't want to hear it anymore. You're a bore, mummy. Just open the door and let us go."

Nasturtium glared angrily at her stepdaughter. Then, she reached back inside her cloak. It was lined with pockets, too, just like Satchmoz's. She drew out a scroll.

"I told you she wasn't a real witch," Caspar whispered to Sunrise.

"Just something that rhymes with it," the boy answered.

Nasturtium read swiftly from the scroll, and it crumbled to ashes in her hand. A blue bolt leapt from her fingertips and struck the wall where the door had been. The stones shimmered, and an instant later, the door was there again.

"Go on, you little brat!" Nasturtium screamed. "But be warned! You've been asleep a long time, and time doesn't work in this castle the way it does out there. Now go on, get out, before I really get nasty! That's what you always called me, wasn't it?"

Esmerelda stuck out her tongue.

The witch leaned over the staircase railing and gave a cackle. "I told you boys you'd pay for waking her up. Well, you will, too. I'm letting you take her!" She threw back her head and laughed so hard her pointed hat fell off and rolled down the steps.

Sunrise and Caspar backed up cautiously and gave a tug on the iron rings. The doors opened easy as you please, and the four of them, with Meezel at their heels, hurried out into the night with the witch's laughter chasing after them. The gate, too, opened with ease.

"You know," Esmerelda said as they stepped out onto the forest path, "she's actually mellowed somewhat." She patted her hair into place again, adjusted her bodice, and put on a pouty little smile. "Now which one of you gentlemen is going to carry me? My slippers weren't made for this kind of ground."

CHAPTER THIRTEEN
THE BIG WIND

THEY HURRIED DOWN THE twisting, narrow path to the Old Forest Road, Esmerelda complaining all the way about the demise of gallantry in the men of Quendor. Every time a branch brushed her face she gave a little scream and clutched at Caspar. Once she tried leaping into his arms. The touch of her body sent a charge through him. But after a half dozen *how dare yous!* and a half dozen slaps to his face, Caspar wearied of being played with. In irritation, he put Sunrise between them.

"Where are we!" she shrieked as they emerged onto the road. She brushed leaves and bits of twigs from the fine fabric of her creamy gown, and frowned at some damage done to the hem. "Look at my dress!"

"Pardon me, Miss," Satchmoz said with polite strain as he stared up and down the old road. "Would you mind terribly shutting up?"

Esmerelda puffed up like a royal peacock on display. Hands stiffly on her slender waist, she glared at the wizard. "Why, who do you think you are?"

The old man caught Sunrise's torch and pulled it close to his face so its red glow shadowed and uplit his sharpest features and made him look like something spectral. "I might be a grue!" he answered harshly, "or a troll, or a kobold, or a brogmoid just looking for a juicy little dish like you to gnaw on. And all I need is your pattering to guide me right to you!"

Esmerelda's gaze darted suddenly into the darkness beyond the torches' light as fear overcame her. She conquered it quickly, though, and tried to recoup her dignity. "Well, you needn't make such a production of it!" she hissed. "If you want me to shut up because I might stir up something dangerous, just say so!"

"Shut up!" all three of her male companions replied at once.

Esmerelda stuck her lip out in a pout until Meezel gave a meow and jumped into her arms. "Nice kitty," she whispered, hugging the ugly little beast close. She wrapped her arms around it as if it were a doll, and kissed the top of its head.

Sunrise and Caspar carried the torches. They gathered on either side of Satchmoz to determine their next course of action.

"I say we go on just long enough to put some distance between this castle and ourselves," Caspar suggested, "and then find a place to spend the night. It's too risky traveling at night."

"Yes, some nice inn," Esmerelda interrupted as she came over to join them. The cat in her arms purred with unashamed pleasure, sounding like a saw drawn slowly through old wood. Eyes half-closed, it practically smiled as Esmerelda rocked it against her bosom. "There should be one not far up the road. The Red Cock, I believe its name is."

The males looked at her in astonishment. "An inn? Are you sure?" Sunrise exclaimed. He closed his hand around the purse of coins inside his belt and jingled it. "With real food?"

"Of course, I'm sure!" Esmerelda snapped. She tilted her head thoughtfully and swayed like a willow limb in a gentle breeze. The torchlight glimmered in her shining black hair. "I remember daddy sometimes had important visitors, and while they stayed with us, their retainers always stayed at The Red Cock."

"Then what are we waiting for?" Sunrise whooped. The youth jumped up and clicked his bare heels. "Wine, women, song!" he cried, "or any two-out-of-three combination!"

"Pardon me," Esmerelda said abruptly, lifting her

nose and stepping between Sunrise and Satchmoz so that she could lead the way northward. "Wouldn't it be better if you men shut up? These are dangerous woods, you know."

Sunrise fell in step right behind Esmerelda, bringing one hand haughtily to his left hip as he exaggerated and caricatured her patrician stride. But Caspar caught a corner of Satchmoz's cloak.

"Pahdon me," he whispered dramatically, allowing himself the small meanness in such mockery. "But considering the effect of Mauldwood on the three of us, what can we reasonably expect from any long-term residents we might run into at this inn?"

Satchmoz pursed his lips as the two of them followed after their friends. "Well, you've the girl to judge by," he answered, ticking off a finger on his right hand. "Though from what you say she's been under a spell and, perhaps, shielded somewhat from its influence."

Caspar made a face. "You mean, that could be the *real* her?"

The wizard gave him a subtle glance and a sympathetic nod as he ticked off another finger. "Then, you've got her stepmother, Nasturtium . . ."

Caspar swallowed. "Nasty," he said, not sure if he'd spoken the woman's name or meant it as a comment.

The wizard ticked off a third finger. "And the kobolds we encountered on the beach."

Caspar rubbed one hand over the hilt of his sword, reassuring himself the weapon was still there, and wondered if it wouldn't be better to sleep in the woods, after all. He might convince Satchmoz, but he knew he had no chance with Sunrise or Esmerelda.

He bit his lip. *"And so Man plunges precipitously toward his Destiny,"* he muttered under his breath.

Satchmoz looked up in surprise. "I know that," he said brightly. "It's from *Sleeping Your Way to Power*, the great Entharion's seminal work linking dreams and imagination to potential for magical ability! Have you read it?"

"No," Caspar confessed. Then his voice softened a

bit. "I learned it from a woman, a very kind woman, back in Djabuti Padjama."

"Oh," Satchmoz commented with a knowing roll of his eyes.

"We were just friends," Caspar chided. His lips drew into a taut line as he resisted the memories. But something in the rustling of the wind through the leaves, or in the gentle grating of the crickets, or perhaps something in Satchmoz made him talk, instead.

"Thyrsobel was very poor," he said quietly. "Her husband had run off, leaving her with two small children and a baby and a house that barely kept out the rain."

"But she was young and pretty," the wizard interrupted, nodding and winking and waving a hand. "I know this story."

"Actually, she was old enough to be my mother," Caspar answered without taking offense. "But she *talked* to me like nobody else in the village ever did. She wasn't from the Peltoid. She'd *been* places." The sudden intensity faded from his voice, and his words softened again. "But it was all in the past for her. Her spirit was broken. She was tired, and she knew it."

Satchmoz laid a hand on Caspar's arm in sympathy. "Not so tired she couldn't fill your head with dreams, I see. That's why you left home?"

Caspar put on a weak smile. He'd told that much of it. He might as well tell the rest. "Not quite," he answered. "You see, Thyrsobel lived pretty much on charity, and there isn't much of that in Djabuti Padjama. Some of the bachelor farmers would give her odd jobs occasionally. Some would give her field work. It was hard, but she managed."

He hesitated, remembering back, even as he kept an eye on the pair ahead of them. "Then, this summer, Jelboz Stumpbiter lost his wife." Caspar leaned closer to Satchmoz and whispered conspiratorially. He was getting into the tale now. "Jelboz and my uncle were tight. They'd sit around all day complaining together about things, both of them miserable as a pair of rotgrubs with only one carcass between them."

He straightened self-consciously, grinning, as he continued. "Well, not a week went by after Jelboz buried his wife. He asked Thyrsobel to come mop his floors for a copper zorkie. The next week he asked her to come clean his windows and wash his clothes for a silver zorkle."

"I can see it coming," Satchmoz said, shaking his head.

"Of course!" Caspar said, raising his voice, then lowering it again. "Anyone could. Poor Thyrsobel did. He asked her how she'd like to make a gold zorkmid, and poor dumb Thyrsobel with three children to feed, who didn't *want* to say yes, *couldn't* say no! And worse, he refused to pay her, afterward!"

Satchmoz's head went back and forth like the pendulum on a grandfather clock. He clucked his tongue. "How did you find out all this?" he asked. "Even if she was your friend, it's hardly the kind of thing a woman brags about."

Caspar spat to one side. "But a man does," he snapped. "Some of them, anyway. Jelboz and my uncle both had a good laugh about it out in the barn one afternoon. Their mistake was not knowing I was in the loft."

"You decided to get even for your friend," Satchmoz said needlessly.

Caspar nodded. "I knew a stream where Jelboz and his pals would go to fish together. I dug a pit near there in my spare time, and for days and days I collected the droppings from all our farm animals. I had to lug it some distance, no pleasant task, let me tell you. Then, one afternoon when Jelboz came to visit my uncle I suggested they all go for an outing.

"I hid out in the woods around the stream and waited, but dressed in one of Thyrsobel's outfits. I'd borrowed it without her knowing. After everyone had their lines in the water I crept a little closer, but not too close." Caspar put a little falsetto into his voice. "*Oh, Jelboz!* I called."

"You tricked him into a pit full of shit," Satchmoz said smugly.

Caspar gave the old man a disparaging look. "You have a way of spoiling a story," he said.

"You have a way of weaving a long one," the wizard answered.

Caspar shrugged. "You're right," he admitted. "Unfortunately, the old fool managed to break his leg when he fell in, and while trying to get him out, my uncle fell in, too. They blamed it all on Thyrsobel. I had to confess to save her from a terrible beating."

"You, they only ran out of town," the wizard commented wryly. "That's peasant justice for you."

"Are the cities any better?" Caspar answered somewhat defensively.

"In the city," Satchmoz replied proudly. "We have courts with judges and juries and everything, where not only can you seek justice, but win valuable prizes and vacations of a lifetime and maybe even your very own dream home!"

"Sounds like a game show," Caspar muttered.

Satchmoz shrugged. "Same thing," he confessed. "Same chance of winning."

They walked a little faster to close the gap that had grown between themselves and their friends. Sunrise and Esmerelda were no longer arguing. They walked side by side, Esmerelda clinging to Meezel, Sunrise holding his torch over them like an umbrella to keep off the darkness. Satchmoz fell in at the girl's right elbow, and Caspar took a position next to him. The road was just wide enough to let them walk abreast.

The wind blew down the road, causing the torches to flare and sputter, and the night air filled with a rasping as the leaves and branches shivered. Through the gaps in the trees the stars shone down, bright as diamonds against the cloudless black velvet sky.

The trees on either side of the road took on monstrous shapes. Thick grasping limbs and gnarly fingers reached out of the darkness. In the gloom and shadows, massive surly giants loomed, ready to snatch the unwary traveler. For all the beauty of the sky, it was the trees that kept their rapt attention. The trees stirred, as if possessed by an eerie life. Branches scraped in the wind, raising a muffled sound like the dry snapping of ancient fingers. Over the trail, a limb wagged slowly back and forth, as if warning them to choose another route. Shivering, they ducked under it and passed on.

A surmin waddled suddenly out of the brush into the road. As the edge of the torchlight fell upon the creature it froze, trembling, its red gleaming eyes fastened upon the unexpected humans.

The entire party froze also, except for Meezel. The cat laid back its ears, gave a low growl, and tried to jump down. Esmerelda wrapped one unyielding arm around her pet and smacked him lightly on the head with her free hand. "Forget it!" she ordered the cat in a firm whisper. "And don't you scratch or snag my dress either!"

Meezel quieted, but he didn't look any friendlier as he stared over her arm at the surmin.

Caspar let out the breath he'd been holding and eyed the strange beast. He'd never seen this black and red variety. A few of the black and purple ones still wandered into the Peltoid Valley now and then, but mostly the land was too open and cultivated to support a surmin population.

The hair on this one was long and crawling with lice. The tip had been chewed off its thin, ratlike tail. The tiny white claws on its four feet, though, gleamed with razor sharpness in the torchlight, as did the tips of the fangs that protruded from its long, snoutish mouth.

It was not the claws or fangs, however, they had to worry about.

"If it lets go a stink," Sunrise whispered, his eyes wide and round with dread, "we're dead meat."

There was no natural, defensive weapon in the world more potent than a surmin's fart. No lion, no hellhound, some said not even a grue would dare attack it for fear of its fragrant retaliation. Though basically a shy forager, it was nevertheless one of the most dreaded of all woodland beasts, and many a farmer, traveler, and woodcutter had lived, albeit barely, to regret a carelessly misplaced footstep.

Now they had nearly made the same mistake. Like a rabbit, the surmin hunched unmoving and frightened in the torchlight. Its red eyes almost whirled with uncertainty.

"Its fart has an effective range of fifty *frobozzits*," Satchmoz reported as quietly and calmly as he could. "There's no way we could outrun the fumes if the little beggar breaks wind."

Caspar gently took hold of the wizard's arm. "It was just crossing the road and got caught in our light," he whispered. "Maybe if we back away slowly it'll go on about its business, and we can go about ours."

Satchmoz caught hold of Esmerelda's right arm, and Sunrise took her left. Linked together, they all took one *very* easy giant step backward. The edge of the torchlight moved with them. The surmin still regarded them uncertainly.

"Fifty *frobozzits* is a long way to walk backward," Sunrise muttered softly.

Meezel raised up again and gave a growl, showing fangs to match those of the surmin. Green fire flashed in his feline eyes. "Quiet, I said!" Esmerelda hissed, giving him a shake.

They backed up a few more steps until the torchlight no longer touched the surmin. A few more steps, and Caspar called a halt. A pair of red eyes low to the road was all that could be seen of the creature. After a few moments and a few wary blinks, the eyes disappeared altogether.

"Do you think it's gone?" Sunrise asked hopefully.

Caspar looked at Satchmoz, and Satchmoz bit his lip. "I'll find out," Caspar said. Alone, he crept forward with his torch. There was no sign of the surmin. "It's all clear!" he called, letting go a sigh of relief.

His friends came forward, too, and Caspar had to grin when he saw the sweat trickling on Sunrise's face.

"My stars!" Esmerelda said breathily as she fanned

herself with one hand. "That was just too thrilling to be told! Eye to eye with a surmin!"

They all chuckled and congratulated themselves on their good fortune. But Meezel, finding himself trapped with only one of Esmerelda's arms, abruptly snarled and twisted free. Before anyone could react the damned cat jumped to the ground and plunged into the brush the way the surmin had gone.

Sunrise and Satchmoz wasted no time, but threw up their arms and ran down the road. Esmerelda, though, grabbed desperately at Caspar's hand. "I've been asleep a long time!" she whined. "Just how far *is* a *frobozzit?*"

Caspar stared in horror after the cat. "About as far as we've come from your castle," he answered hurriedly.

Esmerelda clapped a hand to her mouth, then shrieked, "Oh my staaarrrrsss!" Throwing the folds of her precious dress indecorously over one arm she fled off after the others, running faster and with far greater skill than Caspar would have given her credit for. Still, he might have left her behind had it not meant leaving her totally in the dark, and that he wouldn't do. Instead, he ran at her side and urged her along as best he could, praying that Meezel would run into a bear before he found the surmin.

In no time they overtook Satchmoz. Sunrise had had no such qualms about running off with his torch. The fleet-footed youth could barely be spied farther up the road, his light glimmering in the distance. Esmerelda caught Satchmoz on the right side, Caspar on the left. Together, they pulled the old man along as fast as his feet would go.

"Stop holding your nose!" Caspar shouted at Satchmoz. He slapped the old man's hand away from his needlelike proboscis. "Your lungs need the air!"

Up ahead, they saw Sunrise stumble and fall. Then the boy was up again. Caspar's heart thundered in his ribs as he took more of Satchmoz's weight on himself. Every tortured breath from the old wizard sounded like the ripping of dry parchment, and Satchmoz's eyes were glazed from effort. Esmerelda stared doggedly ahead, doing her best to help.

"Catch up to Sunrise!" he urged her between gasps. "I'll take care of Satchmoz."

She shook her head without looking at him, and moved even closer to Satchmoz to help him along.

Then came the sound they had all dreaded—the long, high-pitched shriek that only a terrified cat can make. It cut like a razor through the sounds of the forest. For an instant, everything grew still. Suddenly, a fluttering rose. Hundreds of birds nesting in the trees around them fled for the safety of the sky.

"Here it comes!" Caspar cried, wishing he had wings as he wrapped his arms protectively around Satchmoz and Esmerelda and drew them close.

A warm wind engulfed them, bringing with it such a noxious smell that Satchmoz fell at once to his knees and gagged. Esmerelda clutched her throat. "No! No!" she whimpered uselessly as she used the hem of her dress to cover her mouth and nose.

Caspar's senses reeled. Pinching his nostrils shut, he stumbled away and fell at the side of the road. He tried desperately not to draw breath. Suffocating was far preferable. The smell covered him, *filled* him. He rolled on the ground to rid himself of it, as if it were flames that he might extinguish. Abruptly, his stomach churned, reminding him of the spenseweed roots he'd last eaten. *Please*, he begged silently, *let me die!* He sprawled on his back in the road dust, then, and let the foulness in the air have its way with him.

He might have stayed there, too, had Sunrise not shaken him.

Caspar had a tough time focusing his vision. Even so, the youth did not look well. Clearly, fast as he was, he'd gotten a good whiff of the surmin, too. Or rather, it had gotten him.

He thrust his torch into the spongy ground at the side of the road. Caspar's torch had extinguished itself in the road dust. "I saw you fall," he said, cradling Caspar's head in one hand as he urged him to sit up.

Caspar supported himself uncertainly on one elbow and turned to stare back the way they had come. He frowned in irritation at the trees and thick foliage. Any other bomb would have left a wide circle of devastation.

Haggardly, he got to his feet, feeling like a limp washcloth someone had hung out to dry. Esmerelda sat in the middle of the road weeping silent tears over her ruined dress. Satchmoz lay nearby. Curled in a fetal ball, his eyes were open, and he watched them.

"Don't come near me," he muttered when Caspar crawled toward him. "You stink." He said it wearily, without any hope or enthusiasm.

"You don't smell like a *dragondil*, yourself," Caspar managed with a weak grin.

"Can we go home now?" the wizard asked, blinking, childlike. "I'll come out if we can go home."

"That's been the plan all along," Caspar reassured him with a pat on the shoulder. "It's still the plan."

Satchmoz let go a long sigh and slowly uncurled. Dust clung to one side of his face as he sat up, and he halfheartedly brushed it away.

"It's ruined forever!" came a plaintive wail from Esmerelda. She held a corner of her dress up to her face as Sunrise bent over her. "I'll never get that odor out!"

Sunrise wrinkled his nose, but reached a hand down to help her up. "That you won't," he agreed. "I'd be more worried about getting it out of your hair."

Esmerelda looked at him with big, wet eyes and lifted a lock of her hair. She passed it under her nose. Tears purled down her cheeks, and her whole face screwed up. "My hair!" she whined dejectedly.

It took time and more coaxing, but at last they managed to get themselves up again and relight Caspar's torch from Sunrise's. If the background stink that now permeated everything was not enough to make them miserable, every time the breeze blew it brought a renewed nausea. Caspar wondered privately if the birds *ever* would return. What was the half-life of a surmin fart?

They had taken but the first few steps when a weak

meow sounded from the brush somewhere behind them. A moment later, Meezel staggered out of the bushes, green eyes swimming, unable to put one paw in front of the other. He took a few steps, hesitated, and fell over on his side. With a cat's quickness he was up again, as if to say to them all, *Hey, I can handle it!* He took a few more drunken steps, then, and tumbled onto his other side. All the while, a tiny pink tongue hung limply out the side of his mouth.

A wicked leer turned up the corners of Satchmoz's lips. "C'mere, cat," he begged, crooking his fingers. "Have I got a recipe for you!"

But Esmerelda knelt down by her pet and swept him into her arms. "Oh, poor kitty!" she wailed. She put her face down next to his and nuzzled him. Then her head snapped up. Clutching Meezel under his front legs, she held him out at arms length and made a face. "Ugh!" she cried in disgust. "You reek!" She gave her cat a shake. "Snap out of it, you stupid beast! I'm not carrying you in this state. You hear me? Shame, chasing after poor harmless surmins! You walk!"

"I'd never call a surmin *harmless*," Satchmoz commented.

"At least, not to its face," Caspar agreed.

"If you want to carry your cat," Sunrise offered benevolently, "I could mount him on a stake."

Meezel let go a pathetic *meow* and stared upward at each of them. In the end, of course, it was Caspar who wound up carrying him.

CHAPTER FOURTEEN
THE RED COCK

IT WAS ALL THEY COULD do to walk next to each other. The surmin's stink permeated their clothes, their hair. It clung to their skin. It made a foul taste that lingered in their mouths.

It was with some trepidation, then, that they noticed a pair of torches burning in the distance. The lights didn't move. They seemed quite stationary. That was all they could see. The travelers were still too far away to make out anything else.

"Well, you can bet on one thing," Caspar said ominously. "Whoever it is, they'll smell us before we see them."

"It might be The Red Cock," Esmerelda said uncertainly. "I don't know." Her gaze rolled upward into the looming trees. "Everything has changed so much."

As they drew closer they saw it was, indeed, the inn Esmerelda had told them about. A pair of torches burned on either side of the entrance. Above the door hung an old wooden sign, its paint chipped and peeling. Still visible, though, was the faint picture of a strutting rooster encircled by a ring of faded blue balls. The inn had obviously seen better days. Light from the interior shone through cracks between the brown, weathered boards that made the walls. The entire structure looked as if a good stiff wind would flatten it.

The door opened suddenly. A head poked out and looked around, an expression of disgust unmistakably etched into the grizzled, bearded face. "What *is* that smell?" demanded a rough voice. "Sheesh!" Another face appeared just under the first, and two pair of eyes turned their way.

"Don't come any closer!" ordered the second face. The door pushed back wider, revealing two men, one taller than the other, both equally fat. Neither looked as if they had bathed or groomed for days, and their garments were in desperate need of repair and washing. The bigger man picked up a club from behind the wall and tapped it on his meaty palm as he regarded Caspar and his comrades. "I'm almost gaggin' all the way over here!" shouted the shorter man rudely. "Get out! Get away wit' ye!"

"Please," Caspar pleaded, stepping a pace ahead of his friends and holding out a hand. "We had a run-in with a surmin . . ."

"That's plain enough, boyo!" snapped the tall man. He pinched his nostrils shut. "An' the critter obviously won, too." He waved a hand toward the woods and raised his club in a threatening manner. "There's no place here for ye stinkers! Off wit' ye, 'fore we bash yer heads!"

Sunrise clenched his fists and stepped forward. "Why, you pair of farts!"

Carefully maintaining his smile, Caspar reached out, grabbed Sunrise, and clamped a hand over the youth's mouth. The boy struggled against him, waving his torch wildly, but Caspar held him in a firm grip. "Moonstroke," he said to the pair as he tapped one finger against his temple. "I beg your understanding. He's young."

"Perhaps, if you could just give us some soap," Esmerelda said reasonably, stepping forward also. "There must be a stream nearby where we could bathe."

"Yeah, there's that right near," one answered. The pair seemed to see Esmerelda for the first time. "Hey," said the taller man, still holding his nose. "This stinker's quite a looker."

Another face appeared behind those two. Three more men, all rough-looking with unkempt hair and beards, leered out the window. One of them picked his teeth with a slender dagger.

"I'm getting an uncomfortable feeling about these guys," Caspar whispered.

Esmerelda leaned closer. "Which ones?" she murmured.

"All six of 'em," Sunrise answered quietly. "I think we should politely back away from this place."

"My sentiments, too," Satchmoz agreed.

The three men in the window disappeared. An instant later, the tavern's door pushed all the way back. All six occupants stepped outside.

"It's been a long time since we seen any girlies in these parts," said the one with the dagger. " 'Less ye count ol' Nasty, which we don't. Haw!"

"Yeah!" said one of the others, an older man in a worn leather apron with a bald head and an unpleasant gleam in his eye. "That Nasty's got a face like hail damage on an ol' barn roof!"

Esmerelda clenched her fists, and her face screwed up in genuine anger. "You watch your mouth, you son of an immoral grue!"

Caspar blinked. After her performance at the castle, Esmerelda was the last person he would have expected to come to Nasturtium's defense. He caught her hand and pulled her back.

"We'll be leaving now," he said quickly with a smile and a wave. He motioned surreptitiously with one hand for the others to start backing away. "Sorry to have bothered you."

"You can go," the man with the dagger said in a low, threatening voice. He gave the dagger a toss. It flipped in the air a few times, and he caught it by the blade. "Ye smell like a dead little worm that crawled up me nose and decided to rot there. But the girlie stays."

"We'll clean 'er up real nice," said the tall man who originally opened the door. He leered at Esmerelda and rubbed his hands together.

With startling speed Esmerelda snatched Sunrise's dagger from his belt and brandished it. "If there's any cleaning to be done," she hissed, "I'll do it! I'll clean you like a catfish!"

The man with the dagger flipped it again and caught it. "Ye any good with that thing, girlie?" he asked smugly, grinning.

Esmerelda straightened indignantly. Then, she tossed her dagger. It flipped three times, and she caught it neatly by the hilt. It was her turn to grin as she answered, "When I'm done they'll call this place The Red Eunuch."

The tall man scowled and made a gesture. In no time the six ruffians spread out and surrounded the four. Weapons flashed from sheaths. One man advanced with a club. One waved a knife. One tapped a short sword on his palm. There was the man with his dagger. The remaining foe didn't need a weapon; his arms and hands were as good as any club.

Caspar's sword came out at once, and Sunrise snatched his dagger to replace the one Esmerelda had taken. In his other hand, the boy brandished his torch. Caspar's eyes shot around the circle. Which one should he take? he wondered. The man with the sword? Or the giant? What did it matter? What chance did they really have against these brigands? All six of them looked like experienced fighters.

"Let's take 'em quick!" one of the men grumbled. "I can't stand the smell!"

"Protect yourself!" Caspar warned Satchmoz, the only one of their party without a weapon.

The wizard frowned and patted Caspar's shoulder. "Oh, don't be melodramatic!" he said. He turned to the man with the dagger, who seemed to be the leader. "We're just going to turn around and run down the road now." He turned back to Caspar and his friends. "Go," he ordered.

Caspar hesitated, unsure he'd heard correctly. "What?"

"Go!" Satchmoz repeated, giving him a push.

"You ain't goin' nowhere, little maggots!" laughed the giant. He spread his arms to block the way to the road and took a step forward. With a surprised shout, he fell on his face.

"Run!" Satchmoz cried, herding his friends through the opening. Esmerelda stepped in the giant's back as they raced for the road. Sunrise pushed his face into the dirt. Shouts and curses filled the air behind them as their foes, intent on pursuit, tripped and sprawled awkwardly on the ground and scrambled to get up.

"You hexed their bootlaces!" Caspar cried gleefully as they sped into the darkness.

Satchmoz nodded. "They'll be up and after us quick enough, though," he said, already breathing hard. "Running is not my sport."

"We should ditch these torches," Sunrise advised.

"Why bother?" the wizard answered. "They'll find us by our smell if they want us bad enough."

"We'd better get off the road, anyway," Caspar suggested. "No point in making it easy for them."

He led the way into the underbrush. It wasn't possible to run. They made their way as quickly and quietly as they could. The sounds of angry shouting drew nearer. In the distance, through the trees and bushes, Caspar saw a torch go by, then another. Everyone crouched low. Sunrise and Caspar did their best to conceal the torches' light.

"They think we're still on the road," Sunrise whispered.

"Let's hope they keep thinking it for a long time," Satchmoz answered.

"Has anyone seen Meezel?" Esmerelda asked, glancing around.

No one said anything right away. Caspar thought back. He'd carried the cat for a long while, but set him down before they reached The Red Cock. Where the cat had gone after that, he didn't know. Nor at the moment did he particularly care, though he didn't say that to Esmerelda.

"Probably off chasing another surmin," Sunrise muttered.

Esmerelda rapped Sunrise lightly on the side of his

head and gave him a stern look. "Don't you be mean to my cat," she warned him.

"You tell 'im, girlie!" said a nasal voice right behind them.

Caspar whirled around, but Sunrise was faster. The boy swung his torch with both hands. The brief light showed them the smug, laughing face of the gray-haired, balding man. He was pinching his nostrils shut with one hand, brandishing his knife with the other. In an instant his expression turned to startled fear. He brought his blade up to block the swinging torch. Then he screamed in pain as a shower of sparks exploded around his face. The impact knocked him off his feet. He hit the ground hard, shrieking and clutching at his eyes. His beard smoldered and smoked.

"I didn't even hear him coming!" Caspar exclaimed, his gaze frantically searching the woods around them.

"These men have probably lived in these woods for years!" Esmerelda pointed out. "If they're anything like the men my father knew, they can sneak up on a deer!"

The man's screams alerted his comrades. Off to the right Caspar saw a torch moving swiftly among the trees. Another light flickered somewhere behind them. Somehow, the man got to his feet and blindly lurched into the darkness. His screams continued to issue from the shadows.

"Keep going north!" Sunrise said, his face fixed with determination. "I'll lead them away!"

Caspar caught Sunrise by the collar and nearly jerked him off his feet. "Forget that!" he ordered, thinking fast. "We stick together!"

They were about to start off again when another light flared suddenly in their midst. Letters of fire seared across the scroll Satchmoz held open in his hands, casting a ruddy sheen on the old wizard's face, filling his wide eyes with a wild radiance as he silently stared. A moment later the flames died, and the page crumbled into ash. Satchmoz brushed his hands, his expression resolute. "Let's kick ass!" he said, grinning.

Caspar rolled his eyes and let go a short sigh. "Let's run, instead," he urged, grabbing Esmerelda's hand.

They charged off among the trees again, choosing a direction away from the approaching torches and the screaming man who could still be heard in the darkness. Low branches scratched at their faces, and roots tried to trip them. Every time a shadow moved Caspar's heart jumped. Every snap of a twig or crackle of a dry leaf underfoot sounded loud as thunder to him. The sweat on his face began to trickle down his neck and chest.

Suddenly there was a loud splash, and Sunrise gave an awkward yelp. His torch tumbled from his grip and sizzled out in a cloud of steam and smoke. The boy cursed, and got to his feet. Sopping wet, in water up to his knees, he turned miserably to his friends. None of them had seen the stream in the dark.

"Better you than me," Satchmoz muttered, drawing his cloak more tightly around himself.

"This must be the stream our rude friends mentioned," Esmerelda said with enthusiasm. "Now I can wash this stink off!" She wasted no time, but began to lift the hem of her gown and pull it over her head.

Caspar caught one of her hands and pulled her dress down again. "Are you out of your mind?" he demanded, his face close to hers. "This is no time for a bath! Those *rude friends* are still out there hunting for us!"

She set her hands on her hips and glared at him. "If you think I'm going another step smelling like the inside of Nasty's slop jar when I have a chance to bathe, then you'd better think again! I'm a lady, and totally unused to this unflattering condition!" She lifted her hem again. "Now get out of my way, Caspar Wartsworth!"

Caspar caught her hand again and stopped her. "Be reasonable!" he insisted. "So what if you bathe? You going to wash your dress, too? It stinks as badly as you do!"

Her eyes snapped wide and Caspar knew he'd said the wrong thing. "You!" she sputtered furiously. "You—farm boy!" Before Caspar could defend himself she lashed out and pushed him off balance. With a despairing moan, he felt his foot slip on the grassy bank. The world gave a crazy spin. He heard the splash at the same time that water rushed up his nose and filled his ears. His last thought as he hit the water was of the torch he clung to. It stood no better chance of surviving than Sunrise's.

Coughing and angry, he sat up, his fingers digging into the muddy bottom. He clutched a handful of it and glanced up at Sunrise, who stood over him.

On the bank, Satchmoz, just visible in the new darkness, held up his hands as Esmerelda glared at him. "By all means," the wizard said in his most placating manner as he backed a step, "take your bath."

He knew it was an ungentlemanly thing to do, but still the mudball made a satisfactory smack as it struck Esmerelda's rump. She jumped, clutching her wounded pride with both hands, and gave a startled, "Oh!"

"Now, ain't ye all just a group o' fun-lovers!"

The short man leaned against a tree close by. He rubbed the blade of his knife idly up and down one of his sleeves, cleaning and polishing it as he leered at them. "I just loves folks what know how to have a good time," he continued, "and what lets other folks in on their fun, too!"

Caspar started to get to his feet, but the short man saw him. "You stay right there, boy!" he snapped. He waved the knife. "I kin split a wild cherry at fifty paces wit' this sticker. You'd be a might easier!"

Esmerelda stuck her tongue out at Caspar. But she moved subtly, and put herself between him and the short man. Her fingers crept up toward the neck of her dress. She tugged it slowly down, exposing just a hint of the creamy mound beneath, and gave a little toss of her head as she wet her lips.

"Come here, big boy," she purred, giving the short man a wink. "I've got something to show you."

With her other hand she raised her dress enough to flash him a little ankle.

The short man stared and wiped at his mouth with the back of his knife hand. He smacked his lips. "Don't play wi' me, girlie," he warned, though obviously he wanted just the opposite. "Ye'll be makin' a big mistake!"

Esmerelda regarded him coyly over one shoulder. "Well, if a girl's going to make a mistake, I always say . . ."—she gave him another wink as the corner of her mouth turned upward in a crooked smile—". . . he might as well be a big one."

The short man gave a whoop and rushed toward her, his arms going halfway around her before Esmerelda's hand moved. At once, the brigand froze. His eyes went wide, and the knife dropped from his grip. Remembering the dagger Esmerelda had taken from him and thrust into her dress's sash, Caspar thought at first she had stabbed him. But the sweat that broke suddenly out on the short man's face, and the breath that hissed from his mouth said otherwise.

"Like that?" Esmerelda said in a voice that bore a surprising resemblance to her stepmother's. "You'll love this, then!" Without any further warning, she let go of what she'd been holding and slammed her knees upward with all her force. The short man's mouth made a round *O* as the little breath he had left hissed from him. He clutched his groin with both hands, sagged to his knees, then fell over on his side in a fetal position.

"These woods just don't have the same class of riff-raff any more," Esmerelda complained as she stepped daintily away from her victim. "I just can't believe the way you men fall for that act!"

"Well, we'll just be sure now not to fall fer it again, stinkums!"

Their leader, the man with the dagger, stepped casually out from behind a tree. The giant melted out of the shadows on his right side. The one Caspar had originally thought of as the tall man appeared on his left. He carried a short sword now. It was hard to see them in the dark. Caspar doubted if his foes had the same problem. He moved his hand under the water and grasped the hilt of his own sword.

Esmerelda put on a pouty look and twitched her hip. "Come here, big boy," she said.

The leader frowned irritably. "Oh give it a rest, ye little bimbette!" he shouted. "Ye'd be funny if ye weren't so obviously an apprentice at danglin' yer bait."

"An apprentice!" Esmerelda shrieked indignantly.

"Don't sweat it!" the leader interrupted. "I'll make ye a master soon enough."

"That's mistress!" Esmerelda shouted back smugly. Then, she clapped both hands over her mouth as the brigands gave evil chuckles.

"As for you boys," the leader said, changing the subject. He looked thoughtful for a minute before continuing. "I think yer bones'll make fine toothpicks after we suck the marrow out."

Caspar had his sword half out of its sheath under the water where it couldn't be seen. Still, he tried to forestall conflict. "Surely you can think of some better use for us!" he said.

The three brigands looked at each other, appearing to think it over. They shrugged at the same time. "Naw," answered their leader. "We got the girlie now." He moved toward Esmerelda.

Esmerelda swiftly stooped and snatched the fallen knife of the man at her feet. At the same time she drew the dagger from her sash. With a blade in each hand, she straightened and faced them. "One more step," she challenged with a sneer, "and I'll be wearing your dangle-bobs for earrings!"

The leader paused, tilted his head quizzically, and looked at her. "Me what?"

Esmerelda frowned and gave her own little tilt of the head. "You know," she said with a hint of embarrassment.

The brigand put on a thoughtful expression, then a light came into his eyes. He looked down, then up at Esmerelda again. "Oh, yeah!" he said with sudden understanding. "Guess I fergot to tell ye, girlie. Me first wife got 'em! Haw!"

He moved toward her, then. Her right hand flashed

upward with the knife. Fast as she was, though, he was
faster. He didn't bother to catch her wrist, just slapped
the back of her hand, and the knife went flying. Before
she could bring her other blade into play, he set the
point of his dagger against her throat, and she froze.

"You really stink, girlie!" he said, voicing it politely,
as if it was a compliment.

Esmerelda was not entirely cowed. "You don't smell
like a field of dragondils yourself," she answered.

Caspar got to his feet with a noisy splash. His sword
remained in the sheath after all. With Esmerelda's life
balanced on a dagger point it was no time for heroics.
He only hoped Sunrise understood that, too. He glanced
at his young friend. There was no sign of the dagger he
knew the boy had.

Then without warning, the world went white. A
stark, painfully bright light stabbed Caspar's eyes. With
a gasp, he covered them with his fists. Esmerelda gave a
sharp scream. Sunrise, too. Even their foes cried out.

"*Aieee!*" the brigand leader shrieked in a voice of
purest terror. "What's happened to me?"

Caspar opened his fists slowly and peered out
through the barest opening. The light was still agoniz-
ingly bright, but subsiding quickly. And it came from the
brigand leader! He was glowing like the heart of a star!
Esmerelda had managed to push herself free, but she
lurched toward the stream with her hand held before her
as if she was blind, a distinct possibility, considering how
close she'd been to the leader.

The tall man and the giant backed away fearfully,
rubbing their eyes and glancing around at the shadows.
Even the man on the ground managed to sit up and
crawl away from his leader.

"It's Nasty!" the giant shouted. "She's around here
somewhere, an' she's put a spell on ye!" Without
another word, he turned and ran away into the woods.

"Hey! Wait a minute!" Satchmoz shouted indignantly.

They weren't listening. The tall man lowered his
sword as he stumbled backward. "I'm not messin' with

Nasty," he told his leader. "If she wants these folks for herself, I'm not gettin' in her way!" He whirled about, too, and chased after the giant. The sound of the two men crashing through the undergrowth gave testimony to their fear.

The brigand leader stared after them. Then, he whirled all about, peering into the forest. "Sorry, Nasty!" he screamed. "I didn't mean it! You want 'em, you got 'em! Just don't leave me like this!" He bent down and pulled his last comrade to his feet. "Come on, Deke," the leader said. "Looks like we got on the ol' bat's bad side again."

The man gave a loud groan as he stood up. He took a couple of limping steps and shot a hateful glance at Esmerelda.

The leader threw an arm of support around his remaining pal. Looking over his shoulder, he said, "You gots me sympathy, folks," he called. "If Nasty wants ye fer herself, ye got bigger problems than us." He smacked his lips. "Too bad. Ain't had decent food in years at The Red Cock. Ye sure would of been good eatin'."

They limped off into the trees. "Damn, damn, damn!" the leader could be heard cursing to himself. "I look like some kind of froggin' saint!"

Caspar and his friends watched the light winking in and out among the old trunks. When they could no longer hear the cursing, they could still see the light weaving through the woods like some ghostly will-o'-the-wisp, getting farther and farther away.

"Harumph!" Satchmoz grumbled, folding his arms across his narrow chest. He kicked at the ground as if his feelings were hurt. "Nasty, indeed!"

Caspar waded up the bank. "Forget it," he told the wizard. "We know it was you that saved our lives." He went to Esmerelda, who stood grinding her fists into her eyes. "Are you all right?" he asked worriedly.

"That was terrific!" Sunrise cried gleefully as he bounced ashore and ran to pick up the dagger the leader had dropped in his confusion. It, too, glowed like a small star. "What did you do to him?"

"Everything's fuzzy," Esmerelda answered Caspar, clinging to him for balance. "For a moment, I couldn't see. It's getting better, though."

"It's called a *frotz* spell," Satchmoz answered Sunrise. "A dash too much *presence,* maybe," he admitted. "So it was brighter than I expected. Still, effective, wouldn't you say?"

The youth nodded enthusiastically. Abruptly, he gave a sharp sneeze.

"I think we've found Meezel," Caspar commented.

"Or he's found us," Sunrise replied as the cat crept out of the woods and leaped into his arms. He sneezed again, and passed the beast to Esmerelda.

She squeezed the cat until its eyes bugged out. "Poor kitty!" she crooned, rubbing her face against his. "Did you get lost?" Then she recoiled and wrinkled her nose. "He still reeks!" she announced to the others. She ran her hand affectionately over Meezel's head a few times, then cradled him on one shoulder as he began to purr.

"I think we could take time to bathe now, if you want," Caspar said charitably.

"Mauldwood just isn't the party place it used to be," Esmerelda answered quietly. "I want to get out of this damned woods. And I think I have a way." Balancing Meezel with one hand, she grabbed a handful of her dress and pulled it up on one side, enough to expose a small black garter she wore on her thigh. There was a folded square of parchment stuck into it. She drew it out and handed it to Satchmoz.

"I snatched this from Nasty's library ages ago," she said with a small sigh. "I always hoped I'd find a way to use it to get away from the castle. But I don't know anything about magic."

"Zork!" Satchmoz shouted excitedly. "This is really a piece of luck! Things are finally looking up, boys."

Caspar pressed closer, grabbing the glowing dagger from Sunrise and holding it over the page. Brilliant blue letters flowed across the parchment in a spidery and antique script. A pattern of arcane symbols bordered the writing. As Caspar studied the pattern, it seemed to move, and the letters themselves swirled on the paper. He tore his gaze away, feeling a slight vertigo, as if he'd looked down from a great height.

"What is it?" he asked, looking from the wizard to Esmerelda.

"*Aimfiz,*" Esmerelda answered, hugging Meezel. "A teleport spell."

"Yippee!" Sunrise cried, jumping up and down. "Borphee, here we come!"

"Please," Esmerelda said plaintively. "This will be my first time ever in a big city. Could we bathe first?"

CHAPTER FIFTEEN

BURBLE, BURBLE . . .

"**H**OW WOULD YOU FEEL about a hot bath, instead, young lady?" Satchmoz asked as he held the scroll closer to the light and peered at it again, "with soap and sponges and fluffy towels, and a glass of wine to sip . . ."

"Stop! Stop!" Esmerelda cried, hugging her cat in both her arms. "Don't tease me!"

"I'm much too old for that, my dear," the wizard answered. "We can all be in the Wizard's Guildhall in Borphee in the blink of an eye."

Meezel purred loudly as Esmerelda nervously stroked the top of his head and rubbed his ears. "But that spell won't take you to a *place!*" she insisted. "It takes you to a *person!*"

Satchmoz let go of one end of the scroll, and it rolled up with a snap. "I know that!" he said sharply. He shook the scroll under Esmerelda's nose. "Who's the wizard around here? You, or me?"

Esmerelda looked down at the ground.

Caspar thought it wise to interrupt. "We're all too tired to argue," he said patiently. "If you can get us to Borphee, then do it now."

"Yeah," Sunrise agreed as he massaged his belly, "before we starve to death."

Satchmoz squared his shoulders and looked at each of them. "Very well, then," he announced. He unrolled the scroll again and held it at the corners. "Everybody stand as close together as you can get and join hands."

"But I can't join hands!" Esmerelda whined. "I've got to hold Meezel!"

Satchmoz frowned in irritation. Then, he let the scroll roll up again and held out his arms. "Give him to me," he ordered.

Esmerelda looked dubious. Pushing out her lower lip, she looked to Caspar, as if for some kind of support, but he gave her none. Finally, she unhooked the cat's claws from the sleeve of her dress and handed him to the wizard.

Satchmoz's frown only deepened as he lifted Meezel in both hands and turned the cat's face toward his own. "You behave yourself, you wretched little beast," he muttered, looking the cat directly in its green eyes, "or I'll shave what little hair you have left and knit a muffler from it."

The cat gave a plaintive meow as Satchmoz shoved him down into one of the many pockets that lined his cloak. At once the garment shifted, and the fastening clasp rose up to exert pressure on the old man's throat. He caught it with one finger and tugged it down to give himself breathing room. "You ought to put that creature on a diet!" he croaked at Esmerelda.

When he could breathe again, he let go of the clasp and opened the scroll once more. "Hold that light up!" he instructed as the others moved together and joined hands. Caspar and Sunrise held the glowing dagger between them. They raised their arms over Satchmoz's head, illuminating the writing on the page. "Grab my arms, somebody!" he ordered as he backed up against Caspar. Sunrise took one of his arms. Esmerelda grasped another just above the elbow.

"If we stand this close for long," Sunrise complained, "I'm gonna gag on the stink!"

"Here we go!" The wizard shouted. He read the scroll, then silently mouthed the words, putting all the strength of will he could muster behind the magic.

A harsh blue light stabbed Caspar's eyes. For an instant, his stomach felt as if it were turning inside out, and his senses whirled as he tumbled through a sky that he knew instinctively was not real.

Then his feet were on solid ground again. Too solid, in fact. The road dust was gone. Cold stone tiles chilled his bare feet and turned his toes upward. "Damn!" he gasped in surprise.

"Wow!" Sunrise exclaimed.

"Aieeee!" Satchmoz screamed in a voice full of despair.

"Aieeee!" echoed another, totally strange voice over the sound of desperate splashing.

Esmerelda gave a giggle as a terrified Meezel gave an angry snarl and leaped, soaking wet, out of Satchmoz's cloak. "Well, you said we'd have a hot bath soon enough," she laughed, bending down to soothe and comfort her poor glowering pet.

Satchmoz cursed. His spell had carried them to someone's bathroom while that person was in the very act of bathing. Perhaps because he'd been holding the scroll, or perhaps because he was the only one who knew personally the individual the spell had brought them to, the wizard had materialized in the bath itself while the rest were left standing around it. Once again, the old man's precious cloak and its valuables were drenched.

Satchmoz screamed in frustration and rose half out of the soapy tub. "Burble!" he shouted, shaking his fist at a pile of white frothy bubbles. "What are you doing taking a bath this time of night?"

A head slowly rose from under the bubbles. A bright pink mohawk crowned that head. Not even the water had slicked down the short stubbly hairs. The face was a pale blue, and though a pair of three-inch fangs jutted up from its lower lip, it wore a terrified expression. Gradually, the fear faded, and a look of recognition took its place.

"Satch!" the creature cried with unconcealed delight. It lunged forward in the large tub, sloshing water over the side, and threw its pudgy arms around Satchmoz's waist. "Burble heard Satch dead!"

"It's a brogmoid!" Esmerelda whispered in wonderment as she stared at Satchmoz's admirer. "I haven't seen one in ages!"

"There's lots of 'em in Borphee," Sunrise told her. "A lot of the warehouse owners work 'em down on the docks. They're cheap labor."

The brogmoid let go of Satchmoz and shot Sunrise a harsh look. Every muscle and vein on its body suddenly popped out as it tensed. "Watch yer mouth, human pup!" the brogmoid growled in a menacing voice. "This ain't no cheap meat!" It glared at him and licked the tips of its gleaming fangs.

"They're also schizophrenic," Sunrise added to Esmerelda, unshaken by the brogmoid's threat.

"But so cute!" Esmerelda replied as she stepped forward and reached out to stroke the pink mohawk.

The brogmoid growled again, its blue eyes narrowing to slits. "Watch it, skirt! I'll bite that hand off all the way down to yer bony little knees!"

Esmerelda recoiled, clutching her hand to her breast, looking shocked.

Satchmoz smacked the brogmoid on top of its head. "Knock it off, Burble!" he snapped. "These are my friends. Now mind your manners and behave yourself!"

The brogmoid looked wounded. Its shoulders slumped, its lower lip sagged out, and it bent its head until it touched the soap bubbles.

Satchmoz stepped gingerly over the side of the tub and stood dripping. His saturated garments clung to him. He gave a low moan as he held his arms away from his body and glanced at the puddle forming under him.

"Satch's friends stink," the brogmoid muttered in a hurt voice that was little more than a grumpy whisper. A little more boldly, he added, "Satch really stink! Phew!"

"Well, we'll all smell better when *you've* drawn four more baths!" the wizard answered testily as he glared at Burble. "Why aren't you in bed, anyway? It's the wee hours!"

"Nobody tell Burble go to bed," the brogmoid

answered in a childlike voice that contained more than a hint of confusion.

"What?" Satchmoz said. He looked around suddenly, then turned back to the brogmoid. "Burble," he said, softening, "where is everyone?"

The brogmoid hung its head again and sniffed. "Burble not know," it answered quietly. "Burble alone. Lonely Burble!" It leaned out of the tub again and threw its arms around Satchmoz. "Good ol' Satch!" it cried. "Welcome back from dead!"

"Who told you he was dead?" Caspar asked, coming closer.

The brogmoid gave him a look that wavered for an instant between hostility and trust. Trust won out. "All over town," it answered, wiping a finger over its nose where a silvery soap bubble clung to the tip. The bubble popped soundlessly. "All know how horny sea serpent ravish Chulig's ship." The brogmoid threw back its head and gave a throaty laugh. "Best story told after war with Antharia."

Caspar raised an eyebrow. "*After* the war?" he exclaimed.

"Righto, Friend of Satch," it answered, grinning as it bobbed its head up and down.

Sunrise leaned on the side of the wooden tub. "How long's it been over?" he asked with interest.

Burble pushed out a lip and looked thoughtful. A blue-skinned hand rose into the air. One finger uncurled and straightened. Then another. Then another. "Two weeks," it answered uncertainly.

"That's impossible!" Caspar shouted, slapping his thigh. He paced around the tub and glared at Satchmoz. "We only left port a couple of days ago!"

"Not so impossible," Satchmoz muttered, rubbing his chin. He wore a look of thoughtful consternation. "It's a ramification I hadn't thought about, though."

"Ramification of what?" Caspar persisted.

The old wizard shook his head. "I'll explain it later," he said as he began to pull wet scrolls from his pockets. "Right now, let's just all get cleaned up and get some sleep. I can't remember when I had a decent night's sleep, lately."

Burble reached for a towel next to the tub and wrapped it about himself as he rose shyly out of the foamy bath. "Pardon, pardon, pardon!" the brogmoid murmured, purpling with embarrassment as it stepped out onto the floor. "Burble draw hot tubs for Satch and friends."

"Wait!" Satchmoz ordered, laying a hand on the brogmoid's shoulder. He cast a quick glance around the bathroom, noting the tile floor, the gold fixtures, the copper mirrors, the exquisitely wrought wooden tub. "Burble, this is Krepkit's bathroom, isn't it? I asked before. Where is everyone?"

The brogmoid squinted its eyes. Visibly agitated, it seemed almost on the verge of crying. "Burble not know, Satch!" it answered plaintively. "Just gone. All gone! Long time now." The creature looked down at the soap suds between its toes as it wrung its hands. "Not tell Krepkit Burble used his bathtub?"

Satchmoz allowed a faint smile as he scratched the top of the brogmoid's head. "Of course not, Burble. It's our secret. Go draw those baths now."

The brogmoid smiled again and began backing from the room. "Righto, Satch!" he answered. "Needs bath bad, Satch does, and Satch's friends, too. Nice and hot, Burble makes 'em, with lots of soap."

Satchmoz shook the excess water from a handful of scrolls before he gave up. "Oh piffle!" he muttered, thrusting them back carelessly into a cloak pocket. "I'll dry them later, or copy new ones from the library." He cast the soggy cloak in a corner. "Let's get you all to rooms, first."

"Who's Krepkit?" Esmerelda asked as she bent over a dressing table in the far corner of the bathroom and examined a gold comb.

"Our foremost enchanter," Satchmoz answered. "The one who called us all together here. Someday, there'll be wizards' guilds all over Quendor. That's Krepkit's dream. But we're the only one right now."

"Why didn't you ask the brogmoid about the war?" Caspar said as the wizard led them out of Krepkit's bathroom and into a most lavish dressing chamber. "I can't believe it said the war was over!"

"Burble is a *he*," Satchmoz told him with a hint of irritation in his voice. "Not an *it*." They passed through a door and into a dimly lit corridor. The wizard left a trail of droplets and wet footprints on the cool stone floor. "And like all brogmoids, his mind is little better than that of a clever three-year-old. Tomorrow, after we've all rested, I'll give you the answers you want."

They turned a bend in the corridor, and the wizard stopped before another door. "This is my room," he said with a wave of his hand. "If no one's here, then there's no reason you shouldn't each take one of the next three rooms. "Help yourself to the closets, too. If you don't find something to fit, we can rummage later. There's bound to be something." With that, he opened the door to his own room, and went inside and left them, closing the door with a soft *thud*.

"I thought once we were free of Mauldwood his mood would improve," Sunrise said lightly to Caspar.

Caspar frowned as he looked up and down the corridor. "I think something's weighing on his mind," he answered, quietly troubled. "Maybe the absence of his guild brothers. Maybe the brogmoid's news about the war being over."

Sunrise shrugged. A genuine smile turned up the corners of his mouth. "Well, I don't know about you, but I feel like a weight's been lifted *off* my mind." He approached the nearest door, turned the knob, and opened it. "I guess I'll take this one, unless anyone objects." When neither Caspar nor Esmerelda did, he bid them goodnight and went inside.

An instant later the door jerked open again. "It's dark in here," Sunrise said nervously. He stared at the dagger in his hand. Only the very dimmest enchantment remained upon the blade, and even that faded completely as he watched.

"Leave your door open," Caspar told him, "and let

the corridor's light shine in until Burble comes back. I'm sure it—I mean, *he*—will provide a lamp or some candles."

"Oh," Sunrise replied doubtfully. But he went back inside, leaving the door open, and sat down stiffly on the side of a large bed. A black streak darted through the open doorway and leaped up onto the bed beside him. Sunrise gave a loud sneeze.

"Meezel!" Esmerelda scolded in a good-natured voice. "You traitor!"

The cat regarded her with round, amber eyes and offered an apologetic meow. Nevertheless, he settled down comfortably against Sunrise's thigh and crossed his front paws on the edge of the coverlet.

The boy didn't say anything, just reached down and scratched the cat between the ears, eliciting a long purr from the beast.

Burble came waddling down the corridor with candles and a lamp, and a stack of fluffy towels. "Draw baths now, Burble will," he told them excitedly. "Take rooms? Bathtubs in each room. Satch's stinky friends pick, and Burble fill good and hot." He waved Caspar and Esmerelda toward rooms. "Be clean in no time," he went on. "Smell brogmoid good!"

"Now there's a thought," Esmerelda whispered to Caspar as she opened the door to the room next to Sunrise's. The brogmoid followed her inside and lit a candle from the lamp he carried, and set it on a table. A pleasant glow filled the bedchamber.

"Hey, can I have one of those?" Sunrise called from his room.

Esmerelda laid a hand in the center of Caspar's chest as he started to follow her in. "Ah ah," she said, clucking her tongue. "A lady doesn't allow a strange man into her boudoir."

Caspar raised an eyebrow. "I'm not a strange man!"

"Honey," Esmerelda answered with a purr not unlike her cat's, "you're as strange as they come." She flashed him a grin and gently shut the door in his face.

"What about the brogmoid?" Caspar demanded through the closed door.

"He's not a man at all!" came the answer through the thick wood.

From farther away, the chamber's bathroom, perhaps, came a gruff and muffled, "Watch it, skirt!"

Caspar gave a low chuckle and went to pick his own room.

Caspar woke up in the plushest, softest bed he'd ever had the pleasure of sleeping in. He hadn't really needed the quilts and blankets or the six pillows, yet there was a kind of luxurious thrill in piling them over and around his body until he was cocooned and nearly buried.

Only a small amount of daylight penetrated the room's shuttered window. He had no idea what time of morning it was when he opened his eyes. It was quiet, and he lay on his back for a long time, reliving the events of the past few days. Finally, he threw back the covers and swung his feet over the side of the bed, stretched, and rose.

The room Caspar had chosen for himself had a bathroom almost as wonderful as Krepkit's. He padded barefoot across the stone tiles and admired the workmanship of the large wooden tub that occupied the center. He still marveled at the way it filled itself with water when he twisted the knob at one end of it. The brogmoid had shown him how it worked.

He'd already had one bath before going to bed, a warm one thanks to Burble. The tub's knob only provided cold water, but the brogmoid had been especially kind and insisted on hauling large kettles of hot water from some other part of the guild hall to make the bath steaming warm. Caspar had spent more than an hour soaping himself, washing away the road dust and the surmin stink, and soaking his weary body.

Bent over the marvelous tub, he bit his lip and cast a guilty glance over his shoulder. It would be a foolish self-indulgence to bathe again. The water would be cold, too, as he couldn't possibly ask Burble to fetch more hot water. Still, he was used to bathing in cold water, having never known anything else. And there was soap left.

Before he could really stop himself, he had the water running, the tub filling, and his toes dangling over the side. Naked, he lowered himself into his bath, too enthralled at the wonder of indoor plumbing to even notice his goosebumps. He snatched up the bar of soap and filled his hair with suds.

"Morning, Friend of Satch!"

Caspar jerked his head toward the door, squinting, barely able to see for the rich lather that menaced his eyes, and prepared himself for a scolding. There was nothing but joviality in the brogmoid's voice, though, so he relaxed. "Good morning, Burble," he answered. "And my name is Caspar," he added as he wiped a dripping hand across his brow to catch the suds so he could see better. The brogmoid was wearing a bright yellow, high-necked sweater with *I love Borphee* blazoned across the front in big black letters. "Caspar Wartsworth. Are the others up, yet?"

"Only Satch," Burble answered from the bathroom doorway. "Other Satch-friends still burrowed deep in covers." He tilted his blue-skinned head to the side, closed his eyes and faked a long, loud snore. "The skirt, she's quite a honker. Might bring down the roof." Burble rolled his eyes and shook his head.

Caspar grinned, wondering how the delicate Esmerelda would react if told she snored. Probably safer not to mention it, he decided. "How did you know I was awake?" he asked.

The brogmoid leaned against the doorjamb while Caspar rinsed the soap out of his hair. "Caspo probably think this ultra-modern top-notch shack, huh?" he said, continuing when Caspar nodded agreement. "Not so modern, though," Burble continued. "When bath water run, pipes all over guild hall rumble like Krepkit's stomach when hungry." Burble shrugged and rubbed his hands together. "So I bring Caspo breakfast. Got rolls and butter, got cold chicken, got apple. Water you already got. But there's that, too, in clean pitcher. All by bedside."

"Gee, thanks," Caspar answered, suddenly realizing how hungry he felt. He rose from the tub and snatched up a towel from a small pile on a stool near at hand. Then, he reached down and pulled the strange cork from the hole in the tub that let the water out. "Where did you say Satchmoz was?" he asked, drying himself briskly.

"In library, or labrador," the brogmoid answered.

Caspar paused and looked at Burble. "Labrador?"

Burble frowned. "Labra . . ." he tried again. "Lab . . . lab." He flung up his arms and put on a frustrated look. "Workplace in basement that stinks like old eggs."

"Laboratory," Caspar supplied, grinning to himself.

"That place," the brogmoid agreed. "Caspo eat, then Burble come back and take Caspo there. Just turn on bathtub. Pipes tell Burble when Caspo ready."

Caspar watched the brogmoid depart, and he smiled with secret mirth. There was something charming about the little fellow with his pink mohawk hair and oversized yellow sweater and childlike manner. He spread his towel upon the side of the tub and went to see about his breakfast. His heart leaped at the size of the platter of rolls that sat with the rest of his meal on a bedside table. He gave a yowl and hurled himself across the middle of the bed. The mattresses gave under his weight, and he bounced a few times, laughing. He didn't even bother with butter. Snatching the first roll, he wolfed it down and brushed the few crumbs from the sheets.

This was the life, he told himself. This was what he left Djabuti Padjama and his uncle's farm for. Sitting cross-legged in the bed, he balanced a roll on his nose while he reached to the bedside table for a piece of cold chicken.

Then his gaze fell on a wardrobe on the other side of the room. Burble must have opened its doors. Within hung garments of glittering silks and satins, robes with splendid embroidery, cloaks and shoes and sashes of every imaginable cut and color. His eyes fairly popped out of his skull. His breakfast momentarily forgotten, he sprang out of bed.

Satchmoz had said to take what clothes they needed, he reminded himself as he pulled several things out at once. It might take some time to decide just what it was he needed most, though. Of course, he'd have to try everything on.

For the first time in days, he found himself whistling a merry tune, and the sound of it filled not only his chambers, but several more beyond.

CHAPTER SIXTEEN

THE EARTH MOVES FOR CASPAR

CASPAR PUSHED BACK the large double doors of the guild hall's library. After pointing them out, Burble had gone back upstairs to take breakfast to Sunrise and Esmerelda. He entered quietly and found Satchmoz bent over a writing table making notes while that strange, multicolored whirling *thing* he usually carried in his cloak cast dazzling light about the chamber.

Satchmoz spared him a quick glance over the shoulder. "Are the others up?" he asked.

Caspar refrained from giving an innocent little whistle. "They are now," he confessed. In fact, neither Sunrise nor Esmerelda had been happy about being awakened by his music, but the promise of food from Burble had readjusted their attitudes.

He cast a gaze about the library. The walls were honeycombed with thousands of square holes into which thick, dusty scrolls had been thrust. Against one wall stood a couple of shelves that contained newer, modern books. On a large table near the room's south corner stood a large wooden table where several hand-drawn maps were displayed.

The carpets on the floor were thick with dust, and dust motes danced in the air. Beams of sunlight shone into the room from windows cut high along the walls near the ceiling. A pair of large cressets, suspended from the ceiling's major beam by stout chains, also gave off light.

On the whole, though, it struck Caspar as a rather

gloomy place. Or it would have, if not for Satchmoz's shimmering infotater.

"What is that thing, anyway?" Caspar asked, coming closer, staring into the wildly spinning colors. He held a hand up to it, and watched reds and blues and yellows stream across his skin.

Satchmoz set down the stylus with which he'd been writing, and put a stopper over the jar of ink. "Krepkit invented it," the wizard answered, rubbing the bridge of his nose with thumb and forefinger. "It's sort of a magical, two-way notebook." He reached out a hand, touched one edge of the swirling colors, and the spinning ceased instantly. "It looks like a child's pinwheel," he pointed out. "All the guild members carry one. No matter where we are we can set it spinning and ask it questions. If the answers are somewhere in this library, the infotater will find them and relay them to us. We can also dictate into it, and it will record what we say."

Caspar touched one of the infotater's delicate-looking blades and gave it a whirl. "How many scrolls in this library?" he asked the device, bending close as he spoke. But no wonderful light and no voice answered him. The pinwheel remained a pinwheel.

Despite his apparent weariness, Satchmoz chuckled. "I'm afraid each one is personalized by Krepkit, himself," he told Caspar. "It'll only work when I breathe on it." To demonstrate, he leaned forward and blew gently on the blades. The infotater began at once to spin and shine until the room once more swam with color.

"How many scrolls in this library?" Satchmoz asked, relaying Caspar's question.

A deep, sonorous voice issued from the heart of the light. "Too many for your bumpkin friend to read in his lifetime," came the answer.

Satchmoz shot out a hand and stopped the infotater. He turned a sheepish grin up at Caspar. "Krepkit has an odd sense of humor," he said by way of apology. "He tries to give these things personalities."

"Krepkit sounds like a real charming guy," Caspar said with a hint of hurt sarcasm. "But why *infotater?*"

Satchmoz gave him a surprised look. "Why, that's obvious enough, boy!" he said. "Because it gives and receives information while it rotates. And speaking of things one could use," he added, gazing up and down at Caspar, "you could use a fashion sense."

Wounded, Caspar held out his arms and did a slow turn. He thought the orange sequined tunic with its high neck and belled sleeves, and the purple silk pantaloons he wore over yellow stockings were quite striking. A silver belt set the whole thing off.

"It's striking, all right," the wizard responded when Caspar muttered his hurt defense. "It could strike a grue dead at fifty paces if the light hit you just right."

Caspar pouted. He'd never seen such fine clothes before in Djabuti Padjama. Despite Satchmoz's snobbery, he still liked his outfit. "Well, you told Burble to burn my other things," he reminded the old man.

"I think I'll tell him to burn these, too," Satchmoz replied, turning back to his table. "But if you must wear them, they'll do until we go out in the streets. Something a little more subtle will be needed then."

"We're going out?" Caspar said with sudden excitement, remembering just how little of Quendor's glorious capital he'd managed to see.

Before Satchmoz could answer a sudden tremor ran through the guildhall. The infotater fell off the desk, its blades whirring. Scrolls shook and shivered in their squared nooks. On the far corner table, the pile of maps slithered to the floor. The cressets overhead began to swing back and forth, causing shadows to dance about the chamber.

"A zorkquake!" Caspar shouted in alarm.

Satchmoz caught him by the arm before he could run from the room. "No, it's not!" he shouted back. "It'll pass."

Sure enough, a moment later the trembling ceased. Satchmoz let go of Caspar and bent to recover his infotater, which he placed back on his writing desk. Then he went to rescue the fallen maps.

"What was that?" Caspar insisted, still somewhat alarmed.

"The Frobozz Magic Tunneling Company," the wizard answered as he straightened the valuable, hand-drawn maps and set them properly on the table again. He returned to Caspar, a sneer on his face. "A bunch of minor enchanters affiliated with Borphee's Engineering Institute."

"What are they doing?" Caspar demanded uneasily. "I thought the house was going to fall on us!"

Satchmoz shook his head. "Naw, the plumbing stinks, but this foundation is rock solid." He straightened all his notes on the writing table, checked his ink jar to make sure it was sealed tight, laid his stylus neatly beside it, and took Caspar by the arm. "Let's have some tea," he then suggested. "I've learned quite a lot this morning that will interest you."

They left the library, and Satchmoz pulled the great doors closed. A few moments later, the wizard led Caspar into an amazing room with crystal walls and a crystal ceiling. Scores of green plants sat on pedestals and tiny tables and shelves. Some hung suspended from posts. The room had a fresh, earthy smell, and the sun streamed down and touched everything with a delicious, sensuous warmth.

Caspar's jaw dropped open. "This is fantastic!" he exclaimed.

"Pretty good," Satchmoz agreed. "Krepkit designed it. He has this thing for growing plants." He pointed Caspar to a table of polished bloodwood. There were four matching chairs around the table. "Be seated," Satchmoz told him. "I'll fetch the tea."

Caspar bit his lip. He approached the table reverently, and ran one finger over the deep ruddy surface. His face gaped back at him from the gleaming finish, and he realized how stupid he looked. But bloodwood grew only in the jungles of far Miznia. A traveler passing through the Peltoid Valley had once shown him a tiny flute made from it, so he knew the table was, indeed, bloodwood. But such a fine piece of furniture from such an expensive material! Why, the Borphee wizards must be rich!

Instead of sitting, he walked to the nearest crystal wall, pressed his nose up against it, and peered out into a large courtyard. A fountain occupied the center. Graceful sculptures stood at various points along pebbled walkways. Flowers bloomed, and topiaries fashioned in wondrous shapes rose up from the ground as if they were lighter than air. Beyond the high garden wall rose the pinnacles and spires of Borphee.

Caspar felt his heart racing as he backed away from the crystal wall. Like a wave rushing over him, he realized that he *was* a bumpkin, just like the infotater had said, and the admission hurt him strangely. He had never seen crystal walls, or bloodwood tables, or bathtubs, or libraries. He glanced at the sleeve of his orange-sequined tunic. It was beautiful, to him, but it was also incredibly garish. He saw that now, and felt ashamed.

He left the chamber and sought his room again in the upper quarters of the guildhall. In Esmerelda's room, he heard the voices of Sunrise and Burble. Quietly as he could, he slipped into his room and quickly changed clothes, donning simple trousers of black cloth, soft black boots, and a white lace-up tunic. For a long moment, he stared at himself in a mirror, not to admire his outfit, but to try to figure out what really lay behind the eyes that stared back at him.

When he left his room again, the voices of his friends could not be heard. He crept back downstairs and returned to the crystal chamber and pushed open the doors. Sunrise and Esmerelda were there with Satchmoz, all seated around the bloodwood table while Burble poured hot tea into tiny porcelain cups and served sweet honeyed biscuits.

He was doubly glad he had taken the time to change his clothes. Sunrise had found common-sense type garments in someone's closet, clothes that might have suited him on a hunt or an outing in the countryside. Of course, everything was a bit big on him, but he had rolled up the sleeves of his brown tunic, and tucked the ends of his forest green trousers into boots. Esmerelda, too, had chosen sensible clothes. There were no women in the guild hall, so she had had to make do with mens' wear. Still, she filled out a blue open-necked tunic quite admirably, and the oversized trousers of a darker blue had a skirtlike drape.

They would have laughed, had they seen him earlier.

Esmerelda looked at him. Her eyes grew wide, and her breath caught in her throat. "You're . . ." Her jaw dropped as she regarded him, and she seemed to have trouble swallowing. ". . . *clean*!" she managed at last.

Caspar blushed as he crossed the room and took the last remaining chair. The honeyed biscuits smelled warm and good, and he helped himself to one as Burble poured tea into his cup. A rich vanilla smell rose from the steaming liquid.

"I approve the change," Satchmoz commented, grinning, as he leaned over and touched Caspar's sleeve. "Very classic."

Sunrise gave them both a look. "What's he talking about?" he asked Caspar.

"Nothing," the wizard answered before Caspar could mention the sequins. He pointed to Sunrise's empty cup. "Have some more tea." He turned back to Caspar. "I figured everybody might as well be present to hear what I have to say."

"Want Burble to leave, Satch?" the brogmoid interrupted. "Krepkit always scoots Burble away when business talk starts. Krepkit gone now, so Satch is boss."

Satchmoz shook his head. "No, Burble. You've been a big help this morning, and I'm not quite the stiff that Krepkit is—or was. Zork knows what's become of him." A troubled expression stole over Satchmoz's face as he steepled his fingers under his nose and peered around the table.

"A lot's been going on," he told them all. "Near as I can pinpoint it, we've been absent from Borphee for nearly two months."

"What?" Sunrise shrieked.

Caspar set his teacup down, rattling the small saucer underneath. "Not more than a week!" he insisted.

Esmerelda shrugged her shoulders. "Don't look at me," she said. "I don't know how long you were rummaging around in Mauldwood. It's always been a strange place." She raised her cup and flashed Burble a sparkling smile. "May I have some more of that marvelous vanilla tea?"

The brogmoid picked up the pot and hastened to refill her cup.

"In fact," said Satchmoz, "you are probably in part to blame."

"I beg your pardon," she countered, eyeing him over the rim of her teacup. She paused to take a delicate sip and swallow. Then she set the cup down. "I am never to blame."

Sunrise and Caspar exchanged glances. Sunrise didn't bother to hide his smirk, and Caspar decided that Satchmoz had been right when he whispered that Mauldwood probably wasn't responsible for Esmerelda's attitude problem. She was as haughty and arrogant as ever.

But Satchmoz deferred. "All right," he answered tolerantly. "We'll blame your stepmother, Nasturtium."

"Nasty," Esmerelda corrected, picking up her cup again and lifting a honeyed biscuit daintily between thumb and forefinger. Not only did she take care to extend the pinky of the hand that held the teacup, but of the hand that held the biscuit as well.

Satchmoz put on a patient smile, sat back in his chair, and nodded. "Nasty, then," he said amiably. He waited a moment to see if she would interrupt again, and finally continued.

"Nasty put you to sleep, my dear, with a time-suspension spell, the like of which I have never seen before. Nor, I doubt, has any member of my guild. Now magic of that sort—any spell, for that matter—must be constantly renewed. Even so, it is not quite stable. It leaks, if you will."

Satchmoz paused and took a sip from his own teacup. Burble hurried around to his side of the table with the pot and promptly refilled his cup.

"The spell was probably cast on the crystal coffin we found you in," he continued. "And at first, the leakage was probably confined to the room where your coffin was kept."

Esmerelda held up a hand and set her teacup down again. "Please," she insisted. "Stop referring to it as my *coffin*. It makes me shiver!"

Satchmoz drummed his fingers momentarily on the arm of his chair. "How about *bier?*" he suggested with just a hint of testiness.

"Beer?" said Burble, setting down the teapot. "Burble fetch beer!" The brogmoid headed for the door.

"Come back!" Satchmoz snapped, stopping the little pink-haired fellow in his tracks. Confused, the brogmoid turned around again. Satchmoz forced a smile. "We didn't mean *drinking beer*," he explained. "We meant *bier*." He spelled it for the brogmoid.

"That really doesn't sound much better, I'm afraid," Esmerelda complained.

Sunrise leaned forward and wrapped his hands around his cup. There was a mischievous sparkle in his eye. "How about *display case?*" he suggested. "Or *cage?*"

Esmerelda kicked Sunrise under the table, and the boy giggled.

Satchmoz blew out a stream of air, pursed his lips, and steepled his fingers again. "As I was saying. . . ." He spoke a bit more loudly than necessary to draw their attention. "The leakage probably affected your *coffin* first, slowing down time inside that. Then the effect spread throughout your room. As Nasty kept renewing the spell over and over, the effect eventually permeated the entire castle. It may even have seeped out into the grounds, maybe the woods itself." Having seized the conversation back, he leaned forward again, and a certain excitement shone in his eyes. "Me, I noticed it the moment we entered the castle doors."

"That was why you whipped out your infotater and sat down in the middle of the floor," Caspar said.

"No," Satchmoz corrected. "That was when I noticed the spatial shift."

Sunrise swallowed the remains of another honeyed biscuit. "The whatial whose?" He sputtered crumbs across the table top. Esmerelda made a disgusted face and flicked a speck from the exposed portion of her bosom.

"The spatial shift," Satchmoz repeated. "The spell that kept kicking us back to the entrance hall, or the library if you were in the upstairs. A brilliant piece of magic, by the way. I've actually managed to decipher it, I think. Can't wait to show it to Krepkit." He beamed as he regarded them. Then, a frown clouded his features. "If we ever locate Krepkit."

"This is all surfing on molasses to me," Sunrise muttered, leaning back, preparing to shove another biscuit down his throat.

"I'll try to be clearer," Satchmoz promised. "Simply put, because of Nasty's magic, time moved much slower inside her castle than in the outside world. We were only there an hour or two, but meanwhile the war with Antharia was fought and won."

Esmerelda looked as if she'd been stung. Her cup clattered down upon her saucer. "Then how long was I asleep?" she asked with a plaintive quaver in her voice. The look in her eye betrayed genuine fear.

Satchmoz bit his lower lip thoughtfully. "I'm not sure," he answered. "Who was Quendor's ruler in your day?"

"*In my day?*" Esmerelda exclaimed, looking more and more frightened as the shock of her situation began to hit her. "That makes me sound like an old woman!" She reached for her cup, then put it down again and began to wring her hands. "Kwisko," she answered finally. "Kwisko was king."

Satchmoz steepled his index fingers and tapped the tips together. "Ah, yes," he said quietly, watching Esmerelda. "Kwisko was Entharion's great-great-grandson. Now, you've awakened in the Year of the Quendoran Age six hundred and sixty."

Caspar nearly dropped his teacup. "But that means . . . !"

". . . she's been asleep . . ." Sunrise shouted, spewing crumbs.

"Almost five hundred years," the wizard affirmed, nodding.

Sunrise half-rose out of his chair and leaned across the table to stare at Esmerelda. "You really *are* an old woman!" he teased.

Esmerelda burst into tears, and the room filled with the sound of her weeping as she buried her face in her hands. Caspar went around the table at once and tried to console her, but it was no use. Esmerelda shrugged him off, determined to cry as long and pitifully as possible.

The men looked at each other helplessly. It was Burble who finally shut her up. The brogmoid waddled around to Esmerelda's side, curled up his fist and gave her a good shot in the arm. It was just enough to startle her out of her mood, and she looked up in disbelief..

"Knock it off, skirt!" the brogmoid scolded. "You're frightenin' Krepkit's plants. And you hit another note like that last wail, an' you'll bring this whole froggin' crystal room down!"

Sunrise nudged Caspar in the ribs. "I like this side of Burble," he confessed in a gleeful whisper.

"You hit me!" Esmerelda rubbed the spot on her arm, unable to believe someone had so mistreated her. She still wore a confused look, though. "Frightening the plants?"

"They got feelin's too," Burble answered roughly, folding his arms across his yellow *I love Borphee* sweater.

"WHO CARES?" Esmerelda shrieked, slamming her hands down on the table so hard all their cups and saucers shook. She leaped to her feet, nearly knocking her chair over as she rushed from the chamber.

"Leave her alone," Satchmoz called to Caspar when he started after her. "She needs time to herself right now."

"Seems to me she's had plenty of time to herself," Sunrise quipped, picking up another biscuit from the rapidly diminishing pile on the plate.

Caspar turned to Satchmoz. "He shouldn't have hit her!" he said petulantly.

It was Burble's turn to look stung. His eyes welled up with big tears. Immediately, he was a three-year-old child again. "Burble do wrong?" he asked as tears poured down his pale blue cheeks. He flung himself down on the floor and hugged Caspar's feet. "Sorry!" he wept. Then he paused long enough to glance up and over his shoulder, as if to see that he wasn't disturbing the plants. When he was sure of that, he cried again, "Burble so sorry!"

"Get up, Burble," Satchmoz said gently, and the brogmoid rose and went to the wizard's side. Satchmoz put one arm around the little fellow's waist and drew him close while he ruffled the pink mohawk with his other hand. "It's not his fault," he explained patiently to Caspar. "There are no females in our guild, and Burble's lived most of his life here. He doesn't know how to behave around them."

Sunrise joined in. "Yeah, ease off, Caspar. She'll survive one punch in the arm." He picked up his teacup, took a quick sip, and set it down again. "Didn't you see that shot she gave that guy in the woods?" he continued, curling a fist and executing a low, slow-motion punch. "Right in the old fellow, if you take my meaning. Despite her teary little performance, Esmerelda's no wilting dragondil."

"I think you're being too hard on her," Caspar snapped.

Sunrise picked up his tea again and met Caspar's cold gaze fearlessly. "I think you'd like to be."

"Stop!" Satchmoz shouted, smacking one hand loudly on the table to draw their attention. "Whoa! Wait! Topic drift!"

Caspar and Sunrise glowered at each other, but they shut up.

"Don't you even want to know about the war?" Satchmoz asked weakly with more than just a hint of exasperation.

Sunrise sat back sullenly. Caspar frowned and began to pace back and forth. Satchmoz let go a long sigh.

"Well, our navy lost the first engagement," he reported wearily. "But apparently, that was planned from the beginning. That's why the galleys carried only the weakest enchanters, like myself. It was all a colossal trick to make the Antharians overconfident and lure them away from their fortresslike island."

Neither Caspar nor Sunrise said anything when he paused, so he let go of Burble and reached for his cup of vanilla tea. "It worked, too. The Antharians chased the remnants of that first force all the way back to Fort Griffspotter. How could they have known the cream of Quendor's fleet and our best wizards were waiting for them there?" He shook his head even as he smiled at the genius of it. "It was hardly a fight. Antharia lost every single ship."

"How did you learn of all this?" Caspar asked without ceasing his pacing.

"Through my infotater," Satchmoz answered. "It's all recorded somewhere in the library."

"That's what you were working on when I came down this morning?"

Again, Satchmoz shook his head. "No. I was writing down the elements of Nasty's spatial shift spell," he informed them, brightening. "The *slow time* spell is beyond me, but the shift, that I've figured out. I need to finish a master copy for the library though, then one to go into my cloak." He put on a big smile suddenly. "I'm going to call it *Satchmoz!*" he said. "My first discovery."

Sunrise made clucking noises. "I thought you said it was Nasty's spell?"

"You," Satchmoz said, pointing a finger, "can be a poop."

"What about that shaking a while ago?" Caspar asked, interrupting again. There was an irritated quality to his voice, and a frown seemed to have permanently etched itself into his features. "You said something about a tunneling company."

Satchmoz leaned back again as Burble picked up the

teapot and commenced to refilling cups. Caspar simply waved the brogmoid away, wanting nothing more to drink.

"The Frobozz Magic Tunneling Company," Satchmoz answered. "In Antharia, Duncanthrax learned of vast tunnels honeycombing parts of the island where various supplies were stored and weapons hoarded." The wizard rolled his eyes suddenly and made a silly face. "Well, from this our fat, red-headed boy decided he could make his own empire larger still by building such a network right here in Quendor, and thanks to the magic of the tunneling company, he's making swift progress. Several tunnels are already complete, reaching as far south as Mithicus, as far north as the wilds of Thriff, and all the way to the Gray Mountains in the west. And he's planning more tunnels."

"The route of one of them goes right under this guild hall," Sunrise guessed.

"He must be mad," Caspar muttered, clenching a fist.

"It goes with the crown," Satchmoz sighed.

"Well, there's something I don't understand," Sunrise said, reaching for the last honeyed biscuit and breaking it carefully in half. "You said Duncanthrax was holding somebody named Berknip hostage to force your guild to help win his war." He raised half a biscuit to his lips, but refrained from taking a bite as he regarded Caspar and Satchmoz. "All right," he continued. "The war's over. Where's Berknip? And for that matter, where's your guild?"

Satchmoz let go another long sigh and tapped his fingers together once more. "I'm afraid, my young friend, that's what I still have to find out."

CHAPTER SEVENTEEN
A STROLL THROUGH TOWN

CASPAR PACED BACK AND forth in his room while Sunrise, stretched on Caspar's bed, stroked a purring Meezel and gave an occasional loud sneeze. Esmerelda had not come out of her room all day, nor did she answer knocks at her door. Satchmoz had locked himself in the library. His search for Berknip and the missing wizards, it seemed, would be a solitary, magical one. The colored light of the infotater could be seen whirling and shifting under the sealed doors.

Burble had served a hot dinner to Caspar and Sunrise, but there had been no sign of the brogmoid, either, since he cleared away the dishes.

Caspar stopped suddenly and stared at Sunrise. The youth looked up at him with a strangely amused expression as he patted the cat between the ears.

"Well?" Sunrise said, cocking one eyebrow the way Caspar often did. "Are you ready to go?"

Am I that obvious? Caspar wondered, caught off guard by Sunrise's question. *Of course I am. I've been pacing for the past hour.* "Damn right!" Caspar snapped, going to the wardrobe and whipping out a thin black cloak he'd already picked out. He grabbed his short sword from the corner where he'd leaned it earlier and strapped that on, too. "Let Satchmoz work his magic, if he can," he said to Sunrise as the boy pushed Meezel to the floor and stood up. "Let's see if we can learn something in the streets."

"Be right back," Sunrise said. He exited the room and returned a moment later wearing his dagger. The makeshift purse full of coins also dangled from one hand.

He tucked it down into his trousers and grinned. "I was getting a little edgy, myself," he confessed.

Caspar went to the window and peered out. The towers of the city were silhouetted against a sky streaked with purple and iodine. The sun had already gone down. Soon, its last light would be gone. A warm breeze brushed against his face.

"Should we leave a note?" Sunrise called.

Caspar shrugged. "Leave one if you want."

"Not me," Sunrise answered. "I can't write."

"What a shame," Caspar said with mock surprise. He patted his pockets. "And I left my pen and paper at home." He moved away from the window and gestured toward the hallway. "Let's go."

They walked quietly side by side down the steps to the entrance hall. No sound came from anywhere in the guild hall. All the lamps had been lit, though, so Burble had to be around somewhere. Caspar crept to the doors of the library and put his ear against the polished wood. He heard nothing within, nor did the infotater's glow shine under the door's edge.

"I think Satchmoz is gone," he told Sunrise, keeping his voice low.

Sunrise pursed his lips thoughtfully. "Maybe we should wait, then," he answered in a whisper. "He may have found some clue."

They looked at each other. Almost at the same time they shook their heads. "Nah," they both agreed.

They soft-padded to the main door, but when Caspar reached out and touched the doorknob, a pair of eyes that shouldn't have been there suddenly snapped open on the smooth surface and winked at him. An instant later, a pair of thick, red lips took form and spoke to them. Its words had a strange, catchy rhythm.

"Hey jack, you bad, you cool, I know!
But the Man, he say not to let you go!
Go back to bed, that where it's at,
An' he'll clue you in when he gets back!"

Sunrise was tapping his foot and clapping his hands to the beat of the snappy patter. Caspar shook his head and regarded the strange, magical face. "A rap at the door?" he said in disbelief.

The door frowned at him and gave answer.

> *"Hey, be you deaf? I'll say it again,*
> *Go back upstairs, back where you been.*
> *I'm a bad-ass door, don't mess with me!*
> *Don't mess with me! Don't mess with me!"*

Caspar felt the heat rising in his cheeks. He'd never been threatened by a door before, and he didn't take very kindly to the idea. He set his hands stubbornly on his hips. "Did Satchmoz tell you to keep us here?" he demanded.

A big smile spread across the door's surface. "Tha's a fac', Jack!"

Caspar grew redder. "And what's going to happen if I just reach out and grab that knob?"

The door gave a low chuckle. "Well, fo' one thing," it answered, still grinning, "Ah'm goin' to get real turned on!"

Sunrise nudged Caspar in the ribs. "I can't believe you're standing here taking lip from a piece of wood," he said, sporting his own grin. "This is ruining my image of you."

"What do you want me to do?" Caspar said, exasperated. "Punch a door in the mouth? I'd probably break my knuckles!"

"Oh, go ahead!" Sunrise insisted. "Give it a cheap thrill. Just turn the knob, and let's go!"

Caspar didn't need more urging. His fingers closed around the knob, and he started to turn it. A sudden, sharp shout made him let go and leap back.

"*Whooaaaah!*" the door sang out.

> *"Sweet babeee! You make me feel so good!*
> *Ah say, you make me feeeelll so good!"*

Caspar shoved a finger in his ear and wiggled it around, trying to make the ringing stop. But Sunrise made a face and ripped the cloak from Caspar's back. "Oh, put a sock in it!" he shouted back. With that, he thrust the wadded cloak straight into the arcane mouth.

The eyes in the door widened with surprise, then crossed as it tried to look down at the gag. It made a few pathetic, muffled grunts and blurbs, then turned a hurt, mournful gaze on the two of them. A moment later, the strange face faded entirely, leaving only a piece of black cloth hanging mysteriously out of the wood itself.

Sunrise grabbed the doorknob, twisted, and jerked the door open. "You just can't let a door give you shit," he explained to Caspar. "They won't respect you if you do."

"Thanks," Caspar muttered, still wondering if he'd lost some hearing. "I'll remember that the next time I run into a door."

They stepped outside and ran across a tiled courtyard, around a tinkling fountain, between two soaring topiaries and up to a pair of stout doors set into a protective wall. Caspar reached out to grab a heavy iron ring and tug one of the doors open. Then, he hesitated and looked at Sunrise.

Sunrise shook his head. "He wouldn't dare," he said.

Caspar gave a doubtful look from the corner of his eye. "It's Satchmoz we're talking about," he reminded.

Sunrise still shook his head. "He thinks we're good boys," he stated with a knowing, mischievous gleam. "He'll think we're back in our rooms where the door told us we should be."

Caspar chewed his lip. "You're right," he said at last. "I've got to break him of that 'boy' business, though."

"Me, too," Sunrise agreed.

Caspar scoffed as he grabbed the ring and pulled the huge old door inward. "But you *are* a boy," he answered, huffing.

Sunrise stepped out into the lane beyond the gate. "You really know how to hurt a guy," he muttered.

"That's right," Caspar affirmed as he pulled the gate closed again. "I learned from some scrawny little whip-master on a ship I once sailed on."

Sunrise's eyes widened, and his jaw dropped. Caspar smiled to himself with wicked satisfaction and did a little quick dance step to avoid the kick his young friend aimed at his rump.

The streets of Borphee were surprisingly quiet, considering that the hour was only a little after sundown. The wind whistled down the lane, stirring dust. Gone were the purple and iodine streaks; the sky was dark, and so were the streets they wandered.

"Do you know where we are?" Caspar whispered uneasily to Sunrise.

Sunrise had lived in Borphee all his life. "The guild-hall is on the southern end of the harbor," he explained. "I lived on the east side. I think I can get around, though."

"We should have brought lanterns," Caspar said, drawing no response from his young friend.

Dark warehouses rose up on either side of them as they turned down a different road. An old boat with a hole smashed through its bottom stood upside-down on sawhorses. A block and tackle creaked and swayed in the black maw of an open doorway. The smell of paint and varnish came to them, mingled with the salty odor of the sea.

They turned another corner and walked out into a much wider street. The warehouses became small shops, and the smell of paint and varnish gave way to the more potent stink of fish and to the buzzing of flies.

"The fish market," Sunrise whispered needlessly. He pointed to his right. "Another block that way, the wharves."

Caspar turned right at the first opportunity and hurried down a short, darkened road to emerge at the edge of a breathtaking sight. He froze in his tracks and clapped one hand to his gaping mouth. His heart quickened.

The air hummed with the sounds of the wind in the guy wires and rigging, and the timbers of mighty ships sighed and moaned as they rode the gently rocking waves. Scores of tall masts rose against the dark sky, painted silvery by a bright moon that hung low over the water. Farther out in the bay another score of ships were anchored in deeper water. Here and there, dim lamplight shone through a few portals, and here and there, a watchman, lantern in hand, walked his watch around a deck. In the far distance, a sailor's hornpipe played merrily.

"This is how I imagined it," Caspar said in a soft voice to Sunrise. "In all my dreams all those nights in Djabuti Padjama, this is how I knew it would be."

"What are you muttering about?" Sunrise asked with a puzzled expression.

Caspar smiled quietly to himself. Sunrise didn't understand. He'd lived here all his life, so maybe he didn't see the beauty Caspar saw. It was easy to take things for granted when they were part of your everyday existence.

"Look at the moon," Caspar urged his friend. It hovered at the edge of the ocean, casting a wide, glittering trail of light that set fire to the cresting waves, big and shining as a new zorkmid.

"I forgot you were a tourist," Sunrise said with a teasing lilt. "But, yeah, there's nothing like a full moon on the ocean."

"I'll make a romantic of you yet," Caspar promised, clapping Sunrise on the shoulder.

Among the great ships were moored hundreds of smaller fishing vessels and pleasure craft. The strangely muffled voices of a few late workers could be heard. In faint lamplight, Caspar spied a pair of burly fishermen folding nets in the bow of a small boat. He paused to watch, mesmerized. To him, fishing had always been a pole, a line, a creek, and a long boring wait.

Abruptly, they came to a street where lamps had been hung from high posts at corners of each block. It led away from the wharves toward the heart of the city. Sunrise insisted they go that way, and Caspar reluctantly agreed. He noticed, however, that Sunrise put one hand on the purse at his belt and kept it there.

"Where are we going?" he asked cautiously as the street began to wind back and forth among a lot of old dark buildings.

"This road's called The Serpent's Back," Sunrise explained. "Lots of bars and restaurants and gambling houses coming up as soon as we're out of the warehouse district. All the fishermen, dock workers, and sailors hang out there. We should be able to pick up some news."

Faintly, the strains of music drifted out of the night. An instant later, they turned a corner, and the last of the dark warehouses was behind them. On either side of the street stood a pair of two-story brick buildings. A sharp whistle blew, and scantily clad ladies lounging in the windows suddenly spied them and came to life.

"Hello, sailors!" shouted several at the same time.

Caspar's eyes widened as one young girl leaned out over the sill of her window and ripped open the front of her blouse. The peals of her laughter rang in his ears.

"Hey, there, cutie!" shouted an older woman, pointing at Caspar. "How tall are you?"

Caspar stuttered an answer. "Five feet, ten inches, ma'am."

She patted her hair into place with one hand, and planted the other suggestively on her hip. "Well, forget the five feet, and let's talk about ten inches!"

"What's she mean by that?" Caspar whispered as he leaned over to Sunrise. "I don't think these are gambling houses."

Sunrise, at home in the streets, his element, answered. "Considering what you could get from those ladies, I'd call it a gamble."

"What are you talking about?" Caspar asked, putting on a nervous frown.

Sunrise looked at him curiously. "You really don't know, do you?" he said with a hint of amusement. "What do they do in Djabuti Padjama for fun?"

Caspar smirked. "They don't believe in fun in Dja-buti Padjama."

"It figures," Sunrise answered. He nodded toward another pair of ladies who called down to them. "Suffice it to say, you can have a good time with them for an hour or two, and three days later your ears fall off."

"My ears?" Caspar muttered, putting a hand to the side of his head. "Uncle told me I'd just go blind."

Sunrise let go a small sigh, took Caspar's elbow and steered him quickly up the street. Nevertheless, ever the gentleman, Caspar managed to smile and wave back over his shoulder, and the ladies on both sides of the street laughed and broke into applause.

A few paces later, though, Sunrise stopped, a look of surprise on his face. Caspar followed the boy's gaze to a door and a sign above it that said *The Blue Whale*. Whatever it was, bar or restaurant, it was plainly closed.

"I know the owner," Sunrise exclaimed quietly. "Barnabas never closes. Especially not at night. *The Blue Whale* is the most popular bar in Borphee."

Perhaps because of the note of distress in Sunrise's voice, Caspar became uneasy. He peered into the dark shadows that surrounded them, suddenly aware of the inadequacy of the street lighting. "I don't mean to alarm you," he said, finding himself whispering once more, "but it looks to me like everything around here is closed."

"Yeah," Sunrise murmured as he went to *The Blue Whale*'s door and tried it unsuccessfully. He turned back to Caspar. "And we're the only ones on the street, too. That shouldn't be. This is the party-place of Borphee."

"I thought we passed the party-place of Borphee," Caspar said with a nervous grin. Back down the street he could still see the brothels. The girls had gone back to lounging and fanning themselves disinterestedly in their windows.

"Something's up, Caspar," Sunrise said in a hushed tone. "Maybe we should head back to the guildhall."

Before Caspar could answer, a patrol of six soldiers came tramping down the east end of the street. Spying the two, one of the soldiers pointed and cried out. "Halt! You're in violation of the King's curfew!"

Caspar and Sunrise shot brief glances at each other. "Shove it up your nose, chicken-porker!" Sunrise shouted before the squad could reach them. Then, they both turned and ran.

"Catch 'em, men!" they heard the soldier order his patrol. "They're galley fodder!"

"Not again," Caspar swore under his breath and he pumped his arms and legs. To Sunrise, "I hope you know this part of town better than they do."

"Trust me," Sunrise answered between gasps. "And make sure you keep up."

The girls in the brothel windows heard the sounds of running feet and shouting. Immediately they went into their routines. One lady removed a silver-sequined bra, dangled it, and waved it like a race flag as Caspar and Sunrise sped by. "The winner!" she screamed at the top of her lungs, and all the ladies laughed. A chorus of boos and catcalls followed as the soldiers gave chase.

Sunrise turned unexpectedly up an alley. Caspar nearly stumbled as he cut to the right, hard on the boy's heels. Up through the old warehouses they rushed.

"Hey, you run all right for a farmboy," Sunrise laughed.

"My uncle raised bulls," Caspar answered between breaths. "When I was little he liked to dress me in red."

A pair of soldiers appeared suddenly at the end of the alley, blocking it. The moon was high enough over the city that its light glinted on the drawn swords they carried. One of the soldiers grinned and tapped his blade on his palm. "Nyah, nyah, nyah," he said with a clever smirk.

"Screw you, too!" Sunrise muttered. He brushed Caspar's sleeve. Caspar made an obscene gesture, and the two of them dived through the open doorway of the warehouse on their left. Almost at once, Caspar slammed into something and felt the breath go out of him with a *whoof* as he hit the ground on his back.

"Get up!" Sunrise hissed, tugging at the front of his

tunic. In a near panic, Caspar managed to get to his feet. In the faint moonlight that shone through an upper window, he saw the wagon he had run into. Sunrise was already straining at the hitch, pushing it across the entrance. In the dark, the soldiers wouldn't see it in time to avoid it, either.

"Come on!" Sunrise urged as he wiped his hands on his chest. They were off again. A pair of stunned cries sounded right behind them as the soldiers crashed into the wagon. Sunrise gave a low chuckle. There was no sign of a door on the far side, but a trace of moonlight filtered in through a shuttered window. Caspar gave it a kick. Sunrise dived headfirst through the opening and rolled to his feet outside. "Oh, oh," he warned, staring to his left as Caspar climbed out.

Another pair of soldiers raced up the street toward them, ordering them to halt. Sunrise and Caspar took off, turning up yet another alley between old warehouses. A rain barrel half full of water stood at the corner. "Help me!" Sunrise whispered urgently to Caspar. Together, they tilted it, and the contents sloshed out into the dusty street. They left the barrel lying there, too.

An instant later, the soldiers turned the corner. "Awwwp!" cried one as he slipped in the suddenly muddy street. Unable to turn in time, he smashed into the opposite wall. "Accckkk!" shouted the other as his knee hit the barrel. He went tumbling head over heels.

Caspar laughed to himself as they watched from a shadowed nook on the next street, and he reached out and rumpled Sunrise's hair. They ran down another pair of streets, and paused behind a pile of crates. They were almost to the wharves, but Sunrise seemed reluctant to go farther. "Too open," he whispered.

They waited for long tense minutes. Moonlight filled the street before them, and they had a good clear view, but there was no further sign of the soldiers.

"That was fun," Sunrise said at last in an easier voice. "What now?"

Caspar raised an eyebrow as he regarded the youth. "My heart's hammering like a crazy blacksmith," he muttered, putting a hand under his tunic and fluttering the material.

Sunrise grinned. "Exercise is good for the heart."

"Not that kind!" Caspar said with a shake of the head.

They grew quiet again, watchful. The street remained empty. The only sounds were the rustle of the wind and their own breathing. Caspar wiped sweat from his face. Finally, when his legs began to cramp, he stood up.

"Borphee's under curfew," Sunrise whispered, rising beside him. "There's never been a curfew in Borphee."

"Duncanthrax's doing," Caspar pointed out. He folded his arms, leaned on one of the crates, and looked thoughtful. It was easy to call up a memory of the fat, red-headed little tyrant. He hadn't forgotten his first meeting with the man. Nor had he forgotten the promise he'd made himself when the *Screaming Queen* sailed out of the harbor with him chained to an oar.

"I don't suppose you know the way to the palace from here?" he said to Sunrise.

It was Sunrise's turn to cock an eyebrow. "Are you serious?"

"Seriously insane, in all likelihood," Caspar answered calmly, "and seriously pissed off. Besides, we promised Satchmoz we'd help find out what happened to his guild brothers. What better place is there to start?"

Sunrise grinned and swallowed at the same time. "Break into the palace? You had any experience at this sort of thing?"

Caspar patted Sunrise on the shoulder. "I don't need experience," he said with a very straight face. "I've got you."

Sunrise pursed his lips. "On one condition," he said at last. "You wouldn't let me keep the hairbrush I found at Nasty's. This time, though, anything I pinch along the way is mine."

Caspar winked at him. "Back in the city and reverting to type."

Sunrise shrugged. "A guy's got to practice his trade," he answered innocently.

Caspar stood straight and stepped from behind the crates into the street. The moonlight washed over him. "You get me into the palace," he said, "and you can steal the throne itself for all I care."

"Too heavy," Sunrise answered without a pause. "The crown might make a nice bauble, though."

CHAPTER EIGHTEEN
A GUARD GETS KISSED OFF

HUGGING THE SHADOWS, they made their way to the palace. It was easy avoiding the patrols they encountered. The soldiers seemed lackadaisical about their jobs, listless at their posts, as if they neither expected trouble, nor cared if it should pass their way.

Caspar felt a sense of dismay, however, as he and Sunrise stared down at Borphee's palace from the high roof where Sunrise had brought them. A tall stone wall surrounded the grand structure, and the grounds were well lit with lanterns and torches. There were several gates visible from their vantage, but all were shut tight and guarded, and though the soldiers all seemed unenthusiastic about their duties, he doubted they would simply step aside and allow two strangers to walk in.

He rolled over on his back and stared up at the moon and the few stars visible despite its effulgence. "It's no use," he whispered to Sunrise. "We're going to need Satchmoz's help on this after all."

"Well, perhaps genius, as well as bravado, was too much to expect," Sunrise sighed as he continued to stare into the palace grounds. A patrol marched by in the street below. "You realize, of course," he continued when the street was empty again, "you've let me down."

"I did have one idea," Caspar admitted.

Sunrise lifted himself on one elbow and met Caspar's gaze. "What was that?" he said hopefully.

"To stand you on the edge, bend you over, and drop-kick you into the palace grounds," Caspar answered without batting an eye. "And while the guards were chasing you, maybe I could sneak in through a gate."

They regarded each other for a long moment. "Nah!" they both said at the same time.

They crawled across the roof, retracing the way they had come until they reached a drainpipe on the far side of the building. After checking for patrols they shinnied down again and hurriedly crossed into an alley. Sunrise knew this part of the city well, every back street and cranny. They had no problems finding hiding places whenever they heard the march of booted feet, and soon they found themselves back at the wharves, where patrols were fewer.

Lamplight still shone dimly in the portals of a few ships, and torches still glimmered on a few distant decks. The wharves held a special magic all their own for Caspar, and he thought he could have spent the night there, listening to the water, the wind in the riggings. But there was business to attend to, and in very little time they made their way back to the gates of the enchanters' guildhall.

As they pushed open the great doors and pushed them shut again a voice called out to them. Esmerelda stood framed in the light from the entrance hall, waving.

"I was so worried!" she exclaimed stepping aside to let them enter. "I heard a rap at the door . . . !"

"Hmmm," Caspar gave the black cloak that Sunrise had ripped from his back and shoved into the magical mouth a sharp yank. It was now a permanent part of the woodwork. Permanent, at least, until Satchmoz removed it. "I guess this is a wrap at the door," he said to Sunrise.

"How did that get there?" Esmerelda demanded, obviously confused. "Where's Satchmoz? Where did you go?"

Before an answer could be given, Meezel bounced downstairs, gave a loud *mowrrrrr*, and leaped into Sunrise's arms. The boy ruffled the hair, what there was of it, on the little beast's head and gave a loud sneeze.

"I think he likes me!" Sunrise said happily.

Caspar shook his head. "He just knows you're allergic to him. Cats are like that. Perverse."

"They are not!" Esmerelda snapped, grabbing her pet and hugging it possessively.

Caspar crossed the entrance hall and went to the doors of the great library. No telltale light showed under the edge, and no voice answered when he knocked. Finally, he tried the knob. Finding it unlocked, he pushed the door open. A little moonlight leaked in through the high windows. There was no sign of Satchmoz.

"Where's Burble?" Caspar asked, turning to Esmerelda. "Is he around?"

"Oh, the brogmoid!" she answered with a nervous, yet haughty look. "I wasn't at all thrilled about being left alone with a creature like that. I mean, it's all right that he's a servant here . . ."

"Oh, grow up!" Sunrise muttered rudely. To Caspar he said, "I'll look for him." He disappeared a moment later in the direction of what Caspar thought was the kitchen.

"Why are you doing this?" Esmerelda demanded in a whining voice when they were alone.

Casper stared at her, struck by her tone and the distress on her face. "Doing what?" he said defensively.

"Helping these people!" she answered, beating her fists in frustration against her thighs. "We could get out of here right now! Just walk out!"

She was on the verge of tears, Casper saw, and a part of him wanted to reach out and hold her. She'd never go for that, though, so his arms remained limply at his sides. "Where would we go?" he asked reasonably.

Her face was full of pain as she whirled away and wrung her hands. "This is Borphee!" she insisted. "This is a big city!"

"Where would we go?" he repeated in calm sympathy.

She didn't turn back to him, but he could see her shaking. Her hands went to her eyes, and finally the tears came. He stepped up behind her then and set his hands on her shoulders. That contact sent a quiver way down in the pit of his stomach. He noticed the sweet smell of her hair for the first time.

"Sunrise and Satchmoz are my friends," he told her softly. "This is their city, and they need my help right now." His voice was a bare whisper, his mouth close to her ear. "I've never really had friends before, so I can't let them down." She leaned back against him as she wept. He gently kneaded her shoulders. "Besides," he continued, "I've got my own score to settle with Duncanthrax."

"Score?" she shrieked, pulling away from him. "I don't care if you ever score! I'm five hundred years old!" She ran wailing up the stairs. The door to her room slammed shut with a force that echoed through the guildhall.

Women, Caspar thought dejectedly. She hadn't heard a word he said. He was beginning to understand why some men went to sea voluntarily.

A soft *bamf* sounded behind him, and a puff of displaced air brushed his neck. "Thank my lucky stars," Satchmoz said as Caspar turned around. "I was half afraid you'd be in the bathtub."

"I was down on the wharves a while ago," Caspar informed him.

The wizard wasn't angry. He wiped a hand across his brow in mock relief. "I could have really been in the deep stuff," he quipped. "That's why I wanted you to stay here. So I'd know where I was coming back to when I cast the *aimfiz* spell." He took off the splendid new black cloak he was wearing and hung it on a peg near the staircase. Its pockets were bulging.

"The city's under a curfew," Caspar reported.

"I know," Satchmoz responded. "You really did go outside, then?"

Caspar nodded, and pointed sheepishly to his cloak where it merged into the woodwork of the door. "Cute spell," he complimented, "but rude. Sunrise stopped its mouth."

The wizard leaned forward to examine the seamless

way the cloth became part of the wood. "Hmmm, I may leave it there," he said, straightening. "It adds a certain conversational something."

"Something," Caspar agreed doubtfully. "You've been searching for your guild brothers?"

"What else?" the wizard answered as he led the way to the library and pushed back the doors. "I've exhausted every magical means I can think of to locate them. So I paid a brief visit to a friend who lives on the shores of the Shallow Sea."

"The Shallow Sea?" Caspar exclaimed while Satchmoz went about the business of lighting lamps. "That's on the other side of the kingdom!"

"I spent part of this afternoon preparing a bunch of *aimfiz* scrolls," the old man told him as he shook out a match and turned up the wick of the lamp on his writing desk. The room brightened. "I had a feeling they were going to come in handy." He sat down in his chair and propped his booted feet on the corner of the desk. "Rub my neck, here, will you, boy?" he said, reaching one arm over his shoulder to indicate the spot. "I'm a bit stiff."

Caspar massaged the spot, and Satchmoz gave a little sigh. "I thought maybe a more skilled enchanter would have better luck. Alas, it wasn't to be. Wherever my brothers are—Krepkit, Berknip, and the rest—either they don't want to be found, or they're sealed away by some powerful magic."

"Mind if we come in?" Sunrise called from the doorway. Without waiting for an answer, he and Burble entered the library. "Burble has a small room downstairs under the kitchen," he told Caspar. "I found him asleep."

"Sorry, Caspo!" the little brogmoid said. He rubbed his eyes sleepily, still not quite awake. "Burble didn't hear Caspo call."

"It's all right, Burble," Caspar said, rumpling the brogmoid's pink mohawk. "We just missed you, that's all."

Burble smiled suddenly, showing the full length of his three-inch fangs. "Really, Caspo?"

Caspar nodded as the brogmoid hugged his leg. He put an arm on Burble's shoulder and left it there as he turned back to Satchmoz. "It seems to me we need to get inside the palace," he said matter-of-factly.

The wizard rubbed his chin, a troubled expression darkening his face. I've considered the same thing," he confessed. "But I can't think of a safe way to manage it. There's no good way to get through that many guards."

"We know," Caspar said. He gestured to Sunrise. "We scouted out the palace earlier.

The wizard tried to hide a worried expression. "I knew my warning wouldn't stop you if you really wanted to go out," he said. "I'm just glad nothing bad came of it."

"But I did come up with an idea," Caspar said. "It depends on you, though. Your magic can get us inside the palace."

Satchmoz took his feet down from his desk and sat up straighter. "How?" he said. "I don't know anybody in the palace."

"I do," Caspar said, pacing to the far side of the desk and holding his hand over the lamp's small flame. The skin glowed redly in the light; the bones of his fingers showed through. "I've met Duncanthrax."

Satchmoz leaped to his feet with a speed that belied his age. "Are you out of your mind?" he shrieked.

"Can I answer?" Sunrise said, holding up a hand.

"No!" Satchmoz shouted.

Sunrise grinned and folded his arms over his chest. "No, I can't answer, or no, you won't send him?"

"There's no other way!" Caspar shouted. They were all shouting now, except for Burble who clung to Caspar's leg as if he were afraid he'd get blown away in a storm. "We need someone on the inside. I'm the only one who's seen anybody in the palace up close and personal. You get me in, and I'll learn as much as I can and get out."

"Or better yet," Sunrise said, getting interested in

the plan, "send me with him. Two can learn twice as much as one."

"You still don't understand *aimfiz!*" Satchmoz shouted as he paced around the room. "The spell will put you right by Duncanthrax's side. He's bound to see you. You'll be in his dungeon faster than you can say, 'Hello, there!'"

Another voice spoke from the library doorway. "I swear, men are so stupid."

They all turned toward Esmerelda. All three swallowed as she strode into the room. She'd changed clothes. Her garments were all black silk. Her trousers clung to every curve of her body, and her lace-up tunic was unlaced to reveal the ample flesh of her bosom. She'd found a pair of sturdy boots in someone's closet. She wore the dagger she'd taken from Caspar, and in the top of each boot she'd shoved another knife, possibly taken from the kitchen. She looked—startlingly different.

Esmerelda marched into the library and took Satchmoz's chair at the desk. "This is the way we're going to do it," she said in a voice that brooked no argument. "And it's going to take all of us." She shot a glance at Burble. "Even you, you little brogmoid, you."

The brogmoid bristled at her tone and immediately let go of Caspar's leg. He straightened his back and glared at her. "Don't worry, skirt," he snapped, clacking his fangs. "I'll do my part."

"Wow, she is so butch!" Sunrise whispered to Caspar.

Esmerelda ignored the comment. She looked at each of them. "You almost had it right, wizard, when you said Caspar would wind up in the dungeon. Well, that's just where we want him."

"He loves you, too . . ." Sunrise managed to get that much out before Caspar clapped a hand over his mouth.

Satchmoz shook his head. "We appreciate your advice," he said, trying to keep his calm, "but don't you think you should leave this to . . ."

"To amateurs?" Esmerelda threw her feet up on the wizard's desk as she leaned back in the chair and openly scoffed. "I've had more experience sneaking in and out of castles than any of you gentlemen. Even Nasty doesn't know how many times I came and went right under her nose. Why do you think she finally resorted to enchantment?" She shook her long hair back and folded her hands behind her head. "It was the only way she could keep me home."

"I'm listening," Caspar told her earnestly. He let go of Sunrise, but warned his young friend with a wagging finger to keep quiet. "Tell us your plan."

"You get arrested," she explained. "Tonight. It's best if we do this at night, and the sooner the better. So let's do it tonight."

"All right," Caspar agreed. "What then?"

"Are you out of your mind?" Satchmoz shouted again.

Caspar ignored him. "What then?" he repeated.

"You get arrested," Esmerelda continued calmly. "Right outside the palace gate. That way, they'll be sure to put you in the palace dungeon because it'll be close. We'll be watching from nearby. Once you're in, the wizard will cast *aimfiz*, transporting us all right to you." She looked at the brogmoid. "Except for you, Burble."

A loud *mowrrrr* interrupted her. Meezel jumped up into her lap, and she stroked the cat idly.

"Sounds like a great plan," Sunrise muttered in disgust. "That'll get us all inside, all right. Inside whatever cell they throw Caspar into."

Esmerelda faked a yawn and tapped her fingers over her mouth. "I assume our mighty wizard here has some spell that could spring a simple thing like a lock."

"*Rezrov*," Satchmoz said. He was beginning to listen, though he plainly didn't like Esmerelda's plan much.

"Whatever," Esmerelda answered with a nonchalant wave. "You just get us in and get the cell door open. Then you wait in the cell for us to return. If we learn anything important we come right back to you, knowing precisely where you'll be. Burble, here, provides the final link. He'll be right here, so *aimfiz* can bring us home."

"Don't you dare take a bath," the wizard warned the brogmoid.

"If a guard comes by the cell . . ." Caspar said quietly, considering the details as he rubbed his chin.

"The guard won't sound the *escaped prisoner* alarm," Esmerelda pointed out, "because the cell won't be empty. He'll see Satchmoz curled up asleep and think it's you. And because we're doing this at night the guards will be a little more relaxed anyway."

Sunrise pursed his lips and nodded appreciatively. "It's really not bad!" he said. "I can't believe she thought of it."

Esmerelda stuck out her tongue.

"I don't know," Satchmoz said, shaking his head worriedly. He walked to a shelf of scrolls and ran a finger over the rolled ends of the dry parchments in their individual nooks. "I feel like I'm getting you all into something I shouldn't."

"Nonsense!" Caspar answered, going to the old man's side. "Duncanthrax has to be stopped. He kidnapped Berknip and forced you enchanters to do his will. That's tyranny. He enslaved Sunrise and me, and lots of other men, too, and chained us to galley oars to fight his war. More tyranny! When was the last time Quendor ever knew war? Now, Borphee's under curfew, and he's building underground highways to carry his tyranny to all of Quendor's seven provinces." He put a hand out and forced Satchmoz to look at him. "We owe it to Quendor to do what we can to oppose this madman!"

"Besides!" Sunrise exclaimed, "why do you think Caspar came all this way from Djabuti Padjama?"

Esmerelda twisted around in her chair and nearly fell over. Meezel gave a startled growl as he jumped clear. "Whose pajamas?" she said.

Sunrise ignored her as he bent down to pick up the cat. "Why, for adventure! This is it!" He barked two rapid-fire sneezes.

Burble, still in his tough-guy persona, stepped up and slammed his hand down on the desk. "I want a bigger part!" he demanded.

"You've got the most important part," Sunrise answered. "Without you here, there's no way to haul our fat out of the fire."

"Let's do it," Caspar urged.

Satchmoz reached out and touched a scroll, and though he picked it up, he didn't quite withdraw it from its resting place. His hand trembled, and the parchment rattled against the wood shelving. "We might not accomplish anything," he whispered uneasily, "except getting caught."

"We might find your fellow wizards," Caspar answered gently.

Slowly, Satchmoz pulled down the scroll, then several more, and carried them to the desk. "Give me a few moments," he said. "We'll meet in the hallway."

Each of them looked at each other, then Esmerelda got up and left the library. Sunrise followed her with Meezel in his arms. Then Burble waddled out, his shoulders sloped dejectedly in disappointment with his role. Caspar patted Satchmoz once more on the shoulder before he, too, left. He closed the library doors as he went out.

Esmerelda pushed her knives deeper into her boots. Caspar and Sunrise were already wearing the weapons they had taken with them on their first outing. Burble paced back and forth. After another sneeze, Sunrise let Meezel down, but the cat continued to purr and rub against his legs.

A few moments later, Satchmoz emerged from the library with a small backpack, which he slung over his shoulders. He went straight to the peg where his wizard's cloak hung and threw that on as well. "I don't much like it," he said as he joined them. "But let's get on with it."

"You know, I kind of miss the talking door," Sunrise confessed as they filed out into the night.

Burble stood in the doorway sniffing, once more the three-year-old. "Goodbye!" he said in a weak, weepy voice as he waved after them. "Goodbye! Goodbye!"

"Remember," Satchmoz called sternly over his shoulder. "No bath!"

Caspar leaned down to Sunrise. "I can hear the sound of running water already," he whispered light-heartedly. He didn't really feel light-hearted, though. He was thinking about what he would do to get himself arrested. He was thinking about the dungeon. He was thinking about Duncanthrax.

Sunrise soon began to lead the way. He knew the city best by night. They avoided the wharves this time. Now that they knew about patrols they stayed strictly to the dark alleys and back streets. It wouldn't do to get arrested before they reached the palace. If that happened the soldiers might decide to haul them to the prison on the south end of town.

Caspar wondered at the hour. The moon still lit the streets in places, but it had slid farther into the western sky. He marveled that the streets were so empty. Borphee was such a large city. Surely there should be a certain number of street people, poor folks who lived and slept in alleys and doorways and such. Then he remembered such people were almost certainly conscripted into Duncanthrax's navy.

For all its size, Borphee was as silent as any field in the Peltoid Valley. He found that oddly disturbing.

Sunrise led them to a secluded park near the palace's main gate. Crouched behind heavy foliage, they stared at the four soldiers on duty there. The men had leaned their lances against the gate. Two of them leaned on it, themselves, while the other two sat in the dirt with their backs against it. They were swapping some tale and laughing. Their muffled voices carried into the park.

Sunrise gave a sudden sneeze, then clapped a hand over his nose before he could repeat it. "Meezel!" he hissed as the cat rubbed up against him. "He followed us!"

Esmerelda picked her pet up and gave him a quiet shake. "Bad cat!" he whispered. "Bad cat!"

"Get him out of my face!" Sunrise warned, desperately trying to stifle another sneeze. It was no use. The sound was like an explosion in the stillness.

Caspar leaped to his feet without a word and darted toward the gate. Alerted by the sneeze, the soldiers saw him at once and grabbed their lances. Caspar slowed to a walk, then pretended to stagger drunkenly.

"Come on out, Kingsy-babe!" he shouted at the top of his lungs. He drew his sword and waved it about in the air. "Gonna give yer tonsils a l'il haircut, yessiree!" He took another step, overbalanced on one foot, and hung awkwardly in the air for an instant. It appeared almost a miracle when he recovered without falling on his face. He did drop his sword, however. Staring at it as it lay in the road, he clappped both hands to his cheeks and sputtered.

The soldiers surrounded him at once. "Oh, lookie!" Caspar cried. "It's the kingsie-babe's babies!" He ran one hand down the front of the nearest soldier's tunic. "Gee, I just love red!"

"Pipe down!" one of the soldiers warned him.

"He's drunk," commented another.

A third soldier grabbed Caspar by the shoulders and tried to straighten him up. "Come on, buddy," he said in a friendly enough voice. "Nobody else has seen you yet. You quiet down and go on home."

"He's violatin' curfew!" charged the fourth soldier. "We got to bust 'im!"

"Oh, let him go," urged the third. "He's harmless enough. Just confiscate that sword and send him on his way. Who's to know we gave some sucker a break? It's a nice night."

"Harmless, am I?" Caspar shrieked, still maintaining his act. He drew back and took a lazy swing at his would-be benefactor. The soldier slipped the punch easily, but as Caspar let the blow's momentum spin him crazily around, he found himself in the man's arms. "Thank you, kind sir!" Caspar said. Then he gave a big wink and kissed the man squarely on the lips.

"Aaacccckkk!" The soldier cried, pushing Caspar

away and frantically wiping his mouth. "Take him away!" he shouted to his comrades. "Lock him up! Aaaccckkk! Ugh! Get me a mouthwash!"

Caspar smiled as he felt hands seize him.

CHAPTER NINETEEN

BREAKING AND ENTERING

CASPAR SAT WITH HIS back against the cool stone wall of his cell. A faint trickle of light from a dim lamp somewhere down the corridor somehow squeezed through the three bars in the narrow window of his cell door. There was nothing to see, though, so he rested and waited. The straw scattered about the floor smelled as dank and foul as he remembered. Loud snores issued from the next cell, and somewhere farther down the hall some poor prisoner wept and muttered to himself.

At least Olio, the large unpleasant jailer he had met his first time here, hadn't been on duty when the guards brought him in. He had no desire to meet that bug-loving giant again.

What was keeping his friends?

He grabbed up a single straw and began breaking it into minute pieces and tossing them across the cell. He found himself thinking of Djabuti Padjama and Thyrsobel. It was easy to admit to himself that, though there was nothing else he missed about his home town, he missed her friendship. He wondered how she was making out. Were she and her children getting enough to eat? Had he made her life harder with the disastrous prank he played on Jelboz Stumpbiter?

He chewed his lip and closed his eyes. No point in asking such questions now.

A soft *bamf* and a puff of displaced air on his face told him his friends had finally arrived. "What took you so long?" Caspar whispered, rising to his feet. He noticed that Esmerelda went at once to the opposite side of the cell. She had that damned cat in her arms!

"Would you listen to his tone!" Sunrise exclaimed to Satchmoz with melodramatic flare, though he was careful to keep his voice low. He turned back to Caspar. "Just how often do you have friends over to a dump like this?"

"Esmerelda thought there was some chance you might be, um, interrogated," Satchmoz explained apologetically as he unslung the backpack he wore under his cloak. "She thought it best to wait a bit, rather than pop up suddenly in the middle of a bunch of guards and their, um, interrogation."

"Interrogation?" Caspar said, glowering at Esmerelda. "Don't you mean torture? You thought they might torture me?"

Esmerelda waved a hand. "Whatever," she answered.

Caspar braced his hands on his hips, his heart hovering somewhere between sublime amusement and genuine anger. "So you *waited* until you figured they were through?"

"Hey," Sunrise said, attempting to mollify Caspar. "You know how she hates to interrupt."

"Do your trick, Wizard," Esmerelda interrupted. She still thought she was calling the shots. "Let's get on with it before this stink gets in my hair."

"I'm ready," Satchmoz said, setting his pack down on the floor. "I've already memorized the *rezrov* spell. Someone better look out that window, though, and make sure nobody's coming. It makes a little light."

Caspar gave Esmerelda a final disgusted look before he went to the window and pressed his nose between the bars. As far as he could see in either direction the corridor was empty.

"Do it," Esmerelda said.

Satchmoz raised his arms, and his voluminous sleeves fell to his thin elbows. "It's showtime!" he hissed. His whole body tensed. His hands closed into tight fists, and he squeezed his eyes shut. Fingers and eyes snapped open simultaneously as a shallow gasp rasped from his throat.

Tiny lines of scarlet force appeared on the door, dividing and sub-dividing. Like thousands of eager insects those lines raced over every inch of the door until the first one made contact with the lock. Then, as if that first one had given some silent signal, the rest raced straight for it. A hazy red light began to form around the lock, growing brighter and sharper as the entire force of the spell concentrated on the mechanism.

Suddenly, Satchmoz tensed up again. "No, no!" he muttered urgently. "Easy! Not too much!"

Caspar watched Satchmoz's face screw up as the wizard fought to get control of his spell, and he took a step back, expecting the door to blow itself off the hinges, and maybe take a good part of the wall with it, too. He'd seen the rather dramatic effects of what Satchmoz called *too much presence* on enough occasions to be wary.

This time, though, there was only an audible click.

"Nearly lost it," Satchmoz said with obvious relief. But there was a smile on his face, too.

Esmerelda pushed open the door and stepped into the corridor, cat in one hand, a knife in the other. She shot a look both ways, then beckoned for them to come out. Only Satchmoz stayed behind. "Be careful!" he urged.

"They brought me in that way," Caspar said to Esmerelda and Sunrise as he pointed to the right. He pointed to the left. "That way leads up into the palace." It was also the direction of the small light, and they soon found a beaten old table with a ceramic oil lamp sitting upon it. A large ring of keys hung on a peg directly above.

"Leave it," Esmerelda ordered when Sunrise started to pick up the lamp. "We'll find light in the upstairs. Take that, and a guard will know something's up."

Mowrrrr, Meezel said agreeably.

"You stick that cat in his face, and a guard might know something's up anyway," Caspar reminded her harshly. "You should have left it in the cell with Satch-moz, if you had to bring it at all."

Esmerelda glared angrily. "Meezel is the only thing I've got that . . . !"

Sunrise brought both hands to his nose. His eyes squinted nearly shut as if he were about to sneeze. Es-merelda bit back any further comment, spun about and stalked on up the corridor. Sunrise flashed a grin and a quick wink at Caspar. He'd faked it.

Before they could follow her, a scratching sounded from the nearest cell door. "Who's out there?" a weak voice called. Sunrise and Caspar froze. No face appeared at the barred window, but the scratching came again. "Hello?"

Caspar bit his lip. "What if he tells the guard he heard us talking?"

Sunrise thought quickly, then went straight to the cell door and dealt it a sharp kick. "Shut up, in there!" he bellowed, pitching his voice as deeply as he could to sound like a guard. "Or I'll come in and break both your legs!"

It was effective enough, if a bit cruel. The occupant said nothing more, and it was unlikely he'd tell a guard what he'd overheard if he thought a guard had been speaking.

They crept up the corridor. There was no sign of Esmerelda. She hadn't waited for them. Caspar cursed. "When we find her," he whispered to Sunrise, "you can break both *her* legs."

"Don't tease me," Sunrise answered.

A familiar staircase led them to an upper level. There was a door at the top, but it was half open. Cautiously, they peeked around. This new hall was lit with regularly spaced torches that rested in sconces on the walls. Close by, a sentry sat slumped over his desk, arms spread upon a scattering of papers.

"Did she do that?" Sunrise mouthed silently, eyes wide. There was no doubt he meant Esmerelda.

A soft snore issued suddenly from the sentry. He was

only asleep. Caspar and Sunrise regarded each other, then tiptoed past the man and down to the first junction.

"Which way?" Sunrise asked.

Caspar raised both hands and pointed across his chest. The sleeping guard let go another snore. It was reminder enough of the danger. Caspar wasted no more time, but turned right.

"You think we should have searched the dungeon?" Sunrise said quietly.

Caspar led the way at a quick, but stealthy pace. There seemed to be no rooms in this particular corridor, nothing to search. "Satchmoz was pretty sure Berknip and Krepkit wouldn't be there. He didn't think any common cell could hold Krepkit."

"If he's alive," Sunrise said unpleasantly.

"I can always rely on you for an uplifting comment," Caspar answered.

They turned down still another corridor. "You act like you know where you're going," Sunrise said.

Caspar nodded. He remembered the way to the rooms Olio had taken him to. It seemed the best starting point.

He found the room easily enough. The door, however, was locked. He tried the knob and frowned. Sunrise merely wagged a finger, urged Caspar aside, and drew his thin-bladed dagger. In no time, he popped the bolt, and they were in.

"A bit dark," Sunrise observed.

Indeed, it was pitch black. Caspar tried to remember the layout of the room. Chairs, he remembered, and a table. Another room beyond. Perhaps there would be a window he could open. The moon was nearly full outside. *That way,* he thought, choosing a direction. Then with a loud crash and a despairing, "Awwwppp!" he fell over a stuffed chair, dragging it down on top of him.

Tiny stars swam in his vision. He gave a low moan. Sunrise's hand was promptly over his mouth. "Shut up!" the boy hissed in his ear. For long moments they remained perfectly still in the darkness, but if anyone heard the racket they didn't bother to investigate.

Sunrise set the chair upright again and helped Caspar to his feet. "Wait here," he instructed.

"Yeah," Caspar agreed. "Maybe this is more your line."

Sunrise slipped away, leaving Caspar to chew off a broken nail. Abruptly, though, he remembered the chandelier that hung overhead with its many candles. Carefully, he felt for the chair he'd fallen over. Then, he stood in it and reached up. His fingertip just brushed the bottom of the thing, but he couldn't reach high enough to snatch one of the candles.

"Sunrise!" he hissed, climbing down again.

His young friend gave a tug at his sleeve. *He moved that quietly!* Caspar marveled.

"If there's a window," the youth reported, "I can't find it. We're screwed in this darkness."

"I know," Caspar answered. "Get up on my shoulders, but watch your head." He crouched down and grabbed one of Sunrise's hands.

"The things I could say," Sunrise muttered as he grabbed Caspar's other hand and put one foot close to Caspar's neck.

"Well, don't say 'em!" Caspar groaned, taking all the boy's weight and struggling to maintain his balance. "This isn't the deck of the *Screaming Queen!*"

"You couldn't tell it from the ride so far," Sunrise shot back as Caspar started to rise and he teetered precariously. He tightened his grip on Caspar's hands. "Ouch!" he said suddenly.

"I told you to watch your head," Caspar reminded him. "That's a chandelier. Reach up and grab a candle. Grab two. We'll light them from a torch in the corridor."

A few moments later they had light to see by. The room was just as Caspar remembered it, big and grandly furnished. It was the room beyond he was interested in, though. At first he had wondered if it might be Duncanthrax's bedroom, but the noise of the falling chair would have awakened anyone sleeping there. He stole inside and held up his candle, the better to see.

He gave a low whistle and beckoned to Sunrise. It

was a library almost like Satchmoz's, with tightly rolled scrolls thrust into honeycombed shelving. Scrolls everywhere. Books, too. In the center of the room stood a globe of Zork. Tacked along the walls were maps of Quendor and its various provinces.

Caspar went to a map he recognized immediately, the province of Frobozz. The map was old, but traced upon it in red ink was a lacework of fresh, new lines. A map of Gurth hung beside Frobozz. It was marked with the same red lines. So was Thriff and Miznia and Mithicus.

"These markings must represent his underground highway," Caspar muttered in disbelief. "It's fantastic! Such an undertaking . . . !" He bit his lip, considering the immensity of the project as he examined another map. "Here's one of Borphee!"

"These look like Satchmoz's scrolls," Sunrise said from the other side of the room. He had taken several parchments down from the shelves. He held them unrolled in his hands. Caspar went to see what he had found.

"Curiouser and curiouser," he said as he bent over Sunrise's shoulder. He couldn't read the language written on the parchments. They did, indeed, look the same as the ones in the guildhall library.

While Caspar studied the scrolls, Sunrise began rifling through the drawers of a desk. "I don't see anything that would help find missing wizards," he announced.

Caspar felt suddenly ignorant and helpless. He let go of one end of the parchments. They rolled up with a crisp snap. "I could be holding detailed instructions to their whereabouts," he said bitterly, "and not know it."

"Let's move on," Sunrise suggested. "We're not going to find anything here."

They took their candles and crept back into the corridor. They had taken less than five paces when booted footsteps sounded from the hallway just ahead. Caspar's heart skipped a beat. He caught Sunrise by the sleeve and pulled him back into the room. He closed the door as softly as he could and shielded his candle so its light wouldn't spill under the door. Crouched against it, he and Sunrise waited.

The footsteps rang crisply on the marble tiles in the corridor outside and passed them by. When they deemed it safe, Caspar eased the door open again and peeked around. Before they took even a step out this time they jumped back inside and crouched down. Three pair of feet ran by.

"That sounded ominous," Caspar whispered.

"Just their morning jog?" Sunrise suggested hopefully.

"Before sunrise?"

"Early risers, maybe," the youth answered. "You wouldn't want 'em running after sunrise, would you?"

Caspar grasped the door knob again. "Nah," he said. "I like you too much."

Sunrise flashed a big smile. "My natural charm," he came back.

They crept out into the corridor yet again. Wisely, they waited a moment, listening, half expecting to dive back inside. The halls were silent, though. But it was clear now that others were awake in the palace. Clear, too, that something was afoot. Men, especially soldier-types, did not run through kingly corridors in the wee hours of morning just for the joy of it.

At the next junction they paused to once more consider which way to go. Caspar had hoped to find a true clue in the room they had just searched. Everything else now seemed a crap shoot. Roll the dice. Even numbers go left, odd numbers go right. Snake-eyes go straight ahead.

His baby was just about to need a new pair of shoes when racing footsteps sounded yet again.

"Damn!" Sunrise muttered.

Caspar looked around frantically. Their former refuge was too far back. His eyes sought the nearest door and found it just in the left-hand branch.

"I hope it's unlocked!" he told Sunrise, rushing toward it.

"I hope it's unoccupied!" Sunrise said, right behind him.

Caspar grabbed the knob and hit the door with his shoulder all at once. Sunrise hit him from behind, and the two nearly tumbled inside. Caspar caught just a flash of scarlet tunic at the far end of the hall as he eased the door shut.

His right hand curled into a fist as he pressed his ear to the wood. He couldn't tell for sure, but it sounded like a squad rushing by the other side of the door. The tramp of boots echoed for long minutes. Finally, Caspar drew breath and looked around.

Sunrise stood a little off to the side, the fingers of one hand thrust into his mouth, his eyes all squinted, and his brow deeply furrowed.

"What a face," Caspar said. "You look like you're going to scream."

Sunrise rolled his eyes. Plainly, he'd thrust his fingers into his mouth to prevent just that. He took them out long enough to explain. "Hot wax," he said, pointing to the hand in which he held his candle. There was wax all over the side of his hand and fingers. "I'd been careful, but it got me that time." He set about flaking the wax off his skin, but no doubt it had been painful at the time.

Caspar raised his own candle a little higher to see where they were. A shimmery fabric on the near wall caught the light and Caspar's attention. He went to examine it and found a rack of ladies' dresses and veils, floor-length tunics, high-collared blouses. Another rack held hundreds of pairs of slippers made from felt and velvet and soft leather. Another rack contained skirts of incredible material, fabrics he had never seen before, with threads of gold and silver that strained toward his candlelight and followed it as he moved.

"No *lady* ever wore these things," Sunrise explained as he joined Caspar. He held up a girdle heavy with attached jewels and metal spangles.

Caspar set down a beaded belt he'd been examining. "The concubines," he whispered, a bit awed by the wealth it all represented. "I met a bunch of concubines the last time I was here." He looked up suddenly, recalling the experience with a certain irritation. "The mouths on those bimbos!" he added.

"Yes, they are talented orators, all," Sunrise answered with an amused grin.

Caspar had a sudden idea. They needed a way to move about the palace without causing undue alarm. As they were dressed now any guard would consider them intruders and raise an alarm. But who would suspect a couple of the king's own concubines?

"Strip," he told Sunrise. He set his candle down on a dressing table and began at once to loosen his own garments. He reached for the nearest skirt, a glistening fabric of cobalt blue. He draped it over a nearby chair as he unlaced his tunic.

Sunrise raised an eyebrow doubtfully. "Don't, Caspar," he pleaded quietly. "This is a side of you I don't want to see."

Caspar tugged his trousers off over his boots. The candlelight gleamed on his pale naked chest as he bent over and stepped into the shimmering skirt. It was a bit tight at the waist, but long enough and full enough to hide his boots. He ran a hand admiringly over the front of it.

"It's just not you!" Sunrise insisted, shying toward the door.

Caspar grabbed a copper-colored garment from the rack and tossed it to Sunrise. "This'll go great with your eyes," he answered, "or around your neck if you give me any trouble. Now hurry up and get beautiful."

Sunrise swallowed, but gave in, and Caspar explained his idea while they both selected their ensembles. When they were done, Caspar looked at himself. The cloth he was wearing was expensive enough to feed a family in the Peltoid Valley for a year, he was sure. He draped a veil around his head to hide the fact his hair was cut short. Then he added another and covered his face.

Left with no choice, Sunrise really got into it. He cast aside the copper-colored dress. Too stodgy, he told

Caspar. Instead, he chose a gold skirt that was split on both sides nearly to the waist. Over it he set the jeweled belt that Caspar had examined earlier. Next, he found a jeweled and fringed halter. He had no breasts, but several pairs of lightweight stockings filled the cups out nicely. Several sheer veils of yellow went around his shoulders, and several more of scarlet disguised his hair and face. He added bracelets and rings from a small chest, then ankle chains and bells from another. "Booty," he told Caspar, grinning.

"Leave the bells," Caspar answered. "We still want to do this as quietly as possible."

Sunrise gave him a sarcastic look. "There is nothing quiet about these outfits," the youth said. He raised the hem of his skirt and turned his ankle teasingly. Three gold chains glittered against the dirty brown leather of his boot. "These must have belonged to a dancer with fat ankles." He batted his eyelashes suddenly. "Do you still like me, Caspar Wartsworth?" he asked, pitching his voice high.

Caspar bit his lip and feigned a worried look. "I think you're too much woman for me, Miss," he answered as he picked up his candle again and headed for the door.

Sunrise mugged a disgusted expression. "Watch your veil," he grumbled, brushing the fluttery material away from Caspar's candle. "You'll set yourself on fire."

They cracked open the door and peeked out. The corridor was empty again. Caspar looked both ways, crept out into the center of the hall, then beckoned to Sunrise. There was no need to sneak now. In fact, it would only look suspicious if they were seen. Instead, they linked arms and swished and sashayed their way to the far end of the hall.

They found the throne room easily enough, but there was nothing there. As Sunrise had noted before, the throne was too heavy to carry off, and there was certainly nothing to hint at the whereabouts of any wizards.

Still, Caspar had come for another reason. He owed

Duncanthrax personally. "Give me your dagger," he said, holding out his hand to Sunrise.

Sunrise gave him a quizzical look, but reached under his veils and into the waistband of his skirt to withdraw the slender weapon. Caspar climbed up into the great royal seat, kneeled there and went to work with the dagger's point. When he finished, he stepped aside and held up his candle with a feeling of smug satisfaction.

In big scratchy letters carved deep into the wood, Caspar's message read, *The king is a fink!*

Sunrise folded his arms across his chest, tilted his head to the side, pursed his lips. "That's your big revenge?" he said.

Caspar felt hurt. "Not all of it," he answered defensively, stepping back to admire his handiwork. "But a little pettiness has its place."

Sunrise ran a finger over the rough gouge marks. "I don't suppose it matters to you this throne is over six hundred years old, dating back to Entharion, himself?"

Caspar's mouth drew into a thin, taut line as he pouted. "It may cause me a qualm or two in a few weeks," he answered. Then, he sprouted a devilish grin. "But not tonight!"

Bootsteps rushed by in the corridor outside the great doors. Caspar and Sunrise threw themselves down behind the massive throne and peeked around its opposite sides. Of course, their candles would have given them away in an instant had anyone opened the doors, but it was fear that compelled them, not rational thought. Sheepishly, Caspar stood up and drew his veil a little closer about his face. Sunrise did the same and did his best to look demure.

The sounds of pursuit echoed in the hall, but no one entered the throne room. There were shouts, and the clatter of armor or weapons, the thunder of swift feet. Then silence again.

"What in the world is going on?" Caspar asked aloud when things were quiet again. They went to the great doors, opened them, and stuck their heads out. The halls were empty.

"I don't know," Sunrise answered. "But I'm beginning to feel left out."

"I think we'd better head back to Satchmoz," Caspar said thoughtfully. "There's too much activity now with the guards on alert. Zork knows why."

"But we haven't accomplished much!" Sunrise protested as he kept a careful watch over his shoulder lest soldiers should suddenly come from that direction. "Besides, I'm just getting used to walking around in this outfit."

"We won't accomplish anything by being discovered," Caspar reminded the youth. "Let's just get out. With Satchmoz's *aimfiz* spell, we can always come back."

Sunrise sniggered at that. "You gonna kiss a gate sentry again?"

Caspar didn't bother to answer. He just set a quick pace back the way they had come. Alert for any sound, they passed the wardrobe room where they had stolen their costumes, then the rooms that Caspar had come to think of as Duncanthrax's library with all its scrolls and maps.

But as they turned the next bend in the corridor they came unexpectedly upon a pair of sentries standing watchful duty at that juncture. Caspar nearly jumped out of his skin when he turned the corner and the two snapped out their lances to bar the way. He immediately drew his veil closer about his face so that little more than his eyes could be seen.

"Stop!" one of the guards barked needlessly, as if the crossed lances were not clue enough that it might not be wise to proceed. Both guards glared from under their burnished helmets. They had an angry, but sleepy look about them, as if they'd just been roused and weren't happy about it.

Caspar looked at Sunrise from within his veil. Sunrise, from under his several veils, looked at Caspar. Suddenly Caspar pitched his voice as high as he could, reached out and clutched the nearest guard's arm. "Oh, thank our lucky stars! We were so frightened with all the commotion!'' He turned to Sunrise and winked. ''Look at these big strong men. Don't you feel safer now, dear?''

The guard snatched his arm back and looked strangely at Caspar. ''What are you doing wandering around this time of night?'' he demanded. ''Don't you know there's an alert on? We've got an intruder in the palace.''

Sunrise stepped in front of Caspar. Being shorter, he passed nearly *under* the crossed spears before he brushed them nonchalantly aside and leaned against the second guard. ''Why, of course we know that, silly!'' He dealt the man a smart slap on the rump and batted his eyelashes prettily. ''After all, where do you think we've been tonight, but with Dunky?''

The guards looked at each other. ''Dunky?'' said one.

''Dinky Dunky, we call him,'' Sunrise answered before Caspar could get a word in. He gave a little giggle. ''But don't tell him that.'' He gave the guard another nudge. ''Just a little gossip between us, all right?'' He held up thumb and forefinger and tilted his head cutely.

''You were *both* with His Majesty?'' asked Caspar's guard with a certain awe.

''Well, you know Dunky,'' Sunrise teased, jumping in once more before Caspar could speak. ''He's such an insatiable beast.''

It probably wasn't such a bad thing, either, that Sunrise was doing all the talking, Caspar reasoned. After all, he had a much higher voice, and he intended to make a point of reminding the little rascal of it later if he got the chance. Right now, he simply concentrated on getting as close to his guard as he could. And it frankly didn't seem to be such a tough job the way the guy was making eyes.

''When the alarm sounded he sent us away,'' Sunrise continued to explain. ''We were on our way back to our own quarters—disappointed and left in the lurch, if you take my meaning, kind sir.'' Caspar kind of marveled at that point as a look of fear stole into Sunrise's eyes and the boy clutched his soldier's arm again. ''But there was a noise back there. Some kind of soft crash! Why, we were afraid to go on and came this way, instead, to find

guards to investigate. You really must go check it out!
Dunky's life could be in danger!''

Good! Caspar thought, full of a new admiration for
his young friend. If he hadn't been so afraid, he might
have laughed at Sunrise's clever performance. In fact,
standing there looking afraid probably lent credence to
the whole story. Would the guards fall for it?

"We can't leave our posts!" Sunrise's guard snapped
suddenly. "Dunky—I mean, Duncanthrax, himself, put
us here!" He looked at Sunrise with abrupt suspicion.
"Are you sure you were with him, tonight?"

Sunrise pressed on valiantly with his game. "I'm just
throbbing with the memory!" he cooed, faking a shiver.

"Yer kind o' cute, girlie," Caspar's guard suddenly
whispered, leaning close to Caspar's ear. "I get off at
dawn . . ."

But Caspar was watching Sunrise's guard. A flicker
of doubt lingered on the man's face. He didn't seem to
be buying it anymore. The fact that Duncanthrax, himself, was up and leading whatever merry chase was running through the palace was enough to convince Caspar
it was time to get out. So there was no more time to
play with these two.

"Oh, Esmerelda?" Caspar said to Sunrise, risking
speech. Then, he clenched his back teeth tight. No sooner
had he spoken the name, intended for Sunrise, but the
sudden realization hit him like a fist. He knew who was
being chased. He had no doubt at all who was being
chased.

"Oh, Esmerelda?" he said, recovering himself, realizing that everyone was looking at him. "Show the nice
guard what you showed that man in the woods." Caspar
winked and nodded.

Caspar's guard put on a leer. His hand slid suddenly
down Caspar's backside. "Heh, heh, heh," he laughed
softly. "Yeah, show us what you showed the man in the
woods."

Sunrise looked at Caspar dumbly, and for a moment,
Caspar feared the boy hadn't caught on. Then, Sunrise
nodded. He clutched the front of his skirt and lifted the

dress the tiniest fraction. "You want to see it?" he asked his guard.

Despite his suspicions, the guard appeared to think it over. He didn't nod, but he didn't say no, either.

"Here it comes!" Sunrise warned him teasingly, raising the hem a little more.

Like a lightning strike his foot lashed upward. The stunned guard's eyes snapped wide. He gave a low, bone-wrenching moan, clutched his groin, and sagged to his knees. "You like that?" Sunrise continued, flouncing his hips in a taunting manner. The guard didn't or couldn't answer. He sank forward and curled up in a ball, his lower lip grasped between his teeth, slobber drooling from the corner of his mouth.

Of course, Caspar was busy, too. As soon as Sunrise moved, Caspar's guard started. "Here now!" he cried. As he grabbed for Sunrise, Caspar stuck out his foot, tripping the man as he pushed him, sending him headfirst into the opposite wall. The guard rebounded, dazed, and dropped his lance. Caspar seized it and swung with the butt end. The guard gave a grunt, fell backward, executed two neat somersaults and lay still on his belly.

"He groped me!" Caspar told Sunrise as he stood over the unconscious guard.

"I'd say you got even," Sunrise answered, not sticking around to argue the point. He gathered his skirts around him and dashed off down the corridor toward the stairway that would take them down to the dungeon. Caspar glanced back only briefly for their candles, which rolled about extinguished on the floor. Too late to worry about a little thing like light, he reasoned. He followed Sunrise, close on his hems.

The guard at the desk was no longer asleep. He leaped to attention the moment Caspar and Sunrise approached. The look on his face at the sight of two concubines was almost amusing. There was no more time to play, though. Caspar went straight to the desk and slammed his palm down on the book of prisoner names.

"Dunky—I mean, His Majesty King Duncanthrax

sent us to find the jailer, Olio," he lied, staring the man straight in the eye from behind his veils. "They've caught the intruder."

Everybody wanted to argue tonight, it seemed. "So?" the guard demanded. "What do they want with Olio? And why come here? The fat old turd's not on duty tonight."

"Duncanthrax said he's here," Caspar insisted, his heart racing. A now familiar sound echoed in the corridor behind them—the rush of booted feet. He improvised, his heart pounding. "He came in the other way, the way they bring in the prisoners. He can identify the intruder." *He can identify me if we don't get out of here,* Caspar thought.

Sunrise stepped forward and crooked his finger at the desk guard. "Can I whisper something in your ear?" he asked sweetly.

The guard frowned, but bent across the desk. Sunrise moved a little closer, cupped his hand to his mouth as if to offer some secret, then caught the chin strap of the man's helmet. With all his young might he jerked the guard's head down against the desk. At the same time, Caspar lunged at the desk, itself, slamming it and the guard back against the wall.

They didn't stop to see what toll it all took on the man. They raced through the door and down the dark steps. Past the cells they ran, toward the dim lamp on the table ahead. Caspar snatched the ring of keys from the peg as they passed it and tossed it through the window of the cell whose occupant he'd frightened earlier. "You're free!" he hissed to the man. "Get out now, and run!"

Of course, Sunrise would later tease Caspar about using the poor man as decoy bait, but Caspar would deny it. He just wanted to do a favor for a poor abused soul, and if the man used the keys to set free a few other prisoners on the way, well, that was grand, too.

Meanwhile, the door at the top of the stairs crashed open behind them. Now there were shouts and curses as soldiers rushed down the steps after them. Sunrise blew out the lamp and pushed the table over on its side in the middle of the narrow passage.

"Satchmoz!" Caspar cried in a tight whisper, wishing his comrade hadn't extinguished the lamp quite so swiftly. "Satchmoz!"

A door creaked open just ahead. "Here!" the wizard answered. "We're here! Hurry up, this cell's got roaches!"

Caspar ran toward the sound of his voice and smashed into the open door. His vision lit up with exploding stars. He would have fallen had Sunrise not caught him from behind.

"I swear, you guys can't do anything right!" The voice was Esmerelda's. She rushed out of the cell to help usher Caspar inside.

"We can't?" Sunrise snapped sarcastically. "I don't suppose you'd know who they're chasing?"

"Never mind!" Satchmoz interrupted. He closed the door behind them and shoved a hand into the backpack he'd brought along. A bright light spilled suddenly out, lighting up the entire cell, no doubt spreading far into the corridor beyond. On the palm of Satchmoz's hand sat a small crystal ball Caspar had seen in the guild hall library, but now it glowed with a powerful radiance. Of course! The wizard must have used a *frotz* spell on it, knowing he would need light to read his scrolls and work the magic that would take them home again.

"You'll give us away!" Esmerelda hissed as she tried to shield the light with her hands.

Satchmoz ignored her. Reaching into the back pack again, he withdrew the single scroll he had put there. There would be no rummaging in his cloak pockets for the proper magic this time. He hurriedly studied. With a flash the *aimfiz* scroll crumbled to ashes. Satchmoz squeezed his eyes shut. Strange words poured from his lips.

Caspar, Sunrise, Esmerelda and Satchmoz all reached out and clasped hands as the noise in the corridor rose to a tumult. With a shout, someone jerked open the cell door. Half a dozen large bodies all tried to squeeze inside at the same time. Someone raised a sword.

A black furry streak leaped from under Satchmoz's cloak. A savage, feline snarling filled the cell, and four clawed feet all sank into the nearest soldier's chest, evoking an unmanly high-pitched scream.

"A demon!" someone shrieked. "They've conjured up a demon!"

The *aimfiz* enchantment surged around the circle. One instant the cell and the soldiers and Meezel were all there. The next instant they weren't.

"EEZEL!" ESMERELDA screamed in horrified dismay.

"Aiieeeee!" Satchmoz screamed as he found himself kneeling soaking wet in the fountain that was the centerpiece of the guild hall's courtyard.

"Oops," said Burble where he sat swinging his short legs idly on a bench beside the fountain. His eyes grew round, and he bit his lip sheepishly as he slowly stood up.

Esmerelda caught Satchmoz by an arm and practically dragged him from the fountain. "We have to go back!" she wailed, giving the wizard a shake.

"No way!" Caspar countered, grabbing Satchmoz's other arm.

Satchmoz, on the verge of being pulled apart, only had eyes for the brogmoid. Big, angry eyes. "Why, Burble?" he shouted at the top of his lungs. "Why here? Why couldn't you wait in the library, or the Crystal Room, or anyplace DRY?"

The brogmoid clutched his hands in front of him, pushed out his lower lip, and looked on the verge of tears.

"Go back!" Esmerelda screamed, tugging the wizard's arm, glowering at Caspar.

"No way!" Caspar bellowed, pulling the other direction.

Sunrise just grinned and watched it all. "Whoa!" he cried. "Split decision!"

"Would you let me go!" Satchmoz cried, taking sudden notice that he was the center of a struggle. With a strength born of rage he gave a shrug and dragged both his tormentors into the fountain with him. Cursing, he brushed his hands together as if he'd accomplished a major chore while Esmerelda and Caspar sputtered and coughed and looked up with utter surprise. Satchmoz didn't say another word, just climbed out and walked dripping into the guildhall with Burble following swiftly after.

"But what about Meezel?" Esmerelda said plaintively. Then she began to cry.

Sunrise rolled his eyes, but he reached out a hand and helped her out of the fountain. "We'll get Meezel back," he promised. "He's a smart cat. He can handle a bunch of guards."

Caspar grunted as he rose, soaked to the bone. "That cat's chopped liver by now," he grumbled.

"Oh, Caspar!" Sunrise snapped, putting on his sternest frown as he wrapped one consoling arm around Esmerelda and steered her toward the guildhall. "Stick an oar in it for a while!"

Esmerelda sniffed as she sneered at Caspar over one shoulder and drew Sunrise closer.

Caspar found himself suddenly alone. He drew a deep breath and found he really didn't mind being alone, either. He plopped down on the bench where Burble had sat and stared at all the wet footprints as he grabbed a handful of his skirt and wrung water. It was surprisingly peaceful. The night air was warm, and there was no other sound but the lulling trickle of the fountain.

No other sound, that is, until Satchmoz stuck his head out the door. "Would you *please* get in here!" he called, his temper only slightly improved.

Caspar gave another sigh as he got up. A life of adventure, he decided, wasn't all it was cracked up to be.

However, when he entered the main hall he found only Sunrise waiting. The youth was stretched on a chair with his hands folded behind his head, still wearing the garments of a concubine.

"Satchmoz and Esmerelda are changing into dry clothes," he told Caspar. Then he lifted the edge of one of his veils. "I figure we'd better change into anything. Satchmoz wants us all to meet in the library as soon as possible. We might be going out again."

"Not after that cat!" Caspar moaned.

"Ease up, Caspar," Sunrise suggested calmly as he bent forward and tugged off one boot. "She's been through a lot, and she thinks the cat is all she's got in the world."

Caspar drew a deep breath and let it out slowly. "We've all been through a lot," he said, on the verge of arguing. But what was the point, he decided. He turned toward the stairs and started up to his room when he remembered his promise to Sunrise. "Too bad you didn't get the crown," he added.

Sunrise followed him up the stairs. "It wasn't a wasted trip," he answered. He shook his hips, causing the jeweled and bespangled belt he wore to shiver and jingle. The jewels were not large, and the sewn gold coins were smaller than normal zorkmids. Still, it represented considerable wealth. "This alone would feed me and my old friends in East Borphee for six months." He shimmied his hips again, and the coins gave a soft rattle. "Shake your booty!" he chanted.

But Sunrise wasn't finished. "And then I got this," he said, reaching the top stair and pulling a small silver medallion on a silver chain from under his tunic. It was about the size of the ball of Caspar's thumb. "Looks like the man-in-the-moon," Sunrise commented, admiring the ornament. "See, it's got all the features." He held it up for Caspar to see without removing it from his neck. "I found it in the desk in Duncanthrax's library. I got a scroll, too. Don't know what it is, but I'm sure I can sell it." He hiked up all his skirts, reached into the back of his trousers and drew out a crushed, wrinkled, but completely readable piece of parchment. "All in all," Sunrise finished, "I think I came away with a small fortune."

Caspar agreed as he examined the scroll. He couldn't

really make heads or tails of it since it was written in the same ancient Quendoran as all of Satchmoz's scrolls. "You should show this to Satchmoz," he told Sunrise. "He'll be able to tell you what it's worth."

He went into his room then and stripped off his garish garments. *Give those to Sunrise, too,* he thought to himself as he kicked the skirts to the far side of the room. *They should bring a few zorkmids and zorkles, as well.*

He went to the wardrobe again and tried to choose a new outfit, but his heart wasn't in it. He felt oddly depressed. Or maybe he was on edge. He couldn't decide which. Perhaps because Esmerelda had worn all black, or perhaps because it seemed to fit his mood, he took down the most funereal garments he could find and pulled them on. In the bottom of the wardrobe he found a pair of soft velvet boots with leather soles, stepped into them, and laced them up. They didn't feel very sturdy, but they were better than wearing his wet ones.

More than anything, he regretted the loss of his sword. The guards had taken it from him outside the palace gate, and he hadn't seen it again. Probably one of them had kept it. Well, it didn't really matter. He had no skill with the thing, anyway.

He went downstairs, arriving in the main hall just as Burble emerged from the kitchen with a large tray of food. "Satch says meet in the Crys . . ."—he swallowed and tried the word again. "In the crys . . ." Again, he stumbled on the word. Finally, the brogmoid shrugged and put on a weak smile. "In the solarium," he said, inclining his head toward the Crystal Room and turning to lead the way.

In the Crystal Room, Burble set the tray on the bloodwood table and excused himself, leaving Caspar alone. Caspar studied the tray with its assortment of fruit, bread, and cheeses, and helped himself to an apple. He took a bite and paced about the room. Beyond the transparent walls there was only darkness.

Esmerelda arrived. She hesitated when she saw Caspar, but summoned her composure and strode to the table. She pulled out a chair and sat gracefully down, looking like an angel in white silk. She picked up a bit of cheese and nibbled it.

Fascinating, Caspar thought, *how different men's clothes look on her.* He approached the table and sat down also. She barely glanced at him. "I'm sorry I snapped at you earlier," he said. "And I'm sorry about Meezel."

For a moment she seemed not to have heard. Then, she looked up from her cheese and forced a tiny smile as she shrugged. "It's all right," she answered weakly. "It's not your fault your brain cell hasn't divided, yet."

Caspar frowned and lapsed into silence. He watched Esmerelda munch her cheese, her gaze seeking out everything in the room except his face.

Satchmoz appeared briefly in the doorway. "Don't get comfortable," he called sharply. He tossed an empty back pack to Caspar. It didn't quite make it and fell limply in the middle of the floor. "Go to the library and fill that with scrolls. Don't worry about which ones. Just fill it. Hurry!" The wizard disappeared toward the kitchen.

Esmerelda snatched up the bag in a graceful sweep and left the Crystal Room. Caspar hurried after, beating her to the library doors, pushing them back. The lamps were still lit; there was light to see by. Esmerelda went to the nearest shelf and held the bag open while Caspar scooped as many scrolls into it as he could gather.

"What's he up to now?" Caspar wondered aloud as he tied the bag securely closed. The back pack was crammed full, but there were still hundreds of scrolls on the shelves. Esmerelda only shrugged. She put her arm through one of the shoulder straps at the same time Caspar put his through the other. A silent, stubborn tug-of-war ensued.

"We're bugging out," Sunrise announced as he came through the doorway. He'd exchanged his skirts for proper attire once more.

"What?" Caspar looked sheepish and surrendered the bag. Esmerelda turned a smug look on him.

"Soldiers will be here any moment," Satchmoz answered brusquely as he entered right behind Sunrise.

He quick-stepped around the youth and rushed to his desk. Opening a drawer, he took out pen and ink and a flat piece of parchment with writing inscribed upon it.

"How do you know that?" Esmerelda snapped as she walked up behind him and stared over his shoulder.

Satchmoz didn't spare her a glance. "What would you do if you thought you'd done away with all the wizards in Borphee, and yet one just popped into and out of your dungeon? You'd send troops to check the guildhall, of course!" He snorted and strode to a sealed box in its own shelf near the map table. From under it he took a key and inserted it into the box's lock.

Caspar nodded and chided himself for not considering sooner that Duncanthrax might seek them out. "Then we should get out quickly," he agreed. "What are you doing there?"

Satchmoz opened the box and withdrew a single sheet of blank, cream-colored parchment. He hurried back to his writing desk with it and set it down carefully beside the other sheet. Twisting the stopper from the pot of ink, he dipped the pen's nib and began copying.

"A spell can't be copied onto ordinary parchment," he swiftly explained without looking up. "It has to be magically treated, or the words will fade as soon as you write them."

"But you've already got this copy," Caspar said, pointing to the original. "We should be getting out."

"Burble's preparing us a bag of food," the wizard said with a shake of his head. "And this," he added, giving a tap with the butt end of his pen to the original, "is the master formulation of the spatial displacement spell we encountered at Esmerelda's castle. I must make a copy. If I use the master, we've lost it."

Caspar had a sudden inspiration. "Make two copies," he insisted. Going to the box, he snatched out another sheet and carried it back to the desk.

Satchmoz looked up sharply. "There may not be time," he said guardedly. "What have you got in mind?"

"Then give me ink," Caspar answered, "and I'll copy it while you work on that one."

Satchmoz set his pen down carefully. "The Old Tongue?" he barked. "Linear Quendoran B?" He dismissed the idea with a shake of his head. "One mistake and . . ."

"I won't make a mistake," Caspar told him flatly. "Just give me ink, and write fast."

The wizard opened his drawer again and passed over ink and a pen. Caspar fell to work at once while the others gathered around to watch. Burble waddled into the library with another back pack, which Sunrise took from him. He, too, moved closer to watch the pair of pens that flew over paper.

"Caspo wizard now?" the brogmoid asked, giving a tug on Sunrise's hand.

Sunrise locked his fingers with the brogmoid's and drew the little creature closer. "Naw," he answered, "but he's got some trick up his sleeve."

There was a sudden furious pounding at the outer gate, a shout, and a demand to open up.

"Time's up!" Satchmoz called, finishing his scroll, tossing a sprinkle of powder over the still-damp ink.

"I'm finished!" Caspar answered, blowing a puff of air over his and turning it toward the wizard. "Let's get out the back door." Satchmoz hesitated only long enough to snatch a new dry cloak from a peg on the wall by the library door. Its pockets were already full.

"What are you going to do with the second copy?" Sunrise questioned as they hurried out of the library, past the Crystal Room and out the door that opened into the side courtyard where stood the fountain.

"You'll see right now!" Caspar answered in a sharp whisper as he signaled them to stop. The sound of splintering wood warned that the outer gate had been breached. Satchmoz was taking advantage of the pause to roll his copy and the master into a tight cylinder, which he shoved into a pocket of his cloak. Caspar handed him his copy.

"The front door's unlocked," Caspar told the wizard. "Wait until they're all inside, then cast it."

A big grin spread over Sunrise's face as he realized

Caspar's intent. Even Esmerelda showed a glimmer of appreciation.

Satchmoz allowed a little laugh. "I love it," he said with a crooked smile. "Every time they open a door or cross a threshold they'll wind up in Krepkit's bathroom."

"How do you know it'll be the bathroom, wizard?" Esmerelda asked as she crouched low and tried to peer back into the house.

"Because I *will* it," Satchmoz answered. "And all magic is an act of will."

Sunrise nudged the old man. "I have the darnedest feeling that you're not bumbling so much anymore."

Satchmoz stiffened and lifted his nose. "Young man," he said indignantly. "I am Satchmoz the Incomparable. I make a mistake now and then. But I never bumble."

Sunrise raised one eyebrow. "The campfire," he said in a low voice, reminding the wizard of the incident on the beach.

Satchmoz gave Sunrise a sidewise glance. Caspar interrupted before an argument could ensue. "Let's sneak around to the front," he suggested. "We have to wait to catch as many inside as we can."

He led the way silently as they crept around the side of the building. He heard a loud crash suddenly, followed by a loud cheer and the rush of feet, and signaled his friends to halt while he stole forward and peered around the corner.

A battering ram and ropes to swing it from lay discarded by the side of the door as soldiers thundered inside, practically trampling each other to get through the doorway. *Fools,* thought Caspar. *They only had to try the knob.*

He almost jumped out of his skin when a hand touched him on the shoulder. It was Satchmoz, bending over him to see, too. The others all pressed around. Burble stuck his head between Caspar's legs.

"One guard!" Sunrise exclaimed in an excited hiss. "They're only leaving one guard outside! I'll take him out!" He started forward, but Caspar caught him by the collar and jerked him back.

"I'm better equipped for the job," Esmerelda said as she cupped her breasts and gave them a lift. She tossed her hair over a shoulder.

But before anybody could stop him, Burble slipped under Caspar and waddled around the corner into plain view. A plaintive mewling sound issued from the brogmoid, and he ground one fist into an eye.

"What the . . . !" Caspar gasped. But Satchmoz shut him up with a curt wave of a hand and watched.

The guard heard Burble at once and drew his sword. Then, seeing that it was only a brogmoid, he relaxed and sheathed the weapon again. Burble wept like a lost child, and the soldier dropped to one knee.

"Come here, little fella!" the soldier said, not unkindly. He crooked a finger, summoning Burble closer. "Come here. What are you crying about? What are you doing here? Huh?"

"Everybody loves a brogmoid," Satchmoz whispered in Caspar's ear.

Burble walked to the soldier and held out his arms, looking so helpless in his yellow *I love Borphee* sweater. He wiped his eyes and gave a loud sniff. The soldier grinned and answered with a chuckle. "It's all right, little fella," he said. "Shame on the folks who left you behind like this. It's all right!"

He reached out and hugged the brogmoid, and Burble returned the embrace. He gave another sniff. His voice reached Caspar plainly. "All right?" he repeated in a meek voice as he let go of the soldier.

The soldier rumpled the pink mohawk atop Burble's head. "Right," he answered.

Burble pushed out his lower lip, and light from inside glinted off the three-inch fangs. "Left?" he said innocently.

The soldier shook his head, grinning like a kid playing with his favorite pet. "No," he said firmly. "Right."

Burble sucked his lower lip back in until his cheeks

puckered, then he let go of it with a pop and shrugged. "All right," he said. "Right it is."

Before the soldier could react, Burble drew back his right fist and delivered a blow of astonishing power. The soldier's head snapped back. The rest of him followed. Sprawled across the threshold, he lay unmoving. Caspar and Sunrise darted around the corner.

"All right!" Burble said with genine satisfaction as he looked at them.

Caspar seized the soldier's feet. Sunrise grabbed his hands. "On three," Caspar said. On two they let the man fly. Through the door he went, and Sunrise slammed it shut. Within, they heard angry shouts. There was no lock on the outside. Caspar and Sunrise both grabbed the handle and braced themselves. Inside, someone gave the door a tug. Caspar and Sunrise slammed it shut again.

"Now!" Esmerelda shouted at Satchmoz. "Do it now!"

"Don't rush me!" the wizard shouted back. He pressed his fingers to his temples. "I've got it memorized," he said, trying to calm himself, and indeed, the scroll was gone. A pile of ash colored the ground at his feet.

The door jerked inward again. Caspar and Sunrise both cried out as they felt the handle slip from their grip. Somehow, they held on. Caspar braced one foot against the side of the building. With a loud groan, he strained to keep the door closed.

"That's it," Satchmoz said abruptly, brushing his hands.

Caspar's pulse throbbed in his ears. His muscles cracked and popped as he struggled to hold the door closed. "What do you mean, 'that's it'?" he demanded through clenched teeth.

Satchmoz gave him a wounded look. "Hey," he said, "every spell can't be a pyrotechnic wonder. I mean, that's it. You can let go."

"You sure?" Sunrise moaned without relinquishing his own grip on the door handle.

Satchmoz folded his arms across his chest. "Trust me," he said.

"You shouldn't have said that," Esmerelda responded, shaking her head.

Caspar and Sunrise glanced at each other. By silent agreement, they let go and sprang back. The door flew open. Three soldiers leaped toward them simultaneously and vanished in midleap. Behind them, another pair of men rushed forward and were instantly transported. A loud crash sounded from the upper part of the guildhall.

In the main hall a roomful of soldiers stared dumbly at each other and at the four people and the brogmoid who stood just outside with their thumbs in their ears and fingers wiggling.

Chuckling, Sunrise started to reach inside to close the door. "Goodnight, sweethearts," he called to the soldiers.

"I wouldn't do that if I were you," Satchmoz warned.

Sunrise snatched his hand back and looked down at his toes, so close to the threshold. "Guess it won't hurt to leave it open," he said.

Caspar blew out a short breath as he turned toward Satchmoz. These soldiers, at least, were no immediate threat. And Duncanthrax would wait, expecting a report, before finally sending more to investigate. That gave them some small breathing room. But they couldn't just stand around in the courtyard. "Where to?" he said to the wizard.

"Down!" said a voice from behind them.

Burble and Sunrise, taking it as a warning, threw themselves on their faces. Caspar, Satchmoz and Esmerelda merely turned at the sound. In the shadow of the ruined gate stood a familiar stoop-shouldered, pointy-hatted silhouette.

"Mummy!" Esmerelda cried with surprising joy.

Nasturtium strode forward, bearing a worn broom in one hand and wearing a most unpleasant expression. "Somebody's shakin' the very damned mortar out of my house!" she said in a bitter, menacing tone. "The whole north tower fell in! Now I mean to find the responsible party." Her voice dropped another octave as she shook a finger under Satchmoz's nose and added, "He better be insured!"

"Or things will get nasty?" Sunrise boldy quipped as he picked himself up from the dirt.

The witch glowered at the youth as if he was a primecut steak that some fool had overcooked. A chilling cackle bubbled suddenly from her lips. She threw back her head, and her fingers curled up like claws. "Don't you worry, little boy!" she cried. "It's Nasty who'll do the gettin'."

Satchmoz frowned distastefully. "Madam," he said with strained patience, "must you overplay your part?"

She jerked her head in his direction and peered at him through squinted eyes. "Hey," she said a bit more reasonably. "It's a bit role. I gotta make the most of it!" She threw back her head again and laughed at her own cleverness before she finally acknowledged Esmerelda's presence.

"So, my pretty!" Nasturtium cackled and hunched her back until she was no more than half her stepdaughter's height. She twisted her neck and peered up at Esmerelda. "How's about a kiss for your poor ol' mumsy?"

Caspar noticed that a number of soldiers had crept close to the threshold. The king's men were staring unpleasantly, but also listening to every word being said. It was a potent reminder that it was time to move elsewhere.

"Do you know the better part of valor?" he asked the group pointedly.

Sunrise pushed out a lip and looked thoughtful. "The fame and free sex it brings?" he suggested.

"Discretion," Caspar informed them. He gestured toward the gate. "Let's discreetly retreat and beat fleet feet downstreet."

Sunrise scratched his head and grinned. "Repeat?"

Caspar shook a fist, impatient with the boy's mockery. "You're meat."

But Sunrise wagged a finger as he raised one eyebrow. "Mistreat!" he shouted. "Cheat!"

"Sheet!" Burble cried, tugging at Caspar's arm.

It took everyone a moment to realize the brogmoid hadn't uttered a profanity. Their eyes followed where the little fellow's thin blue finger pointed.

One of the soldiers was waving a bedsheet from an upper window in an effort to attract attention.

"Sheet!" They all cried at once. Without another word they ran for the gate and into the darkness of the city streets.

CHAPTER TWENTY-ONE

"THEY DON'T CALL YOU NASTY FOR NOTHING"

WITH CASPAR LEADING
the way, perhaps it was no accident they wound up near
the wharves again. Crouched behind a pile of empty
crates in the darkness of an old warehouse, they paused
to catch their breaths.

"I feel like I'm in training for the Borphee ten-fro-
bozzit run," Sunrise said as he wiped a hand across his
sweating face and leaned back against a wall.

Nasturtium pulled a pair of crates down from the
pile, set them on the ground, used her broom to sweep
the tops clean, then motioned for Esmerelda to sit beside
her.

Burble wrapped one blue arm around Caspar's thigh
and clung quietly.

"That looked a lot like my *trizbort* spell back there,"
Nasturtium said to Satchmoz when she had her breath
back.

Satchmoz was bent double with his hands on his
knees, breathing hard. Still, he managed to twist his head
up to look at her. *"Trizbort?"* he replied. "That spell,
Madam, is called *Satchmoz.*"

Nasturtium glared suspiciously. "Well, it looks like
my *Trizbort.*"

"Argue over the patent later," Caspar interrupted.
"We've got more important things to plan right now."

"Damned true, there!" Nasty agreed, pointing a
gnarly finger at Caspar. "Why, my house is nearly

shaken apart. I want whoever's building that damned tunnel under my basement!"

"You know about the tunnel, then?" Satchmoz said, straightening, breathing easier.

"Know about it?" Nasty snapped. "It runs right under me, doesn't it? It only took a little spell to locate it and follow it up here." She hesitated and frowned. " 'Course, it got a little confusing once I actually approached the city. That's why I was flying overhead and happened to see Essie."

Esmerelda elbowed her stepmother in the ribs and muttered an unladylike curse.

"Essie?" said Caspar, arching an eyebrow.

"Flying?" Sunrise said, leaning forward with interest.

Nasturtium leaned forward, too, and gave Sunrise a light rap on the head with the end of her broom and cackled. "A fiery broom with the speed of light, a cloud of dust, and a hearty cry, hi ho!" She made a swooping gesture with one open hand and a sound, *zoooommm!*

Sunrise backed away, rubbing his forehead, and shot a glance at Caspar. "I told you she was a witch!"

"Now, now!" Nasty warned, wagging a finger. "No name calling."

Caspar ignored Sunrise. Whatever magic Nasturtium used, there were certainly no such things as witches. "You got confused," he said to Nasty, "probably because the tunnel you were following ran into several others."

"Others?" she answered, surprised. "There are more?"

"An entire system of underground highways," Caspar assured her. "All under construction. I've seen the maps."

"Where?" Satchmoz said, looking up with interest.

"In Duncanthrax's library," Sunrise answered before Caspar could. "He's got one just like yours."

Satchmoz looked at both the boys. "What do you mean, just like mine?"

"There were a lot of spell scrolls," Sunrise replied.

He reached into the back of his trousers and pulled out the scroll he'd stolen. "Here, I've got one."

"You're sure they were spell scrolls?" Satchmoz demanded. He took the rolled parchment from Sunrise and held it up. It was too dark to see, though, so he moved to a shutterless window. It was still too dark. "Damn," he muttered. "I need some light."

Almost instantly, the tip of his nose began to shine with a soft white light. Satchmoz nearly jumped out of his skin, and Nasty threw back her head and chortled.

"Lookie!" Burble cried gleefully. "A bulbous nose for Satch!"

"Feeling a little light-headed?" Sunrise asked the wizard in an innocent tone.

Once he realized where the light was coming from, Satchmoz was not amused. He stared angrily at Nasturtium, and gave Burble a look that silenced the brogmoid at once.

"Oh, don't glare like that!" Caspar chided, choking back a fit of giggles.

"Madam," Satchmoz said in an icy voice, "you will remove your *frotz* spell from my person at once."

Nasturtium waved a hand in the air and nearly fell backward with laughter. The crate teetered uncertainly under her. Esmerelda shot out a hand to rescue her stepmother from a fall. "Don't worry," Nasty said when she'd recovered her composure, "it'll wear off in a little while. I can do a *frotz* from memory, but it's not as potent as when it's read from a scroll."

"See?" Caspar whispered to Sunrise. "She uses scrolls. I told you she wasn't a witch."

"I want Meezel," Esmerelda grumbled unhappily.

Reminded of the cat, everyone immediately turned serious again. Satchmoz lifted his nose in the air and turned away to examine the scroll Sunrise had given him. "It's a *vaxum* spell," the wizard announced.

"*Vaxum?*" Caspar repeated uneasily. "Wasn't that what you used on the sea serpent just before it wrecked the *Screaming Queen?*"

The wizard harumphed. "Well, yes," he admitted diffidently.

"It was just a mistake," Sunrise said with a forgiving shrug of the shoulders. "Satch never bumbles."

"Sunrise," Caspar said without looking at his young friend, "stick an oar in it."

The boy made a brief show of outrage, rolling his eyes, drawing his arms akimbo, and shaking his shoulders. It was a nice piece of pantomime. Then he skulked back into a corner.

"He'd make a nice gingerbread cookie, that one," Nasturtium commented with a grin as she regarded Sunrise. She wiggled her fingers in the air as if she might weave the spell right then and there.

"Leave him alone, Mumsy," Esmerelda sighed. "Baking was never one of your better talents. Or cooking, in general, for that matter."

"This is an awfully powerful version of *vaxum*, though," Satchmoz said, shining his nose on the scroll again. He handed it to Nasty for her opinion.

"Would you mind sneezing a little light this way?" she asked, beckoning him closer so she could read. "Wow," she added after a brief study, "this could charm the hair off a grue." She handed the scroll back.

"Why would Duncanthrax have this?" Satchmoz wondered aloud, shining his nose into the highest rafters of the warehouse as he tapped the roll of parchment on his palm. He looked at Caspar again. "You say he had lots of these?"

"Yes," Caspar affirmed. "Is Duncanthrax an enchanter?"

"Not the Duncanthrax I knew," the wizard answered. He paced back and forth, wearing a puzzled frown, tapping the scroll on his hand. "But you tell me he has a library of magic scrolls. There's more, too."

"What *more?*" Sunrise asked suspiciously.

Satchmoz bit his lower lip as he paused in his pacing. "Nasty—I mean, Nasturtium—will tell you. After a while, an enchanter becomes sensitive to the use of magic nearby."

Nasturtium nodded agreement. "It's like an itch on the back of the neck sometimes," she said.

"In my case, a tingle inside my head," Satchmoz added. "Well, while you three left me behind in the dungeon cell, my head was buzzing like a hornet on a three-day drunk."

"Somebody was casting spells in the castle?" Caspar interrupted.

"Not in it," Satchmoz answered. "Under it."

"The tunnels!" Nasty exclaimed, rising to her feet. "It's got to be this underground highway you're talking about."

Caspar rubbed his chin. It was his turn to pace. Satchmoz turned to watch him, and the light from the wizard's nose cast Caspar's shadow high on the wall. "You mentioned the Frobozz Magic Tunneling Company," Caspar said. "Maybe you felt their digging spells."

"All the way from Mauldwood?" Nasty scoffed. She leaned on her broom as she shook her head. "Naw, no wizard could sense a spell that far away, let alone one of his meager skills. And if one of the tunnels has reached that far, we have to assume any others have, too."

Satchmoz stiffly ignored her affront. "It was no digging spell," he affirmed. "Whatever enchantment is at work under the dungeon, it is potent and long-lasting."

"All of which brings us back to the question," Sunrise interjected, stepping into the middle of the group. He lifted his hands in exasperation. "Is Duncanthrax some kind of wizard?"

"Seems to me," said Nasturtium, "we're going to have to get into the palace to answer that."

A chorus of groans went up. Only Esmerelda seemed enthusiastic about that idea. "We have to find Meezel," she insisted. "I don't care about all this other stuff anymore. I just want Meezel."

Caspar let go a long sigh as he resigned himself to the inevitable. "How do we get in this time?" he asked wearily. "I'm not kissing any more guards."

Sunrise grinned. "Just close your eyes and think of Borphee," he suggested.

Caspar made a horrible face. "His breath was awful," he said with a shiver. "Sixty percent leeks and eighty percent garlic."

Burble waddled a few steps forward, scratching his head with one hand while he calculated on the fingers of his other. "Caspo, that too much percent."

Caspar made another face and shook his head. "It was certainly too much garlic."

Nasty made several rapid strokes with her broom on the old floor, raising a cloud of dust sufficient to capture their attention. "That's better," she snapped when all eyes turned her way. She glared at Caspar. "You can rattle on about your disgusting little relationships another time. Right now, let's get on with this business. I've got a mess to clean up back home." She turned to Satchmoz. "It sounds like you're planning to get inside using *aimfiz?*"

"It's the only spell I know, Madam," he answered, folding his arms rigidly across his chest, "that can transport this many people inside at once."

"But it requires somebody on the inside already," Nasty said with a dismissing wave of the hand. "All right. There's no need for Cutie-pie here to sleaze his way inside." She gave Caspar another sidewise glance. "I'll be your anchor."

"Good idea," Sunrise piped up sarcastically. "Why should Caspar sleaze his way inside when you can do it, instead?"

Nasturtium glowered down at the youth and wiggled the fingers of one hand. "Yes, a tasty little gingerbread boy, you'll make!"

Burble made a quick move and put himself between Sunrise and Nasturtium. He clacked his fangs threateningly and shook a fist under the old woman's nose. The three-year-old was gone. "Watch yer mouth, skirt!" he warned with a growl. "The kid's my chum, see. You mess with 'im, an' I'll tenderize your flank steaks!"

Nasturtium straightened with genuine surprise and

regarded Burble. "What's this?" she exclaimed with more than a hint of amusement.

"Schizoid brogmoid," Caspar answered.

"If annoyed," Sunrise added, sticking out his tongue, "avoid."

"Stop!" Esmerelda cried, leaping angrily to her feet. "Enough stupid rhymes! I'm getting really annoyed! Our energies are better employed finding my cat before he's destroyed!" She stared at all of them, then flung up her hands in complete despair. "Oh!" she shrieked. "You've got me doing it!"

"Who said poetry can't stir the masses?" Sunrise said with a quiet smirk.

"I think we'd better find the cat before her screaming brings every soldier in town," Caspar stated irritably.

Hearing his words, Esmerelda quieted immediately, but she gave him a look that could have turned oil to ice. "One of these days, Caspar Wartsworth," she half-whispered, "you're going to regret the way you treat me."

Satchmoz caught Burble's hand and pulled him back. At the wizard's touch the brogmoid instantly reverted again. But there was a lurking gleam in his big eyes whenever he looked at Nasturtium. "Madam," Satchmoz said, doing his best to restore calm, "how do you intend to get into the palace?" He made a small gesture toward her broom. "Can you fly that thing?"

"See!" Sunrise shouted excitedly. "I told you she was a witch!"

Caspar clamped a hand over the boy's mouth and held him in an unbreakable headlock. He gave Nasty his best smile.

"Of course I can fly!" Nasty snapped indignantly. "And would you stop calling me *Madam!*"

Sunrise had almost grown calm again, but now he struggled harder than ever to get free of Caspar's grip. A few muffled, unintelligible sounds were all he managed to get out. "Let it lie, Sunrise," Caspar warned. "Let it lie. It's the oldest straight line in the world." Without releasing Sunrise, he gave Nasty another huge, if somewhat disingenuous, smile.

"Hmmmppp!" Nasty commented, turning up her nose. "Well, I'm only in this for the insurance, remember. But I'll fly over the wall and find an isolated space to land. You can all *aimfiz* over when you're ready."

"And how will we know when it's safe?" Satchmoz asked reasonably.

Nasty gave him a contemptuous sneer. "I haven't lived for five hundred years for nothing," she answered. "Trust me."

Esmerelda shook her head. "You probably shouldn't have said that, Mumsy."

"Bah!" Nasturtium said. She gripped her broom in a tight fist and strode from behind the crates toward the warehouse door. At the threshold, she paused long enough to call out to Satchmoz. "You just count to one hundred. That's all the time I'll need."

Nasty hiked up her skirts then and straddled her broom. She lifted one foot and kicked downward several times without actually touching the ground, and one of her wrists made a sharp, twisting motion. A keen roar filled the doorway as a sudden wind whistled around her and swept her wizard's cloak straight out. Her gray hair streamed under the pointy hat, and she gave a cackle as she lifted the nose of the broom a bit higher. Then, like a skyrocket taking off, she shot upward into the darkness, leaving behind a thinly visible cloud of pale smoke and a short trail where the broom's straw bristles had brushed the floor.

Caspar ran to the door and stared upward into the night. Nasty was already out of sight. Only the faintest vapor trail marked her course high over the rooftops. "Maybe it's not such a rational world, after all," he called back to the others.

Sunrise came to his side. "You mean she really is a witch?"

Esmerelda also joined them. "Something that rhymes with it," she answered.

Satchmoz walked to the warehouse door also, but

he kept one hand before his face to conceal the light of his radiant nose. "Well, I think she's quite a woman," he commented.

Sunrise looked up at him with a smirk. "Yes," he said, "I can see you've taken a shine to her."

"She lights up his life," Caspar added.

Esmerelda glanced nervously out into the empty streets. "I hate to sound so businesslike," she said, "but is anyone counting?"

"Burble keep count!" the brogmoid answered. He held up both his hands and showed them all six fingers and two thumbs. "This many, so far," he said. Then, he used the toe of his right boot against the heel of his left and slipped it off. He lifted a foot and wiggled two bare toes. "And this many."

Satchmoz leaned down and rumpled the brogmoid's stiff pink mohawk. "Thank you, Burble," he said, smiling. But when he glanced up at Caspar, he wore a more desperate look. "B-U-R-B-L-E doesn't know how to C-O-U-N-T," he added worriedly.

The brogmoid waddled over to Caspar and tugged on his sleeve until he bent down close. Still proudly holding up his fingers, he whispered sharply in Caspar's ear. "Can't S-P-E-L-L, either," he said with a gleeful note and a quick wink.

Satchmoz wasn't listening. He was searching through his cloak pockets. "I know I put it here somewhere," he muttered to himself. Finally, he pulled out the sought-after scroll. "Here it is." He gave the parchment a shake and it snapped out straight. Almost instantly, it curled up again. Satchmoz gave a low growl and unrolled it with both hands. The light from his nose illuminated the spidery script written on the parchment, and the wizard's lips moved as he read. A moment later, the letters burst into flame, and the parchment swiftly consumed itself.

Esmerelda shouldered the bag of scrolls she'd carried from the library. Burble dashed back behind the crates to grab the sack of food he'd left sitting there. Upon his quick return everyone joined hands.

"Wait!" Satchmoz cried in sudden dismay. He clapped

both hands over his nose. "I can't go like this! I could give us all away with this shnoz!"

They all exchanged looks. "I've got it," Sunrise said. He grabbed the right sleeve of his tunic and gave it a sharp yank. Then, he gave it another. Finally, he turned to Caspar. "Would you do the honors?" he asked politely.

"That's a high-quality, name-brand designer garment," Satchmoz told them. "Made to last."

Caspar grabbed the sleeve in both hands and tried to rip it. "Damn!" he said after his first attempt. He tried again, and the stubborn material resisted. Once more, he tried, audibly groaning as he strained at the task. Finally, he seized the fabric firmly in his fists, gave a determined glower, and planted a foot in Sunrise's stomach.

"Uh, hold it," Sunrise suggested, stepping back quickly as he brushed Caspar's foot away. "I think Esmerelda can help us." He turned to Esmerelda. She was still carrying her knives. "Would you mind, please?" he asked her.

"Not at all," she answered gracefully. But instead of reaching for one of her knives, she reached out, caught Caspar's right sleeve and ripped it cleanly from his arm and over his hand in one vicious jerk. With a curtsy, she handed it to Sunrise, leaving Caspar to stare at his suddenly naked limb.

Sunrise thanked her with a bow. "Bend down," he said to Satchmoz. When the wizard complied, Sunrise tied the sleeve over the lower half of the old man's face, shielding most of the light. Only a small illumination leaked from the top around Satchmoz's cheeks and nose. It gave his eyes a strange look, indeed.

"Wow!" Sunrise exclaimed, admiring his handiwork. "Who is that masked man?"

"That's really not a bad effect!" Caspar said with an appraising nod. "Anybody who sees you coming is likely to run the other way."

"I think we'd better join hands again," the wizard said, his voice only slightly muffled by the mask. "A spell only stays memorized for a short time. I brought several *aimfiz* scrolls, but let's not waste this one." He squeezed his eyes tightly shut. "Get ready," he said.

Bamf!

Nasty was tapping her foot impatiently, her spindly arms folded sternly across her bosom. "What took you so long!" she demanded in a sharp, hissing voice. "A body could die of boredom waiting for you pokeys!"

Caspar let go of Sunrise and Satchmoz and looked around nervously. He swallowed hard at the sight that greeted him. "Uh, you don't look like the one who died," he said in a soft whisper.

They stood in a side courtyard near the palace. Among the flowers and the marble benches, he counted the limp forms of four soldiers. A pair of boots sticking out from behind a rose bush suggested a fifth. He walked to the nearest body and stared at it.

"I guess they don't call you *Nasty* for nothing," Sunrise commented uneasily.

Nasturtium elbowed him aside. "I can see I don't need to turn you into a cookie, after all," she said snidely. "You've got plenty of 'em for brains." She reached Caspar's side and nudged the soldier with her toe. "He's not dead." She jerked a thumb back at Esmerelda. "No more than she was when you found her."

"You mean they're asleep?" Caspar breathed a sigh of relief.

"How many?" Satchmoz asked eagerly.

"Everybody on the open grounds," Nasty answered with a hint of pride. "I got 'em from the air before I landed. Got one more memorized and ready to go for anyone inside, too," she added. "Course, if Duncanthrax is a wizard, he felt this first one. It's a potent spell. Probably jangled his fool head off. He'll be ready."

"You gave us away?" Caspar blurted, realizing what she'd said.

Nasty patted him on his backside and grinned a big, toothy grin. "Don't worry, sweet-cheeks," she told him. "The fun's just beginning."

"Let's find Meezel!" Esmerelda whined.

"Let's find Berknip and Krepkit and my guild brothers," Satchmoz added.

"Let's find Duncanthrax," Nasty said with a soft cackle, "and his insurance agent."

The three of them strode toward the palace, and Burble waddled after them, leaving Sunrise and Caspar staring at each other. "You know," Sunrise said quietly, "it's at moments like this when I think life on the *Screaming Queen* wasn't really so bad. The roar of the sea, the rush of the wind, the snap of the sail . . ."

"The crack of the whip," Caspar reminded him.

"Yeah," the boy answered with a wistful smile. "That, too."

Their comrades were beckoning to them. Satchmoz tugged his mask down three quick times, a signal to hurry up. They'd found a door into the palace.

CHAPTER TWENTY-TWO
SOFT LAUGHTER IN THE DARK

NASTURTIUM DEMANDED that the others wait outside while she and Satchmoz stepped across the threshold and closed the door. Shortly, they opened the door again. Satchmoz's nose was uncovered. A pile of ash lay at Nasturtium's feet.

"Walk quietly," she warned in a whisper. "Everyone *should* be asleep now, but I wouldn't bet the cat's fur on it."

"I want Meezel!" Esmerelda whined.

"A poor choice of words, Madam," Satchmoz muttered to Nasturtium.

Nasty only shrugged. She turned and led the way a few steps along the corridor in which they found themselves. But there were no lamps or torches. Putting on a faint smile, she slipped her arm around Satchmoz's arm and drew him close. "Satchmoz, with your nose so bright," she said, "won't you guide our way tonight?"

"Yes, please, Satch," Sunrise said as he entertwined his arm with Caspar's and batted his lashes, "be a dear."

Burble reached up and caught Esmerelda's hand, but she shook him off with a look of irritation. "I want Meezel," she mumbled petulantly.

"We know, already," Caspar answered sharply. He bent down and took Burble's hand himself and pulled the hurt-looking brogmoid to his side. The corridor was wide enough for them to walk three abreast.

Nasty used Satchmoz as if he were a flashlight as they started forward again. Holding tight to his arm, she steered him this way and that, directed him to look left or right, wherever she needed light. At the first intersection of corridors, she turned him in a circle, shining his nose down each branching passageway.

A soldier sat slumped against a closed doorway in the hall to their left. His lance lay on the floor near his open hand. Caspar might have avoided that direction, but Nasty went straight to him and nudged him with her toe. The soldier gave a sudden loud snore that made them all jump, but gave no other sign of waking.

"Gotcha," Nasty said with a low cackle. She turned to Caspar and Sunrise. "Open that door," she ordered. "Let's see what he was guarding."

Sunrise looked at her suspiciously. "I don't suppose there's any reason why you can't just reach over and turn the knob?" he asked. "You're closest."

Nasturtium let go a small, disappointed sigh. "Just trying to let you feel useful," she answered as she grabbed the knob. "We're a team now. Don't want anyone feeling inferior." She gave the knob a sharp twist. The door, however, was locked. The barest hint of surprise flickered over her face.

"Allow me," Caspar said, stepping quickly forward. His foot shot out forcefully, and the door smashed open. It struck the inner wall and rebounded nearly closed again. He stopped it with his hand. "There," he added with a smug look to the witch as he held the door open for her. "Don't want anyone feeling inferior."

"Verrry good!" she answered sarcastically. "The quiet, subtle approach."

"Your spell worked," Caspar said, stiffly defensive. He pointed at the guard. "Everyone's asleep."

Nasty shook her head and patted his cheek as she passed inside. "Like I said, Cute-stuff, don't bet the cat's fur on it." She beckoned for Satchmoz to follow, for the room within was utterly dark, and she needed his nose.

"What's she hinting at?" Caspar asked the wizard as he passed.

"Duncanthrax," Satchmoz answered simply. "If he's a wizard, as you suggest, he probably sensed the magic she used to ensorcel the outer guards. He'd have protected himself from a second employment of that particular spell."

"You mean, he's awake?" Caspar asked, astonished.

"I believe I said that," Satchmoz affirmed as he went to Nasturtium's side and shined his nose around.

Caspar leaned out and shot a quick, fearful glance up and down the hallway. "Wait right here," he said to Sunrise and Burble. "Keep a sharp eye out."

It was then he noticed that Esmerelda was gone. "Damn!" he cried.

"What?" Nasturtium hissed irritably. "Will you keep your voice down?"

"Damn your stepdaughter!" Caspar snapped, genuinely angered by the witch's tone. "That's what! She's taken off after that cat!"

Nasturtium ran back into the hallway and stared up and down. When she turned back to Caspar, she spoke in a softer tone. "I should have kept a watch on her," she said with more than a little worry in her voice. "She always could sneak right under my nose and never give me a sneeze."

"Speaking of noses," Satchmoz said from the far side of the room, "look what mine's found."

Sunrise and Burble started to come inside, but Caspar motioned for them to stand on guard while he and the witch went to see. It was not the far side of the room at all, as Caspar had thought, but a curtain made of layered veils. Satchmoz parted those veils with one hand and held them back.

Nasturtium gasped. Instantly, she shot out a hand to cover Caspar's eyes. But Caspar brushed her hand away. Half a dozen beautiful ladies lay asleep on soft floor cushions right at his feet. Beyond those, lay another half dozen. The smells of incense and perfume hung in the room. Here and there, a few small oil lamps burned dimly on carefully placed tables. That light, and the light of Satchmoz's nose, gleamed on bared breasts and thighs, on ladies who snored peacefully in each other's arms, on ladies who leaned close together on either side of a hookah pipe. A few wine bottles rolled on the floor. A num-

ber of crystal glasses, some still half full, rested on the
tables near the lamps.

"Looks like quite a party," Satchmoz said with a
grin.

"I'll show you a party!" Nasty snarled. She jerked
Satchmoz's arm and dragged him away. The curtain fell
closed again. Only a soft hazy glow could be detected
through the heavy gauze. Caspar lingered to part the
veils and take one more peek.

"What was it?" Sunrise asked insistently when they
were all in the hallway again.

"Just the harem," Caspar answered when neither
Nasty, nor Satchmoz, supplied the answer. Burble stuck
out his lower lip and started to waddle inside, but Sunrise caught him by the collar of his yellow sweater.

"Burble just curious," the brogmoid said innocently.

"You're curious, all right," Sunrise affirmed as he
took Burble's hand firmly and led him down the hallway
after the others.

Not far beyond the harem, they found another corridor. Satchmoz's nose, noticeably dimmer now, revealed
a narrow passageway that bent out of sight after about
twenty paces. The air was stale, and the walls cool to
the touch. The dusty floor showed numerous footprints.

"Something just occurred to me," Caspar said as
they hesitated at the entrance to the passage. "Shouldn't
we look for Esmerelda? She has the bag of scrolls from
the guildhall library."

Satchmoz muttered something inaudible under his
breath. "I wanted to save something from the library,"
he said in a louder voice, "in case the soldiers ransacked
or burned it."

"You still have all the scrolls in your cloak pockets,"
Sunrise observed reasonably.

That didn't erase the frown Satchmoz wore. "Those
are master copies she's carrying," he said. "And I don't
know what she's got."

Nasturtium patted him on the shoulder sympathetically. "Essie's a sharp girl," she reminded him. "She

knows the value of what she's got. She won't let anything happen to your scrolls."

A low laugh suddenly rumbled out of the darkness. Caspar felt a chill crawl up his neck. Sunrise and Burble found themselves shivering in each other's arms. Nasty's hand tightened on Satchmoz's sleeve as she stared around, searching for the source.

"I didn't like the sound of that," Caspar said to Satchmoz.

The wizard barely glanced at him. "Perhaps you'd have preferred it in a different key?" he suggested, trying to sound brave.

"Yeah," Sunrise agreed. "The key of E, for Exit."

Nasturtium looked at each of them with stern eyes. "I think it's safe to assume our host knows we're here. I've got to go on now. Not just for the insurance, but to find Essie. The rest of you will have to make up your own minds." She didn't wait for them to decide, though. She simply started off into the dark passageway.

Of course, Satchmoz followed her without hesitation, taking the light with him. Unless they wanted to be swallowed by the darkness, Caspar, Sunrise, and Burble had no choice but to follow as well. They hurried to catch up as Nasty and Satchmoz rounded the bend in the passageway.

But the passage soon bent back again, and yet again, becoming as twisting as a snake's back. They passed a tall iron brazier. The cauldron of coals atop it still exuded heat, but no light. Little by little, the floor took on a noticeable downward slant.

Abruptly, Satchmoz's nose flickered and went out. Sunrise gave a soft despairing moan and clutched at Caspar's arm as the darkness crashed around them. The breath caught in Caspar's throat. He couldn't see any of his friends. He felt the hand on his arm, but he couldn't see it. He couldn't see his own hand when he held it up to his face.

"Dark," Burble said needlessly, his voice small and timid.

"Don't panic," Nasty told them. An instant later, a

brilliant flash nearly blinded them. The witch held her broom at arm's length. It shone with a pure white radiance from top to bristled bottom. "I used to hate the dark, myself, when I was a child," she admitted with a wink to Sunrise. "When I started studying magic I knew if I never could memorize another spell, I'd memorize *frotz*. It's saved me a small fortune in candles and lamp oil, let me tell you. And when you own a castle these days, the lighting bills alone can kill you!"

Satchmoz was looking cross-eyed at the tip of his nose, exploring it with the fingers of one hand. "Actually," he said with a measure of regret, "I was getting kind of used to it the way it was."

They continued along the snaking corridor. There were no doors, no windows, no furnishings other than the occasional lightless brazier. The floor continued to gradually descend, however. A strange odor began to seep into Caspar's nostrils. The others noticed it, too.

Abruptly, they emerged into a vast chamber. Not even Nasty's broom could dispell the pervading gloom. Caspar stared aghast at various instruments of torture. A rack stood in one corner. A brown-stained table with heavy leather straps stood in another. Several pairs of pincers and tongs rested upon it. Chains dangled from the ceiling beams, and manacles hung upon the walls.

"Every castle should have a play room," Nasty commented as she admired a set of delicate ivory fingernail spikes. She closed the finely crafted leather case that contained them and set it aside.

"Nothing seems to have been used for a long time," Sunrise observed. He drew his hand through a cobweb, then wiped it on his trousers.

"Zilbo's idea of a good time was an evening of Double Fanucci," Satchmoz reminded them. "Physical pursuits didn't interest him much."

"Maybe Duncanthrax shares that attitude," Nasturtium suggested. "It's stale down here. This place isn't used."

Another low laugh vibrated through the air. Caspar felt the hairs on the back of his neck stand straight out.

He spun around, seeking the source of the laughter, and nearly tripped over Burble. The brogmoid's hair, too, was standing on end. But then, Caspar reminded himself, it always stood on end.

Nasturtium threw back her head and gave a wicked cackle of her own as if she was answering some challenge. The sound of it echoed against the stone walls, just as chilling in its own way as the first laugh.

They found an open doorway on the far side of the chamber. The passage beyond, like the one that brought them here, also snaked back and forth for no apparent reason. It also descended at a gentle rate, taking them lower and lower.

A sudden loud crunch made them halt. They looked sharply around. Burble gazed up at them with wide, sheepish eyes, holding his knapsack in one hand, an apple in the other. A large bite was missing from the fruit. Realizing he'd done something wrong, Burble swallowed hard.

"Hungry," he said meekly.

Caspar remembered the food the brogmoid had set out on the bloodwood table in the Crystal Room and later packed into the knapsack. It had been some time since he'd eaten, but he wasn't hungry now. No one else seemed to be, either, except for Burble.

Under the weight of so many stares, the brogmoid trembled and dropped the apple. It rolled a few paces away and came to rest against the wall.

Sunrise put an arm around Burble's shoulder. "We'll eat soon," he promised.

They started off again, weaving back and forth, the light of Nasturtium's broom chasing away the darkness. They hadn't gone far, though, when they heard the crunch again.

"Burble . . . !" Satchmoz snapped, spinning around.

The brogmoid held up both his empty hands.

"He didn't . . . !" Sunrise snapped back, his arm still around Burble.

Suddenly, they all stared back up the passage. A loud

gulp sounded from the darkness where Nasty's light failed to reach. Then, came that low laughter once more.

Caspar felt a hard lump in his throat. A shiver ran all through him. He tried not to show his fear, though. "Come out, come out, whoever you are," he called, though his voice was little more than a hoarse whisper.

"Uh, I wouldn't do that if I were you," Satchmoz warned him, his gaze fixed on the darkness behind them. "I thought it was just the stale air I was smelling. But now I recognize it."

Caspar tried to control his trembling. "Well?" he demanded. "What is it, then?"

Satchmoz looked at each of them in turn, his gaze hard and gleaming. Then he stared back into the darkness again. "I don't think I'd better tell you," he announced.

"Oh good strategy!" Nasty sneered, glowering at the wizard. "Frighten everybody with some grim pronouncement, then refuse to tell us what's back there!" She raised the straw end of her broom and smacked Satchmoz twice over the head with it before he could throw up his arms to protect himself.

"That's it!" Sunrise cheered. "Beat it out of him!"

"All right! All right!" the wizard shouted, holding up his hands to ward off the next blow. Nasturtium paused in midswing, her broom drawn back like a batter ready to knock his head into centerfield. "I think it's a grue!"

A soft rumbling voice echoed out of the darkness beyond the edge of Nasty's light. *Grue food!* the voice said as if in answer to the wizard.

Caspar felt all the blood drain from his face.

"On the other hand," Sunrise muttered. "Maybe I'd rather not have known."

"A grue?" Nasty said uncertainly. "I haven't seen one of those in ages. Of course, I don't go out at night anymore. Haven't had a date in nearly four centuries."

"I thought they only roamed the deeper woods," Caspar commented. He'd only heard stories about the huge, hairy monsters. Few had ever seen one and lived to tell about it. But patches of dark, wiry hair had been found stuck in the bark of trees where they had scratched themselves. And half-chewed corpses of luckless travelers had been found along forest trails. No beast was more feared in all the land of Quendor. "What's a grue doing here?"

Satchmoz rubbed his hands together nervously. "Probably a watch-pet, I'd guess. With his human guards put to sleep, Duncanthrax has let it loose."

"Pet?" Nasty snapped sarcastically. "Who, in his right mind, would try to make a grue his pet?"

"Who said Duncanthrax is in his right mind, Madam?" Satchmoz answered quietly. "And remember the scroll Sunrise showed us. A very potent *vaxum* spell, which turns hostile beings friendly. Perhaps he's ensorcelled this monster."

"But it won't come into the light, will it?" Sunrise cried hopefully. "Grues can't stand light."

"The boy's right there," Satchmoz said. He nodded to Nasturtium. "Just don't let your *frotz* wear off."

"I've got a better idea," Caspar announced. He caught the end of the witch's broom and plucked a straw from it.

Nasty shrieked in outrage. "What are you doing, you miserable boy?" She drew back and swung the broom at him, but Caspar only caught it and jerked out a few more straws, which made her scream all the louder.

"Shut up, you old bat!" he finally shouted. Stunned by such effrontery, she actually did shut up. He let go of her broom then, and walked with his handful of straws to the very edge of the darkness. Was it his imagination, or could he really hear something breathing close by? He didn't wait to find out. He gave a little flick and sent one of the broomstraws a few paces back into the gloom.

There was a soft shuffle. Something retreated quickly from the straw's small light.

Caspar rejoined his comrades.

"My apologies, Cutie-pie," Nasturtium said genteelly. "That was quick thinking. If we drop a straw

·very so often we might be able to keep that thing at ·ay."

"Until the light wears off," Satchmoz reminded her.

"Not waste time, then," Burble urged, giving Sun-ise's hand a tug. "Go forward. Leave bogey-thing."

"That's got my vote," Sunrise agreed.

Caspar dropped another straw where they stood, and ·hey started down the passage again. He thought of Es-·nerelda, though. With a grue on the loose, he wondered f she was safe. Had she found that miserable cat, yet? ·Ie smiled half to himself, and hoped so. Practically her ·nly redeeming feature was her love for the mangy little ·east.

Every twenty paces or so, he dropped another straw, ·eaving a trail of light that extended behind them. When ·is last straw was gone, he reached for the broom and ·lucked another bunch.

"You're screwing up my aerodynamics," Nasty com-·lained, though she didn't try to stop him. "It'll probably ·ever fly right again."

"Let's hope we all get the chance to find out," ·aspar replied.

The passageway took a sudden sharp downward ·slope. Satchmoz, in the lead near the front edge of the ·ight, put one hand against the wall and, taking small ·areful steps, eased his way down. Nasty followed him, ·hen Sunrise, Burble, and finally Caspar.

Without warning, the wizard's feet flew out from ·inder him. "Awwwp!" he cried, sliding away into the ·larkness below. "Aieeee!" Nasturtium screamed as she ·lipped and slid after Satchmoz. "Casparrrrr!" Sunrise ·houted, his voice swiftly trailing off.

Caspar made a desperate grab for the nearest hand ·ind caught Burble by the wrist just as the brogmoid's ·eet went out from under him. Jerked off balance, Caspar ·umbled head over heels past Burble, landing hard on ·is backside. Shining straws went every which way. ·Entwined, the two of them slid together down a vast, ·lippery tunnel, tossed helplessly from side to sloping side ·as their momentum bore them faster and faster along.

"Some fun!" the brogmoid squealed breathily in Caspar's ear.

"Helllppp!" Caspar shrieked uselessly. The walls battered him. He hit his head, his elbows, his knees. Stars burned through the red haze that filled his vision. Around and around he spun, unable to find any purchase on the strange smooth substance that made the tunnel. Down into darkness he hurtled.

It stopped with a suddenness that sent a shockwave through his spine. He spilled out of the tunnel into a heap on a cold hard floor. Burble's elbow was in his gut. Sunrise's left heel was in his right eye. Somebody's cloak, either Satchmoz's or Nasty's, half covered his head.

A lot of groans filled his ears, and not all were his own.

"Ahhh," Caspar moaned, rising up on one raw elbow and peeking out from under the hem of the cloak. It turned out to be Satchmoz's. Sunrise struggled to his feet also. He rose slowly, then limped about, clutching his rump. The slide had worn a hole clean through the seat of his trousers and scraped off some flesh, too.

"Everybody all right?" Satchmoz asked painfully as he pulled himself to his hands and knees and looked around.

Nasty pushed out her lower lip and blew an upward puff of air at the hair that spilled over her eyes. She reached out one hand for her hat. It lay on its side, its point bent nearly at a right angle. Scowling, she set it on her head and pounded it into place. Stiffly, obviously feeling all the aches and pains of the ride, she got up and recovered her broom. "I'm really pissed now," she warned them, straightening her cloak.

Caspar looked around. The light from Nasty's broom reflected back at them, magnified many times by the glass walls of the chamber in which they found themselves. The room was round. The mouths of several more tunnels could be seen at even intervals around the chamber.

Before them, though, stood a huge crystal door. Unlike the rest of the chamber it was not perfectly smooth, but faceted. It gleamed and shimmered with traces of red, green, and gold fire. Whenever Nasty moved her broom, the fire shifted, creating new brilliancies and fantastic radiances. There was no knob, no knocker, no keyhole. Yet, there was no doubt that it was a door.

"It's like a giant diamond," Sunrise exclaimed, his aches apparently forgotten as he stepped closer and gingerly touched it. "If I had a chisel, a chunk of this could set me for life."

At that moment, the light from Nasty's broom winked out, plunging them instantly into total darkness. Before Caspar could even gasp in surprise, he heard a *shooosh* in one of the tunnels, and a *thump* as something hit the floor.

Then, he heard a familiar low laugh, and every hair on his body stood on end.

A cool, terrifying voice rumbled on the far side of the chamber, like a soft harsh wind through the trees of a very old forest.

It said, *Grue food!*

CHAPTER TWENTY-THREE
THE UNDERGROUND HIGHWAY

PAIR OF HUGE, LUMI-
nous eyes blinked open in the darkness and regarded
them. Again, the monster growled. *Grooooooo*, it said in
that strangely sonorous voice.

Just *grooooooo*, Caspar realized suddenly, not *grue
food*. That had only been his imagination. The new bit of
knowledge didn't really comfort him, though, because
grue food was exactly what they were about to become.

"We're gonna get eaten," Sunrise uttered in barely
contained terror. "And not even in a nice way."

Before Caspar could answer, a voice that he barely
recognized as Burble's spoke from the center of the
room. The three-year-old was gone; the tough-guy was
plainly in control. "Forget it, bubba!'" the brogmoid
warned. There followed a sound that could only be Burble's three-inch fangs clacking together. "Nobody and no
thing chows down on my buddies."

The grue gave a low growl. Burble snarled. There
was the sound of a brief commotion, a loud *smack*.
Something heavy hit the wall or the floor. The moan
that followed was distinctly brogmoid.

"Burble!" Sunrise cried.

Caspar felt the grip of panic as Sunrise rushed past
him. He tried to grab the youth and missed. "Sunrise!"
he screamed. The boy had no chance at all against the
grue. Damn the darkness! Caspar couldn't see! What was
that scuffling?

The monster's roar shook the whole room. Those big
luminous eyes turned toward them once more, burning

with malevolence. Caspar was sure this time it said *grue food!*

"Your breath stinks, and your mother was a polar bear!" Nasturtium shouted. She gave an evil-sounding cackle, and Caspar heard her shifting about in the darkness. "How about a little fire, furball?"

The chamber exploded with a blinding white radiance. The grue's roar turned to an inhuman screech of fear and pain. It was no fire spell the witch had thrown, She'd *frotzed* the beast! The grue shone with an achingly intense light that the crystal walls of the room magnified and reflected. Every inch of the grue, every limb, every claw, every hair on its body screamed with light.

Caspar shielded his eyes, but tried to stare between his fingers for a look at the monster. No one had ever seen a grue and lived to tell it, he remembered. Yet, so intense was the white glow that he couldn't bear it long, and the form within was indistinct.

The grue gave another ear-shattering cry. Maddened, it launched itself around the chamber.

"Look out!" Satchmoz called, releasing his grip on Sunrise's collar. Apparently, he'd stopped the boy from rushing to Burble's aid. The wizard pushed Sunrise one way, and he dove the other as the grue ran straight at them.

Caspar hurled himself to the side as the grue charged him. The monster ran straight into the wall, roaring. Then, as if the wall was its enemy, it lashed out with massive fists, pounding at the crystal. Bursts of astonishing brilliance erupted from each impact, but the wall held.

The grue spun about, fanning the air with mighty limbs, wailing with terrible agony. It spied Sunrise and ran at the boy. Quick thinking saved him as Nasturtium hurled her broom low and caught the creature's legs. The grue hit the floor with a tremendous force and rolled into the opposite wall, barely missing Sunrise with a sweep of its arm. Caspar caught him and pulled him to a safer corner even as, from the corner of his eye, he watched Satchmoz drag Burble by the brogmoid's ankle to the farthest side.

Caspar could barely force his eyes open. Watching the grue was like staring into the sun! He clung to Sunrise, ready to move again when the beast charged.

"What's that smell!" Sunrise shouted in his ear over the grue's pain-wracked roaring.

Caspar didn't have time to answer. The grue got to its feet and turned, throwing off lancets of stabbing light with every movement. Through squinted, watering eyes, Caspar tried to anticipate its attack. Bracing himself, he prepared to hurl Sunrise out of harm's way. That's when he saw the slender dagger in the boy's hand. Of course! The very one Caspar had given him! It was a better lock-pick than a weapon, but he grabbed it from Sunrise, and pushed the youth toward Satchmoz and Nasturtium.

"Here!" he screamed, leaping into the center of the room, waving his arms to draw the monster's attention away from his friends. "Over here, you flea-bitten bag of bones!"

The monster swung around, flailing with its arms, its agonized roar reaching a deafening pitch. But though it turned toward Caspar, it didn't attack. Within the glow, it threw back its head and wailed, seemed to clutch itself. Confused, it whirled about again and ran into the wall. It beat its fists on the crystal, flung itself on the floor, kicking. Rolling, it sprang up and hurled itself at another wall. Satchmoz, Nasturtium, and Sunrise, dragging Burble, scurried to get out of its way.

A potent odor now filled the chamber. Burning hair, Caspar realized, sniffing, and burning flesh. Grues hated light. It burned them. And this light, this *frotz*, was consuming the grue! Coils of smoke swirled in the white glow, becoming darker and thicker. The grue screamed. With all its might and fury it smashed at the walls, striving to escape the room and escape the light.

Clutching the dagger limply, Caspar watched as best he could through the crook of the arm he raised to shield his eyes. He coughed as the smoke filled his lungs, and he backed a few paces away. The smell threatened to make him sick. Still, mesmerized, he watched.

The monster's claws raked at the wall as it sank to its knees, its screams taking on an almost human pitch. Then, suddenly, it leaned its head against the wall, its screams ended. For the first time, Caspar noticed a faint, sizzling sound, a popping as flesh bubbled and burst. The white glow did not subside. Only the shadow at its heart grew thinner and smaller and lost its shape altogether.

Finally, only a charred and formless mass remained. A few bones poked up here and there, all glowing as brightly as ever.

"Guess I overdid it on the *frotz* a little," Nasturtium conceded. Among all the shocks of the grue's attack, perhaps the biggest shock was seeing that the witch was actually trembling.

Satchmoz patted her sympathetically on the shoulder and slipped one arm around her. "A bit too much *presence*, but you were excited," he answered in a consoling tone as he drew her close. "You saved our lives."

Sunrise bent down beside Burble who was just beginning to stir. There was an ugly blackening bruise on the brogmoid's right cheek where the grue had batted him aside. "Flea-bitten bag of bones?" Sunrise said with a weak grin as he glanced back at Caspar.

Caspar shrugged as he handed back Sunrise's dagger. "I don't offer myself as a sacrifice that often," he replied, kneeling down to examine Burble's bruise. "You can't expect originality under that kind of pressure."

But before they had a chance to recover and regroup, a voice came shrieking down one of the tunnels.

"My groooooo!"

An instant later, Duncanthrax, himself, popped neatly and gracefully into their midst, emerging from a tunnel opening with an agile and acrobatic little roll startling for one of his girth and minuscule stature. He sprang lithely to his feet, like a man who practiced this sliding business regularly and enjoyed it. His face, though, was as red as his hair and beard, and his eyes gleamed with anger. "My poor groooo!" he wailed, shaking a fist as he stared at the remains of his pet. "You'll pay for this, you fools!"

Caspar didn't miss the cloak that Quendor's king wore, nor the scrolls that protruded from some of the lining's pockets. Royalty or not, all he thought about was the threat this plump little mockery of a man posed. Curling one hand into a hard fist, he moved.

Duncanthrax stretched out a hand and made a sweeping gesture. A strange euphoria engulfed Caspar's senses. Instead of striking the king, he found himself in Duncanthrax's arms, back arched, head flung back, his heart pounding as he stared up into the deepest blue eyes he had ever seen.

"I love you," Caspar sighed dramatically, and he meant it too.

"Of course, you do," Duncanthrax answered with barely contained politeness. "That's how my *vaxum* works."

"We love you, too!" Nasty cried passionately.

"Me too, me too!" Sunrise rushed forward, caught the king's sleeve and danced up and down.

Over in the corner, Satchmoz nodded agreement while Burble, sitting against the wall, folded his hands over his heart, sighed, and batted his eyelashes.

But I don't really love him, Caspar thought to himself. Inside, as if through some kind of spiritual fog, he knew he hated Duncanthrax. Yet, every expression of that hate transformed itself to an act or word of admiration.

"That's quite a *vaxum* you've got there," Satchmoz complimented, looking like a puppy starved for the attention of its master.

Duncanthrax released Caspar and made a little bow toward the old wizard. "So very glad you like it," he answered with formal courtesy. "One does so appreciate praise from one's peers."

Caspar found it hard to think for the fog that encompassed his thoughts. He loved his king, he knew that. Doted on his every word, worshipped the breath he exhaled. That red beard was the dearest sight he had ever beheld. Had Duncanthrax asked him for a pedicure he would gladly have chewed his lord's toenails with his teeth and been grateful for the honor. So did he love Quendor's ruler.

And yet, he knew, in some deep part of himself, that Duncanthrax had cursed him, called him *fool,* only moments before. Something about the death of his pet, that heap of shining ash in the corner by the wall. Now, though, he was so . . . *polite!*

Suddenly, Sunrise pulled out his slender dagger. For the briefest instant he clutched it tightly and a dangerous fire flickered in his young eyes. It swiftly faded. Love radiated there. "A gift, my king!" Sunrise proclaimed, kneeling and presenting the blade.

Duncanthrax nodded and extended his hand for Sunrise to kiss. "Accepted with gracious pleasure," he responded, making a genteel flourish with the thin dagger. There was the barest hint of menace in the gesture. For a moment, Caspar felt the fog lifting from his mind, but the mists closed in again. It was but a delicate, sweet, and graceful turn of his beloved king's most perfect wrist.

"I've seen you before," Duncanthrax declared, turning to Satchmoz. "You're one of the guild's most minor wizards, as I recall. No offense intended, you understand. Is that not so?"

Satchmoz made a sweeping bow and straightened with the most sublime smile upon his face. "Satchmoz is my name, Majesty," he admitted, "and it is as you say."

The king made another bow, and wearing an equal smile, he asked, "How is it that you escaped my notice, then? That you are not in Antharia with all the lesser wizards?"

A look of surprised appreciation lit up Satchmoz's face. "Ah, I begin to see, Most Awesome Emperor of Earth and Sky!" he proclaimed with a look of awe. "You stranded some of my brethren on that distant island to put them out of your way. A brilliant plan! A stroke of genius!"

"But Most Wise King of Kings!" said Caspar. "We

had heard that the wizards helped defeat Antharia's fleet at Fort Griffspotter in northern Frobozz!"

Duncanthrax's smile turned into a genuine grin that stretched from ear to ear. Shaking with silent mirth, he hopped back and forth from one foot to the other. "That required only your seven most powerful masters," he answered with self-congratulatory glee. "They who even now with their mighty powers dig my underground highways! Was there ever a more clever king than I?"

"Your underground highways?" Satchmoz threw back his head and laughed heartily. "Krepkit, himself, that prissy old show-off? Digging? He's actually doing *work?*" He clutched his belly, he laughed so hard. When he caught his breath, he added, "You are not only clever, Most Beatific Master of My Affection, but just!"

"That is, indeed, brilliant, Lord of my Life and Loyalty!" Caspar cheered.

"Magnificent!" Nasturtium chimed in.

Sunrise clapped his hands. "Duncanthrax is the smartest!" he announced grandly.

Burble rose uneasily to his feet, rubbing the bruise on his cheek. "Pretty good," he admitted.

Duncanthrax glared at the brogmoid. "Pretty good?" he snarled.

For another instant the fog seemed to lift from Caspar, and he saw the evil look his king directed at Burble. But then, his heart went out once more to his Majesty as Duncanthrax seemed to relent. He smiled broadly, went to Burble, and stroked the pink mohawk.

"I do, indeed, remember you, little one," he said more gently to Burble. "You are the wizards' mascot and the keeper of their winecups. Always underfoot, I'm told, and always forgiven."

Burble grinned with embarrassment and hung his head. "That's Burble," he answered sheepishly. "Everybody loves Burble."

"No, no!" Duncanthrax corrected, wagging a finger. "Everybody loves *me*. We must keep that straight now. You all love me, and you'll do anything for me, won't you?" When they all nodded enthusiastically, he turned back to Satchmoz. "Now, I must be certain I've over-looked no one else. Once more, how did you escape from Antharia?"

"I never made it to Antharia, Faultless and Most Perfect Ruler of my Beating Heart," Satchmoz explained. "My ship, under Captain Chulig's command, went down before ever we left the Quendoran coast. Attacked by a sea serpent, we were, and my friends and I . . ." he pointed to Caspar and Sunrise, ". . . washed up on the edge of Mauldwood."

Satchmoz would cheerfully have continued his story in full detail, but Duncanthrax cut him off with a curt wave. "Then you would be galley slaves," he said, addressing Caspar and Sunrise. Again, the fog parted, and again it closed in as the king put an arm around each of their shoulders. "I'm so glad that you survived to continue in my service! You, too, shall help to build my highways. They will link every major city and castle in Quendor and the outlying provinces, and when they are complete, scores and scores of my soldiers shall pay each of them a wonderful surprise visit. Then, my rule will truly be complete. Won't that be wonderful?"

They all applauded and agreed that it would.

"But why is it necessary, O Magnificent Commander of My Beating Heart?" Caspar inquired.

Satchmoz tut-tutted and frowned at Caspar. "I already said, 'My Beating Heart,' " he reminded in a side-whisper.

"Oh," Caspar responded, momentarily disconcerted. Then, he smiled at Satchmoz. "A thousand pardons." To Duncanthrax he repeated his question. "Why, O Magnificent Commander of All Other Organs in my Body?" He turned a very superior smile toward the old wizard.

"Now don't fight over me," the King of Quendor chided goodnaturedly. "Soon, all will be revealed to you. But for now, we must concentrate on the highways. Nothing is more important than the highways. Right?" He waited for everyone to agree. "And you are all ready to do your part. Right?" Again, a panting enthusiasm from his ardent admirers. "And you're eager to get started. Right?"

Sunrise leaped up and waved his hand wildly back and forth. "Choose me, Most Precise and Perfect Potentate of Purity and Peace!" He jumped up and down. "Choose me!"

Nasturtium, too, began to dance around and wave her hands. "Use me!" she urged. "I have magic skill, too! Let me dig, Most Sovereign Suzerain of Silliness and Simple Pleasures!"

Burble began to bounce up and down, his squat, powerful brogmoid legs carrying him high into the air. He clapped his three-fingered hands and clicked his heels. "Use me!" he sang. "Use me!"

Caspar found himself waving his own hand in the air. "Use me!" he demanded. "Abuse me, even." He hesitated suddenly, bit his lip and thought hard. "Uh, how about, uh . . ." he bit his lip harder, then stuck a finger in the corner of his mouth, his mind a total blank. Then, his eyebrows shot up. "How about, 'Most Happy and Harmonious Hetman of our Homes and Hearths, Herald of all our Hopes, and all-around Heavy Dude?' "

His friends stared at him, and a moment of silence hung in the chamber as they thought about it. Sunrise and Satchmoz both held out a hand and wiggled their fingers doubtfully while Nasturtium puzzled over it, and Burble scratched his head.

"Well, I like it," Duncanthrax proclaimed. He clapped his hands together. "Let's get to it, then!" He reached into a pocket of his robe and drew out a slender black wand. Even Caspar knew that wands weren't much favored by enchanters, being unreliable in their ability to retain their magic. Nevertheless, Duncanthrax strode up to the great diamond door and touched it with the wand's tip. A shudder went through the chamber as the door slowly opened.

Beyond lay a great blackness.

"Those who labor in my name are very far along now," said Duncanthrax. "But perhaps together we can start a new tunnel." He made a gracious gesture toward

Satchmoz and Nasturtium. "The enchanter and the enchantress will do the digging," he announced. "I'll provide a sufficient supply of the magic scrolls needed to move the earth. The rest of you will assist in whatever way they require. Is that all right with everyone?"

It was so kind the way he asked for their consent, Caspar thought, when as their king he could have simply ordered their compliance. Caspar loved his monarch more than ever and gazed at Duncanthrax adoringly.

Then, before they could move beyond the door and into the darkness of the tunnels, a shrill scream ripped through the chamber. Despite its volume, it came from far away. But it rapidly drew nearer. A moment later, Esmerelda swept out of one of the chutes that descended from the upper palace levels. Wide-eyed, she hit the floor feet-first, but such was the momentum of her slide that she ran shrieking straight at Duncanthrax. She threw up her arms to protect herself from the inevitable collision, and knocked the King of Quendor flat on his ass! She, herself, tripped, tumbled head over heels, and lay on her back.

"Mumsy!" she cried, spying Nasturtium.

Sunrise bent down and extended a hand to help her up. "Welcome back, O Beautiful and Buxom Bimbo and Bearer of Bewailments, Bellyaching, and Bad Attitude!"

Satchmoz broke into applause. "Oh, I say!" he shouted. "I like that one!"

Duncanthrax sat up. His Most Perfect Face contorted suddenly with anger as he glared at Esmerelda. "You clumsy, stupid girl!" he raged. "You dared . . . !" Abruptly, he stopped and clapped a hand over his mouth. "Oops," he muttered, gazing at each of them. Slowly he rose to his feet and backed away.

The *vaxum* ensorcelment dissolved like a dew in strong sunlight. Caspar shook his head to clear it. He looked down at Esmerelda, at Satchmoz, wondering what had happened to break the spell. He looked at Duncanthrax as all his old anger reasserted itself, and plenty of new, besides. His fingers curled into fists.

"Oh, thank you!" Satchmoz said, wheezing as if a

heavy burden had been lifted from his chest. He rubbed a finger over one temple, trying to clear the effects of the spell. "It only takes one harsh word to blow a good *vaxum* straight to blazes."

Duncanthrax continued to backstep into the Crystal Room. Surreptitiously, he slipped one hand back into the pockets of his cloak, seeking a scroll.

"Oh, no you don't!" Caspar shouted. Desperately, he threw himself at Duncanthrax.

But before he reached the king, another sound, an inhuman whining wail echoed from the chute where Esmerelda had just emerged. Spinning crazily, scrambling frantically for some purchase on the tunnel's glass surface, Meezel came shooting out. At the last possible instant the cat managed to leap from the very lip of the chute. Like a black streak it flew through the air, claws opening, extending.

Duncanthrax screamed as Meezel landed on his back. The cat screamed in feline panic. Esmerelda screamed as Duncanthrax whirled, frantically trying to beat the little beast loose with his wand. Fabric ripped. Meezel's claws shredded Duncanthrax's cloak, and drew blood from the terrorized monarch's neck. Duncanthrax tripped over the charred remains of the grue and stumbled into the wall forcefully. Still Meezel hung on, wide-eyed.

Whether Duncanthrax finally unfastened his cloak, or whether Meezel's weight pulled it from his shoulders, or whether the cat's rending claws tore it loose, was unclear. But suddenly the cloak came free. With a loud feline wail, Meezel hit the floor, tangled in the folds of the garment. Duncanthrax glanced in dismay at his loss, then saw Caspar and the others closing in. Without hesitation, he darted to a section of the wall and struck it with his wand. It swung open long enough to reveal a staircase before it crashed shut again.

Duncanthrax was gone.

Meezel poked his head out from under the hem of the cloak and stared around. He opened his mouth and let go a single *mowrrrr?* Esmerelda swept him up in her arms and hugged him until his eyes started to bulge out.

Sunrise crept up beside her, reached out a hand, and patted the cat's head and made cooing sounds. Without warning, Sunrise gave a series of sharp sneezes, but he continued his stroking and petting.

"Good work, Meezel," Caspar muttered, giving the cat a pat, himself. Meezel trembled quietly on Esmerelda's shoulder and tolerated the touch.

"Where'd you find him?" Satchmoz asked as he bent down to retrieve Duncanthrax's cloak.

"Where I thought he'd be," Esmerelda confided. "In the dungeon, not far from where we left him. In fact, I have the feeling he's been terrorizing the place. Several of the sleeping guards showed scratch marks on their hands and faces."

"You shouldn't have slipped away from us," Nasturtium scolded as she joined Satchmoz. Together, they began to empty the pockets of Duncanthrax's cloak.

"Not love Dunko-tracks anymore," Burble said. He was standing in the middle of them all, so short they'd barely noticed him down around their legs.

"He's right, there," Sunrise pointed out as he rumpled the pink mohawk. "If Essie hadn't slunk off on her own, she might have gotten caught in the same spell we got caught in."

"And if you use that name again," Esmerelda said stiffly to Sunrise, "you're going to wish you were still caught in it."

Satchmoz and Nasturtium were on their hands and knees, bent over three piles of scrolls, a small key ring, a bottle opener, two zorkmids and a zorkle, and four lint balls. "*Katpil* digging spells," Satchmoz said, indicating one pile of scrolls. He pointed to the second pile. "*Vaxum* spells." He pointed to the third. "And this. I don't recognize it."

"*Plasto*," Nasturtium informed him. "I've only seen it once. It's a disguise enchantment. Lets you look like someone else." She opened up one of the *plastos*, looked it over with a squint and slipped it into one of the pockets of her own cloak.

Satchmoz watched her with surprise, then did the

same, taking one of each. Then, almost as an after-thought, he began shoving them all into his pockets. "We really can't leave these lying around," he said.

"And don't leave those lying around, either," Caspar said, pointing toward the chute from which Esmerelda had emerged. The bag of scrolls she'd been carrying lay there where she'd dropped it. Sunrise hurried to snatch it up.

"He didn't have much of an arsenal," Nasty commented as she rose and rubbed her knees. "Only three spells."

"Don't forget the wand," Caspar reminded, lending a hand to steady her.

Nasty shrugged. "That's just a key," she answered. "Probably doesn't do anything except open his private doors."

"Speaking of doors," Esmerelda said with a suddenly bored tone as she inclined her head toward the entrance to the underground highways, "I've got what I came for. Is that the way out? It smells like someone burned a steak in here!" She glanced toward the remains of the grue and wrinkled her nose.

"Krepkit!" Satchmoz murmured half to himself. He gave himself a little smack in the forehead. "Berknip! They're down there somewhere!" He got up quickly and moved toward the great diamond door. But he stopped on the threshold and stared into the blackness. "Uh, Madam," he called, turning toward Nasty, "could you possibly provide us with a bit of light again?"

Nasty let go an exaggerated sigh. "Well, I suppose I could break off one or two of the grue's bones. They should shine for quite a while yet."

"How about something a little less grisly?" Caspar suggested as he handed her her broom.

The witch gave him that *picky-picky-picky* kind of look before she pursed her lips and looked around. Then, without asking, she drew the knives out of her step-daughter's boots and *frotzed* each of them. She handed one to Caspar and one to Sunrise.

"What about me?" Satchmoz asked.

"Don't worry, snookums," the witch said, taking him by the arm. "You're with me." A moment later, her broom blossomed with light again.

They moved past the diamond doorway and into the darkness of Duncanthrax's underground highway. The tunnel was vast. They couldn't see the ceiling, and only found the sides when they lined up and walked shoulder to shoulder. The ground beneath their feet was smoothly paved, and an entire structure of supports was in place to carry the weight of the earth overhead.

"How far do you think it goes?" Sunrise asked quietly. His voice echoed off into the far distance.

"At least as far as Mauldwood," Nasturtium reminded him. "And according to Duncanthrax, that's just one highway."

"Remember the maps," Caspar added, trying to keep his voice low so it wouldn't echo. "There were all sorts of branches and forks and intersections."

"He can't have completed all those, though," Sunrise answered disbelievingly.

They walked on without speaking for a while. The only sounds were the ringing of their footsteps on the pavement and the loud purr coming from Meezel as he rested on Esmerelda's shoulder, content to have done his part.

A sudden *crunch* made them all give a start. They stopped in their tracks and turned slowly. Sunrise and Burble had dropped back a bit. They both held apples. Burble tried to hide his behind his back.

"Stick an oar in it, Caspar," Sunrise snapped before anyone could object. "We're starved."

Caspar licked his lips as he stared at the apple. "Uh, me too," he admitted.

Everyone was hungry. Finally, Burble got to open the pack he'd been carrying around since they fled the guildhall. As they continued on they munched a short meal of fruit and cheese and drank from a canteen of water.

"I've been meaning to ask," Caspar said to Satchmoz as he licked the last crumbs from his fingers. "With this sensitivity to magic you say all enchanters possess, why didn't Duncanthrax detect us when we broke into the dungeon the first time?"

Satchmoz swallowed a last bite of apple and tossed the core over his shoulder, becoming the first litterbug in Quendor's long and enduring history. "Well," he answered carefully, "because the spot where we materialized—a cell in the dungeon—was so far away from wherever he was at that moment. Nor was it the kind of really powerful, far-reaching spell that Nasty—I mean, Nasturtium—used to put the grounds sentries to sleep."

"It just wasn't as powerful a spell, period," Nasturtium interjected.

Caspar rubbed his chin. "But you were able to sense the Gate—the diamond door—all the way up in the cell?"

"Oh, not just the door," Satchmoz corrected. "This whole complex! It's all magical, all these tunnels!"

Nasturtium ran a hand over the back of her neck. "Yep," she agreed. "You should just feel it. I've got a real buzz."

"Quiet!" Sunrise ordered suddenly. "Look!"

Far ahead, a light shone faintly in the darkness.

CHAPTER TWENTY-FOUR

NO PLACE LIKE HOME

THERE WERE LOTS OF
lights, they discovered. Torches, cressets, braziers, oil
lamps were placed all around. Caspar and company had
come to the end of the line, at least as far as the pavement was concerned. The tunnel traveled on into the
vast darkness.

Hundreds of people—men, women, children of all
ages—labored enthusiastically to mix mortar, to trowel
it out, to place the bricks that formed the road bed. Some
carried food to the workers. Some ladled out cups of
water. A few rested on blankets, but the work obviously
never stopped. Everyone wore smiles.

A woman approached them, bearing in each hand a
heavy can of some black, oily substance. It was plain her
arms could hardly handle the strain. Her eyes were dull
and lifeless as she gazed at them, but she flashed a huge
grin.

"Welcome, friends!" she cried. "Welcome to the
Great Labor! Join in! Join in wherever there is work to
be done!"

Caspar tried to avert his eyes. The woman's dress
was torn half off her body. Her knees were scarred and
cut from kneeling on the bricks. Her elbows were crusted
and scabbed. She smelled as if she hadn't washed in
weeks.

He couldn't stop himself, he pitied the woman so
much. The effects of Duncanthrax's *vaxum* were plain
upon her. Remembering Satchmoz's remark about harsh

words, he leaned close and whispered something very rude and personal in her ear.

She dropped the heavy cans at once. Black liquid splashed in all directions, and Caspar jumped back to avoid it. For an instant, the woman glared in anger, but that emotion swiftly faded. Confusion took its place, and fatigue. She looked around fearfully, then quietly fainted.

Caspar caught her in his arms, dragged her away from the spreading puddle of thick, black goo, and laid her gently on the ground. A score of workers passed blindly around, but paid no attention at all as they proceeded with their tasks. The sound of hammering and bricklaying and road-paving went on unabated.

"No wonder the streets of Borphee were so empty," Sunrise said, standing over Caspar and the unconscious woman. "Half the city must be down here."

"It's obscene!" Esmerelda exclaimed.

"Well, what can we do about it?" Caspar demanded sharply. He looked around for someplace safe to put his new charge. It was his fault she'd collapsed. He couldn't just leave her lying in the middle of all this activity. And once he'd gotten her to a safe place, what then? There were so many people, and who knew how many more in other tunnels? "We can't just go around whispering dirty words in everyone's ears!"

"Get her over to the side," Nasturtium suggested. "There are some blankets spread on the ground over there. Put her down on one."

Caspar saw where the witch was pointing. The woman was light as a feather as he picked her up. Her form was emaciated. Though there was food to eat, none of the workers seemed very interested in it. Only the Great Labor mattered. Almost on the point of tears with anger, he carried her to the blankets and laid her gently down. The blankets, of course, were filthy, but there was little traffic nearby. At least nobody would step on her.

"I feel bad about leaving her there!" Caspar said, rejoining his friends as a pair of laborers rolled wheelbarrows of bricks past them. Caspar spared them a glance, then did a quick double-take. "You!" he screamed, enraged. He seized one of the men by the throat, causing the overturn of a wheelbarrow. Bricks clattered out. The nearest workers all dropped whatever they were doing and began to gather the bricks.

Caspar barely noticed. "I'll kill you!" he shouted into the face of his victim. It was Duncanthrax's throat he had his hands locked around. Red beard, red hair, and all.

But Duncanthrax barely resisted. Caspar felt hands breaking his grip, pulling him away. Voices urged him to let go, to calm down, and the rage subsided a little, long enough for him to stand back and take a good look.

It was Duncanthrax. There was no doubt about that. But all his fat was gone. His red hair was matted and tangled and dirty. His gaze was just as lifeless as the other workers. But even as Caspar watched, something stirred in the little man's eyes. With a trembling hand, he reached up and rubbed his temples. Then, he rubbed his throat where Caspar's fingerprints showed lividly.

"What's going on?" Caspar asked Satchmoz.

The wizard watched with interest. "I think, 'I'll kill you!' can be classified as harsh words."

"*Vaxum?*" Caspar's hands curled into fists. "What in Zork is this?" he demanded. "Is this Duncanthrax, or not?"

"The real Duncanthrax, I'll bet," Nasturtium answered. "It's coming clearer now. The *plasto* spells we found, remember? Somebody—some enchanter—has been using magic to impersonate this man."

"And whoever he is," Esmerelda observed as she stroked Meezel on her shoulder, "he's getting away."

The real Duncanthrax looked around in confusion. "I've got to get my tonsils checked," he mumbled to himself, one hand still massaging his throat. "Where am I? Who are you?" He stared at each of them in turn, then looked down at himself. The rags he wore caused him to wrinkle his brow in disgust. Then, his eyes widened with surprised joy. "Wow!" he exclaimed. "I'm svelte! I've never been thin in my life!"

"A little thin upstairs, too, from the sound of you," Nasty said. "Maybe you'd better sit down."

"Sit?" Duncanthrax replied. "I can't sit, Madam! Why, they made me king yesterday. I must have duties . . . !" The confusion caught up with him again. He looked at his rags again, swept his gaze around the tunnel. "I . . . ! I mean . . . !" He turned to them with an expression of genuine pain.

Esmerelda sidled closer to her stepmother. "You know, he's really kind of cute," she whispered a little too loudly. "Well, he would be if he was cleaned up." She put one thumbnail to her lips and chewed it thoughtfully as she ran her gaze up and down.

"I just saw him out of the corner of my eye," Caspar said to Satchmoz. "I thought he was trying to sneak up on us. Maybe grab his scrolls back, or something."

"It was understandable," the wizard answered. "But the question now is, if this is the real Duncanthrax, who is the other fellow?"

Duncanthrax licked his lips as he regarded Esmerelda. He drew a deep breath and let it out slowly. He no longer seemed as concerned with the state of his attire. He straightened his spine and lifted his head a bit higher. Even so, he was considerably shorter than the object of his attention.

"Drespo Molmocker," he said to Satchmoz without looking around.

Satchmoz's jaw gaped. "The president of the Frobozz Magic Tunneling Company?" he gasped. "Are you sure? He's such a minor magician!"

"That might explain why he only had three spells," Nasturtium suggested with a careful eye to her stepdaughter.

"All I know is," Duncanthrax interrupted, "is that Drespo is the last person I remember being alone with. It was right after the coronation. He had this mammoth project he wanted to interest me in." He looked around the tunnel and threw up his arms meaningfully. "Guess this is it. But I said no. The cost was far too great."

"So he ensorceled you and stole your throne!" Esmerelda said sympathetically. She balanced Meezel carefully on one shoulder while she went to Duncanthrax's side and put her arm around him. His face was practically in her bosom. "You poor man. You must feel terrible. Let me console you." She pushed his face right into her cleavage.

Nasty watched it all, her brow furrowing, eyes narrowed. She rubbed her chin.

"But Drespo?" Satchmoz replied in astonished disbelief. "How could he ever get a *vaxum* of such power?"

"You've improved, haven't you?" Caspar reminded the wizard reasonably. "You couldn't start a campfire properly when we first met. But you've learned. You've gotten better. Maybe Drespo has, too."

"And maybe he's been planning this for some time," Duncanthrax added, looking up red-faced from those globes of white flesh. "Hiding his true power and waiting for the right opportunity. Zilbo had been king for a long time. A thousand little mistakes might have tripped Drespo up if he'd tried to impersonate Zilbo. But I was king for less than a day!"

"And everybody who knew you suddenly found themselves chained to oars on ships bound for Antharia," Caspar commented, remembering the so-called *political prisoners* he'd been chained with on the *Screaming Queen*.

"Say there!" Satchmoz cried suddenly. "What's Burble up to?"

Caspar spun about seeking the brogmoid. The little creature was no longer among them. Instead, he was off across the tunnel tugging on some man's sleeve. The worker bent down. Burble cupped a hand to his mouth and whispered something. A strange look came over the man as he straightened. He dropped the shovel he held.

There were other men and women nearby, all wearing confused expressions. One man, reacting angrily, seized a mortar box and flung it. The curses he shouted had an instant effect on those workers nearest him.

"Uh, I uh, ah . . . taught him a new word," Sunrise admitted as he watched Burble. "A phrase, actually."

"What word!" Satchmoz demanded. "What phrase!"

Sunrise glanced at Esmerelda and Nasturtium as he sucked his lower lip. "Uh, I don't think I'd better say it out loud," he answered. "Not in the company of ladies."

"Whatever it is," Caspar observed, "it's breaking the *vaxum* spell."

But Satchmoz began to wring his hands in concern. "There's no place for them to go down here, though. We haven't found any exits. Even if we go back to the Crystal Room, there's no guarantee we can find and open the door that Drespo used to escape."

"There are tools down here," Sunrise noted. "We can take the room apart if we have to."

"Those walls resisted a grue's fists and claws," Caspar reminded Sunrise unpleasantly.

Some of the laborers started to gather around. They looked weary and haggard. Some looked very angry. Most merely looked confused. A little boy with matted blond hair and brown eyes came up and grasped a handful of Nasturtium's skirts and leaned his head against her leg. For an instant, she looked as if she might rip his head off for his presumption, but then the old witch merely reached down and stroked his hair. The boy put a thumb in his mouth and closed his eyes.

Meezel leaped suddenly from Esmerelda's shoulder. He hit the ground and bounded instead into Sunrise's arms. Sunrise gave a loud sneeze.

"These are my people," Duncanthrax said, turning to Satchmoz. He kept Esmerelda's hand in his as he gazed at the worn faces of those who stood around them. More and more were gathering close. "Is there anything you can do for them?"

Satchmoz raised one eyebrow. "They are my people as well," he reminded his king. "But these are not the only ones we must consider. There are at least a score of tunnels just like this one. No doubt many of Borphee's citizens are slaving away in those. And my guild brothers are among them."

"Is there anything you can do, Satchmoz?" Esmerelda asked with a sudden display of compassion. She stepped forward and touched the old wizard's hand gently.

Satchmoz hesitated and bit his lip. He paced back and forth a few times. Then he chewed the nails of one hand. Lines of concentration furrowed his brow. Everyone watched him expectantly. Even Nasturtium.

"There may, however, be one way to save us all," he announced finally. "It might work, but it might not. If it does, it will take everyone's cooperation."

"Oooooh," Nasty cooed with a note of mockery in her voice. "Sounds like a work of Great Magic. What have you got up your sleeve, you cute old buzzard?"

Satchmoz gave her a bold wink, but the look of worry still did not leave his face. "Actually, you old bat," he answered tartly, "it's up *our* sleeve, since it involves a spell I stole from your castle."

Naturtium feigned shock. "Stole? From my castle?"

Satchmoz nodded. "The spatial displacement spell. I didn't steal it, really. I just analyzed its components and made a few changes. Surprisingly, I seem to have an affinity for that spell. It resonates inside me. I think I'll be able to memorize it, soon. I've never been able to do anything else from memory except tie shoe-laces."

"That's the way of magic, dearie," Nasty said with a cackle. "Totally predictable unpredictability."

Duncanthrax interrupted. "Well, get on with it, then. If you can get us out of here, let's get." He drew Esmerelda into his arms and gave her a squeeze. She answered with a quiet giggle. "Some of us have plans for the evening," he added with a lewd grin.

"They make such a cute couple, don't you think?" Sunrise whispered to Caspar.

Caspar leaned closer to Sunrise. "I don't understand it," he admitted with a frown and maybe just a touch of irritation. He wasn't really jealous, just puzzled by her behavior. "They've only just met."

Sunrise gave a very low chuckle and pointed subtly toward Nasturtium's feet. A fine pile of ash lay there. "I don't know what it was," the youth said, "but I'll bet that had something to do with it."

Caspar hadn't seen Nasty even reach for a scroll, let alone actually cast a spell, but he didn't doubt the witch's subtlety. There had been plenty else to occupy his attention, too.

"Gather around!" Satchmoz called to everyone. He waved his hands in the air, summoning all to come closer. "Gather close. I want everyone to take part in this."

The wizard reached into one of the pockets of his cloak and pulled out a scroll and unrolled it. He looked at it for an instant, then let it roll up again. "Damn," he said, thrusting it back into a pocket. He tried again, and again drew out the wrong spell. "I never should have shoved all Drespo's scrolls in here!" he grumbled to himself.

It was a false complaint, Caspar thought as he waited impatiently. Satchmoz had never been able to find anything in those pockets on the first try.

Unfastening the clasp at his throat, he spread the garment on the ground and began pulling out scroll after scroll. Cursing, he examined them quickly and tossed them over his shoulder.

Burble, back from his self-assigned duty, scrambled to gather the discarded scrolls again. He picked them up and clutched them in his arms, running back and forth, wherever a scroll happened to land. But there were far too many for his small limbs, and still they kept coming from those seemingly bottomless pockets. With an exasperated sigh, he tossed them into the air, and kicked another pile with his foot, scattering them.

Sunrise watched the wizard, and he watched the brogmoid. Suddenly, he took from his shoulder the bag of scrolls he'd been carrying, the scrolls from the guild hall library. "What the Zork did he ever want with these?" he asked with a merry laugh. Burble frowned at him, then kicked a scroll that was lying on the floor. Sunrise laughed again, grabbed the bag by the bottom and slung it around his head, scattering scrolls everywhere.

"Men!" Nasturtium laughed, her eyes on Satchmoz's

exposed rump. She looked as if she were seriously considering giving it a good kick. "You'd think a wizard of your caliber could learn to alphabetize!"

"Here!" the wizard cried triumphantly, leaping up with the proper scroll clutched in his fist. He gave Nasturtium a smug look and raised his nose a trifle higher. "I just had time to transcribe this copy from my infotater notes before we fled the guild hall."

"You say you got this spell at my castle?" Nasturtium snapped goodnaturedly. "All these people aren't going to wind up in my hall, are they? I can't feed this many people."

"Not to worry, Madam," Satchmoz answered. "But something's going to happen. Something wonderful." He unrolled the scroll and glanced at it. Then, he added, "At least, I hope."

Someone set a box before the wizard, and he stepped up on it to address the assemblage. He looked almost noble of stature, standing there, gathering the citizens of Borphee to himself, his gaze sweeping over the crowd. Caspar didn't have the heart to tell him that the seat of his trousers was ripped wide open. If he'd just kept his cloak on . . . Instead, Caspar covered his mouth with a hand and suppressed any remark.

"Now, all of you!" Satchmoz proclaimed. "This will take a massive act of will. All our collective concentration. Close your eyes now. Tightly. And concentrate. Say to yourself over and over. There's no place like home. There's no place like home!"

Sunrise brushed past Caspar and tugged on Satchmoz's sleeve. The wizard tried to ignore him for a moment, but Sunrise persisted until Satchmoz stepped down from the box. "What is it?" he snapped. "Everybody's waiting!"

Sunrise shrugged apologetically. "Well, it's just that I live in East Borphee," he said.

Caspar stepped forward, too. "And I don't have a home," he reminded his friends. "I can't go back to Djabuti Padjama."

The wizard knew at once what Sunrise meant and

patted him sympathetically on the shoulder. "Oh," he answered. "Well, thanks for reminding me. You and Caspar, and you also, Madam and Esmerelda, you think of the enchanters' guild hall. You too, Burble. Concentrate on that."

Satchmoz got back on his box again and turned to the crowd. "Remember, we have lots of friends and family in the other tunnels. We've got to amass energy enough to free them, also, so really concentrate. Squint those eyes and furrow those brows!"

He sounded like a cheerleader for the Borphee snaggleball team, Caspar thought. But the workers did as he said. They closed their eyes tightly, set their jaws, and screwed their faces into horrible expressions, all looking as if they'd just eaten brussels sprouts.

There's no place like home, the crowd began to chant. At first, it was a low rumble, but it spread from man to woman to child until everyone took it up. From a low rumble it became a roar. *There's no place like home, there's no PLACE LIKE HOME, THERE'S NO PLACE LIKE HOME!*

"Like the guild hall," Caspar substituted. He reached out to clutch Sunrise's hand. Sunrise gave a loud sneeze, then another, before joining his hand to Caspar's. Caspar tried to ignore the dampness in Sunrise's palm. "The guild hall," he muttered. "The guild hall."

Satchmoz unrolled the scroll again. He read it silently on his high box, his lips moving, his finger trailing down the page. The scroll burst into flame then, a bright flaring fire. Caspar never saw the ash hit the ground.

Satchmoz sat in a chair moved into the garden especially for him. His feet were propped up on a high pile of cushions, and cushions had been placed against his back. He smoked a pipe and blew a ring high into the air as he sighed.

Berknip sat on his lap. The little boy clapped with excited glee as the smoke ring drifted off. He had appeared in the guild hall with the rest of Satchmoz's guild brothers, dirty and ragged, but in good spirits.

Satchmoz had never mentioned that Berknip was a child. Caspar had chided him about that.

"That's why it was so important to find him," Satchmoz had answered. "Only a child, and already he's discovered five new spells. Berknip will be one of the greatest enchanters of our age."

"And you'll go down as one of its greatest heroes," Sunrise had answered.

Two days had passed since the Great Magic that freed everyone from the underground highways, and things in Borphee were just showing signs of returning to normal. A debate had been held in the palace as to what to do with the tunnels, and at Satchmoz's urging a decision was made to complete them. The idea, he argued, was good, to link all the great cities of Quendor with one massive road system. As for the cost, that could be offset by selling space on the walls to merchants who wished to advertise their businesses.

The order had gone out to Antharia to free all the lesser wizards of the guild. Duncanthrax, however, was adamant on the issue of Antharia, itself. As long as it had been conquered he intended to keep it and that was that.

Caspar leaned back on the rim of the garden's fountain and folded his arms across his chest as Satchmoz blew another smoke ring and Berknip clapped. Suddenly, the little boy pointed his finger and the smoke ring changed shape, becoming a bird. It hovered in the air until a light breeze scattered it.

"That's six," Satchmoz said nodding and smiling at the child. "He's never done that before." He winked at Caspar.

"You think you could teach me magic someday?" Sunrise said from the bench where he reclined, basking in the sunlight.

"We might try a spell or two sometime," the wizard answered. "But you and Caspar are going to be pretty busy with your new duties as the king's roving minstrel and his assistant. You'll be Duncanthrax's good-will ambassadors to the outlying provinces and lands far away." He looked at Caspar and pursed his lips. "And I suspect you'll be very busy, too. I don't think Duncanthrax approves of your friendship with his bride-to-be."

That suited Caspar just fine. He'd always dreamed of seeing new lands. And as a minstrel, too! A musician! With his pockets full of the king's coins and fine clothes on his back and the doors of every court open to him. Sunrise to keep him company, too. As far as he was concerned, this adventure couldn't have worked out better.

"He has my gratitude," Caspar answered, "and my sympathy. With Essie for a wife and Nasty for a mother-in-law, he's either going to be the happiest man alive, or . . ."

"Or the most bellicose king Quendor has ever known," Sunrise finished, sitting up, grinning. "You're right, Caspar. He has my congratulations or condolences, whichever is more appropriate."

The seven master wizards of Borphee's guild filed through the side door from the kitchen into the garden. The first bore a small folding table, which he opened before Satchmoz. Smiling, he made a curt bow and turned away. The next set down a bottle of wine and three beautiful crystal chalices. The third wizard placed a tray of rolls and a tub of butter. Smiling, he tossed a napkin over his arm, bowed, and departed. The fourth set down a small roasted duck. The fifth placed three plates with knives and forks on the table.

"Bring a fourth place setting for Berknip," Satchmoz instructed pleasantly. "I think he'll eat with us."

The fifth wizard beamed and hurried to obey.

The sixth wizard bore steaming bowls of potatoes, beans, and spenseweed tubers. Satchmoz only glanced at Sunrise to see the look on the boy's face. "Leave the potatoes and beans," he said, "but throw those out. If we never taste spensweed again we'll all be happy."

The seventh wizard came forward then. He was the only one who did not smile. In fact, he practically scowled as he set a small black case down beside Satchmoz's chair within easy reach. When he straightened, he did not bow. He glared. Then turned and strode away.

"Krepkit isn't a happy camper," Caspar observed as he watched the head of Borphee's enchanters' guild retreat from the garden.

Satchmoz sighed heavily as he leaned forward to pinch off a bit of roll. He held it to Berknip's mouth, and the child took a tiny bite, his big eyes watching every move Satchmoz made. "First of all," Satchmoz said, "he's embarrassed about being tricked and captured by the president of the Frobozz Magic Tunnel Company. Everyone's laughing about it. It's not something he'll live down soon."

"Second of all," Caspar interrupted, "he's not happy that you, a supposedly minor wizard, saved his fat. Or that Drespo Molmocker has apparently managed to make a clean getaway."

Satchmoz nodded sagely as he tapped his index finger to the tip of his nose. "Thirdly," he added as a gleam of mirth lit up his old eyes, "some of the other wizards are pressuring him to give up his bedroom. Someone told them how much I love that big bathtub."

Sunrise coughed and rubbed a hand over his chin and took a sudden interest in the flowers that grew beside the bench.

"That's what I thought," Satchmoz muttered, grinning.

They each took a plate and began to feast on duck and potatoes and beans. It was not the fifth wizard who returned with a plate for Berknip, but Burble. He also carried a cup of water for the boy to drink. Meezel came fast on his heels. Without so much as a *mowrrrr*, he jumped onto Sunrise's lap and settled himself.

Sunrise gave a sharp sneeze as he stroked Meezel and held a strip of duck-meat for the cat to chew. The old cat looked much healthier now. With the help of one of the wizards, his hair had grown back over the bald spots, and the broken ear had straightened. "I couldn't believe Esmerelda let me keep him," Sunrise said, sneezing again.

"Essie have only Dunko-tracks on mind," Burble said, stroking the cat, too.

"Well, she certainly has her stepmother to thank for that," Caspar replied as he lifted a drumstick and began to munch.

"Nasty just wanted to see her in a good marriage," Satchmoz said somewhat defensively. "But I did warn her not to try any love-spells on me."

"You're going to see her again, then?" Caspar asked with amused interest.

The wizard shrugged. "Why not?" he answered. "She hasn't had a date in four hundred years, and I've never had one, period. What could be more perfect?"

Burble began dancing from one foot to another. "Satch in love with Nasty! Satch in love with Nasty!" he sang.

Satchmoz leaned forward casually, ripped off the duck's remaining drumstick, and thrust it in Burble's mouth. The brogmoid gave a look of surprise that quickly turned to pleasure. "Ummm, good!" he exclaimed. Without bothering to chew, he swallowed it, bone and all.

"You know, I keep thinking about all those scrolls we left in the tunnels," Sunrise confided a little uneasily as he sipped from his glass of wine. He was a bit young for wine, yes, but after all, he was an ambassador now. And it *was* a special occasion.

Satchmoz swallowed a small bite of potato and took a drink. "I have the darndest feeling," he confessed thoughtfully, "that those scrolls are going to turn up all over the kingdom, and in the darnedest places, for many years to come."

When the meal was finished, Satchmoz put Berknip down and gave him a little pat on the backside. Berknip gave a short, shy giggle and ran across the garden and through the kitchen door.

"Now, then," Satchmoz said with a satisfied sigh. "Nice day, good food. What say you, Royal Minstrel? It's time for a little music." He reached down and lifted the small black case that Krepkit had carried to him. He put it on his lap, lifted the latches with his thumb and took out a small trumpet.

"Satchmoz!" Caspar exclaimed. "I didn't know you played the trumpet!"

"Of course!" the wizard answered. He put the horn to his lips and blew a short riff, his fingers flying skillfully over the keys. "Why do you think they call me Satchmoz?"

In the bestselling tradition of
The Hitchhiker's Guide to the Galaxy™

ENTER THE
INFOCOM™ UNIVERSE

THE LOST CITY OF ZORK
Robin W. Bailey
75389-8/$4.50 US/$5.50 CAN

THE ZORK CHRONICLES
George Alec Effinger
75388-X/$4.50 US/$5.50 CAN

STATIONFALL
Arthur Byron Cover
75387-1/$3.95 US/$4.95 CAN

ENCHANTER
Robin W. Bailey
75386-3/$3.95 US/$4.95 CAN

WISHBRINGER
Craig Shaw Gardner
75385-5/$3.95 US/$4.95 CAN

PLANETFALL
Arthur Byron Cover
75384-7/$3.95 US/$4.95 CAN